AF227882

LIGHTNING

DO NOT ENTER
DANGER!!
KEEP OUT

LIGHTNING

A NOVEL

MICHAEL RAY EWING

Grand Canyon Press
Tempe, AZ

Copyright © 2025 by Michael Ray Ewing

All rights reserved.

No part of this publication may be reproduced, distributed, or transmitted in any form or by any means, including photocopying, recording, or other electronic or mechanical methods, without the prior written permission of the publisher, except as permitted by United States copyright law. For permission requests, contact the publisher at Grand Canyon Press, Tempe, AZ.

www.GrandCanyonPress.com

The story and all names, characters, and incidents portrayed in this novel are fictitious. No identification with actual persons (living or deceased), places, buildings, and products is intended or should be inferred.

Cover design by Damonza.com using licensed images from Shutterstock and AI – Midjourney

Interior image via www.Stock.Adobe.com: ID 245405393 © Noel; ID 571022564 © Chris; ID137407199 © Chris; ID 263862243 © studioloco; ID 227083202 © vikusandra.

Publisher's Cataloging-in-Publication

(Provided by Cassidy Cataloguing Services, Inc.).

Names: Ewing, Michael (Michael Ray), 1962- author.

Title: Lightning : a novel / Michael Ray Ewing.

Description: Tempe, AZ : Grand Canyon Press, [2026]

Identifiers: ISBN: 9781963361063 (paperback) | 9781963361056 (hardback with dust jacket) | 9781963361070 (hardback imprinted cover image) | 9781963361094 (epub) | 9781963361087 (kindle) | 9781963361100 (digital online library edition) | 9781963361124 (digital online direct access) | 9781963361117 (downloadable audio file)

Subjects: LCSH: Genetic engineering--Fiction. | Phoenix Metropolitan Area (Ariz.)--Fiction. | Heroes--Fiction. | Villains--Fiction. | Auditory hallucinations--Fiction. | Suspense fiction. | LCGFT: Thrillers (Fiction) | Detective and mystery fiction. | BISAC: FICTION / Thrillers / Suspense. | FICTION / Science Fiction / Genetic Engineering. | FICTION / Action & Adventure.

Classification: LCC: PS3605.W554 L54 2026 | DDC: 813/.6--dc23

Printed in the United States of America

Registered with the U.S. Copyright Office, www.copyright.gov

To my Arizona writers' group

Outside of a dog, a book is man's best friend. Inside of a dog it's too dark to read.

— GROUCHO MARX

CHAPTER 1

Lightning detonated with a crackling fork, followed by a sizzling, celestial *boom*. A thread of smoke rose from the rusty corrugated roof of a dilapidated block building. Behind that building, Adam Barnett staggered sideways and collapsed against a low stone wall. Blue sidewinders of electricity needled along his arms, and air whooshed from his lungs. The next flash illuminated a narrow desert valley, its rocky bottom an obstacle course of creosote, mesquite, and chest-high weeds. Steep mountains rose above the remnants of an abandoned copper mine, its distant, cone-shaped tailings illuminated in bursts of lightning and then obscured by driving rain. He was in the mountains, but where? Wheezing, a hand on his chest, Adam struggled to catch his breath. His ears rang as if he were trapped beneath a huge, tolling bell. He'd once heard of a golfer struck by lightning. The lightning had traveled from the guy's nine iron through his body, exiting his calf. Had something similar just happened? Adam's right foot hurt like hell. He pulled the foot onto his knee. Between the shoe's muddy cleats, he saw a small, black hole and stuck his finger through it, touching a wound.

"Ow!" he said.

He was about to take off his shoe when a black shape raced from the darkness. Adam shielded himself with his hands and got a wet tongue all over his face.

"What's this?" he asked. "Where'd you come from?" The dog wagged its tail, splattering Adam with mud.

"Hey, mutt, you're killing me here." The rain was warm enough, but he was already soaked and didn't need the dog slobbering all over him. "If you want to make yourself useful, give me a hand up."

Adam meant to push the dog away, but it turned and stiffened its legs, just as if it was doing what Adam asked. Adam grabbed on to its ruff, a thick mane that felt like steel wool. Its head was wedge-shaped, its legs long, and its body heavy and powerful. The moment Adam regained his balance, the tongue started up again.

To keep the dog from jumping up, Adam blocked it with an arm. "Okay, okay! I get it. You're glad to see me."

Every muscle in his body ached, and he felt weak. What on earth was he doing out in the rain, and why in this remote spot? He waited for an answer but it didn't come. Had the lightning short-circuited his brain? Not entirely. He knew his name. Adam Barnett.

With Adam's face out of reach, the animal began licking his legs. The rough tongue burned Adam's scraped knees. "Stop with the mopping. You like licking mud?" Then, thinking he'd spoken too harshly, he scratched the dog between the ears. "What's with the mopping behavior?" He looked into the animal's luminous eyes. "You're a big one, aren't you? Are you a dog or a pony? Maybe you can tell me what's going on?"

The dog whimpered up at the sky.

"Yeah, maybe we should get out of the rain."

Almost as if the dog could understand him, it loped off toward the building. Adam limped around to the front. The sliding door stood open. In the back corner, near a workbench and a stack of wooden boxes, water poured from a hole in the roof. The rafters smoldered. The dog sat on its haunches next to an old Chevy pickup.

Stepping inside the building, Adam tripped over a mountain bike. This looks new, he thought, and picked it up. The bike had a front and rear suspension, big, knobby tires, and oversized disc brakes. The strap beneath his chin cut into his jaw. He unclipped it and held a bike helmet in his hands. He looked down at his biking jersey, red and black and covered in mud. Thirst made him grab instinctively for the tube of his hydration pack. He brought it to his lips and sucked, but the water was gone. He must have covered a lot of ground before stopping here, and he didn't remember any of the ride.

He lifted the bike with one hand. There was no mistaking the reverse pivot suspension or the bike's elegant curved lines. It was one of his custom-built Defiant RIP mountain bikes. Before he had won all the awards, one of the bike magazines had written that the RIP was the most beautiful bike ever designed. Since then, he'd made sure all his bikes had Defiant RIP painted on both sides of the down tube. The best way to sell bikes was to get bikes out on the trail so riders could see them in action.

Adam had been working on manufacturing a second-generation carbon frame, but he hadn't painted this bike, and ordinarily he wouldn't take a prototype out on a trail, especially if bad weather threatened.

Whining, the dog nosed its head under his hand.

"What happened, Mop?" he asked the dog. "Why would I be out here riding in the rain?"

He squeezed the tires. Still inflated. He poked his head out the door and looked at the sky. Lightning jumped from one black cloud to another. Maybe not a good idea to go riding out in that. Better to get his bearings, a high point to stand on that would allow him to look for familiar landmarks—Camelback or Four Peaks or South Mountain with its brightly lit antenna farm.

An old mining road zigzagged uphill, and Adam, favoring his injured foot, began the laborious climb. The monsoon had turned the muddy ruts into a rivulet of rainwater, gravel, and swirling mesquite beans. Winded and brushing rain from his face, Adam stopped on a small plateau with a lightning-scarred mesquite clinging to its edge. The road continued on, but his chest heaved. Behind him stood a mine shaft cut into the mountain, and above him, another. Barely seen in the stormy gloom and waist-high weeds, ancient mining equipment—gear wheels, sections of track, and an ore cart—had been left to rust. Looking down, he saw that the valley held more of the same—a rusty steel tanker car the size of a semi and buildings with missing roofs. A drilling rig that might once have stood upright tilted at a forty-five degree angle. A piece of it crashed to the earth. Maybe lightning had struck it, too.

With a hand protecting his forehead, he panned the horizon. Far away and to his right glittered the faint glow of city lights. In every other direction the sky was dark with clouds obscuring the peaks.

Mop sniffed the wind. Tail between his legs, belly scraping the road until he was almost crawling, he edged toward the mesquite, its skeletal limbs twisting up into the sky. Mop growled. The dog was big and heavy, with a powerful chest and long jaw. A lot of teeth in that mouth, Adam thought, realizing how little he knew about the animal.

The dog's growl ended in a whine. Trembling and staying low to the ground, Mop backed away.

"For Pete's sake, it's just a tree, Mop. If you need to lift a leg, pick another one," Adam said. "Here. I'll show you there's nothing to be afraid of."

Trying to see through the deluge, he stepped closer to the tree. The limbs shook, groaning in the gusts of wind. Warm rain washed over Adam's shoulders but a finger of unease slid down his back. The rain turned cold. Pressed into the mud in front of the tree was a human footprint.

Adam crouched down for a better look. It was hard to see clearly in the dark, but the print was narrow and long, almost as if someone had been walking around in bare feet. The rain had not yet washed away the outline of the toes. Why would anyone walk barefoot in the desert? All the plants had spikes and thorns.

A distant, wavering howl, unlike anything Adam had ever heard, floated on the wind. Adam stood. Hackles raised, Mop backed downhill.

The howl sounded again, only closer. Whatever it was, it was coming fast.

Mop grabbed the hem of Adam's shirt with his teeth.

Thrown off balance, Adam flailed. "Let me go! I can't move if you keep pulling!"

Mop let go. Adam staggered, nearly falling, then steadied himself. He had to get out of there. He had no idea how or why he knew that, but he did. The howl sounded again. Adam, favoring his injured foot, sped into an awkward run. Behind him, at the top of the road, the cry turned into an eager, yowling shriek. Had it gotten his scent?

He hobbled as fast as he could past the old mining equipment, his broken shoe squishing with each step. The ramshackle building appeared. He veered sideways toward it, lost his footing, and splashed down into a ditch. Mud filled his mouth and nose. Mop grabbed his shirt and dragged him into the dense, chest-high weeds. On hands and knees, heart hammering in his throat, Adam scuttled into the building. Mop bolted past and cowered behind the truck.

Adam spied a broken length of pipe and snatched it off the floor. He lifted the pipe and stood, teeth bared, hands clamped, the hairs on the back of his neck standing straight up. Just for an instant, as wind flattened the bushes, he thought he saw something big race past.

Suddenly the temperature changed. The rain outside felt warm again. Mop, edging forward, sniffed the wind. Adam lowered the pipe and stepped outside. Wiping rain from his face, he squinted, looking down the valley.

"Hey, Mop, did you see that big, dark shadow?" he whispered. "What just ran past us?"

CHAPTER 2

Like a deadly dragonfly, the Sikorsky Black Hawk roared through the lightning storm. Major Blain Jacobson did not like flying, especially this close to the ground. As the Phoenix monsoon bucked the helicopter violently about, he gripped his armored seat with one hand and his assault rifle with the other. He hated helos. They were slow, noisy, and took too long to take off and land. He had been shot down in four helos, the last in Yemen after an Al Qaeda RPG blew off the bird's tail rotor.

Now, he was flying over the McDowell Mountains' rolling foothills, heading west over creosote flats split with rain-filled washes. Another few minutes east and they would be in the North Scottsdale Pinnacle Peak area, where multi-million-dollar mansions, world-class spas, and country-club golf courses dotted the picturesque hills. Jacobson had been an Army Ranger for almost thirty years. He had fought the Russians in Afghanistan and then later, the Taliban. In between he had battled Iraqis, Iranians, Hezbollah, ISIS, and Al Qaeda affiliates in Syria. North Scottsdale was the last place on earth he would ever have expected to make a combat drop but then he'd never expected to be taking orders from an officer who'd never faced combat.

"I don't want any heroes!" Looking back at the faces of the heavily armed men, Admiral Bill McDermott, a Commissioned Corps officer in the US Public Health Service, shouted over the roar of the engines. "Get the security system back online, find out the status of the labs, and pull out. Without the grid, we're blind. If you run into hostiles, cover your six, and we'll dust you out. Got it?"

McDermott, wearing a white, open-neck shirt with black shoulder boards striped with gold, was arrogant enough to think he could play with the big boys. Whatever lingo he'd picked up came from *Top Gun* or *Black Hawk Down*, Jacobson thought, trying not to chafe at orders coming from a man who'd earned his stripes by getting a PhD. A Navy Admiral wouldn't have earned his stripes without a good deal of time at sea but Public Health Admiral? What had he ever fought but microbes? Wondering what awaited them at Biodosius Labs, Jacobson looked at the faces of the heavily armed men around him.

The men nodded. Jacobson watched McDermott's expression, noting the scar that started at his hairline and curved back across his left temple. With an injury like that, the admiral was lucky to be among the living, so maybe he had done some sort of black ops active duty, the kind of thing that wouldn't appear on a public record.

Jacobson switched his gaze to the woman who sat next to McDermott. Dr. Riya Kumar was East Indian, barely five-feet-tall, and had dark skin, dark hair, and impossible-to-read dark eyes. She wore dress flats and a charcoal business suit with a metallic thread that glinted in the dim light. Oddly, she did not look uncomfortable in the Black Hawk but simply stared down at the armored deck, a faint smile on her lips.

The visor of McDermott's gold-embroidered hat cast a shadow on his face. He leaned toward Jacobson. A scowl hardened his jaw. "Major, you're going in as an observer only, understand? You're only here because General O'Dell insists. Lieutenant Sanchez will be running the operation. If this goes sideways, I don't want an additional liability."

Liability? What was the guy talking about? Jacobson saw his own reflection in McDermott's blue aviators and didn't answer. Arguing about his role with a Commissioned Corps Admiral wasn't worth the air. Unless McDermott was willing to risk losing General O'Dell's funding, Jacobson was going in. The Sikorsky bucked sideways in the wind, spraying them with rain. Jacobson would have never guessed Arizona could have such violent storms. The night sky flashed and boomed around them as if they were in a war zone.

He gave the admiral's team a final appraising once-over. He was at least fifteen years older than any of the others, and he was the only one with a wedding ring. It was a good bet that none of the others had dependents, while he had five children at home, every one of them looking like his wife—which was a good thing as far as he was concerned. Sheryl was a slender, sunny woman with hazel eyes and an unfailing smile, while he was intense and easily twice her weight, with rough hands, unbowed shoulders, and deep squint lines around his eyes. Smiling wasn't easy for him, and people shied away.

The team wore night-vision goggles and carried Colt M41A assault rifles that fired high-velocity 5.56 mm rounds, ammo that was good against body armor and at punching through doors, walls, and pretty much anything else. Lieutenant Antonio Sanchez was in his early thirties. Sergeant Anderson, the only man bigger than Jacobson, was in his late twenties. Corporal Griffin, their medic, looked like he should still be in high school. Specialist Layton handled communications. Warrant Officer Hallett was their computer expert. Though both Layton and Hallett had acne on their faces and reminded him of teenagers playing video games in their parents' basements, a careful look at their expressions revealed something completely different: they were hard men trained for combat.

And they were frightened.

The recon at Biodosius scared him, too. The last time anyone had heard from the National Institute of Health's satellite research center had been hours before—just after the start of the second shift on the long Labor Day weekend. Phone calls to the facility had gone unanswered. Emails were ignored. Even now, at two in the morning, satellite images showed dozens of cars in the parking lot. None had moved an inch since the previous evening.

Jacobson glanced again at Dr. Kumar's odd smile, wondering what she knew that she wasn't saying. Earlier that evening, she had given him a quick examination. She kept it to the basics. Sit down, stick out your tongue, breathe deeply. She peered into his eyes, felt his lymph nodes, and gave him three shots that burned his veins and gave him a low-grade fever. Every trip overseas required a round of new inoculations and boosters, but he'd never needed shots for deployments in the States. Puzzling.

The cockpit lights blinked. The co-pilot, holding two fingers over the Black Hawk's complicated center console, killed the lights. Jacobson lowered his night-vision goggles and switched on his rifle's holographic sight. His goggles electronically amplified available light, including light not normally visible to the human eye. This allowed him to see in almost complete darkness, a huge advantage over anyone without the same technology. With the goggles, Army Rangers ruled the night. They knew it, and their enemies quickly learned it, to their dismay.

He tried to concentrate on the task at hand but felt troubled. His disquiet had started when he had been diverted to Williams Air Force Base to meet General O'Dell. As far as Jacobson had been able to find out, O'Dell had served one tour of duty in Iraq, not when Jacobson was there, but well after, when Saddam's statues had been toppled and the political officers were brought in to reconstitute a government.

In person, O'Dell had turned out to be heavyset, florid-faced, and impatient. A former ROTC lieutenant proud of his service record, he had risen through the ranks by overseeing the development of the Army's latest high-tech tools. Of course, some of those tools turned out to be essential—like night-vision glasses—so front-line troops like Jacobson owed men like O'Dell a debt.

The general had lost contact with his researchers at Biodosius. O'Dell had invested millions of his division's budget in McDermott's research and wanted Jacobson to go into Biodosius and find out what had happened. Now, McDermott was calling the shots, and O'Dell wasn't even here.

In the meeting with O'Dell, Jacobson had brushed aside his misgivings about the command structure. Then came the visit to Dr. Kumar, she with the Cheshire Cat smile and burning shots. Normally he would have dismissed his uneasiness as nothing more than pre-op jitters, but the feeling was only growing worse as they neared the drop-off point. This was not shaping up to be an ordinary mission.

The Sikorsky lifted slightly, and he caught the glint of Biodosius's twelve-foot security wall through his goggles. The building was a new four-story structure that looked more like a high-tech corporate center than a government research lab—not that he'd ever been to one, but when Covid hit, he'd seen them on TV. The pilot landed in the empty rear parking lot. Jacobson followed Lieutenant Sanchez and his team out into the rain. The Black Hawk lifted smoothly up into the air and, seconds later, disappeared into the roiling clouds.

"Keep proper spacing and don't bunch up," Sanchez ordered, the rain making it hard to hear. "There are civilians inside, so watch your fire. You see something, don't keep it to yourself. Sergeant, you have point. Major, you have our six. Let's go."

Jacobson fell in at the rear of the squad and jogged across the parking lot. The sweet scent of wet sage filled the air. In the gusting wind, the ghoulishly green branches of palo verdes swayed like dancers.

They climbed the metal stairs to the loading dock. Specialist Hallett swiped a magnetic card at the reader next to the security door. Nothing happened. Sergeant Anderson moved forward, slid a flat-edged pry-bar against the doorjamb, and pulled. Metal popped, and the door opened.

Jacobson smelled blood. A woman in hospital scrubs lay sprawled by the door. Tangled hair fell around her battered face. Judging by the smears on the floor, she'd dragged herself down the hall in an attempt to reach the security phone.

Corporal Griffin checked her pulse, turned over one of her arms, and examined her legs.

"Admiral," he whispered into his microphone, "we have a dead female civilian. Her wrists are broken, and her stomach and Achilles tendons are sliced through."

"Understood," McDermott answered over the roar of the Black Hawk's rotors. "Proceed to the security office. I need the grid operational."

"Yes, sir."

Jacobson turned toward the darkened hallway. Who would cut open a woman's stomach, break her wrists, hamstring her, and then let her crawl to the phone?

They followed the trail of blood. On either side were locked lab doors, only accessible with the swipe of a keycard. Except for the squeak of their wet boots on the tile, the building was eerily silent. There was no hum of lights, no quiet sigh of air conditioning, no ringing of phones.

The blood led into a lab. Inside were the bodies of two more women and a man. All three had died in the back corner. A desk had been thrown out of the way. Smashed test equipment lay scattered about.

"Admiral, we have three more dead civilians," Griffin whispered into his radio. "All have defensive wounds on their arms and hands. Their throats were cut."

"Understood. Proceed to the security office."

Jacobson backed out of the lab. The team made its way down the hallway. One lab had the door completely torn from its hinges. Another had a shattered window. Inside each room were dead employees. Some had been killed quickly. Others, like the first woman, had been left to die slowly.

What had General O'Dell gotten him into? O'Dell's instructions had been specific. Locate the dogs and get the embryos. Whatever else was N. H. P.—not his problem.

They crept past the cafeteria toward the front of the building. They turned a corner. The bodies of doctors, lab technicians, nurses, secretaries, administrators, and maintenance workers choked the hallway. The killer or killers had cut them down as they ran for the main lobby. A workman, his overalls sliced open, had died clutching his bowels. A doctor had his eyes torn out. Two nurses in scrubs lay sprawled in the hallway, terror on their bloody faces. A security officer sat slumped against a wall. A semi-automatic pistol lay on the tile next to him. The sulfuric, fecal smell of rotting bodies filled the air.

Jacobson had dealt with the horror of war most of his adult life. More than once, he had counted the dead by the number of limbs. But this was not an airstrike on a village in Afghanistan. They were in beautiful Scottsdale, Arizona where things like this did not happen.

Sanchez touched his radio, his voice a whisper so that the sound wouldn't carry.

"Admiral, we're almost to the lobby. A lot of civvies died in the hallway. They were making a run for the exit."

"Understood, Lieutenant. Proceed."

Trying not to step in the fluids pooled on the floor, the team moved silently through the bodies. The lobby was empty except for a second dead security officer lying on the floor next to his Glock pistol. Specialist Hallett went into the security office behind the front desk. Security monitors covered one wall, each labeled with a zone identifier. There were more cameras than monitors. Gray CAT-5 cables snaked from the monitors to a rack that held a dead networking switch.

"Admiral, the power's been shut down," Hallett whispered into his radio. "We can turn it on, but if we do that, they'll know we're here."

"That's a risk we must take," McDermott said. "Sanchez, deploy a defensive perimeter and get the power up. As soon as the network is operational, my techs will log in and parse the video log files to see what happened. Watch the security monitors after they come up. If anything's going to move, it will be after the power is turned on."

While Hallett worked on the power, Jacobson examined the dead security officer. Thanks to his goggles, the dim light from the lobby's windows was almost as bright as full daylight. Jacobson counted the bullet casings scattered on the floor and then looked at the hallway leading to the cafeteria. He couldn't quite work out the angle of the attack. The employees had been running toward the lobby when they had died. But how had the officer been killed? He had an excellent defensive position. Anyone coming up the hallway would have been bottled up between the walls. Even if the killers used the fleeing researchers as human shields, the guard should have been able to defend himself.

Jacobson glanced around the lobby, trying to think. If he had been the killer, he wouldn't have gone after the officer in the hallway. He would have stayed at the far end, peeped around the corner, and killed the guard with a headshot. The hallway was less than fifty yards long, and, with a holographic site, it would have been a no brainer. But the killer had not stayed back. The officer had emptied his entire clip.

Blood had pooled under the guard's head, and his neck had been slashed. Jacobson caught a glint of metal at the guard's throat and leaned down to remove an empty shell casing from the top of the officer's shirt. He found two more shell casings on his stomach.

Jacobson tipped his head back. His blood went cold. The attacker hadn't come after the officer from the hallway. The officer had been hit from above. The ceiling was full of bullet holes.

He moved around to the officer's feet, his back to the hallway. Light from the high, narrow windows illuminated the grisly scene. In the grit of the ceiling's fallen fire retardant, he saw footprints. Bare footprints.

He motioned to Sanchez.

"There were at least two killers," he whispered. "One chased the employees into the hallway by the cafeteria while another dropped out of the ceiling here to cut off any escape. They then converged on the staff in the hallway from the front and back. That's why none of them made it out."

Jacobson lifted his gaze to Sanchez's face. "One more thing. There are bare footprints in the fire retardant. Whoever hit the officer did it without shoes, probably so they wouldn't make any noise."

"I need to call this in."

Jacobson grabbed the lieutenant's elbow. "What's going on?"

Sanchez scowled at Jacobson's fingers, and his mouth hardened above his helmet strap. "You want answers, Major? Have O'Dell take it up with McDermott."

Sanchez went over to Sergeant Anderson and pointed up at the ceiling. Anderson retrieved a ladder from the security office, climbed up, and pushed aside a ceiling tile.

"Sir, there's a maintenance crawlway up here with lots of pipes and wires," he whispered down. "I can see maybe ten yards."

Sanchez snapped his fingers at Specialist Layton, easily the smallest man in the squad. "Get up there and keep them from hitting us. The rest of you keep an eye on the ceiling. There are lots of ducts and conduits they can hide behind. I don't want any surprises."

Jacobson moved to the head of the hallway leading to the cafeteria. He didn't know the men around him, but after what he'd seen, he wasn't about to let anyone else cover the approach. Except for the lobby and the ceiling, the hallway was the only way to attack them. He took up a position on the left side of the hallway entrance and peered into the darkness, his scope sweeping the walls. Who could kill with such precision and speed in their bare feet?

"Admiral, we've set up a defensive perimeter," Sanchez whispered into his radio. "We're ready to power up."

"Proceed."

"Yes, sir. Everyone, lights-off."

Jacobson pushed his goggles up onto his helmet. For a second, he was blind in the darkness, and a horrible vulnerability gripped him. There was ambient light coming from the high narrow windows behind him, but it wasn't enough to see down the hallway. He wondered if the killers had attacked after turning off the power. It made sense. Most people were fine with waking up in a darkened bedroom in the middle of the night and stumbling to the bathroom, but put them in a forest or in a rocky canyon in utter darkness, and they were helpless.

The lights switched on. With the goggles, the killings had been in flat-relief shades of gray. But with the lights on, he saw the blood-splattered floor in brilliant color. Bullets chewed the walls. Chunks of drywall lay on the tile. Some of the fallen had been shot—at least one had been hit in the head—but most of the dead had been killed with an edged weapon. Killing with a knife was much more personal than a bullet. Nothing was more intimate than taking a life up close where you could twist the blade and watch the other person die.

Whoever had done this liked to kill, he realized. And, more than that, they liked to kill intimately.

CHAPTER 3

Thompson's going to die!

Victoria Stewart awoke with Dark's snarl in her head. Not again! She looked around the bedroom, just to be sure he wasn't some ghost, hiding in a corner, but no, everything was as she had left it: jeans draped across the back of a chair; her bra on the chair's seat; boots on the floor. Outside, lightning flashed through the pouring rain. Whether from nerves or the leftovers she'd tried to eat for dinner, her stomach rebelled. She staggered to the bathroom and leaned over the toilet, vomiting. At the sink, she poured mouthwash and rinsed out the taste of bile.

She lifted her bloodshot eyes to the mirror. "What's wrong with me?"

A lifetime ago, she had been beautiful, with strawberry-blonde hair and pale skin that freckled in the summer sun. She had inherited her mother's delicate nose and hazel eyes and her father's quick intelligence. But that had been before her mother's suicide, before the narcos killed her father, and before Victoria's world exploded in a fireball.

Dark was not one of the bad guys who killed her father—that much she'd figured out. He never talked about running drugs but, like them, Dark was heartless and determined, and now he was about to kill someone else, a man, she thought, although "Thompson" could just as easily have been a woman's last name.

Back when she first began hearing Dark's voice, she had warned the sheriff that there was a killer on the loose, but when she couldn't identify the victim by more than a first or last name—or, most often, no name—the sheriff had written her off as a psycho. And as for Dr. Young from the county's Victim Services department, the woman could offer no rational explanation, only a sympathetic smile and an offer to refill her meds or put her on something stronger.

More than anything, Victoria wanted to be believed. She wanted a knowledgeable person to say, "Yeah, that happens—killers do invade your dreams, and we'll help you find out why." Unfortunately, the one person who would have believed her implicitly was her dad, and he was dead.

She could always call Special Agent Doug Monroe, the new guy in her life and the one person who'd consistently shown up in Mayo Clinic's burn unit. He liked her. He liked her a lot. She could tell how he felt by the way he looked at her when he didn't think she would notice. But how many three a.m. calls would it take before he told her it wasn't going to work out?

"He'll listen," she insisted, then laughed because listening wasn't the same thing as doing something about it.

Shivering, she hugged herself. "I just want my life back!"

Or maybe not.

She wrenched opened the medicine cabinet and took out the brown plastic container of Valium. Paying her medical bills for the months in the burn unit and trying to keep her head above water, she'd run through her father's life insurance. The ranch was failing. While she'd been in the hospital, the narcos, trying to drive her off the land, had killed her stock. Worst of all, the nightmares kept coming. She tried to remember when she hadn't felt exhausted and couldn't.

Victoria shook out the pills and cupped them in her palm. How many would it take to finish what Blackjack Joe had started three years ago? The pain, the despair, the helplessness would end. She could finally get some sleep, and if she was asleep—or dead—she wouldn't care. Maybe that's what her mother had felt, that the pills would bring her a measure of peace.

But if she took her mother's path, then the latest incarnation of Blackjack Joe's old gang would have free rein, crossing back and forth across the backroads of her ranch in ATVs. When the narcos killed her father, the DEA had surged agents to the north, but when Joe and his gang vanished, the DEA decided the ranch lands of northeastern Arizona were too remote. Nogales to Yuma, that was where they'd find the big shipments—drugs packed in crates delivering tequila, clothing, and auto parts.

The agents were right about the ranch being remote. Her father, Vern Stewart, had grown up on the land and thrived on solitude and the routines of ranching—repairing fences, herding cattle, branding calves. As a young man, he had enlisted in the Marine Corps and served in the Third Force Recon Unit, dropping behind enemy lines in Vietnam. He would have reenlisted if Victoria's grandfather hadn't died. Vern returned to the ranch and with him came his new bride.

Lilly, Victoria's mother, hadn't been happy living in Arizona. She had grown up in the gentle maple-covered hills of New Hampshire and never adjusted to the bleak cinder mesas and the forlorn, whistling wind. And that wasn't all. Victoria remembered her mother saying she was constantly being "evaluated and found lacking." Vern's mother had set a high standard, and the comparisons grew even more pointed after the steely matriarch's death. Victoria's grandmother had been part of the tight-knit Mormon ranching community in Apache County, and the women, even the young ones, regarded Lilly as an outlier. She had trouble making friends and withdrew into her clouded thoughts. Finally, she decided there was no point in continuing to live.

Good grief! It was cowardice to take her mother's way out. Victoria poured the pills back into the plastic container. Besides, she loved the ranch. How many times had the narcos tried to kill her before her .308 sent them scurrying away like the rats they were? *La Puta Loca*—Crazy Bitch—they called her, the nickname a badge of honor. The key, as her father had taught her, was to always keep moving. Shoot and move. Find another spot, shoot, and move again. By the time reinforcements arrived, she would be gone and waiting where they wouldn't expect her, scope to her eye and finger on the trigger.

She could not just stand idly by while Dark killed someone else. In life, you couldn't always pick your fights. Sometimes, fights picked you.

———

She sped northwest across the Black Knob. Lightning flashed across the heavens in blinding white-blue forks of celestial brilliance, the thunder so close it shook the car as she drove. Millions of years ago, volcanoes had rained down hell on the northeastern Arizona plains. Wind, rain, snow, and heat had eroded the landscape into bleak cinder prairies broken by bright sprays of prairie fire and green islands of pine.

She gave the Range Rover more gas, and the SUV banged along the gravel ruts that cut across the Knob. The windshield wipers, turned up as high as they could go, fought valiantly against the thunderstorm. She had gotten the Rover months before, but she rarely drove it and kept it parked out of sight where it couldn't be seen from the air. The Range Rover was done entirely in gaudy red, from its lurid red-leather interior to its glittering candy-apple paint. Blackjack Joe, the head of the narcos, had bought the Range Rover fully loaded from a dealer in Vegas and had spent untold thousands in custom accessories such as a hydraulic lift-kit, skid plates, twelve-speaker surround sound, high-def video, and more chrome than a Vegas hearse. The fool had even engraved the fuel injection shroud with the most god-awful rap poetry Victoria had ever had the misfortune to read. She'd been tempted to dump the vehicle down a sinkhole but had held back, thinking that, one day, she might need an all-terrain vehicle with the speed of a race car.

She sped into a herd of elk. Hands clamped on the steering wheel, tires churning for traction, she stabbed the Rover's brakes. The elk scattered, and a yearling sprang into the pines.

"Slow down!" she snapped. "You won't be able to help Thompson if you spin out!"

She mentally froze at hearing the name a second time. Thompson. Not anyone she knew.

"I'm insane," she muttered. "And, besides, I'm late." How she knew that Thompson's life hung in the balance was a mystery, but if she didn't move her sissy ass, she was going to miss the show.

***

She skidded onto Arizona 273 and hit the rocker switch under the dash to lower the Rover for road use. Hydraulics whining, she sped east. Blackjack Joe had been a son of a bitch of the lowest order, but she had to give the bastard credit. The Range Rover could handle anything off-road then transform into a cruiser with the well-mannered aplomb of a Caddy on a Sunday drive.

Twenty minutes later, she stopped at the junction of Arizona 260. The asphalt was still black and wet from the storm, and it would be an hour until the sun came up. Now what?

A big silver RV turned left in front of her. Startled, she saw that the driver had flipped on his dome light so that she could see his admiring thumbs-up. Before he could make eye contact, she gunned the Rover and cursed. Driving around in a dead man's eyesore wasn't a good idea, especially since Blackjack Joe was one of the most wanted narcos north of the Mexican border. However, on this particular occasion, the Rover was exactly what the situation called for. Her heavy-duty truck wasn't built for speed, and she needed speed, especially since she had no idea what she was getting into.

She had nearly reached the turnoff for her ranch when the man's face from the RV abruptly clicked into place. She stood on the brakes, slid hard onto the shoulder, and wrenched the Rover around. She knew the driver! How she knew, she didn't know. She just did.

Ten minutes later, she reached the junction again. Using both lanes, she skidded left on the wet road and accelerated. From the paved road, single-lane dirt driveways led into the pines. She slowed at each turnoff to check for fresh tracks before speeding on. Minutes crawled by until she found a fresh set and followed the tracks into an unnamed, muddy road. She bounced past three logging cuts until she saw the dim lights of a cabin through the trees.

After hiding the Rover behind a windfall of downed trees, she grabbed Blackjack Joe's Uzi from the gun tray and jumped out into the mud. Dressed in his Kevlar vest and her shooters' goggles and stocking cap, she ran through a grove of wildlings and stopped. Hidden behind a rocky outcrop stood an old cabin with smoke curling from its chimney. The walls had once been faced in blond pine, but mold and moss had turned the siding black. In front of the cabin sat an old, mud-splattered GMC pickup. Tracks from the RV circled the cabin and headed back toward the main road. She'd missed it.

She swore and debated what to do. She could return to the Rover and follow the RV back to the main road, or she could see what was inside the cabin.

She waited, trying to prod whatever sixth sense had compelled her to venture out on such a stormy night. Thankfully, the storm was moving southwest towards Phoenix, and the rain was tailing off. What should she do?

She crept around to the back porch. Through the kitchen window, she saw a sink of dirty dishes and a kitchen table covered in pizza boxes. Inside, a TV blared a game show, and an announcer listed the prizes contestants could win if they correctly answered questions.

A tear slipped down her nose. Was she crying? She backhanded it with her glove and tried the back door. She was here but too late. Whatever insanity had driven her to this cabin waited inside.

The back door was unlocked and swung inward. Jumping forward and grabbing the retreating knob, she found herself in a kitchen that smelled of bacon and burnt toast. A skillet full of congealing grease cooled on the counter. She eased around the table. Sitting on a couch, a big man with dark, greasy hair and an even darker beard jeered answers at the TV. He was eating from a paper plate and using his fingers.

She watched him eat, telling herself to leave before he noticed her. The mountains were full of cabins. Some guy eating bacon and eggs was not unusual. He might be a slob but that didn't mean he had done anything wrong.

The man's cell phone rang. Leave now, she told herself. Couch put down his plate, muted the TV, and reached toward a side table.

He picked up his phone and put it on speaker. "Yeah?"

"Is it over?" a voice asked.

Victoria stiffened. She knew that voice.

Couch swallowed. "Not yet, boss. He's a player but he won't last. You want to ask him how he's doing?" Couch picked up a bit of bacon rind and threw it at something on the floor. "Have you handled the other problem yet?"

"Flight's working it. It won't be long."

"You want me to finish up here and drive over?"

"Just handle your end. No mistakes."

Couch smiled. "No worries, boss. I have a nice deep hole in the cinders picked out."

Dark didn't reply for a few seconds.

"Have you seen somebody up there?" he finally asked. "A woman maybe? Anybody nosing around?"

Couch chuckled. "A woman around here? I wish."

"Something isn't making sense. Look around and call me back. Do it now."

The connection dropped.

Victoria froze. Dark had asked Couch if he had seen a woman nosing around. Was he talking about her, and if so, how did he know where she was? She only heard Dark in her dreams, but he talked about her as if he had seen her on some kind of psychic video channel.

"What's going on?" she asked.

Mouth open, bits of egg in his beard, Couch gaped back at her.

Two strides took her across the kitchen. Beyond Couch lay a man on a green tarp. Tiny, desperate hiccups escaped the gag in his mouth, and his fingers pressed a stomach wound.

Victoria switched her gaze back to Couch. The automatic in his hand boomed. A bullet whipped over her shoulder. The next one went past her cheek, and the last one tugged at her hair. The Uzi bucked in her hands. Couch spun sideways, tripped over the man on the plastic, and fell into the TV. DVDs spilled onto the floor. The Uzi kept firing, the bullets chewing up the wall, the window, and the blinds.

She ran forward and kicked away Couch's automatic. One of her bullets had gotten him in the leg, another in the ribs, and the last one in the neck.

"What's his name?" she demanded. "Tell me and I'll call for help. Do anything else and I'll watch you die!"

Couch blinked. "Thompson. His name's Will Thompson."

Victoria glanced at the man curled on the plastic and felt a surge of anger.

"Not him, you idiot! I already know who he is. Who's the man on the phone?"

Couch opened his mouth, lips moving, but nothing came out.

"What?"

She knelt to put her ear by his mouth. His arm snapped up. Two of his fingers caught her by the throat. She gagged for an instant, and then her father's training took over, and she brought her elbow up and down into the inside of his elbow. His fingers let go and she leapt up, breaking his nose with a hard sideswipe of the Uzi's butt. She kicked his wounded leg and ground her boot into the bullet hole. Fighting the narcos had taught her how to play this game.

"Who is he?" Her voice cracked with anger. "Why is he in my head?"

Couch hiccuped through the blood in his mouth. "...kill you." She laughed. "You think that scares me?"

Doubt entered Couch's eyes. But then he hiccuped again, the air in his lungs hissing silently out. Very slowly, he sagged onto the floor.

"No!" She dropped the Uzi and grabbed him by his shoulders. "Who is he? Tell me who you were talking to!"

No response.

She had been so close! A few more seconds and she might have found out who had turned her sleep into nightmares.

Maybe Thompson would know. He gasped shallowly through his gag, each breath held only an instant before he snatched the next. With brown eyes and hair and a medium build, Thompson wouldn't have warranted a second look, apart from his wound. He had been shot in the stomach. How long ago, she couldn't tell, but his skin looked gray, and sweat beaded on his forehead.

Forcing a smile, she rested a hand on his arm.

"Hey, it's going to be fine, okay? I'm Victoria. I'm going to call an ambulance and they'll patch you up."

She pulled out the gag.

"Help them." His eyes fluttered. "They took them. In the RV."

"What? Who are you talking about?"

He stared up at her, pleading. "My wife and girls. They're going to kill them."

CHAPTER 4

Even if the rain stopped, Adam wasn't sure he could make it back to civilization, wherever that might be. He felt horribly weak, and his right foot burned. Plus, what if that thing doubled back? Mop pushed his head under Adam's hand. The dog was limping.

He lifted the dog's paws and felt the pads, split and cracked. "What happened to your paws, boy?"

Mop whined, glancing at the doorway. Adam shivered.

"Do you have a name? When I was a kid, I had a German Shorthair named Cooper. He used to get cracked paws if he ran too long on the road after my bike."

Why could he remember Cooper and not how he'd gotten here? Judging by his bike and clothing, he had been out riding. But why had he ventured out on a rainy night? Mountain biking was a dangerous, extreme sport in the best of circumstances, but riding in the dark without a light was beyond foolhardy.

And right now, he needed a way out. He didn't want to be around if the howling thing came back. He limped over to the old truck and reached for the door. A jolt of static electricity jumped from his finger to the metal handle. The air hummed with static.

Gritting his teeth, he pulled open the door. The smell of dust rolled out of the cab. A key sat in the ignition. He slipped off his hydration pack and tossed it across the cab. With his left foot on the running board, he hoisted himself onto the seat. As far as he knew, it wasn't his truck. So what if he was stranded out in the middle of nowhere after getting struck by lightning? The truck didn't belong to him.

Or did it?

He had no idea.

Muttering, he pressed the clutch, shifted into neutral, and turned the key. He put his foot on the gas. The pain rose from a four to a ten, but the engine didn't turn over.

"Well, that's no big surprise," he said to the dog. "It's probably been sitting here for years." But, then, why would the key be in it? Maybe it did belong to him or to someone he knew.

He limped to the front of the truck, found the release, and lifted the hood. The engine was a dark, greasy lump in the gloom. The truck had an air filter, flywheel, valve covers, and battery. Everything seemed to be there, for all the good it would do him.

"Any ideas?"

The dog wagged his tail. "Well, that'll help."

Not holding out much hope, Adam checked the battery cable. As he wiggled it back and forth, he heard a *click* and one of the headlights switched on. It was dim, but the lamp was getting juice. Letting his injured foot drag, he hoisted himself onto the truck's sagging Naugahyde and turned the key. The engine groaned. He pumped the gas pedal. The engine groaned again, sputtering, each rhythmic cycle like the pulsating pain in his foot. The truck was his only way out of here, and he had to keep pumping the accelerator in hopes that the alternator still worked and could charge the battery. Engines were complicated, even old engines, and he hoped the motor oil hadn't turned to sludge.

"C'mon," he pleaded, "turn over."

The engine caught, died, caught again, and slowly, like an old man getting out of a warm bed on a frosty winter morning, groaned to life. An oily blue cloud of smoke shot from the tailpipe.

After sliding out of the truck, Adam picked up his bike and put it in the truck bed.

"C'mon, Mop! We're leaving!"

———

Keeping the truck in second gear, he followed a rutted mining road down the valley. The truck's springs were in bad shape, and the Chevy banged and swayed with each turn and bump. The drum brakes shrieked, metal on metal. The rain stopped, which was a good thing because the truck's wipers were in a sad state, but it hurt to use his arm, and he had to manhandle the big steering wheel one-handed as if he were driving a fire truck. The cab smelled like wet dog, and he pulled over to roll down the windows and let in the fresh desert air. Mop stuck his head out the passenger side, tongue lolling like a flag in the wind.

"Geez, dog, your drool is dripping down the door."

The terror and panic that had consumed Adam earlier had faded. No one would blame him for seeing things, because he didn't have to tell them. He just needed to find a way out of the mountains.

He switched on the AM radio and slowly turned the tuner knob until he found a classic rock station. Bob Seger's familiar growl filled the cab.

"Do you like rock and roll?" he asked the dog.

Mop cocked his head to one side at the question.

"Well, that doesn't tell me anything," Adam said. "What we have here is a communication issue." As he said *communication*, he pointed to himself, and when he said *issue*, he pointed at the dog.

Mop snorted and stuck his head back out the window.

As he drove, Adam wondered if he looked as bad as he felt. His eyes were bloodshot, his muddy hair plastered against his skull, and when the lightning strike happened, the shoulder of his biking jersey had turned molten, blistering his skin.

Looking behind him to make sure he wasn't being followed, he stopped the truck again, shifted on the seat, and felt one-handed for his zippered pouch. Rummaging inside, he pulled out his cell phone, wallet, and keys.

"I'm an idiot!" he swore. "A total idiot!"

Mop gave him a doggy grin.

"Well, if I'm an idiot then what does that make you? An idiot's hound."

His phone was dead. Fried by the lightning, no doubt. He put it aside and opened his wallet. The license had been issued to Adam Barnett. He lived in Defiance, Arizona. The picture on the license was the same as the reflection in the pickup's mirror, only younger. He was thirty-eight, had brown hair and blue eyes, did not wear corrective lenses, and could drive a car or motorcycle. He stood six-two and weighed a hundred and ninety. Everything on the license matched his memory, but nothing told him where he was or how he'd gotten there.

He placed the wallet on the seat. Back to an analogue universe, he thought. He couldn't be close to home. Defiance was located in the mountains northeast of Globe. There were no mesquite trees or creosote bushes, which meant he'd probably driven down to Phoenix to ride his bike. Where had he parked his truck? Not near the mining building or the mine itself.

He checked his keys. The first went to his old Corvette, the second to his brother's Dodge pickup. The third key unlocked his bike shop,

Defiance Cyclery. The last and most important key went to his Ford F-150.

He sighed and, lacking options, resumed driving. The ruts eventually ended at a slightly wider set of ruts. To the right, they went up. To the left, they went down. He stopped and looked in both directions.

"Where to, Mop?" he asked. "Uphill is toward the lights. I don't see anything to the left. I wish I had a map."

Mop pawed at the truck's pushbutton glovebox. It clicked and fell open.

Had Mop somehow made the connection between needing a map and the glove box? It was one thing for a dog to do tricks. He had heard about dogs doing everything from assisting the blind to waterskiing. There were watch dogs and guard dogs and dogs that were so loved by their owners that they left their pets everything in their wills. It was amazing what a professionally trained dog could do. But how had Mop known a glove box was the most likely place to find a map?

"Did you open the glove box on purpose?" he asked. Adam waited. Mop panted. A new song came on the radio.

Mop dripped saliva on the seat.

"Fine, Lassie. Normally I would freak out if my dog knew how to open a glove box and find a map, except, as far as I know, you're not my dog, so you can open any glove box you like. Plus, in case you missed it, I got zapped by few billion volts of electricity, so I'm not really thinking clearly. But the last thing we need around here is a barking cat-chaser. Got it? Also, just to be clear, I'm not cleaning up your slobber off the seat."

He stopped again. In the glove box he found a Phelps-Dodge baseball cap, a tire gauge, fast-food napkins, a receipt for a tire that was almost as old as the truck, and a copy of *Life* magazine. The pages were stiff and curled, but he could still read the date. June 1961. For a crazy second, he almost wondered if he had gone back in time.

"The way you're dripping on the seat, maybe we should tear a hole in a few of these napkins and put them over your head like a bib," he suggested.

At the bottom of the glove box, his fingers felt leather, and he pulled out a heavy drivers' atlas, the kind he remembered his parents keeping in the trunk of their car. The atlas was old but readable under the dome light. He shoved everything else back in the glove box and slammed it shut.

He frowned at the dog. "Good thing I thought about looking in there for a map, hey?"

Adam waited for a reaction, but Mop settled himself on the seat as if readying himself for a scenic Sunday drive.

Adam opened the atlas to the index in the back, searched for the city of Defiance, and flipped pages to east-central Arizona. It took a minute to find the tiny dot halfway between Globe and Show Low, high up in the mountains. He traced the map with his finger along the roads to Globe and then back to Phoenix. Then he looked out the window.

"Judging by the saguaros on the hillside, we're probably some-where in the Sonoran Desert." He brushed his fingertip sideways across the map. "That's the good news. The bad news is that it's a big desert. It stretches from California to New Mexico and south into Sonora, Mexico. I've been scuba diving in San Carlos, Mexico, and that's five hours south of the border, and it all looks like this. Do you know where we are?"

Mop thumped his tail.

"I'll take that as a no."

He threw the road atlas onto the dash. Without a starting point, a map was worthless.

He put the transmission into gear and rattled the truck up the rolling, cactus-covered hill. If there were lights, then hopefully there would be a sign of some kind, so he could figure out where he was.

Cool wind smelling sweetly of rain and creosote blew through the open window, and he found himself humming with the songs on the radio.

"So why can I remember all these songs, but I can't remember where I am or what happened?" he asked the dog.

Like a wife bored with her husband's stale jokes, the dog looked out the window.

The road turned steep. The old Chevy steadily lost speed on the incline. The higher they climbed, the more the temperature dropped, and Adam began to worry about gas, because they sure weren't going to find a gas station out here in this desolate wilderness. The saguaro, mesquite, and juniper gave way to ponderosa pine. Wisps of cloud drifted silently past. Driving up into the clouds, it was almost as if they were on top of the world. Adam told himself to relax. No way was that thing coming all the way up here. Suddenly, Mop backed away from the window and whimpered, crowding against Adam's side.

"Whoa, mutt, are you trying to drive?"

A wailing howl drifted out of the darkness.

Adam's heart skipped a beat then hammered to life. He slammed the accelerator to the floor. For a second the old truck nearly stalled before it shambled forward, its lone headlight stabbing the darkness. The needle on the speedometer flicked upward. Mop turned circles on the seat. Adam snapped the transmission into third. They needed speed.

Mop barked, and something out of a nightmare bounded from the pines. In the dark, Adam couldn't get a good look, but what he saw was enough for him to frantically shift into fourth. The thing left the trees and leapt onto the muddy road behind them. The truck began to shake, and Adam could feel them slowing. They were doing close to thirty, but the thing, whatever it was, had a hand on the tailgate.

The road started down the far side of the hill. Their speed inched upward. The Nightmare howled behind them, the sound rising into a scream. Adam risked a quick look in his rearview mirror. Maybe they were going to get away. The road curved around a rocky outcrop, and suddenly there was a cliff in front of them. Adam shouted and hit the brakes. Nothing happened. He stabbed the pedal. A rumbling vibration shot up his leg. The left front drum brake caught but the right did not, and the truck veered sideways through the gravel toward the cliff beyond. He wrenched the wheel the other way.

"Not good!" he screamed.

He forced the truck down into second and frantically turned the steering wheel with his working arm. The engine bellowed. The pick-up's suspension bucked sideways through a hard switchback. The bike slid across the pickup's bed and crashed against the side. Adam pushed on the brake pedal as hard as he could. If he downshifted and reduced his speed, the engine could blow a gasket or throw a rod, but if he left the transmission in second, they wouldn't stay on the road. The truck careened around curves.

Tires churning the gravel, he skidded through the first switchback. Standing on the brakes, he turned into the skid and braced against the seat. There was no railing, just a drop-off. In any other vehicle, the road wouldn't have been a problem, but in a sixty-year-old truck with bad brakes, a sagging suspension, and worn-out tires, it was suicide.

The vibration in Adam's foot became a jackhammer. Pain shot up to his thigh. The next turn appeared in his lone headlight. If the truck scraped against the cliff, would that slow them down or kill them?

"Hold on!"

He put all his strength into the brakes and frantically circled the fire engine wheel hard to the right. Mop lost his balance and flew against the dash. Gravel boomed in the rear wheel wells. He yanked the wheel left, into their slide. The front left tire reached the precipice. He spun the wheel the other way. The truck shuddered, front end dipping on ruined springs. The road straightened, then they were through the turn and picking up speed toward the next one.

"This is not fair!"

He pumped the brakes. No reaction at all. He might as well punch a hole through the floorboard and drag his foot. They were going too fast. The truck would never hold the next turn.

He pulled next to the cliff face, braced himself, and threw an arm around Mop. The road veered off to the right. He desperately turned the wheel. The engine wailed, the sound rising into a tortured bellow, and then, as suddenly as it had dropped down the mountain, the road abruptly leveled out. Gasping, he shifted the truck into third.

"You okay?" he asked the dog.

Mop warily put his nose back out the window.

Adam risked a look in the side mirror. All clear. But what on earth could be that big and fast? The Nightmare hadn't moved like a bear. A bear ran like a freight train: powerful, unstoppable, legs shorter in front than in back. This thing had run like a leaping mountain lion. Except taller.

And upright.

CHAPTER 5

Jacobson was grateful that his orders were straightforward: get the embryos, get the dogs, and get out. Sanchez and his men had a bigger and potentially riskier job—making sure the lights and security system were operational. The moment he'd come through the front door, stepping over and around dead bodies, he'd known this mission was seriously undermanned.

Ordered to keep a temporary watch on the hall, Major Jacobson risked a quick glance at the rest of Sanchez's team. Sergeant Anderson waited against the other wall, his dark eyes sweeping across the corpses. He hadn't shaved since the previous day, and whiskers darkened his jaw. Corporal Griffin, their medic, opened his pack and checked his equipment. In the light from the lobby windows, his brown hair looked almost black. Neither man looked unnerved, but Jacobson had been in combat long enough to know that all soldiers have an instinct for survival that tells them they're in danger.

Lieutenant Sanchez, approaching quietly, turned off his microphone. "Major, can I have a word?"

Jacobson nodded. Sanchez, signaling Corporal Griffin to take Jacobson's place, headed for the security office. Boots crunching on the fallen fire retardant, Jacobson followed him. Specialist Hallett, the computer expert, sat in the security office in front of a computer. He was switching the feeds from one camera to another. He had taken off his helmet, and his pale hair and blue eyes made him look like a choir boy.

"We don't have much time, so I'll be brief," Sanchez said quietly so his words would not carry beyond the office. "Admiral McDermott wants the security grid operational. I need your opinion of the situation before we leave. The security network was shut down before the attack, so there's no video of what happened. The eastern section of the building's security network, zone one, is still offline. The two zones in the back, three and four, are also offline. Only our zone, zone two, is operational, and that's because we powered up the network switch. It was turned off."

"Did someone power off the other network switches?" Jacobson asked.

"No way to tell from here, sir," Hallett answered from in front of the monitors. "They could have been disabled multiple ways."

"How many cameras are offline?"

"There are thirty cameras per zone. Three zones are offline, so ninety altogether," Hallett said.

"What about the research labs in the basement?" Jacobson asked.

"The network in the basement is not operational."

"So there's no video on what happened?"

"No, sir."

Not good, Jacobson thought. The dogs were down there.

Hallett moved the computer's mouse to another window, showing a list of video files. "Every video camera writes its own file in its own directory on the security file server. All files are replicated offsite every hour." He clicked on a file. "This is the video file of the lobby yesterday evening at 17:45. If I let the video jump at three-second intervals, you can see the network go down."

He started it running, and Jacobson watched figures walk back and forth through the lobby until the video stopped.

"That's when the switch shut down in the wiring closet," Hallett said. "It happened two minutes before the power to the building dropped. Without the network, none of the cameras could write their files."

"They disabled the network so nobody would know they were coming, and then they dropped into the lobby, killed the security guards, and cut the power," Jacobson said. "All in two minutes?"

"Yes, sir."

"How did the guard know someone was up in the ceiling?"

"I don't know, sir. Maybe he heard something."

"What security zones are working in the building?" Jacobson asked.

"Our zone is operational," Hallett said. "Everything on the second, third, and fourth floors is also operational."

"But the network in the basement is offline, along with the other three zones on our floor?"

"Yes, sir. None of the security switches respond to a ping. They're probably powered down like this one was."

Jacobson turned to Sanchez. "Our lack of information is a critical problem."

The lieutenant was in his early thirties, but the unease in his eyes was as old as war itself.

"That's why I wanted to talk to you, Major. I would like your opinion on how to proceed. We don't know if anyone made it out alive, if the killers are still here, or if there's anyone left who saw what happened."

"How long until the rest of your team arrives?" Jacobson asked.

"Three hours," Sanchez said. "They're airborne from North Carolina."

Jacobson glanced out at the bodies in the hall. Some of the dead had surprised expressions. Two had bled out and looked as if they'd simply fallen asleep. Most had died running for their lives.

He lowered his voice. "Whoever killed these people had the element of surprise and used it effectively. They knew the layout of the building and how to limit security's ability to make good decisions. Knocking out the network before the attack did not happen by accident. Worst of all, whoever did this knew there'd be someone coming to investigate. They'll try and ambush us—probably from the ceiling or maybe as we transition from a live security zone to a dead one. They'll try to get us moving one way and then hit us from another, probably from behind, since most of the killing was done that way."

"How would you proceed?"

"I would call in local help. At the very least, have the police secure the perimeter until your unit arrives."

"The local police don't have the training or clearance for this. McDermott won't go for it."

"Yes, but they can secure the exterior of the building without having to see what went on in here. A lone gunman or a couple of guys having a bad day did not shut down the security network for multiple zones all at the same time. This was a planned, coordinated attack."

"What you want is above my pay grade. I can request it, but that's it. What else before we move?"

"Put Sergeant Anderson in front and pair him with someone who has good hearing. Keep Layton up above in the maintenance ceiling. Eyes above are critical. If the killers follow the same pattern, they'll feint in front to hold us, then hit us from the rear and come again from the front. That's what they did here in the lobby. It worked once, and they'll try it again. I'll cover our six. You stay in the middle where you can see. Kill the lights and go dark. Use the darkness to our advantage. The killers did. We don't want to be blind like the employees in the hallway."

"If I turn off the lights, Admiral McDermott won't be able to see anything on the security cameras."

"Whoever did this knew about the cameras. If they took them out once, they'll do it again. Plus, if they control what we see, we'll react the wrong way. Tell McDermott to turn off the cameras above us. The killers are most likely watching."

"Is that possible?" Sanchez asked Hallett.

"Of course it's possible!" Jacobson snapped. "They already did it once. Do you think it's a coincidence that the lights are on but none of the network switches are operational except for the one showing us? McDermott's over-reliance on the security cameras is going to get us killed."

Angry, he left the security room and reclaimed his old spot in the hallway. Sanchez closed the security door and got on the radio with Admiral McDermott. Two minutes later, he came out.

"Get ready to move," he whispered. "We're going to power up the network switches. Hallett has the locations and wiring closet diagrams on his tablet."

"And the lights?" Jacobson asked.

"We'll use our night vision if they go down. The security team needs to be able to see."

Jacobson didn't argue. It would only have caused problems if he did. The decision was out of Sanchez's hands.

Jacobson made sure his goggles were turned on and lowered them to the rim of his helmet. Leaving them on would drain the battery, but he didn't care. He always carried extras. Being blind could kill him.

Sanchez deployed his men—Anderson and Hallett up front as

recommended, Sanchez and Griffin in the middle, and Layton up above in the ceiling. Jacobson brought up the rear. Sanchez nodded at Anderson. Stepping over bodies and making their way to the cafeteria, they crept slowly back down the brightly lit hallway. In the glaring lights, Jacobson felt exposed, and he was relieved when they reached the end of the first main hallway. Another long, empty hallway led away to the right. To the left was the entrance to the cafeteria.

"Layton, we're at the junction of the two main hallways," Sanchez whispered, cupping his hand around his microphone. "What's your position?"

"Just above you, sir. I can see you through the seams in the ceiling tile."

"Has anyone been up there?" Sanchez asked.

"Yes, sir. The fire retardant has been disturbed by someone crawling in it."

"Anything blocking your ability to move forward?"

"Just ducts and pipes and electrical conduits, sir," Layton said. "Some places might get tight. I'll let you know if I run into roadblocks."

Sanchez nodded. "Roger that. Everyone, move forward to the network closet."

Staying close to the walls, they stole silently around the corner. Unlike the other hallways, this one was clear of bodies. The unmarked networking closet door had an electronic lock. Hallett swiped his card. The lock clicked, and he pushed the door open. Two network racks occupied most of the space. Telephone wires snaked down the wall to a telephone patch panel mounted on the wall.

After withdrawing his tablet from his pack, Hallett called up the building's schematics and tapped the screen.

"Lieutenant, the security network switch has been shut down," he whispered to Sanchez, standing beyond the open door. "The power cable's been removed. The voice and data equipment don't appear to be damaged. Only the network switch is powered off."

"Can you start it up?"

"Yes, sir. Stand by."

Jacobson looked up at the ceiling. A slow minute crawled by before Hallett got back on the radio. "Admiral, please confirm operational status."

The roar of the helicopter sounded over the radio. "Stand by."

Moments later, the roar of the helicopter returned. "Team, grid one's security cameras are online. Proceed to the second wiring closet while we go through the feeds. We'll update if we see anything."

Hallett exited the closet, shutting the door behind him. Anderson led the way down the hallway toward the back of the building. Three hazardous-chemical aid stations appeared. A hazmat suit and the scattered contents of a chemical medical kit lay next to a dead lab technician. Jacobson stepped over the hazmat suit. Had the guy been trying to put that on?

The next two doors had red hazardous-materials signs posted on the walls. One of the lab's steel doors had been twisted partially off but was still attached by a reinforced hinge. Jacobson examined the misshapen steel. What could exert that much force? In combat, the easiest way through a door was to either shoot out the hinges or use an explosive breeching charge. Civilian first responders, like firemen, used specialized pry bars to get through doors. Given enough force, even a crowbar could break a steel door, but he had never seen a door opened like a can of tuna.

"Admiral, are you seeing this?" Sanchez murmured.

"We see it, Lieutenant. Proceed to the second wiring closet. Be advised, you are leaving zone three for zone four. You'll be on your own until the next set of cameras comes online."

"Roger that."

They moved around a corner and crept past an empty conference room.

Sergeant Anderson stopped at the next door, sniffed, and looked inside. "Admiral," he whispered, "we have a lot of dead civilians in an office area."

"Survivors?"

"None I can see."

"Acknowledged. Proceed to the wiring closet."

Anderson crept past the open door. Sanchez and Griffin did the same. Jacobson reached the doorway and felt his stomach tighten. He had been around combat for most of his adult life, but it hadn't prepared him for what he saw inside. Dead men and women were everywhere. Overturned chairs, phones, and furniture were scattered among the dead. An overhead florescent light hung above the doorway, throwing the surrounding area into partial darkness. Beneath the shattered light lay ceiling tiles. The door had a self-closer and an electronic lock, but a fallen chair kept the door from swinging shut. The smell was worse than in the lobby.

Jacobson started to move past but stopped. He couldn't explain why, but something bothered him about the room. He retreated to the other side of the doorway, next to the card swipe. A yellow sign, flung onto the carpet, said, "Ask Me a Wellness Question!" Face down, a woman, covered in blood, sprawled next to the door.

"Sanchez," he hissed, "hold up."

Sanchez turned around. With a hand over his microphone, he asked, "See something?"

"I need a minute. Something's not right."

The thunder of the helicopter crackled over McDermott's radio. "Is there a problem, Major?"

Jacobson tried to keep his voice low but loud enough for McDermott to hear. "I'm not sure, sir. Something's odd."

Impatience entered McDermott's voice. "We're dark here, Major.

We cannot provide aid until the security cameras are brought online. Sanchez, how far are you from the second wiring closet?"

"Fifty feet, sir."

"Close up the perimeter, Jacobson. Once the cameras are online, we'll send you back if we see anything."

Jacobson didn't argue. All he had to do was get the embryos, find out about the dogs, and get out.

"10-4. Moving up."

He moved past the door. Nothing lunged at him from the gloom.

When they reached the network closet, Hallett swiped his access card and disappeared inside to power up the switch.

Jacobson put a hand on Sanchez's shoulder. "Lieutenant, I want another look at the office area."

"Why?"

"I don't know."

"If someone gets inside our perimeter because you're out of position, we'll be compromised."

"I know."

Sanchez turned to Hallett. "Is the switch up?"

"It'll be another minute before it's operational."

"All right, Major," Sanchez said. "You have until McDermott tells us to move."

Jacobson led the way back to the office. Nothing had changed. Dead men and women lay where they had fallen. In the white, gritty dust thrown by the fallen fire retardant, Jacobson saw bare footprints.

"There are footprints in the fire retardant from the broken ceiling tiles," Jacobson whispered to Sanchez. "The office staff ran this way as a group, probably because they were being chased from behind, but they were cut off when one of the killers dropped down through the light tray." He pointed at the fallen light. "That's why the staff are all facing away from the doorway. They tried to retreat the way they'd come and got hit from both directions."

"They were bottled up?"

"Yes. Terrified people don't think straight. They congregate in herds, like sheep. The killers exploited that."

The roar of the helicopter crackled over the radio. "Hallett, the security cameras are operational, but we're getting packet collisions on the network. Are you sure you powered up the right switch?"

Hallett slung his weapon over his shoulder and brought out his tablet to look at the schematics. "Yes, sir. I checked the number with the schematic. It was the only thing in the closet that was turned off."

"The video from the cameras is very choppy. Can you shut it down so we can try to isolate the problem? The network schematic might be incorrect."

"Yes, sir."

Sanchez straightened. "You heard the admiral, Major," he whispered. "Back to the closet."

Jacobson got to his feet and took one final look at the room, the fallen light, and the broken ceiling tile.

"Wait."

Sanchez scowled, but Jacobson cut him off. "Look at the chair."

The roar of the helicopter came over the radio as McDermott clicked on. "We can't see a thing here, Major. Move back to the closet. We need the switch shut down."

"Admiral, there's a chair holding the office door open."

"So?"

"It's lying on top of some broken ceiling tiles."

"Which means?"

Jacobson hissed the words as fast as he could. "Everything the killers have done here has been about attacking from multiple directions, sir. They did it in the lobby, and they did it here. The dead cameras, the powered-off switches, the slow network. I'm certain all of this has been a setup to get us bottled up right here, right now."

"How do you know that?"

"The door, sir. The chair holding it open is on top of the ceiling tiles."

"So?"

"It was put there after the killer dropped out of the ceiling, sir. They propped the door open."

The lights went out.

CHAPTER 6

It has been said that a bad day fishing is a better day spent than doing anything else, so James Barnett decided to try his luck in his favorite fishing hole under the Diamond Creek Bridge. It had rained hard all night, and the heavy downpour had turned the normally placid creek into a torrent of rumbling boulders, rusted cars, dead animals, and anything else the creek could get hold of.

He wore a black, sleeveless T-shirt and jeans pushed into his hip waders. In one back pocket was his multi-tool. The other held a pair of diagonal cutting pliers he used to cut fishhooks. The water had dropped, but every step through the swollen creek was still a treacherous scramble from the bank to the bridge's middle abutment. Loaded down with items large and small, he juggled a fishing pole, tackle box of hooks, leaders, sinkers, flashlight, and a can of corn. He placed his gear on the abutment's concrete ledge.

He propped the flashlight so he could see what he was doing, and opened the can of corn. Threading five kernels onto the hook, he hummed an old song by ZZ Top. Now he was ready.

A couple of hours fishing and he'd be able to face the day—and whatever pissy mood his ex-wife would be in. When he got back to town, he'd pick up Bailey. Her mom, Cindy, needed the day to get ready for her wedding, and she didn't want their daughter underfoot. He'd bring Bailey back to the bike shop, flip the OPEN sign, and hope that Adam would show up.

Adam had gone down to Phoenix to test a new carbon bike frame and hadn't come home last night. He hadn't answered his cell phone, which was worrisome enough, but Adam had gone riding in the desert where the daytime temperature was only slightly less hot than the surface of the sun. James told himself not to worry. His brother was an experienced rider in peak physical condition. He had probably gotten caught in the storm or forgot to charge his phone.

Testing the slippery rocks beneath his feet, James pushed off, heading toward a deep hole just downstream from the abutment. When his feet were set, he cocked his wrist and cast his line over a submerged log. The strike was immediate and hard. The tip of the rod whipped down toward the dark water, the fish dove under the log, and the line snapped.

"Well, that was fast," Adam said. "Somebody must be hungry."

He reeled in the snapped line, still whistling the tune under his breath, attached another leader to the end of the line, squeezed on a sinker with his tool, and tied a hook to the leader. He baited the hook, set his feet, and cast the hook over the log. The rod dipped, the fish dove, and the line broke again.

He frowned and reeled in the broken line. What could snap a twenty-pound line? Apache trout? Channel cat?

He put on another leader, sinker, and hook, tossed the bait over the log, and resumed humming. It was a beautiful morning, and the fish were biting. This time he tried to keep the fish from diving under the log by holding the pole up as high as he could, but the fish would have none of it. The rod dipped, the fish dove, and the line snapped.

He swore and waded back to the abutment. He had been here five minutes and already lost three leaders. He had plenty of hooks and sinkers, but not many leaders. Propping the fishing pole on the ledge, he rummaged through his tackle box until he found the spool of the two-hundred-pound line he had used for marlin fishing in Mexico. He swapped out the twenty.

"Try breaking this," he said.

He attached his last leader, hook, and sinker to the heavier line. He had just cast his bait over the log when he heard a scream and looked up to see a woman plummeting from the bridge. She had dark hair, a pinched, terrified face, and wore a business suit. Someone had wired a block of cement to her ankles. She screamed one long, horrifying shriek as she fell. She saw him, and desperate hope blazed in her eyes. Then she hit the water.

The impact of her body wrenched at his fishing pole and yanked him headfirst into the storm-swollen current. Icy water closed above his head, and a horrible weight filled his waders. Trying not to scream the air out of his lungs, he fought to reach the surface. Pain laced up his chest. The log caught his left boot, and he spun sideways, trapped between the weight on the end of the line and the snag that had caught his boot. Tiny suns exploded behind his eyes.

For an instant he almost let go of the rod, but then his left hand grabbed the log. His air nearly gone, he tore at his trapped boot and wrenched it free. His head cleared the water, and he got one good, desperate gasp of air before he sank down into the hole. Water swirled and churned, the cold burning his skin. He flailed downward for what seemed like forever until he hit bottom. The starry sky was a tiny, dim light above his head.

Desperate hands clutched his shirt. Hair brushed his cheek, and then the woman's terrified face loomed in front of him. A torrent of bubbles burst from her lips. He let go of the pole and grabbed her jacket collar. He hadn't gotten more than a quick gasp before being pulled under. He needed air.

He kicked upwards and didn't move. Her weight, combined with the water in his waders, kept him anchored. Panic seared his mind. In that icy hell he couldn't function without oxygen. He let go of her, pushed off the bottom, and used his arms, but she had his legs in a death grip. He pushed her away. If he could just get free, he could swim to the surface, grab a breath, and swim back down to her.

She released his legs. Despair and stoic acceptance of her fate clouded her eyes. Bubbles exploded from her mouth. She shuddered, her body convulsing. If he left her, would the current sweep her away, or would the concrete block hold her in place? He grabbed her jacket and kicked off the bottom with all his strength, one hand tight on her jacket, the other reaching for the surface. All his will and determination went into scissoring his legs.

His grasping, desperate hand grabbed the stub of a branch. One-handed, he pulled the two of them slowly up to the log. His head finally broke the surface. Sweet, blessed air coursed into his lungs. He crawled over the log, dragging the dead weight of the woman's body until he collapsed against the abutment. Her eyes were flat, unseeing slits. Water drained through blue lips.

He tried to grab her nose with his fingers to give her mouth-to-mouth but could not. He was so cold and exhausted his fingers wouldn't obey. Shouts sounded from the bridge. A hard, sharp crack sounded. A bullet skipped off the water. Whoever had thrown her off the bridge had seen him.

He pulled her around to the other side of the pillar, her back against his chest, and linked his hands under her diaphragm, made a fist, and pulled up. Water exploded from her mouth. He waited. She didn't move. He did it again. She coughed, gagging.

"Just breathe," he told her.

"K-knew you w-would come," she stuttered. "S-saw it in your face."

"I didn't have a choice. You landed on my line and pulled me in."

She looked young, maybe mid-thirties. Dark hair plastered her head. And who would wear a business suit in northern Arizona? Real estate agent? Banker? In normal circumstances she would have been attractive, but now she looked half-drowned.

He grabbed bolt cutters from his toolbox and, grasping her thighs, submerged and groped his way down to her ankles. He cut the encircling wire and shot up to the surface. Another sharp crack sounded. A bullet hit the abutment and whined away.

He looked up at the underside of the bridge. Too dark to make out the shooter. He could be anywhere.

"Can you walk?" he asked. "Whoever threw you off the bridge knew exactly where to drop you into that hole. That means they know how to drive down here."

"I-I think so."

As they staggered into the current, she held onto him. He felt horribly cold, and his teeth chattered. He wanted to find someplace warm. Stumbling, he fought his way across the creek. Halfway to shore, he tripped and fell. She pulled him upright.

They finally reached the bank and staggered from the water. He fell to his knees in the warm dirt, completely spent, but each second of delay brought danger closer. Sitting, he yanked off the waders. Each boot came off with a squish.

Three sharp barks sounded. The bullets hissed past.

She clutched his arm. "Stand up! We have to go!"

He tried to stand and fell back to his knees. Exhaustion had his chest in a vise.

She pulled him up, both hands under his arms. "Where's your car? I'm not going to let them take me again!"

He pointed into the trees. Her face tight with effort, she dragged him forward. One step at a time, with her arm around his back, he staggered into the pines. It was only a minute or so to his car, but it felt much longer.

When she saw it, dismay flooded her face. "This piece of junk is your car?"

"It's not a piece of junk," he gasped. "It's a frame-off '59 'Vette."

"I don't know what that means."

"It means the car was completely taken apart and restored." He dug the key out of his pocket. "I borrowed it from my brother Adam. My pickup's getting the rear differential oil changed."

"Great, I got saved by a car nut."

He popped the trunk and pulled out a pair of jeans and sneakers from Adam's gym bag. He sat on the chrome bumper, then took off his sodden socks and pants and slid his legs and feet into the jeans and sneakers. Pulling off his own T-shirt, he shrugged into a sweatshirt from the bag. The shirt was dry and warm and felt wonderful.

"There's a pair of sweats and some T-shirts." He passed the bag to her. "Get out of your wet clothes. Once we start driving, the air is going to turn your clothing to ice."

"Doesn't the car have a heater?"

"It doesn't work. Adam hasn't installed the new heating core."

She turned her back and unbuttoned her blouse. He put the key in the Corvette's ignition. The new engine kicked over with a rumble. He shifted into neutral and set the brake. Better to leave it idling in case they had to make a fast getaway. Then he returned to the trunk and pulled Adam's twelve-gauge automatic shotgun from its leather case. He looked up to see her gaping at the weapon. She had pulled on the sweatshirt and removed her slacks but hadn't put on the sweatpants. Her bare legs were pale in the darkness.

"Does your brother always carry a gun in the trunk of his car?" she asked.

"He does today." He pushed three-inch magnums into the magazine.

"What's special about today?"

"My ex is getting married. The only person her brother Mike hates more than me is my brother Adam."

"And you're both going to the wedding?"

"It's expected."

"Why would this Mike guy hate Adam more than you?"

"Because of an accident that happened a few years back." He leaned the shotgun against the bumper and watched her lace up a pair of racquetball shoes, three sizes too big.

"No such thing as forgive and forget?" she said.

"Not in Mike's universe," he said. "Why would someone throw you off a bridge?"

Her eyes danced away. "I don't know. They gagged me and put a hood over my head."

"Where did they grab you?"

"At a Mexican restaurant in Show Low. I was on my way up for the Labor Day weekend. I have a friend who lives up here."

"Where do you work?"

"I work for a medical company in Scottsdale." Her eyes danced away again. "We do stem cell and gene therapy research."

Not a good liar, he thought.

He opened a box of shotgun shells and filled his pockets. "Would they want to kill you because of your job?"

"I can't see why."

Another lie. Okay, so he had rescued a liar, but that didn't mean she deserved to be killed. He finished with the shells and pointed north. "See those headlights coming our way? That's the people who threw you off the bridge. They're on the dirt road coming in. It runs just south of us on the other side of that hill." He pointed up at the small, round hill to his left. "With any luck, they'll stay on the road and go past us. How many of them are there?"

"Two."

"Weapons?"

"I couldn't see through the hood."

James pointed to the trees to his right.

"Hide behind those pines and wait for me. When you see me running downhill, jump in the car. If I don't come back, drive for help."

"What are you going to do?"

"Give them a reason not to follow us."

"Are you a policeman or something?"

"No, but I don't like people shooting at me."

———

He jogged uphill through the black volcanic rocks, and when he reached the top, he scrambled down the other side, picking his way through the boulders. Headlights approached. He crouched in a cluster of young pines next to the dirt road. He heard the roar of an engine. A white panel van slid around a curve, back tires churning for traction in the cinders. Two men sat in front. The one by the passenger window pointed toward the glowing flashlight James had left sitting on the abutment.

James waited until they had sped past, switched off the shotgun's safety, and put a shell in the driver's side rear tire. The tire exploded. The van skidded sideways, engine roaring, and crashed into a tree. He put another round through the back window, then started up the hill. A questioning shout rang out behind him.

He had gotten about halfway to the top when a bullet whined past his ear. Another sheared off a branch by his elbow, and then an automatic rifle started barking. He swore in surprise, ducked, and, with his arms around his head, zigzagged from boulder to boulder. Whoever they were, they were amazing shots, especially considering the darkness. He dodged behind a sapling, changed direction, and heard the hiss of a bullet followed by a sharp crack. The sapling splintered and fell. The next bullet whizzed by his head, and he threw himself down onto the soft bed of pine needles. Bullets shrieked past.

Dragging his shotgun—no match for their firepower—he finally reached the boulders at the top. He dove behind the biggest and then ran down the other side of the hill. The woman was nowhere in sight. Had she panicked and run off? He reached the car and threw the twelve-gauge onto the passenger seat.

He got behind the wheel, put the transmission in gear, and started up the dirt track, leaving his headlights off. The shooters had at least one automatic rifle and knew how to use it. If the men had been armed with handguns, he would have placed odds on the shotgun, but an automatic rifle was something else altogether. If she didn't show up by the time he reached the main dirt road, he would have to leave her and go get help. He had no idea who the kidnappers were, but they were better armed, could see better in the dark, and were much better shots than he had expected.

He had almost reached the road when the woman ran out of the darkness. He slowed down, and she jumped in.

"I thought they'd killed you until you came running out of the rocks," she shouted over the engine.

"They have automatic weapons. Did you know that?"

"No."

"You sure you don't know who they are?"

Her eyes flicked away. "I told you no."

"You must have heard something on the drive up."

"All they talked about was football. Nothing but football."

If she didn't want to talk about it, he wasn't going to force her.

"My name's James Barnett."

"I'm Monica."

She didn't offer her last name. He felt another stab of frustration.

He had risked his life to save hers, yet she didn't trust him with her full name.

As soon as he reached the asphalt, he felt under the floor mat for his cell phone and watch. "Here," he said, handing her the phone. "The moment we have cell service, call 911."

She clutched the cell phone to her chest. "I don't want the police involved."

"Why not?"

"I don't have time. I need to reach my car before noon, or my career is over. We can bring in the police after I get my research."

"The people who kidnapped you won't be at the river for long. I shot out their tire, but they'll have a spare."

"I don't have a choice!" The words snapped out. "I've given up everything for my research, and it's worthless unless I get to my car. I know it sounds crazy, but the less you're involved the better. The people trying to kill me won't hesitate to kill you if you get in their way. Just drop me at my car, and forget you ever saw me."

"Where's your car, again?"

"Show Low."

Show Low! What did she think he was, an Uber driver? "That's two hours out of my way. I need to pick up my daughter at my ex's before she accuses me of sabotaging her wedding. Plus, if we go to Show Low, I'll have to turn around and come back this way. If those guys saw the 'Vette, which they probably did, they'll come after me. You might not know anything about cars, but Corvettes are rare up here in the mountains. We'll go to Defiance, get my truck and daughter, and I'll take you to your car."

"You would do that for me?"

"Yes."

He glanced at his watch and floored the accelerator. She wasn't ready for the new motor's power, and her head snapped back.

"Are they after us?" she asked, whipping her head around to look behind them.

"No. But they aren't the only danger. Believe me, and I know this from personal experience, nobody except for the groom wants to be anywhere near Cindy on her wedding day, and I'm going to be late picking up my daughter."

CHAPTER 7

Looking for Couch's cell phone, Victoria Stewart patted him down. Blood seeped from the wound in his throat. If she could find the phone, she could see Dark's phone number. With any luck, there might be a name and address in his contacts. The phone must be somewhere on the floor.

Under the table, a floor safe stood open. Inside were stacks of money, neatly bundled in paper wrappers. Surprised, she stared at the bills and debated what to do. Couch wouldn't need the money, but she did. Every day fighting the narcos had sent her deeper into debt. Lately, she'd had to choose between filling her propane tank or buying groceries.

Her empty stomach decided the question. She found a shopping bag and stuffed the money inside. On hands and knees, she ran her fingers beneath the furniture and found Couch's gun and a dirty plate.

The ring of a cell phone shattered the silence. It had fallen between the couch cushions. She snatched it up, hoping there would be a name on the display. RESTRICTED, it said.

She thought about answering but didn't. Surprise was her best option, especially until she figured out who Dark was and what he was planning. She stuffed the phone in her pocket and picked up her shell casings. Then she left the cabin, hurried to the Rover, and threw the money on the passenger seat.

They took them in the RV. My wife and girls.

That's what Thompson had said. She turned on the headlights and followed the RV's muddy tracks to the main road. The driver had turned west.

This stretch of highway ran between bleak cinder mesas and islands of ponderosa pine. If the RV stayed on the main road, she could overtake it. The road slowly rose to go around a hill and started down the other side. Far-off taillights shone in the darkness. As she drew nearer, she made out the RV's lumbering bulk. She maintained her speed and passed without looking at the driver. Soon, the RV fell behind her and out of sight.

Ten minutes later, she found a gravel pullout. After hiding the Rover in the trees, she removed her .308 from its gun case. In the Rover's gun tray, she found a suppressor and screwed it onto the end of an Uzi. She tucked her hair under a stocking cap and pulled it low over her high-contrast shooting goggles. Two stun grenades, a 9mm pistol, tactical gloves, and a knife completed her preparations. She took her weapons and ran into the trees.

She didn't have long to wait. With each rise and fall of the road, the RV lumbered toward her, the vehicle rocking gently back and forth. The man who had given her a thumbs-up sat in the driver's seat. She saw his face in the RV's dashboard light and, through the .308's scope, watched him get closer and closer.

"Here we go," she whispered.

She took a breath, let it out, and gently squeezed the trigger. The rifle bucked against her shoulder. The passenger rear tire exploded. The RV swerved back and forth, the driver fighting for control as the tire tore itself apart. He slammed on the brakes and muscled the RV off the road and into the pullout.

Victoria switched the .308 for the Uzi and dodged through the trees. The RV's stereo blared, and even through closed windows she heard the thump of hard rock. The side door screeched open. The driver, carrying a flashlight, jumped out. He was young and tall and wore jeans, cowboy boots, a white T-shirt, and a baseball cap. He stopped at the flat tire, aimed a flashlight at it, and pushed the ball cap up on his forehead.

"What did I hit?" he wondered aloud.

Now I've got his attention, Victoria thought. But what next?

Thompson had said the men had his wife and daughters, but she saw no sign of women. The blaring music made it impossible to hear footsteps inside the RV, and she couldn't just kill the driver. She could have the wrong RV or, god forbid, could even be imagining the whole thing. Less than three hours ago she had been having trouble sleeping, and now she was thinking about shooting a man she didn't know.

The driver returned to the RV and came out lugging a toolbox. Victoria picked up a rock. It hit the gravel near his boots. He dropped the toolbox, and his head snapped sideways.

"Put up your hands, sir," she called out, motioning upward with the barrel of the Uzi.

He lifted the flashlight, eyes sharpening as he saw her. His face was lean. A shaggy mane of blond hair fell on his shoulders.

"Well, aren't you a pretty picture with all those freckles, Shortcake," he drawled. "What are you doing behind that big tree with a gun?"

"Lower the flashlight and put up your hands."

A good-natured smile split his face. "Hey, I know you, Shortcake! You were driving that fine candy Rover earlier! You and that SUV make a pretty pair. How about coming out and saying a proper hello? My friends call me 'Flight,' but you can call me whatever you want."

His drawl was easy and natural. Uh oh, she thought. Just a tourist.

The RV's side window exploded, showering glass across the turnout. A bullet hissed past her ear. With a yelp, she ducked away, falling onto the pine needles and rolling. When she looked up, the flashlight lay in the dirt, and Flight had disappeared around the back of the RV. While she'd been standing with her shoulder against the tree, he had been calling out her position.

"You still with us, Shortcake?" he shouted.

She raised her voice. "Yes, sir."

"Good. You and me gonna have some fun then."

Another rifle shot thundered from the RV and splintered the branch above her head. Crouching, she duck-walked to a larger tree, ten feet away and closer to the rear of the RV. The next bullet landed behind her.

Like John Wayne in a gunfight at high noon, Flight, with a double-handed grip on a Desert Eagle, jumped out from behind the RV. He squeezed off three wild shots, the big gun booming and kicking upward with each recoil. He grinned and leapt back to safety.

"How was that, Shortcake? You like my big gun?"

The big gun wasn't what she was worried about. It was the rifleman inside who had her worried. She examined the exterior of the RV. The window by the side door had blown out. That had been where the shot came from. She searched the curtained windows for the shooter's silhouette but the darkness and the angle of the RV made it impossible to see the RV's interior. If she could keep Flight talking, then maybe she could take her shot.

"Flight, what are you doing with a cannon like that?"

"Having fun, Shortcake." He chuckled. "My gun's always ready for a good time, if you know what I mean."

"Size doesn't matter, Flight. 'Course, I'm sure that's not the first time you've heard that from a woman."

He barked out a laugh. "And we had fun, fun, fun 'til I took your Rover away."

She slid behind a bush. From her spot low on the ground, she saw Flight's boots below the RV's undercarriage. He stepped out from behind the rear tire. She glanced at where he had jumped before. Would he be stupid enough to do the same thing again?

Pick your spot, then shoot and move. That's what her father had taught her and how she had terrorized the narcos. Never do the same thing twice and always do the unexpected. Don't let them get comfortable, and never get pinned down.

She lifted the Uzi and waited.

Gun held in both hands and elbows locked, Flight leapt out from behind the bumper. His boots hit the ground and she fired. Flight spun sideways in an odd, jerking dance and crumpled to the ground.

The rifle boomed again. The slug slammed into a pine. She sprinted out of the trees to the back of the RV. The rifle cracked again, and the bullet flew over her head. Rifles were great at shooting from a distance, but they were lousy up close. That's why she had swapped out her .308.

She stopped by the RV's rear bumper and took a quick look at Flight. Her bullet had torn open his chest. She picked up his Desert Eagle, shook her head at the beast, and flung it into the trees.

"Not so fun, fun, fun now, are we?" she murmured.

But what now? If the woman and kids were inside, she had to be careful. The bullets she used weren't as big as the .50 caliber monsters fired by the Desert Eagle, but her hand-loaded, high-velocity jacketed rounds would go through anything that wasn't armored. That's what she had used with the narcos' vehicles. But if she fired indiscriminately through the RV, she was liable to kill the hostages. That was why the police used hollow points. They hit their target and stopped. Jacketed rounds did not.

She slid past the tire Flight had ducked behind and crept around the bumper decals. The RV rocked slightly on its springs. She threw herself to the ground. The rifle cracked, and the bullet tore through the wall where she had hunkered down. The rifle roared again, and the next bullet cut through the RV's lower wall into the dirt. She threw herself under the vehicle. Flight had been an idiot, but the person inside was smart. The next bullet went through the undercarriage and exploded into the gravel next to her shoulder. She slithered sideways toward the front of the RV. The shooter kept firing blindly, each bullet cutting through the RV's floor. The rifle boomed again. The bullet struck the RV's steel chassis and ricocheted back inside.

She squirmed out from beneath the RV, pulled a stun grenade from her vest, and threw it through the broken window. She covered her ears and opened her mouth. There was a thunderous, explosive whap and a sudden hiccuping lack of air pressure. The remaining windows detonated outwards in showers of glass.

Uzi tight against her shoulder, she came through the side door. A man with salt-and-pepper hair lay on the kitchen floor in front of a closed bedroom door. The air reeked of gunpowder.

Where the ricocheting bullet had caught him, blood pooled under his hips. She picked up his rifle, ejected the clip, and threw it out the window.

"Where's the woman and kids?"

His dilated eyes blinked, and he didn't answer. Stun grenades were designed to cause temporary blindness and disorientation but his eyes did not look like someone who had been blinded. They were soft and unfocused. She checked his wound. The ricochet had torn through his femoral artery. He sighed, the air rattling in his throat, and lay still.

Fighting the druggies, she had seen a lot of death. It wasn't like TV. There was nothing noble or dignified. Just pain, blood, and confusion.

She had one grenade left. If there was a third bad guy, he could shoot through the door and kill her. Alternately, she could go around to the back of the RV, shoot out the rear window, toss in the grenade, and use the roof ladder to climb up and look inside.

She knew what the police would do. They would cover the windows with snipers and use a bullhorn to talk to whomever was inside. They would have ten or twenty cops and maybe even a helicopter so that they could see what was going on from above.

But all she had was herself. If someone drove by and saw Flight on the ground, the police would be on their way. How would she explain what had happened? She'd spend the rest of her medicated life in a federal lockup.

She kicked open the bedroom door, then darted through with the Uzi hard against her shoulder. The back of the RV held a bed, a bathroom, and a closet. A woman with a ripped blouse lay gagged on the bed, her arms above her head and wrists handcuffed to the wall. Tears streamed down her face. Two small girls cowered on the floor. Both were gagged and tied.

Victoria lowered her weapon.

"You're going to be all right, ma'am," she told the woman. "You're safe."

She pulled off the woman's gag and plucked the dishrag from her mouth.

The woman sobbed. "Are my girls okay?"

"They're fine," Victoria said. "What's your name?"

"Jan Thompson." Tears spilled from her eyes. "They took my husband! They shot him and took him away!"

"He sent me. That's why I'm here. He held on long enough to tell me where you were."

The blood left Jan's face. "Is he...?"

"I didn't get there in time. I'm sorry."

Body shaking, Jan started to cry. Victoria draped a towel over Jan's torn blouse. Jan bared her teeth and thrashed against the cuffs.

"Get these off me!"

"You know where the keys are?"

"The older one had them."

Victoria started to leave but saw the girls and cut them free with her knife. The oldest couldn't have been more than three. Victoria reached out to comfort her, but the girl recoiled.

"It's okay," Victoria said. Her voice was rougher than she wanted it to be. "Climb up next to your mother."

Victoria went to the big man lying just outside the bedroom door. Strands of salt-and-pepper hair had fallen into one unfocused eye. Her hands shook. The asshole had almost killed her. She was lucky to be alive.

The man had a keychain around his neck. Not wanting to touch him, she lifted his head. Was this Dark, the voice that invaded her dreams? She wished he'd spoken instead of leaving her with yet another missing puzzle piece.

The key was too big for the handcuffs. She tried the side door, but the key didn't fit. Mystery upon mystery. She pulled open cabinets. Inside the kitchen storage closet, bolted to the floor, stood a gun safe. The key opened the lock. She whistled. Whoever the men were, they knew their weaponry. There were handguns, a tricked-out tactical shotgun, and two Heckler & Koch assault rifles.

She picked up a rifle. Did these guys launder money for the narcos? Did they rob banks?

She returned the H&K to the safe and pulled out a brown legal-sized envelope full of money. What would money launderers or bank robbers want with Thompson?

"Did you find the key?" Jan called out.

"Not yet. I found some guns. The keys could be anywhere. Let me keep looking."

She closed the envelope and stuffed it in her coat pocket. Her entire body trembled, the aftermath of the adrenaline rush, and she touched her chest, feeling the all too familiar pull of scar tissue. Now that the excitement had died down, she was going to have to live in her body again. Mentally and physically exhausted, she wanted to get back to the ranch. Every minute she delayed her departure increased the chances of something going wrong, but she couldn't very well leave Jan Thompson handcuffed with two small children.

Opening the side door, she stepped out into the darkness. No key, no bolt cutter, no hacksaw in the toolbox. Flight lay sprawled in the dirt, a startled look on his face. Off in the distance she saw headlights and heard an approaching car. How could the authorities understand what had happened when she didn't understand it herself? She dragged Flight behind the RV and used his flashlight to retrieve her shell casings. She left the Desert Eagle where she had thrown it. The police could pick it up.

She dropped the Uzi in the Rover's gun tray and put the money in Couch's shopping bag. As she worked, a car zoomed past without slowing. She returned to the RV and slipped the key back around the dead man's neck. If he was Dark, then maybe his death would put an end to the dreams. But even though that was the outcome she'd long desired, his death left her angry. She still didn't know why or how he had so completely penetrated her thoughts.

In the back room, the girls had crawled up next to their mother.

"I can't find the key," Victoria told Jan. "Their toolbox doesn't have a bolt cutter. The police will have to unlock you. I'm sorry." She took a breath, trying to keep the desperation out of her voice. "I need to know something. Why did they kill your husband?"

Jan stared at the ceiling and swallowed. "I don't know what exactly happened," she finally managed. "Will said there was an accident at his job. He wouldn't tell us anything else except we had to leave."

"Accident?"

"He wouldn't talk about it. He and his former boss picked us up, and we headed up here. They knew someone who lived in the mountains. They thought we'd be safe until they could figure out what to do." Tears rolled down her cheeks. "We were coming out of a restaurant in Show Low when they jumped us. Will tried to fight them, but they shot him. That's all I know. None of it makes sense."

"What does your husband do for a living?"

"He's a medical biologist. He works in a lab. Most of his day is spent looking in a microscope. Why would anyone want to kill someone like that?"

Victoria felt dizzy. It couldn't be a coincidence. The odds were just too great.

"Did your husband work for Biodosius?"

Jan gaped. "Yes, he did! How do you know that?"

"And they do stem cell research?" Victoria clutched at the scars on her chest. The narcos had killed her once. She had died when they fire-bombed her truck, and only a medical miracle had brought her back. "Like, for burn victims?"

CHAPTER 8

Something big and fast came through the office doorway and hit Lieutenant Sanchez with a bone-shattering crunch. Sergeant Anderson went down, his helmet spinning across the hallway. The ceiling exploded, and a third shape landed next to Corporal Griffin. He stumbled backward, holding his throat. Hallett dropped his tablet and tried to get his rifle off his shoulder but was lifted off the floor and slammed into the wall.

"Sanchez, what the hell is going on in there?" Admiral McDermott demanded over the radio. "I can't see anything!"

Something grabbed Jacobson by his helmet and threw him down the hallway into a wall. His headset smashed with the impact. A dark shape lunged at him. Jacobson dove away. Something sharp caught his vest. One of his flash grenades clattered to the floor. He threw himself through the open office door, crashed into the chair holding the door open, and fell sprawling to the floor. The door swung closed behind him with a gentle, firm *click.*

The grenade detonated with a thunderous boom. Even with a wall between him and the explosion, the explosion made his ears ring. He fumbled his goggles over his eyes, untangled himself from the chair, and staggered toward the door. The flash grenade would end this mayhem. Anyone in the hallway would be incapacitated for at least five minutes, more than long enough for him to kill them.

He was reaching for the doorknob when a shoulder smashed into the metal from the other side. He stopped in disbelief. It wasn't possible. Flash grenades were designed to overwhelm the photoreceptors in the eyes and cause severe balance problems by disturbing the fluid in the ears. Even if the killers had closed their eyes and put their hands over their ears, they wouldn't be able to stand up, let alone fight. He had used stun grenades in combat and had even been stunned a few times in training. They were extremely effective. Nothing could recover that fast.

Something screamed, the sound shrieking into a howl, and a body smashed into the door again. Jacobson brought up his rifle and emptied the clip through the metal. Another howl sounded down the hallway. Something struck the wall so hard that drywall exploded into the room.

Jacobson ejected his spent clip, slammed in a replacement, and fired, sweeping the rifle horizontally across the door and the wall until the magazine clicked empty. He ejected the clip, slid in a fresh one, and, jumping over bodies and equipment, hurtled into an adjoining office. Unlike the building's rear exit where people had died like slaughtered sheep, the office staff in this room had tried to fight off the attackers by pushing desks against the door.

He clambered over the barricade, butt-pushed the furniture aside, and opened the door. He was in the northwest corner. If he headed toward the south lobby, he might run into whomever or whatever had shut off the lights. The loading dock was behind the killers to the north, so that was out. The west exit would give him his best shot. Of course, running would leave Sanchez and his team behind, but he couldn't help them, not when the killers could hit him from multiple directions. Besides, they were almost certainly dead. He needed to call for help.

The locked door behind him exploded with a crash. An angry cry rang out. Jacobson broke into a sprint. His pursuer leapt over the barricade and slid across the hallway floor. Jacobson fought off the desire to look back. He heard the rasp of eager breathing, the churning of legs, and dove around the corner, sliding on the tile as if he were stealing home base. As he slid, he pulled a fragmentation grenade out of his jacket, yanked the pin, and threw it back around the corner. The grenade clattered on the tile. A long second went by, and then it exploded. Shrapnel struck the walls and floor. Dust, fire retardant, and wiring rained down from the ceiling.

Wheezing sounded from around the corner. Something heavy was dragging itself down the hallway. Another howl sounded from inside the office area, followed by more running footsteps. A second howl answered from where Sanchez and his men had died.

Jacobson staggered to his feet. He stumbled into a run and turned left into the next hallway, then right. Labs, offices, and conference rooms flew past. A shriek sounded behind him, maybe a half-dozen turns back. Another answered, this one closer and to his left. For a moment he thought about finding a hiding place, but they knew the building, and he didn't.

An exit sign appeared. He followed it to the west lobby and saw a pair of heavy glass doors. Two female security guards lay on the floor. He shot out the hinges of one door, pushed it out of the way, grabbed one of the women's purses, and stumbled outside.

The rain had not let up. Cowering under the deluge, he sprinted for the parking lot, shifted his rifle to his left hand, and searched the purse with his right. As a married man, he had gone through his wife's purse hundreds of times, and it was never easy. He pushed the wallet out of the way and dug through some makeup and an appointment book. No keys. He upended the purse and shook the contents onto the asphalt. A flash of lightning illuminated a keychain. He snatched up the keys and aimed the largest, with a big letter "H," at the parking lot. When he clicked the lock button, lights flashed and a horn chirped. At least he had the right lot.

Pressing the alarm button, he ran through the cars and finally skidded to a stop in front of a Honda Odyssey. He swore. He was going to escape a pack of killers in a minivan. Maybe he should pick up some milk on the way home.

The lobby's glass doors exploded behind him. He unlocked the van and got inside, dropping his rifle on the passenger seat and removing his pistol. The rifle was a far better weapon for most things, but not if he was driving. He stabbed the keys into the ignition and started the engine. Kids' music blared through the speakers. He smacked the stereo's power button. The music cut off.

He threw the transmission into reverse. The minivan lumbered sedately backward out of the parking spot. He spun the wheel, stopped, put the transmission into drive, and hit the accelerator. The van floundered and then lurched forward. He reached the end of the row and made a sharp left. A sippy cup in the center console went flying, lost its lid, and spilled juice. He risked looking out the side window. Three shadows raced diagonally through the rain. They clearly had the advantage. He had to avoid the cars and landscaping, while they could go over anything in their way.

He gave the van more gas and accelerated through the darkness toward the exit. The back window shattered. He snatched up the pistol, thumbed off the safety, and fired blindly over his shoulder.

The main security building loomed through the rain. He wrenched the wheel, banged over the curb, and crashed through the exit's traffic control arm. A red traffic light appeared.

"Dammit!"

He dropped the pistol, grabbed the Honda's wheel with both hands, and used all four lanes to turn left onto the city street. The tires lost their traction on the wet asphalt. The van's big rear end began to slide. He wrenched the wheel the other way. A running shape appeared outside his window. Something big and dark smashed into his front bumper. It rolled up over the hood and hit the windshield before the momentum of the van's turn sent it tumbling away.

Jacobson flattened the accelerator. The van groaned forward, wheels spinning through the puddles. Another red light appeared. He ignored it and sailed through. The faster he went, the harder it became to see through the rain. He groped around the steering column, pulling levers until the wipers finally switched on. The glass cleared, and he centered himself in his lane.

Expensive Scottsdale subdivisions and the occasional golf course flew past. Then he saw a McDonald's on the corner. Jacobson pulled into the parking lot and circled around until the SUV faced the street.

He steadied his hands on the steering wheel and tried to order the jumbled images of killers dropping from the ceiling and tearing victims limb from limb. No enemy he'd ever fought could shrug off a flash grenade or bend metal doors or run fast enough to chase down a speeding car.

Shaking his head, he took a cell phone from his vest pocket and dialed. "It's Jacobson," he said. "Reporting in."

"Where are you?" O'Dell asked.

"In Scottsdale," Jacobson said, smirking at his face in the rearview mirror. No point in mentioning McDonald's.

"Well, if you're in Scottsdale, why is no one answering the radio?" General O'Dell demanded. "Is there any sign of the dog? What about the embryos?"

The dog and the embryos? He had to be kidding. "We didn't get as far as the basement," Jacobson said. "We were attacked."

"What about McDermott's men?"

"They're all dead, sir. Whatever's in there, it killed them. Everyone on McDermott's team."

CHAPTER 9

Adam headed toward the distant lights. In the dark, he had no idea where he was driving, but at least he was moving away from the Nightmare that hunted him.

The further he went, the worse the road became. Decades of rain and erosion had washed away the dirt, leaving mostly rocks. With each bump, the Chevy's suspension shuddered. The truck did not have power steering, and every turn of the wheel felt like a white-hot branding iron pressed against his wound. Mop balanced on the seat, head out the window and nose sniffing the wind.

The ruts finally joined a slightly better road, and Adam shifted out of first. As if the storm was upset that it hadn't killed him and wanted a second chance, thunder echoed over the mountains. Pine trees gave way to junipers and finally cactus and creosote bushes. He spotted a Tonto National Forest boundary marker and stopped to check the road atlas. The Tonto National Forest was huge. It stretched from the Phoenix city limits north to the Mogollon Rim and east to the San Carlos and Fort Apache Indian Reservations. It was so large it had eight federally protected wilderness areas inside it. If the sign and the saguaro cactus were to be believed, he was probably somewhere east of Phoenix and west or south of the Four Peaks Wilderness area. But exactly where, he did not know.

He threw the atlas back on the dash and continued driving. The road entered a canyon. Runoff from the storm had turned the normally dry wash into a torrent of muddy water. The canyon slowly widened, and he eventually reached a dirt road that had actual dirt on it instead of just rocks. There was no clock in the truck, and his melted phone had no way of tracking time.

Faint lights glowed to the left. The landscape gradually flattened, and, for the first time since taking the truck, he was able to shift into third.

The lights slowly grew brighter. He circled a hill and reached a paved road. He exhaled and slumped against the seat. Fleeing a Nightmare in a sixty-year-old wreck, he had somehow made it.

He turned toward the lights and accelerated. With the smooth road and higher speed, Mop lay down on the seat and rested his head on Adam's knee.

"Where did you come from, mutt? Anything you would like to share?"

Mop thumped his tail.

"You're a dog of few words, aren't you? Cat got your tongue?" He snorted. He wouldn't want to meet the cat that could take Mop's tongue.

The lights grew brighter until they lit the horizon. A boundary sign for Mesa appeared. Mesa was an eastern suburb of Phoenix, but what had he been doing there in the middle of night? There were dozens of mountain biking trails in the area; however, as far as he knew, none went as far up into the mountains as he had gone. Only miners and cattle ranchers went that far.

Okay, so he had escaped, but what now? He could find a hospital and get treated. Getting struck by lightning was no trivial thing, and he was lucky to be alive. He could find a phone and call his brother or parents to come pick him up, or maybe his friend Paul Moody. Paul owned a garage and ran a towing service. He and Paul could load the Chevy on Paul's car hauler and return it to the mine, and then—if Adam could remember where he'd left his pickup—he could drive his own truck home. But what about the Nightmare? Whether it was a figment of his imagination or not, Adam would return with a gun.

He sighed and kept driving. The truck had made it this far. If it died, he could flag someone down and call for help.

He reached a strip mall with a gas station and pulled up to a gas pump. He looked horrible, so he put the baseball cap from the glove box over his muddy hair and tried to look like it was no big deal to be driving a sixty-year-old truck with tags that had expired decades ago. He probably should call the police—but, then again, maybe not. He was driving a stolen truck. Nearly dying wouldn't matter. Plus, if he started yammering about seeing the boogieman, he would get hauled off in a padded ambulance. Why would anyone believe him when he didn't believe himself?

Shifting into neutral, he listened to the engine grumble and looked out the side mirror. Mesa wasn't Phoenix, but it was still a good-sized city. He couldn't imagine the Nightmare running through people's yards or dodging traffic. Arizona was a concealed carry state, which meant that almost anyone could carry a weapon without a license. If that thing came howling through town, someone would bag it and hang it on their wall as a trophy. Ignoring the sign that said to cut the engine before fueling, he topped off the tank with regular. That should get him home.

The moon was hiding behind the clouds as he drove east, past Apache Junction. An hour later, he reached the copper-mining town of Superior. East of Superior, the road entered a narrow, steep canyon with towering cliffs. In the dim beam of his single headlight, he saw tiny hamlets appear and disappear. Legs twitching, Mop whimpered softly as he slept. The dog looked completely worn out.

They reached the industrial mining town of Globe at six in the morning. The sun leapt over the mountains and turned into a blinding disk of flame. Adam lowered the Chevy's sun visor, but it didn't block the glare.

"Hey, Mop, what do you think? Any sunglasses in the glove box?"

Mop lifted his head off the seat.

"I could use some sunglasses. Maybe there are some in the glove box."

Adam waited. Mop yawned.

"Yes, sir, it sure is bright. Sunglasses would be welcome."

Mop stretched. His paws touched the dash, and he closed his eyes.

Adam sighed. "Fine, you can go back to drooling in your sleep."

He checked the glove box for sunglasses, but there were none. Squinting through the glare, he headed northeast out of Globe and into the mountains. The further he went, the higher the elevation became, until ponderosa pines flanked the road, and the air turned cool. The engine pinged, forcing him to downshift into a lower gear. A truck this old needed leaded gas. He willed the old truck onward.

He finally reached the Haystack Butte overlook where tourists pulled off the road and took pictures of the canyon's steep red-and-orange walls and the pale, copper-colored Salt River cutting through the bottom. The slanting morning sunshine turned the air a hazy gold. Sixteen miles later, he turned at the Defiance Historical Marker and followed the jagged mountain ridge until it ended in the boom-bust former mining town of Defiance, Arizona.

"Hey, Mop, wake up. We're home."

———

Defiance had begun as a small mining camp but eventually became one of the richest copper and sulfide mines in the Southwest. In the early twenties, the veins played out. The town was largely abandoned until a colony of artists took up residence. Tourists slowly followed until, at the turn of the century, Defiance had its first gourmet bakery. On Friday nights, weekenders rolled into town, partying in the renovated saloons until Sunday afternoon.

He drove into the historic downtown, with its eighteenth-century mix of Spanish and Victorian buildings, and rattled past the entrance to the lower Silent Black Mine. The Silent Black Mine, named after the German miner Theodore Black, who discovered copper in Defiance, had once been the deepest sulfide mine in the United States. The mine shafts, two miles deep, followed a vertical vein of copper created by an ancient volcano.

Six days a week, Black tyrannically drove three shifts of miners deeper and deeper into the bowels of the earth until the air became so thick with dust from the widow-making jackhammers that hundreds of men drowned as their lungs filled with quartz dust.

Day after day, deeper and deeper, the miners delved until they unexpectedly broke open the mountain's toxic heart. An entire shift of miners, sixty-four in all, died of carbon monoxide poisoning. None made it out alive, and the mine eventually closed.

Black died years later, but perched high above Main Street, on a ridge where it still lorded over the town's ordinary citizens, stood the beautiful mansion he had built. The Black Mansion—white because of the color of the bricks used in its construction—was a four-story Victorian styled loosely on a picture torn from a book of children's fairy tales. As a child Black had loved that book. Though the mansion was over a hundred years old, tourists were still stunned by its grandeur.

Adam kept his speed down and made sure he didn't hit any of the early morning out-of-towners who seemed to think nothing of jaywalking across the narrow, winding road as they sipped coffee and window-shopped the jewelry and antique stores. He continued up Main Street past the Defiance graveyard where hundreds of the miners killed by cave-ins, murders, and silicosis had been buried. A sign had been erected on the fence advertising ghost tours. Mop got to his feet on the vinyl seat and shook, spraying dried mud.

"Geez, next time, warn me, okay? Your tail is a whip."

Adam passed the tourist information building with its huge banner advertising the weekend's Taste of Defiance festival. He pulled the Chevy into Paul's Automotive. Paul Moody, the owner, walked out of the garage carrying a coffee cup. He had dark hair, grease-stained hands, and the muscular shoulders of someone who worked hard for a living. He squinted at Adam and his face lit up.

"Only you, Adam!" he called out. "You go riding in the desert and come back driving this old girl! What happened this time? You look terrible, so you must have had fun."

"Big storm last night. I got struck by lightning. Everything's fuzzy."

The humor left Paul's face. "Are you all right?"

Adam pulled his jersey to one side so Paul could see the burn. Paul blanched.

"Whoa, that's a first, even for you. You should have called so we could have picked you up. Everyone started getting worried after you didn't come home. James said you had probably made up with Cathy and stayed with her, except she hadn't seen you and didn't want to."

Adam grimaced. That had been a bad breakup, even by his standards. Most of his girlfriends worked their way up to throwing things: dishes, CDs, bike parts. Cathy had started there.

"The lightning melted my phone, and I couldn't remember where I parked my truck, so I had to hot-wire this old thing. I found it at an abandoned mine. Do you know happen to know what trail I went biking on?"

"James said you went down to ride Cat Sick."

Adam pulled the atlas off the dash and traced his finger along the

Bush Highway linking Mesa and Saguaro Lake. Judging from the trip out of the mountains, he had somehow ridden his bike from the Hawes Trail System more than thirty miles northeast through some of the worst terrain on earth. In the middle of summer, temperatures rarely dropped below a hundred degrees, even at night. It was a terrible ride, even on a world-class bike like the RIP, and he didn't remember any of it.

"James has been trying to get hold of you," Paul said. "He dropped off his truck to get the differential fluid changed and took your 'Vette fishing. He wants you to pick Bailey up from Cindy's so Cindy can get ready for her wedding. You do remember the wedding is today, right? Cindy will go nuts if you forgot."

Adam, tired, grimaced and closed his eyes. The last thing he wanted to deal with was his ex-sister-in-law.

Paul glanced at his watch. "You'd better scoot. What are you going to do with this old girl?"

"I don't know. We could haul it back to the mine and then drive my pickup home. It will take some time to find the mine again though. It was raining and dark, and there are hundreds of those old mining camps in the mountains. The road out was horrible."

"Then you'd better get your pickup today and deal with the Chevy when you have more time. Hop out, and I'll pull her around back."

As soon as Adam took his foot off the accelerator, the engine let out a sputtering cough and died. Paul got in and turned the key. Nothing happened. Not even a click.

"How did you get it to run?" he asked.

"I tightened the battery cables, and it turned over."

Paul got out. "I'll jump it. You'd better get moving before Cindy comes looking. Why your brother married her is beyond me."

Adam opened the door and slid out, trying not to put weight on his foot. Pressing it on the accelerator had been hard enough.

CHAPTER 10

Admiral McDermott's liaison officer was a Hispanic woman with the unlikely name of Summer Day. Carrying a rifle and armed with a pistol, she had muscular shoulders and skin the color of beaten copper. A rubbery scar cut across the left side of her neck, and she had an uncomfortable way of walking, like a cat tiptoeing across a sparking electrical line. Behind her aviator glasses, her eyes moved ceaselessly back and forth as if she were afraid of being jumped.

She led Jacobson into the hanger. Outside, six of Admiral McDermott's Black Hawks warmed up. Quite impressive, Jacobson thought, given that McDermott was a flag officer with public health, not the Navy, but he supposed commissioned officers might need to have access to armed men during, let's say, an outbreak of dengue fever or some other health emergency. Still, he was impressed that McDermott had assembled this much firepower. How didn't matter. The show of strength should improve the odds.

As he followed Lieutenant Day to the helos, Jacobson took a second look at her scar. Keloid scars like hers could only have come from a very deep wound. Not to be nosy, but he had to ask. Maybe they'd served in the same combat zone. "When did you get shot, Lieutenant?"

"Sir?"

"The wound to your neck. When did you get it?"

Day stopped and pushed the aviators up on her forehead. "Two years ago, sir. We were chasing some insurgents in Yemen and came under sniper fire. Command called in an air strike, but they never did find the shooter."

Jacobson, feeling the rotors' vibration beneath his feet, wondered if Day had gotten treatment for post-traumatic stress. "Why the sunglasses?"

"Ever since I was revived, light bothers me. The treatment affected the pigment in my eyes."

"Lucky you made it."

A full five seconds went by before she replied, her voice so quiet that Jacobson almost didn't hear her. "Yes, sir, I'm lucky all right. I'm the luckiest woman in the world."

What an odd comment, Jacobson thought. She pulled down her aviators and pointed toward one of the Black Hawks.

General O'Dell waited inside. A short, stocky man, the general, in his late fifties, had a crew cut that matched his wide jaw and perfectly square head. Barrel-chested, he had already strapped in. An entourage of his men had boarded: three members of his senior staff, along with a four-man security detail and two orderlies to fetch coffee, except that today there wouldn't be time for a coffee run.

O'Dell glanced up from the laptop on his knees. "McDermott's agreed to let you lead the return assault. He's giving you seven squads. Don't take any unnecessary risks. I'll be monitoring your helmet cam and the radio. Get the security grid online, find out what happened to my assets, and get out. McDermott will handle the rest. I don't want you getting caught up in this mess. Do you understand?"

"Yes, sir, but where is he?"

General O'Day pointed to one of the other Black Hawks. "But don't worry. Lieutenant Day is McDermott's liaison officer. She'll have a team with her to ensure your safety. That's her job. Let her do it."

Jacobson buckled himself into an armored seat, grabbed the harness with his left hand, and held onto his rifle with his right. Lieutenant Day climbed into the seat beside him, and the Black Hawk lifted into the sky. The night before, it had been pouring rain but the storm had passed and the air was cool, which was saying something considering that it was August.

He watched Glendale, North Phoenix, and finally Scottsdale pass beneath him and wondered why the government would put a top-secret research lab in the middle of Scottsdale's golf courses and expensive, master-planned subdivisions. From what he'd seen yesterday, the killers weren't anything you'd want roaming around Scottsdale's Fashion Square.

The pilot brought the Black Hawk in low over Biodosius's south block wall and circled around to the front, landing on the lawn. The other helos had already landed. Soldiers ran toward the front entrance. Lieutenant Day jumped out, and Jacobson followed. The Black Hawks lifted off and thundered up into the sky. In seconds, the predawn stillness returned.

A soldier, rifle against his shoulder, pulled the front door open and moved into the brightly lit lobby. The rest of the troops followed. Jacobson went last, blinking and hoping his eyes would adjust to the brightness.

The dead security officer lay on the floor, empty shell casings still scattered on his chest. Jacobson waved over the squad assigned to cover the ceiling maintenance area.

"We've got to keep the ceiling's maintenance area clear," he told them quietly. "If anyone sees or hears anything, I want to know about it. Understand?"

The men glanced nervously at the dead employees in the hall and climbed up the same ladder Layton had used a day earlier.

Jacobson adjusted his microphone. "Command, we've secured the lobby. Have you gotten anywhere with the cameras?"

"Negative," McDermott answered. "Getting minimal packet throughput. Everything's still locked up. You'll need to go to the wiring closet and fix it."

So it wasn't just get the embryos and get the dogs—get in and get out—like yesterday. Now, it was get the security system up and running, the very thing that Jacobson had foreseen as being dangerous. The lack of a clear command structure could be a problem, especially with both men hovering above his head. Jacobson waited to see if O'Dell would countermand McDermott's order, but when he didn't, Jacobson ordered a squad to hold the lobby and led the remaining men toward the cafeteria. The men took hard looks at the dead. Jacobson had warned them before they went in, but there was a difference between being told something and experiencing it firsthand.

Eyes sweeping the silent hallways and ears straining for the slightest noise, he headed toward the second wiring closet. If the killers had messed with the wiring, and he was pretty sure they had, then all they needed to do was wait for Jacobson to show up. He was glad not to be doing this mission on his own.

With Lieutenant Day beside him, he reached the end of the main northeast hallway. He took a breath, braced himself for what he was about to see, and peered around the corner toward the administration area. Lieutenant Sanchez had been slammed upright into the wall so hard he'd gone partially through it. Embedded in the drywall, he stood motionless, chin slumped against his chest, as if he were asleep on his feet. Griffin, the medic, had bled out on the floor from a slashed throat. Hallett lay on the fallen ceiling tiles next to his broken tablet. Sergeant Anderson sprawled on the floor with his helmet at a weird angle.

Jacobson bent down for a closer look and abruptly realized that Anderson had been decapitated. All the more reason for caution.

He examined the corridor, trying to reconstruct the sequence of events prior to the ambush. The door to the office area had been propped open. One of the killers must have hidden in the office cubicles until it was time to attack. Another had waited around the corner from the wiring closet. The third had killed Layton in the ceiling and had moved into position above. A fourth had turned off the lights. Once the lights were off, the killers attacked as a group.

"This is where the first team died," Jacobson quietly told Day and waited for her response. She nodded slightly. Her sunglasses bothered him because it made it harder to pick up her nonverbal cues. "Until we bring up the networking switch, we won't have any help from the security cameras. Keep your eyes open. They could be waiting to ambush us again."

Feeling exposed in the bright light, he slipped around the corner. He was tempted to turn off the lights, but O'Dell had ordered him to leave them on. Unfortunately, if he could see, then so could the enemy, and Jacobson didn't like fair fights.

Rifle against his shoulder, thighs tensed, he crept forward, eyes sweeping the room. The smashed office door, or what was left of it, hung on one hinge. The broken light tray dangled over a dead woman, her business suit so bloody it was hard to see what color it had been. He held up a hand, motioning for the men behind him to stop, and crouched by the office door. The bodies lay where they had fallen during the initial attack. Empty brass casings littered the floor where he had fired through the door and wall. The chair that had propped the door open lay on its side. He had tripped over it in the dark. Everything was exactly as he remembered. What had he been expecting—that the killers would rearrange the stage for Act II?

"Major, we've found Layton above your position," one of the men in the ceiling reported over the radio. "His neck's broken."

"Understood." Jacobson nodded and motioned Day forward. "Take your men and another squad past the wiring closet. Cover the far corner and hallway. Stay close to the walls so you don't disturb any tracks."

"Yes, sir."

He waited until they were in position, then moved forward to examine the hallway floor. He found a bloody footprint by Griffin's head and crouched for a closer look. The footprint was clearly outlined from the toes to the heel. He found a second footprint in the middle of the hallway and two more where one of the killers had run through the door.

"Command, we're in the office area," he whispered into his microphone. "Sanchez and his team are dead. There are three different sets of footprints in the fire retardant."

"Are you sure on the number?" McDermott asked.

"Yes, sir. Three different sets. Counting the one that turned off the lights in the security office, that means there are a minimum of four of them."

"Acknowledged. Proceed to the wiring closet."

"Yes, sir."

Jacobson led the men down the hallway where Day and her team waited. Two techs carrying laptops went inside the wiring closet. One tech in camouflage and a helmet went straight to a laptop sitting on the shelf of a network rack. Using a serial cable, one of the techs connected the laptop to the switch's diagnostic port, then typed on the laptop's keyboard. Error messages scrolled up the screen. The two techs whispered. The second tech moved a finger along the top row of switch ports and reached for a cable.

"Hold!" Jacobson snapped. "Stop!"

The tech froze. Jacobson moved into the closet. "Step back. I want to look at the cables."

Jacobson examined the switch, the rack, and the cables. Most of the cables went up into the ceiling, but some of them linked the switches together.

"Major, what are you doing?" McDermott demanded.

"Checking the equipment for IEDs, Admiral. Stand by."

He wasn't an expert in computer networks, but he had a sixth sense about traps. The killers had hours to prepare. The closet was a logical place for an ambush.

"What cable were you going to unplug?" he asked the tech.

The tech pointed. Jacobson ran a finger along the wire. It left the switch and looped up into the rack and came back down to plug into another port. He removed his helmet, leaned in as close as he could to the switch, and looked up. He sucked in a breath and waved the tech over. He pointed to the ceiling.

The tech's eyes widened.

Jacobson called Day into the closet. "Lieutenant, there's a grenade hanging from the top of the network rack. Pull everyone back to both ends of the hallway. I'm going to disarm it."

"We have experts who can do that, sir. General O'Dell was specific in his instructions concerning your safety."

"I can do it."

She stared at him from behind her sunglasses before finally nodding. "As you wish, sir."

The techs followed her out. Carefully, with his left hand, Jacobson wrapped his fingers around the grenade and pin. With his right, he seized the cable. The cable had been pulled tight, making it difficult to unplug. Pushing gently, he put pressure on it. The cable was attached to the grenade's pin. He kept the pin from moving and gently worked the cable's switch-end free. It let go with a click. Then he fed the cable through the grenade's pin and, making sure it wasn't wired into anything else, pulled the grenade down from its hiding place. He unzipped one of his pockets, put the grenade away, and zipped it up again. He waved the techs back inside.

"The grenade's been disarmed." He glanced at the laptop. The errors had stopped scrolling up the screen. "Command, can you confirm usability?"

"Usability confirmed," McDermott answered. "Packet throughput has returned to normal levels. What was wrong?"

"They looped the switch, sir," the tech with the computer said.

"What does that mean?"

"They plugged both ends of a cable into two different ports on the same switch, sir."

"Isn't the network smart enough to handle that problem?"

"The spanning-tree protocol was disabled, sir, so it didn't shut off the compromised ports. The switches are interconnected so the errors flooded the network."

"How many people would know how to take out the network like that?" Jacobson asked.

The two techs looked at each other. "Not many," the second one said. "Especially disabling the protocol. They knew exactly what cable we would unplug."

Jacobson frowned. The more he got into this, the less sense it made. It was one thing if someone got angry at their supervisor or coworker and went on a killing spree, but another entirely to coordinate a mass killing in the workplace, especially where a specific set of skills was needed to make it work.

"Admiral, are all the cameras operational on the floor?" he asked.

"Yes. We're going through the feeds now."

"Permission to investigate the hallway where I killed one of them, sir."

"Stand by while we look at the cameras."

Jacobson heard clicks as McDermott searched the files, and then McDermott's answer. "Major, the cameras and lights are not opera-tional in that hallway. It might be another trap. They could be expecting you to go there to look for the body. I recommend extreme caution."

Jacobson looked at Day. "Ready?"

"Yes, sir."

He took point again and led the way forward. At the next hallway, he turned left and moved quietly down the hallway to the next junction. Ahead of him, he saw something shiny, the pin from the grenade he had thrown a day earlier.

Motioning for Day and her men to stay back, he crouched by the corner and peeked around. The fragmentation grenade had exploded twenty feet in front of him. It had blown holes in the walls and ceiling. Drywall, broken ceiling tile, and fire retardant had spilled on the floor. Smears of blood ran down the middle of the hallway. When the grenade exploded, the killer had fallen to the floor and slid, smearing blood through the debris.

He summoned Day to come closer. Walking on the balls of her feet, she tiptoed to his side.

He pointed around the corner. "Take your team to the other end of the hall. The office is down there. Cover the approach. Hug the walls and don't disturb the debris. If you hear or see anything, fall back. We'll make our stand where we can cover both hallways."

She summoned her team and moved forward. Jacobson waited for them to get into position. Lowering his night-vision goggles, he slipped into the darkened hallway. Eyes on the floor so that the lights at either end of the hall didn't blind him, Jacobson crouched at the first trace of blood. It was as if a barefoot painter swinging an open gallon of rust-colored paint had sloshed its way down the hall. He followed the blood to the far end, where Lieutenant Day waited with her men, and then he stepped back against the wall and lifted his goggles.

"Command, there's blood on the floor, but no corpse. Whatever it was, it was moving fast when it went down. The thing slid about fifteen feet to the corner. That's where the blood ends."

A long moment went by before McDermott responded. "Why do you keep saying *it?*"

"After it got to the corner, sir, it got to its feet and chased me. I can see footprints."

"So?"

He thought about the mangled doors and how a flash grenade hadn't disabled the killers.

"There's no way anyone could have bled that much and still had the strength to run. Something about this doesn't make sense."

CHAPTER 11

Victoria Stewart thought about what Jan Thompson had told her—that her husband had worked for Biodosius, the same company that had saved Victoria's life. Right when Victoria's life hung in the balance, Monica Belles, her college roommate, had brought Victoria to the research institute's critical care unit.

Victoria thought about calling Monica but didn't. If the police had any reason to think that Victoria had helped Jan Thompson, they would pull her phone records. Mobile phones communicated much more with the telecommunications infrastructure than most people realized. Some phones even did it when they were turned off. That's why she always physically removed her phone's battery when not in use. If the police placed her at Couch's cabin or the motor home, that would be it.

The motor home's blown tire had split and separated from the rim. She peeled back the pieces and carried them to the Rover's cargo area. Once she was away from the main road, she would pull over, cut through the rubber, and remove the bullet. That way the authorities couldn't track the tire to her .308. Her father had taught her how to swap out barrels and firing pins to create different bullet striation patterns, but the FBI had ballistics experts. The less evidence she left, the better. That's why she had worn a man's coat and why she had slipped her shoes inside men's size twelve boots.

She drove west, away from the approaching dawn. She didn't think Jan Thompson, or her girls, had seen the Rover from inside the motor home. Hopefully the rock music had drowned out Flight's references to the Range Rover and him calling her "Shortcake." But either way, she needed to leave the asphalt. There weren't many roads in the Pinetop-Lakeside area, and what roads there were would soon be crawling with sheriff's cars.

She turned onto the first Forest Service Road she came to and sped into the sheltering pines. Most Forest Service roads were built to allow access to natural resources. None of them had been built with the idea of getting anywhere in a timely manner, but at least they would get her home. With luck, she might be able to make it without anyone knowing she had left her ranch.

For the next three hours, watching the road in front of her, the road behind, and the sky above in case the Feds were doing surveillance, she drove. Normally she appreciated the Feds' help, but not today. The FBI and DEA had been after Blackjack Joe for years and knew he owned a candy-apple Rover, but they didn't know he was dead. The only way the SUV could stick out any more than it already did was to mount a spotlight on top.

But had she covered her tracks well enough? Was there something more she could have done? She'd picked up the bullet casings, worn gloves during her search, and picked up the tire. As far as Jan Thompson was concerned, the only thing Jan knew about Victoria was that an unknown person had appeared out of nowhere, killed her captors, and then asked questions about her husband's job. That was the good news. The bad was that, even though Victoria had tried to disguise her voice, odds were good that Jan would have identified her as a woman. There were very few people in eastern Arizona who could kill three armed and dangerous men without incurring a scratch. If Jan told them she'd been saved by a woman, the list grew even shorter. The authorities knew her. They knew how good she was with weapons.

She swore under her breath and gripped the Rover's wheel. She hadn't asked for this. She had enough problems without chasing someone she only knew from nightmares. Rumor had it that Juan Padilla, the Sinaloa Cartel's main northern enforcer, had put another bounty on her head, and the last time that had happened, Blackjack Joe had blown her up. It had taken weeks to get out of critical care unit at Biodosius and months of hellish reconstructive surgery in Mayo Clinic's burn unit.

But, finally, she had walked out, returned to the ranch, and made Blackjack Joe pay dearly for what he had done. She had gotten lucky with Couch, Flight, and the guy with the rifle, but fate had a way of evening the scales.

She shifted on the Rover's seat and sighed. She should quit the ranch. Sell off the land and leave. There wasn't anyone keeping her there. Buzzards were her closest neighbors, and as for friends, to have friends you had to be a friend, and when you vanished off the face of the earth to stay alive, friendships died.

And, now, keeping the ranch was a matter of pride. The ranch had been in her family for three generations. The Stewarts had survived wildfires, predatory banks, and tax collectors, and she wasn't going to run away like some city slicker who folds up at the first sign of trouble. The land connected her to her parents and grandparents. Ranching was in her blood. But her resolve came at a cost. Since getting out of the hospital, she had become someone she barely recognized. She had taken the fight to the traffickers and, one by one, made them pay, but with each death a bit more of her had died inside.

She found an isolated spot far from prying eyes, stopped the Rover, and pulled out the motorhome's tire. Using her knife, she cut into the side of the rubber. She found the mangled bullet and threw it into the pines, and then she buried the tire in the cinders. She did the same with her boots. She had bought them used from a thrift store in Williams. They couldn't be traced to her. With any luck, the authorities would see the boot prints at the cabin—maybe even at the motorhome—and think she was much bigger and heavier than she was.

Another half hour and she reached the broken fence that marked the edge of her property. To keep the narcos out her father had tried locking the gate, but they had cut through the lock. He had blocked off the gate. They cut through the fence on either side. He dropped boulders in front of the fence. The druggies simply found another section of fence that wasn't protected.

The situation worsened until it grew violent. Sometimes her father used a backhoe and dug pit-traps for the narcos to drive into at night. Other times he shot out their tires or radiators. But in the end, it didn't really matter what he did. If it was easier moving drugs on the back roads than on the interstates, the traffickers would keep looking for a cross-country route.

She reached the Black Knob and drove across the mountain's eroded flank. On the other side of the mountain, the road dropped into a narrow canyon of ponderosa and sycamore. She followed the road until she reached a rocky track that led into another canyon. The road ended at a prospector's cabin built into the side of the canyon wall. After the narcos had firebombed their house, she and her father had moved into the ranch's original cabin.

The cabin had been built by her grandfather and perched above a small creek. The grove of shade sycamores that lost their leaves in the winter gave it a warm, southern exposure. The walls were constructed of stone thick enough to turn a bullet. She had put on a new metal roof that a Molotov cocktail or wildfire couldn't ignite. Power came from a solar array at the top of the ridge, and the solar panels charged a Powerwall battery in the cellar. Phone calls were made using the satellite dish on the roof. So far, the narcos hadn't figured out where she lived.

She parked the Rover under a rocky overhang where it could not be seen from the air and pulled a camouflage cloth over it. Exhausted, she lugged her money and weapons through the trees. Inside, she disabled the security alarms. The house was outfitted with a world-class system that monitored the cabin and the surrounding canyon. Her father had spared no expense in upgrading the cabin, but, in the end, the precautions hadn't helped him.

Too tired to carry her equipment to the panic room in the cellar, she dropped her weapons on the floor. The Uzi and the .308 would need new barrels and firing pins to change the ballistic signatures. Tomorrow's job. If, by some miracle, that was Dark she'd killed, then she might finally get a good night's sleep.

In the bedroom, she stripped off her coat and the Kevlar vest, men's jeans, and T-shirt. Exhausted, she staggered to the shower and stood shaking as hot water sluiced over her shoulders.

"What have you done to me, Monica?" she moaned. "Did you save my life for this?"

She toweled off and stumbled to bed. She was asleep before her head touched the pillow. She dreamed of him again. This time Dark's enraged fury swept her into a psychic firestorm.

I'm going to find you, bitch, and when I do, I'm going to kill you!

CHAPTER 12

Before going down to the basement where the research labs were located, Jacobson wanted to sweep Biodosius's first floor. By now, he had the schematics of the building, including all the exits, practically committed to memory. Yesterday, he'd had no reason to go to the east wing—his tablet showed meeting rooms and offices—but as soon as Lieutenant Day pushed open the wide fire doors, he found himself in a small hospital. All the patient-rooms were empty because the patients, bandaged and with IVs trailing from their arms, had been slaughtered and dragged into the hall. The team fanned out to sweep an empty operating room, a small analytical lab, and a room with a MRI machine, all cleverly fitted into space about the size of an urgent care office in a strip mall. Behind the counter of the nursing station, he found two doctors in scrubs and several nurses, some still masked, others killed while trying to hide beneath the counter.

Jacobson frowned and looked at Day. "What's with the hospital setup, Lieutenant?"

"It's a critical care facility," she said, nodding to a gowned patient at her feet. "That could have been me on another day."

"Is this where you were treated after your injury?"

She nodded and seemed about to elaborate, but stopped. "Are you satisfied the first floor is clear, sir?"

"Yes," Jacobson said.

"Then that's all that should concern you."

So that's how it is, Jacobson thought. Need to know.

He followed Lieutenant Day and her team down to the basement. The lights were off, so they wore their night-vision goggles to do the search. Even though Jacobson trusted the darkness, he felt vulnerable. After yesterday, the killers knew how they would be equipped. A quick flip of a light switch and they would all be blind.

The fire doors at the bottom of the basement staircase stood ajar. The air smelled of blood, but it was the underlying current of unease that bothered him the most. The killers had taken out Sanchez and his team before they knew what had hit them. Sanchez had weighed more than two hundred pounds, yet someone—or some *thing*—had physically picked him up and slammed him into the wall.

With two teams crowded behind him in the stairwell, Jacobson rolled a flash grenade through the doors and pulled them shut. The flash exploded. Day and her team went through, moving left. Another squad deployed to the right. A central hallway stretched into darkness, cutting the basement in half. There were six labs in the basement, three on each side. Labs 4 and 5 contained O'Dell's research. The rest of the basement belonged to McDermott. A dozen or more people lay dead on the floor.

At the first lab, Jacobson tried the doorknob. It was unlocked. He removed another flash grenade, rolled it inside, and shut the door. The grenade exploded. Day kicked the door open and went inside. Long rows of lab tables stretched into the darkness. Hunkering down to make himself a smaller target, Jacobson crept through the computers, beakers, and microscopes. Nothing moved or attacked them. The only sounds were the creak of boots and the team's hushed breathing. Except for a fallen cup of coffee on the floor, nothing looked out of place, and there were no bodies.

They reached the rear of the lab without incident and returned to the central hallway. According to the blueprints on Jacobson's tablet, the second lab on the left, Lab 3, was the largest room in the basement and housed the building's data center. He rolled another flash grenade through the door and followed Day's team inside. Hundreds of computer racks stretched into the darkness. Each rack held at least twenty thin, rack-mounted computers. Cables connected the servers to a network switch at the top of each rack. Network and power cables ran from the top of each rack to cutouts in the ceiling tile. None of the computers had power, and the room was eerily silent.

He pointed right and left. "Two men to each row."

When Lieutenant Day and her men were in position, he started slowly down the center aisle. The racks were taller than he was, which made it impossible to see from one row to the next. The air smelled faintly of cleaning fluid, almost as if a janitorial service had come in for their usual night duty. His boot soles squeaked on the floor.

He reached the end of the row. There were more rows than he had men, so he spread them out again and went back and forth through the rows they hadn't covered. It was better not to think about how exposed they were. With no way to see from row to row, the killers could easily avoid their sweeps and get behind or above them.

They finished the rows and returned to the entrance of the data center.

He touched his radio. "Admiral, we finished our sweep of the data center but it's not secure," he reported. "The ceiling and raised floor are full of power and network cables and ducts for the air conditioning. Every room and the maintenance crawl areas need to be reswept."

"Understood, Major. Continue your initial sweep. Once power is up and all the cameras are operational, we'll go through the building again."

"10-4."

Jacobson returned to the basement's central hallway. The third lab on his side of the hall, Lab 5, looked smaller than the other labs. Inside were medical examining tables, locked cabinets of medication, heart monitors, Xray equipment, and more computers. In the back stood a steel security door with a yellow hazard decal. The electronic lock had a small red light, the first sign of power he had seen since coming down here. Mounted above the door and recessed in the wall was a touch screen.

"Admiral, I'm at the cryogenics lab. The door has power."

"Roger that. Proceed with entry."

Jacobson removed McDermott's security card from his pocket and touched the plate. The door clicked open.

"Watch out for the light," he told Day and her team.

They turned away from the door. He lifted his goggles, kneed the door, and stepped inside. After the darkness, the lights in the room blinded him. One wall held three liquid nitrogen storage tanks. Another wall had an air handling system with a computer display on the front that showed the particulates per cubic foot. The display had the number 847 on it, but the moment he entered the room, the number began to go up and an alarm started beeping. He shut the door.

"Admiral, the room still has power from the emergency battery. An alarm just went off from the air handler."

"You are contaminating the air, Major. Ignore it. Once you leave, anything you brought into the lab will be scrubbed out. What's the temperature of the cryogenic storage tanks?"

"Minus one hundred and ninety-six degrees centigrade."

McDermott let out a sigh loud enough for Jacobson to hear it above the radio's static. "Proceed to the robot for the inventory."

Jacobson went to the computer console. Leaning his rifle against the wall, he bent over the keyboard and started the robot software. The software's graphical user interface appeared on the screen. He clicked on the INVENTORY button on the right menu pane. The screen cleared, showing the storage tank's embryo inventory.

"Sir, I have the storage inventory up on the computer. There are five columns. What am I looking for?"

"Each row contains a number, name, description, date, and status," McDermott answered. "The status field should either be red or green. Please read off any that are red."

Jacobson did as he was told. All the rows were green until he reached the last screen, and then from that point forward, everything was red. He relayed the information.

"Are you sure of what you're seeing, Major?" McDermott asked. "What row are you on?"

Jacobson read off the number.

"And everything from that point forward is red? Nothing is green?"

"Yes, sir. Negative on green."

"Stand by."

McDermott spoke with someone, and then O'Dell's voice came over the radio. "Major, repeat the last ten rows that are green."

Jacobson did as he was asked.

"And nothing else has a green status field from there to the end of the inventory?"

"That's correct, sir. Is there a problem?"

"We're missing inventory. Can you check the robot's security log and read off when it was last accessed and what they did? The security tab is in the top right corner of the display."

Jacobson found the tab and clicked. A log of users appeared.

"Do you see the admiral's user ID with today's date?"

"Yes, sir."

"Are there other users on the list from today?"

"No, sir. Everything else is from yesterday or older."

"Click on each user with yesterday's date and tell me what they did."

Jacobson did as he was told. When he finished, there was a long silence before McDermott got back on the radio. His voice sounded strained. "Major, can you count how many inventory-eject statements Candice Chamberlain executed yesterday?"

Jacobson relayed the information.

"Who is Candice Chamberlain, and why would she take all the embryos?" O'Dell asked McDermott.

"She's a second-level medical technician. She works in the lab. Maybe she realized there was a problem and moved the embryos some-where else. Maybe she was forced to remove them. There's no way of telling until we go through the security video."

"Can Major Jacobson access the video from the lab?"

"No. It's on the server in the security office. I'll have my team look for it."

"Major, what are the time stamps on the eject operations?" O'Dell asked. "Are they before or after the power went down for the building?"

Jacobson looked at the eject commands. "After, sir. All of them are after six p.m."

"There won't be any video," O'Dell said.

"No, sir."

"Okay, we'll look at the logs in more detail later. Exit out of the soft-ware, then proceed to Lab 4 across the hall to confirm the status of the other assets."

Jacobson did as instructed and left the lab. The doors clanged shut behind him, the magnetic security lock clicking into place. For a second, he couldn't see anything, and then he lowered his goggles.

"We're to proceed to Lab 4," he told Day.

According to Jacobson's tablet, the first two doors were for Lab 2 and the last doorway was for Lab 4. He reached for the doorknob, but Day stopped him.

"Sir, that's Lab 6. Lab 4 is the door by the stairs."

"Are you sure, Lieutenant? That's not what the blueprints say." He lifted his goggles and brought out his tablet. "The first door on the left is Lab 1. The first and second doors on the right are for Lab 2. Lab 4 is the third doorway on the right. There is no Lab 6."

He held out the tablet. Day looked unsure. He wasn't going to waste time quibbling about which door was which. The longer he stood here, the greater the chance of an ambush. Jacobson put his tablet away and opened the door.

———

The room, two hundred feet long by thirty wide, had a low concrete ceiling. Arrayed on both sides of the room were holding cells. Each cell had a wall of glass, a sleeping pad, a toilet, and a sink. In the first cell, a woman lay on a pad.

"What is this?" he asked Day. "Where are the dogs?"

At the sound of his voice, the woman rocketed off the pad and smashed into the glass, screaming and flailing wildly in his direction. The woman's white shirt and pants looked like they had been vomited on. Tangled, matted hair hung across her face. Bruises covered her body.

He leapt back and snapped up his rifle. He didn't see the occupant of the cell behind him until the man threw himself at the glass. Jacobson spun sideways, trying to keep both people in his sight. The man beat crazily on the barrier, using both his hands and feet and even his head until his forehead split and blood streamed down his face. Even though he screamed, only whispers of anguish penetrated the glass. His eyes were almost entirely white.

Jacobson whipped his head around. What on earth? The next cell sat empty, but the following two were occupied. The occupants attacked the walls as well, hands scrabbling and clutching madly at the glass.

Jacobson quickly checked the rest of the cells and returned to Day's side. There were twenty cells in all. Twelve were occupied. The other eight were empty.

"Lieutenant, what's this?" he whispered. "Where are the dogs?"

"We're in the wrong lab, sir. This is Lab 6."

"There is no Lab 6."

"Sir, I don't think your tablet got updated with the correct schematics."

As blood dripped down his face, the man with the split forehead retreated from the glass and crouched to stare at Jacobson with his white eyes. Both hands were twisted and looked as though he had broken them during a futile escape attempt.

Jacobson got on his radio.

"Command, there's confusion about where we are. My tablet says we're in Lab 4, but Lieutenant Day thinks we're in Lab 6."

"What are you seeing?" McDermott asked.

"I'm in a large room with twenty medical cells. Twelve of the cells are occupied by seven men and five women. The occupants are alive but extremely agitated. I don't see any signs of General O'Dell's assets."

"What door did you go through?" McDermott asked.

"I'm in the second lab on the right side of the basement, sir."

"Major, you are in Lab 6. You are not cleared for that lab. Exit immediately."

Jacobson started to protest but McDermott cut him off. "Lieutenant Day, are you with Major Jacobson?"

"Yes, sir."

"Escort Major Jacobson into Lab 4. If there are further questions about him finding his way, bring him immediately to the security office."

Jacobson opened his mouth to object but stopped. All he had to do was report on O'Dell's assets and get out. This was McDermott's mess, not his. The less involved he got, the better.

Day stepped forward. "Sir, if you will come with me."

Jacobson followed her back to the basement's central hallway. A dozen or more of McDermott's men stood talking; two laughed at a joke. One man was even checking his phone. Jacobson thought about warning them not to drop their guard but didn't. They weren't his men.

Day started to go to the first door on the right, but Jacobson stopped and took out his tablet. "Wait."

He lifted his goggles onto his helmet and turned the screen toward her. He flicked the blueprints back and forth so he could see the entire basement.

"Show me Lab 6," he said, holding out the tablet.

Day swallowed, the rubbery scar on her neck moving. She took the tablet but didn't look down.

Taking it back, Jacobson sighed and lowered his goggles. "I don't like it when people hold back information, especially when my life is at risk. Do I make myself clear?"

"Yes, sir. I believe the access to Lab 4 is through the first doorway on the right by the stairs. I'll show you."

He followed her through the first doorway. Inside were two doors, each with a sign. The door on the right said Lab 2. The door on the left said Lab 4. Jacobson paused outside the doors. The metallic smell of blood hung in the air.

"Have these labs been checked?"

"Yes, sir."

She opened the door to Lab 4 and waited.

"You're not coming in?"

"No, sir. Other than the initial sweep team, General O'Dell left specific instructions that only you should be given access."

Jacobson lifted his rifle and stepped through the door. The walls were painted bright primary colors that wouldn't have looked out of place in a day-care facility. A large padded rubber mat covered the floor. Arrayed across the mat were various agility items such as hoops, ladders, tables, tunnels, and weave posts. The wall on the left held bins of pet toys. Letters of the alphabet had been pinned to the wall. Along the wall on the right were computers, videoconferencing equipment, a sink, and two storage cabinets. The back wall had a door that led to an outdoor dog run and three large wire crates.

The occupants two cages had been torn apart until there was little left that was recognizable. The dismembered bodies of the office workers had been bad, but this was somehow worse.

"General," he said, "I'm in Lab 4. Two of the assets are dead."

When O'Dell answered, his voice rasped over the radio. "On the front of each crate is a serial number. The same number should be on the collar of each asset. Read them off."

"It won't be easy, sir. The dogs are in pieces. The crates are a mess."

"Understood, Major. Proceed."

Jacobson hesitated and then lowered his rifle to the floor. He looked at his leather combat gloves, then went to the storage cabinets and rummaged inside. There were no surgical gloves but there were cleaning supplies, and he found some rubber gloves. He put them on and crawled inside the first crate. The reek of blood and excrement made him gasp. He picked up a severed paw and the remains of a leg and put both against the side of the crate. Under the dog's chest cavity, he saw the animal's head, crushed against the crate's bottom. One of the dog's eyes was still in its socket but the other was missing. Bits of teeth lay splintered on the floor. What could apply so much force that teeth would break?

He located the dog's collar, backed out of the cage, and hurried to the sink. He turned on the water and stuck the collar and his rubber gloves and arms under the water until the blood and gore washed down the drain. Why would someone tear a dog apart?

He left the sink and went to the second cage. An Australian cattle dog had retreated into the back corner when it was attacked. Jacobson reached through the metal bars and moved skin and limbs aside until he located the collar. He cut it off with his knife, rinsed both off in the sink, and removed the rubber gloves.

He read the serial numbers over the radio.

"Any sign of the third asset?" O'Dell asked.

"No, sir. There are only two dogs in the lab."

"Understood. Please secure one of the missing asset's personal articles and meet me in the security office for additional briefing. I'm coming in."

"Sir, the facility is not secure. I can't guarantee your safety."

"I'll take the risk."

Jacobson picked up a piece of the missing dog's pillow and put it in his pack. Out in the central hallway, he collected Day and her men and went upstairs to the main lobby.

Jacobson had left an entire squad behind to guard the security office, but only two of the men remained.

"Where are the other men?" Jacobson asked.

The two sentries glanced at each other. "Admiral McDermott reassigned them to the sweep teams, sir," one finally answered.

"How many are up watching the ceiling?"

"None. They were reassigned. The admiral said they weren't needed."

"I want both of you up in the ceiling. The killers always attack from above."

The two men glanced uncertainly at each other. "I'm sorry, sir, but the admiral ordered us to watch the lobby. You'll need to clear new orders with him."

Jacobson stomped over to the lobby's conference room. General O'Dell and his staff sat around the table with Admiral McDermott. O'Dell saw the look on Jacobson's face and walked out with a man wearing a dark blue windbreaker with the letters FBI emblazoned on the front.

"General, can we talk outside?" Jacobson asked quietly.

O'Dell nodded. Once they were outside, Jacobson let the door swing shut. The rising sun had turned the building gold.

O'Dell held out a camera. "Here's another helmet cam, Major. Swap it with the one you have so we can go through the video of the cryogenic robot's inventory."

Jacobson exchanged the cameras.

O'Dell turned to the FBI agent. "Special Agent Terrance, this is Major Blain Jacobson of the Army Rangers. Jacobson's going to assist us in the recovery of the missing asset. You'll be working closely with him until the problem is resolved."

Terrance smiled and stepped forward. He was tall and fit with the athletic build of someone who had played varsity sports in college. He wore dark jeans, a Kevlar vest, and a baseball cap that had the FBI emblem on it. Slung across his back Jacobson saw a folding-stock AR-15 rifle. A 10mm Glock semi-automatic handgun sat in a well-used holster on his right hip. The wedding band on his finger was the first Jacobson had seen since he had started this mission the night before.

"I've been monitoring your webcam video, Major," Terrance said. "Fine work in there. Have you had any formal forensics training?"

"No, sir."

"Major Jacobson is a man of many talents," O'Dell said. "I had to call in a lot of favors to get him here."

Terrance nodded. "Major, there's a helicopter inbound to take us to the Hawes Recreation Area in the Tonto National Forest. There's been an incident we need to investigate."

"What happened?"

"McDermott's techs found this." Terrance held out his phone. Jacobson watched security footage of a man and a large black dog running across the Biodosius parking lot. Holding his side, the man wove unsteadily through the parked cars. Under his right armpit, blood stained his white shirt.

"When did this happen?" Jacobson asked.

"Just before 6 p.m. Friday. Eight minutes before the building's power went down."

"The dog got out?"

"Yes, it did, and I'm going to take you to its last known location."

CHAPTER 13

Adam opened Mop's door, and the dog bounded from the cab. Then Adam picked up the hydration pack, carrying it by the straps rather than easing it onto his shoulders. While keeping a watchful eye on the street outside, he washed up in the restroom at Paul Moody's garage. He was more than a hundred and fifty miles from where he'd started, and he had traveled through some of the most desolate country on earth. Even so, he didn't feel safe. At any moment the Nightmare could come bounding out of the trees.

His eyes looked bloodshot. He used his fingers to comb his hair, but what he needed was a shower and a change of clothes. No, scratch that. What he needed was a hose to get all the mud off.

He made do with the restroom sink. The lightning strike had burned off his left eyebrow and the hair on his arm. With one finger, he pulled his biking shirt's collar aside. The blisters on his shoulder looked much worse than the time he'd gone snorkeling down in Baja. He let go of the collar and grimaced.

Mop barked at the sink. Adam turned on the faucet, and Mop pushed inside for a drink of water.

"The toilet isn't good enough for you?" Adam asked.

Mop lapped up his fill, backed out of the restroom, and shook, throwing off clods of mud.

Handing Adam an orange power cord to use for a leash, Paul said it was okay if Adam left the bike in the garage. Adam could have ridden the bike, but he had no idea how Mop would behave. Riding a bike while holding a makeshift leash with a dog that thought nothing of bolting after stray cats was not something he wanted to risk.

He tied the power cord around Mop's neck, and the dog struck off down the road. There wasn't anything Adam could have done to stop him, short of being dragged, so he let Mop lead the way. Even so, he felt ridiculous. His gaudy biking shirt was bright enough to be seen from space and an advertisement for every biking vendor and product there was. His padded shorts looked normal on the outside but were damp and chafed where it counted. The broken cleats on his biking shoes made him unsteady, and his right foot felt he'd stepped on a white-hot railroad spike. Mop jerked him sideways to the front door of the Hillside Diner. With the hydration pack in one hand and Mop's leash in the other, he could barely keep his footing. Adam hadn't been expecting the abrupt turn and nearly fell. The smell of frying bacon wafted out the open window.

Mop whined at the door.

"We don't have time for this," Adam said halfheartedly. "We can eat at home."

Mop barked.

Adam sighed. The food smelled good, and he was hungry. "Fine. Let me see if I have enough cash."

He took out his wallet and counted his cash. Mop whimpered, eager for the door to open. Adam hesitated. "I don't think dogs are allowed inside. You're going to have to stay out here. I'll bring you something to eat."

Mop sank to his haunches by the door, leaving Adam holding the electrical cord. Even if there'd been a hitching post out front, he doubted the cord would have held the dog if it made up its mind to leave.

"Okay, Mop, you're on your best behavior. You run off chasing cars or something, and I'll just have to disown you before I own you. Got it?"

The dog gave a quick bark that sounded like *okay*.

Adam limped inside. The café had been in business for more than sixty years, and even after a few remodels it still looked the way it had in the fifties: exposed brick walls, chrome fixtures, and solid oak tables and chairs. Red-and-white Mexican tile covered the floor, the booths were made of burgundy vinyl, and each booth had a wall-mounted, old-fashioned jukebox. He waited to be seated, glancing around as the smell of hash browns and eggs washed over him.

A couple sitting near the door tried to get their kids to eat, a truck driver drank coffee and fiddled with his phone, and two workmen wearing T-shirts and white canvas pants attacked their sausage and eggs. Next to them, Kate Lansing, the mayor of Defiance, sliced straw-berries with a steak knife, then arranged the slices on her cream cheese bagel. She was attractive, with hazel eyes, dark hair, and the natural, engaging smile of someone who enjoyed working with people. Defiance was a small town, but Adam hadn't been formally introduced.

One by one the customers glanced up and gaped at him. Kate Lansing sliced one final strawberry and added the pieces to her bagel, then looked up. Their eyes met across the silent room, and she smiled. Adam was suddenly intensely conscious of his appearance. She wore a navy-blue business suit and a blouse so celestially white it glowed. Every inch of her was trim, prim, and proper, while he looked like he had face-planted in a pigsty.

Carrying a coffee pot, Ashley Wilson, the owner of the Hillside, hurried over. "My, goodness, Adam! What happened?"

"I got caught biking in the storm last night. I know I look like a wreck, but can I get something to eat for me and my dog?"

"You have a dog?"

"I found him out biking. He's on the sidewalk."

She opened the door to look. "Wow, Adam! What kind of dog is he? He kind of looks like a mix of black Lab and retriever."

Wagging his tail, Mop got to his feet.

"Watch out, his tongue is a lethal weapon," Adam warned.

Mop politely offered a paw. Ashley laughed, shifted the coffee pot to her left hand, and shook it.

"Aren't you polite! Do you do tricks?" she asked, scratching under his chin. "You want something to eat? Are you hungry?"

Mop barked and turned in a quick, excited circle.

"Take him to the back patio," she told Adam. "No one will care if he's there. I'll get him some scraps from the kitchen."

"You hear that, mutt?" Adam said. "You won't have to eat grizzly for breakfast!"

Mop, the cord trailing behind him, bolted around the corner. Adam watched him go and gave Ashley a shrug.

"I guess we'll meet him there."

"Did you know he was going to do that?" she asked.

"No."

Adam followed Ashley through the café to the back patio.

Mop waited outside, tail wagging excitedly.

"Well, aren't you smart!" Ashley laughed. "Did Adam find you or did you find him? Do you know any single men as well behaved as you?" Giving Adam a smile, she turned, heading back to the kitchen. The door closed behind her.

It was chilly in the morning breeze. Wishing he had a jacket, Adam crossed his arms and shivered. On the opposite side of the street stood Donny's Art Studio and Supplies. Paintings of Southwestern landscapes stood on small easels in the picture window. Next to it, White

Mountain Curio advertised unique gifts. Its window had an antique tricycle, a glass beverage set of hand-blown decanters, and sparkling displays of semi-precious jewelry.

Since he was a regular, Ashley brought out his normal order of bacon and eggs, grits, toast, a side of fruit, and a glass of orange juice along with scraps for Mop. She put Adam's plate on the table and Mop's on the ground.

"Let me know if you need anything else," she said. "I'm glad you didn't break your leg again." She turned to leave and then paused. "Oh, before I forget, James called looking for you. Cindy wants to drop off Bailey so she can get ready for her wedding. You do remember about the wedding, right?"

He sighed. "Yes, I remember the wedding. I just don't *want* to remember it. There's a difference."

She laughed and scooted back inside.

Mop attacked his food, the scraps vanishing so quickly that Adam wondered if he was going to eat the plate. Licking his lips, the dog gave Adam a mournful look until Adam tossed him a piece of bacon.

"Enjoy it, mutt. From now on you must earn your keep. Do you have any job skills? Has anyone hooked you up to a plow?"

Adam forked up his eggs and watched the mountains change from blue to green under the rising sun. Mop got to his feet, trotted to the door, turned the knob with his teeth, and went into the cafe.

Adam had a slice of toast halfway to his mouth. "Mop! Come back here!"

He lurched out of his chair, each step sending a jolt of pain through his foot. At first, he thought the dog was making a break for it, but Mop, dragging his makeshift leash, veered through the tables toward Kate Lansing. When Adam had first seen her, she had been slicing strawberries, but now she was talking to a heavyset man wearing a dark suit, gray silk shirt, and burgundy tie. He held a manila folder in one hand and gestured angrily with it as he spoke.

Mop stopped between Kate Lansing and the man and lifted a paw. Kate stopped speaking and blinked at the dog in surprise.

"Where did you come from?" she asked.

Mop swished his tail across the tile. She shook his paw, and Mop pushed his head under her fingers. She ruffled his dirty ears.

Adam hurried over. "You don't want to touch him, Miss. He'll get mud on your skirt. We were out biking last night and got caught in the storm. C'mon, Mop, let's go back out on the patio."

Kate smiled again, and Adam's stomach did an abrupt, vertigo-inducing flip. Her hazel eyes caught him.

"That's an odd name for short-haired dog, Mr. Barnett. I've been meaning to drop by your shop and congratulate you on the awards you've won for your bikes. That's quite an honor. Things like that don't usually happen in towns this size. Have you decided what you're going to do for manufacturing? We're always looking for ways to diversify the local economy."

"Um, uh, not yet."

"We just opened a business development center to assist small businesses. You should take advantage."

The big man, as wide as he was tall, looked from Adam to the dog. His custom-fitted suit was expensive and barely contained his heavy shoulders. Adam was taller, but the other man had at least a hundred pounds on him.

"You should control your animal," the man said.

"He ran inside while I was eating." Adam picked up the cord. "He won't hurt you. He's well behaved."

"I didn't say I was afraid of it. It's interrupting our conversation. We were talking."

"I think he just came over to say hello," Kate said, scratching Mop's short ears. "Didn't you, boy?"

Mop fanned his tail.

She glanced at her watch, gave her half-eaten breakfast a regretful look, and got to her feet. "Speaking of interruptions, Mr. Kwei, I have things to do in the office. Coordinating the Taste of Defiance is a lot of work. I'll relay your zoning concerns to the board."

Kwei clenched the folder. "Mayor Lansing, I've already gone before the board twice. You're a lawyer. I want you to do something."

"What exactly did you want me to do, Mr. Kwei? The area's homeowners have made it clear they don't want timeshare condos in their backyards."

Scowling, Kwei tried to step around the dog. Mop turned to face him. Adam saw Mop's muscles tense and realized, again, that he knew next to nothing about the dog or its temperament. If Mop decided to attack Kwei, Adam couldn't hold him back.

"What am I going to do with six hundred acres I can't rezone or subdivide?" Kwei asked.

"I would enjoy it," the mayor said. "It's a beautiful piece of property."

Kwei's face flushed. The folder trembled in his hand.

Kate's liquid eyes hardened. "If you would like to discuss this further, you can make an appointment with my secretary, or you can request another meeting with the board."

"I don't want to make another appointment."

"Then have a pleasant day, sir."

She slipped coolly past, trailing her nails across Mop's broad head.

"You have a nice dog, Mr. Barnett."

He smiled. "Call me Adam."

"I will if you'll call me Kate."

She smiled, and he was aware again of his muddy clothes. What was a woman that attractive doing in a tiny town the size of Defiance? The place barely had a stop light.

When the door closed behind her, he said, "Okay, mutt, you've had your fun with the pretty woman. Let's finish eating and go home. You can have the rest of my toast."

Mop ran for the patio door. Adam watched him go and tried to recall what he'd said. It was one thing to tell a dog to stay or roll over or play dead, but as far as Adam knew, he hadn't looked or gestured at the patio. Dogs often recognized short phrases—*go for a walk* or *bring in the paper*—but only after months of training.

As a kid, he'd taken Cooper, his German Shorthair Pointer, out hunting for ducks, geese, and pheasants. The dog had a good nose for birds and was smart enough to understand most hunting commands such as *hold, fetch, stay,* and *flush.* But Cooper would have never known what a road map was or to go to the patio without being told. Mop had somehow understood Ashley when she suggested that Adam take Mop around back. Maybe Ashley had glanced at the patio through the cafe's glass door. At the very least, those skills suggested Mop was good at picking up both verbal and nonverbal cues.

All of this brought up a question he hadn't had time to think about. Where had Mop come from? Both Paul and Ashley had never seen the dog before. Had someone lost him in the desert, and he'd found his way up to the abandoned mine? Was there a connection between the dog and the Nightmare?

He limped back to the patio and lowered himself awkwardly into his chair. Stiffening up already. He reached for his fork. The toast was gone. The rest of his breakfast was still there, but the two pieces of bread were missing.

He looked at the dog. "Did you take the toast?"

Mop licked his chops.

"Is that tongue language I'm expected to understand? Drool for *yes* and slobber for *no,* is that it?"

He waited.

Mop whined at Adam's plate.

Adam sighed. "I just hope you didn't lick my food."

He had just speared a piece of cantaloupe when the patio door burst open and Adam's ex-sister-in-law, Cindy Benedict, stomped over to the table. She wore a tight T-shirt, tight shorts, and an annoyed scowl on her attractive face.

"There you are!" she snapped. "Where's James? I've been looking for him for the past half hour!" Her eyes flicked over his muddy shirt. "Were the two of you out biking?"

"Paul said he went fishing."

Cindy threw up her arms. "That is just so absolutely perfect! He knows how important today is to me, and he's run off!"

His niece, Bailey, walked around Cindy and sat down in a chair by the table. "Hi, Uncle Adam."

"Mermaid Girl Squirrel." The words popped out of his mouth before he could think about them.

Bailey smiled. "You haven't called me that since second grade." She lowered her voice. "Watch out. Mom is stressed."

"Weddings are stressful."

Bailey was a fourteen-year-old version of her mother, with blonde hair, thin, coltish arms and legs, freckles, and blue eyes. She wore shorts, sneakers, and a Defiance Cyclery golf shirt. She turned and saw Mop. "Whose dog is that?"

"Mine, until someone tells me different. His name is Mop. You can pet him if you like."

"Wow!"

Cindy draped a dress over a chair and stepped back to spear Adam with her eyes. "That is Bailey's dress for the wedding. Do not forget it. Do not get mud on it or slop from whatever sty you've been rolling around in. The wedding is at five. The reception is at six-thirty. You, James, and Bailey need to be at the wedding at least an hour early. None of you will be late."

She said each sentence as if Adam didn't have the ability to understand more than a half-dozen words at a time. She inspected his appearance, and her mouth settled into a tight line. "What happened to you? You're a mess."

"I was out biking and got caught in the storm."

She crossed her arms and tapped her foot. "You know what your problem is, Adam? You don't respect yourself. Every time I look at you, I wonder why you lived and Jeff didn't."

Adam opened his mouth to tell Cindy exactly what he thought of her statement but saw the alarm in Bailey's eyes.

He had never been shy about his feelings toward Cindy and her family. His animosity had contributed to James's and Cindy's divorce. But seeing the distress on Bailey's face gave him pause. He didn't know if it was because he felt horrible after his night from hell or if he was just too worn-out to rehash the same tired arguments. Whatever, there were more important things to worry about. If Cindy wanted a piece of him, she could get in line behind whatever had chased him out of the mountains.

"Do we always have to do this?" he asked quietly. "What happened to Jeff was fifteen years ago. Can't we just move on?"

Surprise showed on her face, but then the look of disgust returned. "We don't move on because you killed my brother."

"It was an accident."

"He died because of your actions."

Adam sighed. "Would you like something to eat? They say breakfast is the most important meal of the day. Have a seat and relax. I'll have Ashley bring you whatever you want."

Cindy gave him another surprised look but rapidly composed an icy scowl. "No thank you, Adam. I'm not hungry. Don't be late to the wedding, please. And I don't want another stupid Walmart gift card."

She left without another word. Adam waited until she was gone and smiled.

"You didn't get her a gift card to Walmart, did you?" Bailey asked.

"No."

"What did you get her?"

"I got her two Walmart gift cards."

Bailey laughed.

Ashley came out a couple of minutes later, bringing two strips of bacon. She handed them to Bailey and returned to Adam's table.

"Be careful with Cindy," she advised. "The only person crazier than her is Mike." She glanced at Bailey, who had taken Mop over near the patio railing. The girl had started teaching Mop to wait patiently while she put a piece of bacon on his nose. "Keep Bailey out of it," Ashley said. "She's a great kid, and I'd hate to see her get hurt. My sister went through a divorce a few years back, and her kids are so confused they're going to be in therapy the rest of their lives."

Mop stared unblinking at the bacon. "Wait…wait…wait…go!" Bailey said.

Mop snatched the bacon.

Bailey laughed, clapping her hands. "Did you see that, Uncle Adam! He's really, really smart!"

Ashley smiled. "Funny how you see a dog and you just can't help but feel good." She bent over and scratched Mop's chin. "Do you want to come home with me, sweetie?" she crooned. "You can give my tabby cat a heart attack. I don't think I've ever seen a dog with as big a head as yours."

"That," Adam muttered, "is the understatement of the year."

CHAPTER 14

The Black Hawk thundered over the confluence of the Verde and Salt Rivers, heading east toward the Tonto National Forest. The terrain was densely forested, but the trees thinned the further they got from the water. Between the rivers and the mountains ran a valley with one large, dry ravine. Even with the heavy rain the night before, the ravine had no visible water, and the undergrowth was mostly cactus and the occasional ironwood or mesquite.

Strapped in and leaning out the door, Jacobson watched for ambush points and tracks in the dirt. In combat, even one set of footprints would keep them from landing unless they knew the area had been secured. An RPG or SAM—or even a well-aimed bullet—could take down a Black Hawk. Considering all the armor they carried, helos were surprisingly fragile.

As usual, General O'Dell had brought his entourage: two senior staffers, a four-man security detail, two orderlies, and Agent Terrance. That made ten passengers. With a crew of four, the Black Hawk could hold up to eleven, so that left an empty seat where Lieutenant O'Day or Admiral McDermott might have sat. Apparently, neither one of them wanted to play dogcatcher. One of the staffers, a major, texted on his phone while the other staffer stared moodily at the deck as if he missed his office. The two orderlies were both under twenty and grinned as if this were an outing to Great America. Jacobson doubted any of them had ever been shot at.

Two sets of tracks cut across the valley's sandy soil. The first had been made by a bicycle, probably a mountain bike, and was hard to follow, but the second set of tracks was much easier to see. It wasn't a trail by any stretch of the imagination, but even from the air, he could make out individual footprints.

Flashing emergency lights appeared on the Bush Highway. The two-lane road was narrow for a highway and snaked through the mountains following the Salt River northeast to Saguaro Lake. With the mountains in the way, Jacobson couldn't see the lake, but he had seen pictures. He was still amazed at how quickly the desert sprang to life after a rain. Before he had flown into Phoenix, he had assumed everything would look like the deserts of the Middle East, but the Sonoran landscape was lush and green. Saguaros dotted the hills.

"You don't like flying?" Terrance yelled over the roar.

Jacobson shifted his gaze to the FBI agent sitting across from him. Terrance looked relaxed in his sunglasses and FBI cap. He'd stretched out his long legs as if riding in a helicopter was the most normal thing in the world—which meant it wasn't. The agent had a slight accent— Georgia? Arkansas?—Jacobson couldn't quite stick a pin on the map.

"I would put your feet flat on the deck, sir," Jacobson warned. "We catch a gust of wind, and you could break an ankle sitting like that."

Terrance brought his legs up. "How long have you been a Ranger?"

"Twenty-nine years, sir."

"All of them in combat?"

"Yes, sir."

"I've never seen anything like what happened at Biodosius. It'll keep a lot of people busy before it gets cleaned up."

Jacobson nodded. He liked Terrance. They had very different jobs, but Terrance had an air of quiet competence that was reassuring. That was why O'Dell had brought him in. O'Dell didn't mess around when he needed help, and O'Dell would need a lot of help to get to the bottom of this.

Everything Jacobson knew about Biodosius bothered him. Admiral McDermott was the government's top neuroscientist, and although Jacobson didn't know exactly what that meant, he did know that McDermott truly believed he was right about everything. Those kinds of brilliant but fatally flawed individuals had, for good and ill, changed the course of human history.

But absolute power corrupted absolutely, and just because the neuroscientists at Biodosius could tweak a dog's genome didn't mean they should. Had McDermott released a monster into the world? Someone or something had picked up a two-hundred-pound soldier and slammed him so hard into a wall that he had died, and then that thing, whatever it was, had climbed the same wall in its bare feet. Those same bare footprints appeared in the dirt below.

———

How much longer could McDermott and O'Dell keep this under wraps? It wasn't just the dog. Eight poor wretches had gone missing from the cells in Lab 6. Maybe that's why McDermott hadn't come along. Maybe he'd taken out teams to try to find them, but good luck with that. Jacobson was glad for an easy job. All he had to do was find a dog.

As the helo descended toward the rendezvous point, Jacobson saw a Maricopa Sherriff's deputy waiting at an emergency pullout. Jacobson lowered his combat goggles and made sure his feet were flat on the armored deck. The pilot set the helo down with a gentle bump, the rear wheels touching down first so that the helicopter wouldn't pitch forward onto its big, round nose. Rifle up against his shoulder, Jacobson jumped out into the blowing dust. His goggles protected his eyes and allowed him to take immediate stock of their surroundings. To the northeast, behind him, the highway snaked up into the mountains. To the southeast, in front of him, sat county emergency vehicles, their lights flashing. To the west were the Verdi and Salt Rivers. To the east loomed the Tonto National Forest.

Weapons at the ready, O'Dell's security detail spread out around the Black Hawk. O'Dell jumped down, followed by his officers and orderlies. None of the staffers had goggles, and they blinked and squinted in the dust. Terrance's sunglasses didn't help. Holding his cap, he moved out from beneath the rotors. As soon as the men were clear, the chopper lifted smoothly off the ground and thundered up into the safety of the sky. A couple of early morning drivers on the highway gaped at the helo and nearly crashed as they veered into each other's lanes.

A Maricopa County Sheriff's deputy, in brown pants and a khaki shirt, stepped nervously forward. He was younger than Jacobson and stood just under six feet in his boots. If he'd come upon the killers from the lab, the deputy's Kevlar vest, 9mm sidearm, and yellow Taser would have done him no good. Pinned to the shirt above his left breast pocket was his badge, but Jacobson had already seen that the killers didn't respect authority—or life itself.

Agent Terrance turned to O'Dell. "General, this is Maricopa County Deputy Swartz. I've worked with him in the past and called him this morning to assist us with the missing asset. Deputy Swartz, this is General O'Dell."

"General, sir, can your men lower their weapons?" Swartz asked. "We have civilian traffic on this road and people will stare and cause an accident. It's bad enough with the flashers."

O'Dell nodded and waved a hand at his security detail. They slung their rifles but kept their hands close to their sidearms. Jacobson reluctantly did the same.

"Can you tell us what you've found?" Terrance asked.

Swartz led the way to the cluster of emergency vehicles parked by the side of the road.

"Sometime last night, a Dodge Durango driven by the deceased, Alan Baltimore, lost control on the highway and crashed into the ravine. Sometime later, after the crash, he was killed by an unknown assailant."

"If no one saw him crash, how was he found?" Terrance asked.

"A couple on their way up to Saguaro Lake saw some buzzards and stopped to take pictures. Once they saw the wrecked SUV, they called 911. They were pretty shaken up. It's a mess down there. There's a seriously deranged lunatic on the loose."

"Has anyone been in the ravine yet?"

"I went down to see if anyone was alive. Once I realized it was a homicide, I secured the perimeter and held off from doing anything more." He glanced around at the soldiers. "What's your involvement with the deceased, General?"

"There was an incident last night at a federal medical research laboratory in North Scottsdale," O'Dell answered. "Dr. Baltimore fled the facility with a valuable medical research dog. We're trying to find it."

The deputy frowned. "You're here because of a *dog*?"

"Yes."

"For what kind of research?"

"Blood disorders, leukemia, that sort of thing." O'Dell nodded at one of the staffers. The staffer opened his briefcase and handed over a picture. "The dog we're looking for is a large mixed breed. It looks like a combo of retriever and black Lab. On the back is a description of the animal's size, weight, and color. Before last night's accident, there were only three dogs in the entire world with his genetic makeup. Now he's the only one left. He's worth millions. It will take years to replace him."

Swartz inspected the picture then flipped over the photo and read the description. "The dog weighs one hundred pounds?"

"Yes."

"Is it dangerous?"

"No. It was not involved in Dr. Baltimore's death."

"Was the dog in the SUV with the victim?"

"We believe so," Terrance said. He held out his phone so Swartz could watch the video he had shown Jacobson earlier.

"He's bleeding in his armpit," Swartz said. "Was he shot?"

"We don't know," Terrance answered. "All we know is that Baltimore fled the facility with the animal in his vehicle. Property records show he owns a boat. He might have been heading up to the lake when he went off the road. We'd like to examine the ravine for signs of the missing dog."

"Will you be taking control of the investigation, General?"

"I won't, but someone else will."

Swartz nodded. "In that case, sir, I can't let you into the crime scene without authorization. However, if you want to look for signs of the dog, you can see the SUV from the top of the culvert over there." He pointed to a large culvert that ran under the highway. "Stay behind the railing and don't disturb anything. I'll be the one homicide will yell at if anything happens."

"Don't worry about that," O'Dell said smoothly. "If we cause a problem, have your superiors talk to me, and I'll get it resolved. Time is of the essence. The dog is not used to the desert. If we don't find him, the heat will kill him."

Swartz led them to the culvert. Jacobson heard the low buzzing of flies. He stopped by the guardrail and looked down. The terrain below was narrow, rocky, and steep. The sides were overgrown with bushes and trees, but the bottom was mostly sand and rocks. Even with the rain the night before, it was dry. The Durango had gone off the embankment and crashed into the bottom. The SUV's front doors hung open. Body parts lay scattered across the ground.

"I'm not sure what bothers me more about this," Swartz said. "The fact there's someone out there who's capable of doing this or that none of you look surprised at what you're seeing."

There was an awkward silence as everyone glanced at everyone else.

"Do you mind if I climb up on the guardrail?" Jacobson asked. "I won't disturb anything."

Swartz looked uncomfortable but nodded.

Jacobson jumped lightly onto the guardrail, removed his binoculars, and focused in on the ravine. Glass, plastic, and metal lay everywhere. What remained of Alain Baltimore's torso slumped sideways on the truck's leather seat. One of his legs and parts of an arm had been torn off and lay on the sand by the Dodge's open door.

"There are footprints on the top edge of the culvert and in the ravine," Jacobson said, pointing down. "I think whoever did this, climbed over the guardrail and jumped down."

"That's a thirty-foot drop," Swartz said.

Jacobson pointed to a mesquite tree growing out of the side of the ravine. A bit of fabric had caught on a thorn. "That might be from the killer's clothing."

Swartz squinted at the fabric and shook his head. "No way. That's at least twenty feet out from the guardrail. There's no way anyone could make that jump. They'd break a leg."

"There are no other tracks west of the crash, sir, and the footprints are pointed east. If he didn't jump off the culvert, how did the tracks get there?"

"Maybe they climbed part way down the embankment and jumped."

"That's certainly a possibility," Jacobson admitted.

"So, the killer went into the ravine and killed Baltimore," O'Dell said. "What happened then?"

"He followed the dog and a bicyclist east into the mountains," Jacobson said.

"What? A bicyclist? How do you know that?"

"I saw the tracks from the air as we came in. There are two sets of bike tracks cutting across the valley. The first is from a mountain bike. The tracks led into the ravine. The second set has a bike, a dog, and human tracks heading east from the ravine." He pointed at the mountain on the other side of the valley. "I think someone riding their mountain bike saw the accident. I believe he cut across the valley to the ravine and tried to help Dr. Baltimore. Instead of coming back here, the bicyclist and the dog headed across the valley toward the mountains. The trail cutting across the hillside is called Horse Tail. It's a difficult trail built by mountain bikers. It has some nasty climbs and dangerous, exposed areas."

"How do you know all that? Have you been here before?"

"No, sir." Jacobson removed his tablet from his pack and brought up a map on the screen. "As we were flying over here, I looked up the area. There are topographical maps, but I found even better maps on mountain biking websites. They go into a lot of detail." He held out the tablet. "Horse Tail starts at the north end of the Hawes Trail System, which is south of here. The trailhead parking lot is about two miles from here at the side of the highway."

"Okay, that's useful information, but why didn't the mountain biker just take the road back to the parking lot? Why go cross country?"

"I don't know, sir. Maybe the killer was chasing him."

"Or chasing the dog," Terrance said.

General O'Dell scowled. "But why is the killer following the dog? That makes no sense."

"Maybe Dr. Baltimore had something the killer wanted," Jacobson said, "and maybe the doctor gave it to the mountain biker."

CHAPTER 15

Adam paid for breakfast. He, Mop, and Bailey walked the remaining two blocks to his bike shop. Bailey held Mop's electrical cord while Adam carried Bailey's dress. Mop could have gotten loose at any time, but Bailey barely had to hold the cord.

"So that's how it's going to be?" Adam muttered to the dog. "You drag me down the mountain through the mud, but with her you're a prancing show poodle?"

His shop occupied the first floor of the historic Jess Fielding Boarding House on the corner of Quarry Canyon Road and Main. The red block letters of DEFIANCE CYCLERY arched across the window. Other windows advertised bikes, gear, and notices for area bike races. On the front door, Adam had taped a poster reprinted from the cover of *Dirt Rag Magazine*. It showed him leaning over his bike's handlebars and jumping off a boulder. The cover of the magazine said, "Bike of the Year!" In smaller lettering were the words "Inside the Revolutionary Defiant RIP."

Bailey unlocked the front door. She flipped the switch three times before the lights came on. Living in a hundred-year-old building meant there was always something that needed to be fixed.

Adam removed the cord from around Mop's neck. "I'm going upstairs," he told Bailey. "Can you get the register money out of the safe, or do you need me to do it?"

She rolled her eyes. "Please, you always treat me like I'm a kid. This place would fall apart without me."

"It would not."

"It would too. Ask Dad."

He stuck his tongue out at her. She did the same back at him.

He hobbled through the office, past the stacks of orders, overdue bills, contracts, and other things he needed to finish. The rear of the store had racks of parts, bikes, and frames in various states of assembly. Adam dropped his muddy hydration pack on the floor, next to an umbrella stand and a wooden orange crate overflowing with biking shoes. Normally, he and his small staff of part-time help would be busy assembling bikes for shipment, but with the holiday weekend, the workshop was deserted. He moved through the racks to the building's rickety staircase and started up, favoring his hurt foot. Mop bounded past him.

Even though Adam didn't own the building, he and his brother had gone ahead and converted half of the upstairs rooms into a family room, kitchen, utility room, and bathroom. The arrangement was supposed to have been temporary and easily reversible, but after three years, he, James, and Bailey still hadn't found a house they could afford. Every cent Adam made from bike sales went into buying more parts so that he could build and ship more bikes so he could buy more parts. It was a never-ending cycle, which meant they were stuck in this makeshift apartment. The floorboards sagged, the plumbing leaked, and the electrical wiring was knob-and-tube. He had complained endlessly to the building's owners, but they weren't responsive. They knew the building wasn't up to code, but they also knew it was a fantastic location in the historic district. Cindy Benedict referred to the living arrangement as "her daughter's jail cell death trap," and she refused to come up upstairs. That was fine with Adam and even more fine with James.

James hadn't gotten a legal separation when he was going through his divorce, and Cindy had used their joint credit to go shopping. As the primary source of marital income, James had been stuck with spousal maintenance, child support, and her debt, while she enjoyed her new clothes, jewelry, and home furnishings with her soon-to-be husband. As a result, neither James nor Adam had a credit score high enough to get a business loan.

Adam hung Bailey's dress in her closet and went down the creaking hallway to his room. The boarding house had been built for maximum occupancy. The rooms could barely accommodate a twin bed, and he turned sideways to reach his closet.

Living in the boarding house always made him question his choices in life. He had a degree in engineering, owned a business that let him do what he loved, and had garnered awards for his bikes, but he still lived in a wreck and couldn't afford to move. To keep his head above water, he constantly juggled money. He spent every minute of every day trying to somehow get ahead, while every day falling further behind. It had been weeks since he'd had a day off and months since he had even gone out on a date. He liked having someone in his life, but simply didn't have enough time to maintain a relationship—unless that person wanted to help out in the shop. Cathy, his last girlfriend, had initially thrown herself into spring cleaning the dusty corners and tidying the shelves, but when Adam went off on bike rides, rather than taking a weekend in Flagstaff, she stopped spending her free time helping at the shop. When women broke up, they behaved like resentful, underpaid employees.

Trying not to bump his shins on the bed frame, he found a clean pair of shorts and a Defiance Cyclery polo shirt and carried them down the hall. Because of the mine shafts that ran beneath the streets, the building's foundation had settled, and the hallway sloped.

Mop followed him into the bathroom and pawed at the shower door.

"You want a shower?" Adam asked.

Mop barked.

He sighed. "All that mud on you will clog the pipes. They barely work as it is."

He dragged a trashcan over to the shower and got in fully clothed. The lightning had ruined the shirt and the shoes, so they were the first things thrown in the trash. The biking shorts were in better shape, so he reached outside the shower and hung them on a towel hook.

Once he'd taken off his clothes, he turned on the shower and let Mop inside. The dog dutifully stood under the water with his head down. The shower did not have a hose attachment, which made it hard to bathe the dog. It was also crowded. Whoever built the shower must have believed people didn't need to move around as they lathered up. But given the circumstances, it was surprisingly easy washing Mop. Adam used more shampoo and soap on Mop than he probably needed to, and the dog stood, resigned, while Adam scrubbed.

"So, what kind of dog are you?" Adam asked as he got his first real look at Mop without the mud. "You sort of look like a cross between a black retriever and a bear. In a moment of weakness, did your mother have an illicit affair? If so, that would explain a lot!"

He chuckled. Mop ignored him.

When he was done, the dog finally looked clean. He toweled Mop off and stepped back.

"You can shake now."

Mop lifted a paw.

"Not that kind of shake, genius. I don't want you getting water all over the bathroom. The other shake."

Mop lifted the other paw. Adam sighed and tried to imitate a dog shaking. Mop grinned. Adam stopped.

"Okay, you tell anyone I did that, and you'll play fetch in traffic." He put Mop's towel over the side of the shower. "You've been well behaved so far, and I'm going to assume you aren't going to get water all over the place."

He opened the door. Mop leapt into the hall and shook, spraying water.

Adam swore. "What part of 'well behaved' didn't you hear?"

Mop looked at Adam then shook again, his paws sliding on the tile.

"Do that again and you'll find yourself at animal control!"

Mop tore down the hall. Grumbling, Adam finished his shower. Mop burst into the bathroom, did a couple of circles, snatched a clean sock off the floor, and raced off again.

"Hey! I'm going to need that!"

Using only his good arm, Adam toweled off. He exited the shower, combed his hair in the small mirror over the sink, and shaved the scruff from his face. Without the mud and facial hair, he almost looked presentable. The dark would hide his bloodshot eyes. Dress pants would hide his scraped knees. His right arm had a round, swollen bruise on the bicep, almost like a scorpion sting, but his shirt would cover that and the burns on his shoulder. As for his foot, he'd drive over to the wedding in tennis shoes and then change into dress shoes. He checked the mirror again. Overall, he felt...not as good as he looked. Hot and achy, as if he had the flu.

He poured hydrogen peroxide onto a pad of folded toilet paper and dabbed gingerly at his shoulder wound. "Ouch," he muttered. He squirted bacitracin on a gauze square from the medicine cabinet, then taped the gauze in place. He eased the shirt over his head and put on his pants.

It was much harder to treat his foot than his shoulder. Walking flexed the sole, so the wound hadn't closed. On the bathroom tile, he saw dime-sized spots of blood. Leaning against the wall, he smeared bacitracin on the bottom of his foot, bandaged it, and wrapped his foot with tape. Putting his weight on his heel, he hobbled to his bedroom and rummaged through his closet until he found a pair of old Converse Hi-Tops. He folded a handkerchief for extra padding and then laced his right shoe extra tight. This would hold him until he could get his foot looked at by a doctor.

After he'd finished, he clomped down the stairs. Bailey had opened the store. A man in shorts, an aloha shirt, and a Suns baseball cap had brought his bike in for repair. Bailey had lifted the bike onto the repair stand and listened while rapidly switching gears. She picked up a tool, made an adjustment to the front derailleur's limit screw, clicked rapidly through the gears again, then took the bike off the stand and wheeled it to him.

"Try it now."

The man took the bike out back and rode it around the parking lot. When he returned, he said, "That fixed it. What was wrong?"

"You had too much sag in the rear shock, so the chain lost tension when the shock engaged, causing the chain to switch rings. I think you also moved the limit screw the wrong way trying to fix it."

The man looked surprised. "For someone so young, you really know your stuff. I guess I took too much air out of the shock the last time I rode. I wanted a softer ride without feeling like a pogo stick."

"Next time leave the air alone and adjust the rebound." She showed him how to adjust the shock.

The customer turned to Adam. "I would love to own one of your RIPs. The reviews are amazing. I wish I'd known about them when I was in the market for a new bike."

"We hear that a lot."

The customer paid for the repair then took his bike and wheeled it out the front door.

Bailey returned her tools to the workbench and gathered delivery boxes from the office. Mop lay down on the floor behind the service counter and licked his fur. The smell of wet dog joined the smell of lubricant and rubber.

Adam heard the roar of an engine and looked up to see his old Corvette skid to a stop at the front curb. James and a woman he didn't recognize got out. James, mud-caked, looked like he'd gone to marine boot camp. The woman looked even worse. Blonde hair flattened by wind, she wore Adam's gym clothes and new basketball sneakers. James pushed open the door.

"Home sweet home," he told the woman, stepping aside to let her enter.

Bailey ran over. "Guess what, Dad! We got a dog!"

"What?"

"We got a dog!"

"Since when?"

"Since last night! Uncle Adam found him out in the desert! His name is Mop, and he's the smartest dog ever! Come see!" She pulled James behind the service counter. "Watch this!"

James dumped his cell phone and keys on the counter and leaned over. Bailey told Mop to untie her shoe. Mop carefully took the end of one of her shoelaces in his mouth and pulled. The knot came undone.

"Now the other one."

Mop did as instructed. Bailey laughed and bent down to give Mop a hug. "Did you see that, Dad? He's really, really smart!"

"If he's so smart, he wouldn't just untie your shoes," Adam said, "he'd tie them."

"Don't listen to him, Mop," Bailey said. "Uncle Adam doesn't know how smart you are, but I do."

Mop licked Bailey's nose.

Adam came out from behind the counter, and James told him about the early morning fishing trip and the men with guns. He turned to the woman. "Monica, this is my brother, Adam. He owns the Corvette."

Smiling, she stepped up to the counter to shake Adam's outstretched hand and abruptly stopped, eyes widening. The blood drained from her face. She took an involuntary step backward. Adam followed her gaze to Mop. From his place behind the counter, the big dog, his nostrils flaring, stared up at her. Then he uncoiled off the floor, growled, and bared his teeth.

Monica took another step back, fear flooding her face. She snatched James's phone and keys from the counter and bolted toward the door.

Mop leapt to his feet. His shoulder hit Bailey and sent her sprawling. He cleared the service counter in a single leap but knocked over a container of Presta tire-valve adapters. The small plastic adapters exploded on the floor, and when Mop landed, his paws went out from under him. He crashed into a row of bikes.

"Mop!" Bailey cried.

Monica wrenched open the door and sprinted to the Corvette. Mop untangled himself from the bikes and reached the end of the display cases. He grabbed the doorknob in his teeth. Outside, Monica jumped in the car. She gunned the engine and squealed out of the parking spot, roaring around the corner onto Main Street and disappearing.

James grabbed an aluminum bat from under the counter and moved between Bailey and the dog. Mop let go of the doorknob and twisted around to face James, a growl rumbling from his chest. Hindquarters low to the ground, his shoulders tensed, the dog looked as if he were about to fly at James.

Adam hobbled between them, holding out his hands. "James, put the bat down. He knows what a weapon is. I think he might be a lost service dog of some kind."

James lowered the bat and backed toward the counter. Mop

relaxed. Adam held out his hand, and Mop padded over to lick his fingers.

Wincing, Adam crouched down to look Mop in the eyes. "What just happened, boy?"

Mop whined and turned toward the door. "Do you know her?"

Mop barked.

Adam sighed. "Things would be so much easier if I knew how to speak Dog."

"Will someone tell me what is going on?" James demanded. He still carried the bat in one hand. The other held Bailey back from going around the counter. Adam had known his brother his entire life and knew he wasn't afraid of anyone or anything, but looking at Mop, there was fear in his eyes.

Before Adam could reply, the shop's phone rang. He limped over, saw James's cell phone number on the caller ID, and picked up.

"I'm assuming you have a good reason for taking my car."

"I do," Monica said. "I can't explain right now, especially over the phone. Where'd you get it?"

"I bought it six years ago from an automotive junkyard in Phoenix. I've been restoring it ever since."

"Not your car, dammit!" she snapped. "The animal! Where did you find it?"

"Oh, sorry. I went mountain biking yesterday in the Tonto National Forest, and I got hit by lightning. My memory's kind of loopy."

"Was anyone else with him?"

He had no idea what he had or hadn't seen the night before, but if he had to make a choice between the dog and the woman, he would have taken Mop's side. "I'm not sure," he said. "I woke up in the mud barely knowing my name. Why?"

"The best thing you can do is put as much distance between you and it as possible. You have no idea what it is."

"Why do you keep referring to Mop as an *it*?"

Her voice cracked. "I can't explain right now and certainly not over the phone." She took a breath. "I'm sorry about taking your car, but I really need something from my vehicle. It's horribly important. If I don't get it soon, years of my work will be undone. If you keep the police out of it, I'll pay for the use of your car. How does a thousand dollars sound?"

"I don't want your money. I'd rather know what's going on."

"You don't want to know. Look, I'm grateful that James saved my life. Most people wouldn't have gotten involved. He's a decent guy. I wish we would have met under different circumstances, but there are people involved in this who'll kill me if they're not stopped."

"Maybe you should talk to James."

"I don't want to talk to James! Well, I do, but not right now. I know I'm not making any sense, but I'll call your cell and let you know where you can pick up the car and the money." She took another breath. "After all of this is over, tell James I'll apologize in person. Maybe we can have dinner somewhere nice. I'll explain everything."

Before he could tell her his cell was fried, the connection dropped. Adam hung up.

"Was that Monica?" James asked.

Adam frowned. "It was."

"Why did she run off like that? I told her I'd pick up Bailey and give her a ride to her car."

"I guess she didn't want to inconvenience you."

"How so?"

"She's paying me a thousand big ones for the use of my car. At this rate my money problems will all be solved."

CHAPTER 16

General O'Dell wasn't one to just sit around once he'd decided on a course of action. They climbed inside the Black Hawk, and he ordered the pilot to take off. "You," O'Dell said, pointing to Jacobson. "Sit by the door and keep an eye on the ground with your binoculars."

"Yes, sir," Jacobson said, sliding off his seat and situating himself so he could see the ground below and just ahead.

The Black Hawk had dual GE T700 turboshaft engines and could fly at a top speed of over one hundred and fifty knots. It took only seconds to cross the valley.

They followed the tracks around Lone Mountain and cut across Bulldog Canyon. As the pilot veered east into a narrow canyon, Jacobson picked up the dim, barely visible trail. Behind them the terrain had been mostly rolling hills, but, in front, mountains like jagged teeth shot into the white-hot sky. The cool morning air had already jumped ten degrees, and General O'Dell's face was turning red. This heat was nothing compared to Baghdad, Jacobson thought, one of the hottest places on earth, and he amused himself by picturing O'Dell as a lowly captain patrolling Baghdad's streets.

Looking down with his binoculars, he followed the trail as it cut across the side of a mountain and crested a saddle between two rocky knolls. Jacobson couldn't imagine how anyone could ride a bike over such rocky, uneven ground. He could have hiked it—in the early morning, not the heat of the day—but there was no way someone riding a bike could make it over that kind of terrain, and yet they had.

As the trail gained elevation, junipers and pine trees appeared. Miles roared past. The remains of buildings and ancient, rusted mining equipment came into view. The mining camp lay in a narrow valley located below two peaks of shattered rock. Three mines had been dug into the mountain, one at the bottom of the valley, another at the top of a small hill, and a third high up. A zigzagging trail had been cut into the cliff and connected the three mine entrances. Most of the structures in the valley had collapsed, and little remained but rusted metal and rotting wood. One block building still had four walls and a corrugated roof. It backed up to the road that led to the upper mines.

Jacobson leaned out of the Black Hawk and pointed. "General, the tracks end by that building."

O'Dell gave the order, and the pilot set down onto what had once been a dirt road but had long ago turned into an overgrown pair of rocky ruts. The staff officers and orderlies stayed behind, but everyone else jumped out, including O'Dell and his bodyguards. With its engines booming and echoing between the peaks, the Black Hawk roared up into the sky.

Jacobson searched the valley, scanning the mining equipment and undergrowth for threats. At the other end of the valley, a long section of rusted steel—maybe from a collapsed drill rig or water tower— jutted at an angle from the ground and reminded Jacobson of a broken finger. The size of a semi-trailer and rounded on both ends like the tanks used to transport propane or natural gas, an industrial tank had been left to rust in the shade of an open shed. The tank might once have been a boiler, or maybe not, because why would miners need to heat water? Nearby stood a slag heap of ash-grey sand. Shoulder-high weeds grew everywhere. Jacobson didn't like it. There were too many places an assailant could hide. O'Dell's security detail was competent at what they did—which was protecting the general—but none of them had combat experience. The only adversaries the orderlies had ever killed were in video games, and the staff officers were only good at combating the clutter on their desks. That left him, and to a lesser extent, Agent Terrance, to handle killers who could jump thirty-foot culverts in the dark and who thought nothing of tearing solid steel security doors apart.

"If something happens, it'll happen fast," he quietly told Terrance. "Be ready if it does."

Terrance nodded and thumbed off the safety of his AR-15.

Jacobson led the way to a building the size of a double-wide garage on a 1920s bungalow. The wind, smelling of pines from the mountain tops, moaned past.

"The mountain biker fell off his bike here, sir," Jacobson said, crouching down and pointing to some marks in the mud. "You can see where his hands and handlebars hit."

"Was he attacked?" O'Dell asked.

"No, sir. I'm only seeing his footprints and the paw prints of the dog. Maybe he was exhausted. It's been almost thirty miles from the accident, the last twenty on a mining trail that was never built for a bike. I can't believe either of them made it this far. It had to have taken them half the night."

Sighing, he stood and followed the tracks to the front of the building. Rainwater seeped through a hole in the metal roof and dripped onto the concrete floor. A workbench leaned crookedly against the back wall. Stacked wooden boxes containing core samples occupied another. Fluttering in the breeze, a piece of black plastic hung from a crossbeam. Behind him, on the far side of the valley, a rock clattered down the side of the mountain and clanged onto metal. Jacobson swung his rifle toward the sound.

"Whoa, easy there, sport," one of the bodyguards said, holding up a hand. "Let's not get excited."

Jacobson nodded. They were in no imminent danger. The bodyguards could see all the way down the valley.

"Let's take a look inside," he told Terrance.

They stepped into the shade, and Jacobson leaned down to inspect some muddy bike-tire tracks on the cement. He picked up a pipe. "It looks like the mountain biker crawled through the doorway with the dog and turned to face the road," he said. "You can see his knees and handprints. There's mud on the pipe from where he held it."

"Last stand?" O'Dell asked.

"Maybe, but I don't see any blood."

"How do you know it's the mountain biker's footprints? It could be anyone's."

"He's wearing biking shoes, sir. They have a metal plate on the bottom where they snap into pedals." He straightened up and pointed at the footprint. "You can see the plate if you know what to look for."

O'Dell raised an eyebrow.

Jacobson handed over his tablet with a picture of a mountain biking shoe on it.

"You're extremely thorough, Major."

"Yes, sir."

The breeze moaned through the open doorway again, fluttering the plastic. The old building creaked. Jacobson watched the sunlight streaming through the holes in the roof. There was a feeling of menace in the air. He couldn't explain it, but something wasn't right. He had long ago learned to listen to his instincts. They'd kept him alive.

Tire tracks left the building. Jacobson followed them through the chest-high weeds and out to the rutted road. He noticed something in the dirt and stopped. In one of the ruts, clearly seen in the mud, were bare human footprints. Some were spaced far apart. Whoever had left them had been running. Others were close together. The tracks were of different sizes.

"General, sir, permission to speak freely?" he asked.

"Go ahead."

"I know I'm an outsider on your project, sir, but what's going on? When I first saw footprints crossing the flatland by the highway, I thought the killer was wearing those shoes that have the toes. Supposedly they make you feel like you are running in your bare feet." He pointed at the footprints. "But these weren't made by a shoe, sir. How can someone run for thirty miles in their bare feet?"

O'Dell scowled, irritation settling into the lines on his face. "I don't know. I'll need to talk with McDermott."

Jacobson glanced at Terrance.

The agent shrugged. "Don't look at me. The deeper I get into this mess, the less I want to know."

Jacobson sighed. "With the rain, it's hard to tell how old the tracks are. I'd guess maybe three or four hours. Could be less depending on when the rain stopped. But at least we now know why the mountain biker came all the way up here. He needed to retrieve his vehicle."

"Vehicle?" O'Dell said.

Jacobson pointed to fresh tire tracks in the mud. The tires still had a good amount of tread.

Terrance crouched over them and pulled out his cell phone. "We can run the tread patterns to see what kind of truck he drives."

"So that's it?" O'Dell demanded. His face was even more flushed than it had been earlier in the helo. "You think the mountain biker drove off with the dog?"

"Yes, sir."

"But it doesn't make sense! Why would someone park their truck up here and ride all that way back down to Phoenix on that godforsaken trail and then come back? Are you absolutely certain we followed the right tracks?"

"Someone on a bike and with a large dog came this way, sir. Whether it's your dog or someone else's, I can't say at this point, but they were followed by multiple sets of bare feet like what I saw at Biodosius."

"But there's nothing here!" O'Dell exploded in frustration, gesturing around at the weeds and rusting equipment. "We're halfway to the damn moon!"

He closed his eyes and rubbed his nose. Jacobson doubted he had slept much in the past two days.

"Let's table this and move on," O'Dell finally said. "We're running out of time. Every second we delay puts the dog further out of reach. What do we do now?"

"We follow the truck tires, sir. With any luck, we'll catch the truck before it makes the highway. If not, we'll find out what kind of tires the truck is using and track them down. It won't be easy or fast, but the Bureau has the resources."

"Can you do that?" O'Dell asked Terrance.

"Given time and manpower, yes."

O'Dell took out his radio and snapped at the pilot to pick them up. The Black Hawk stopped circling and started up the valley, the sound of its engine rumbling back and forth between the surrounding peaks. The building groaned and popped in the breeze. Something scratched on the metal roof.

Jacobson leapt away from the building and squinted up through the glare. The sun blinded him.

He pushed Terrance's back. "Move into the open."

Wood moaned, metal tore, and the roof collapsed. Decades of dust and dirt exploded out the open doorway in a choking cloud. One of the security men standing in front of the doorway ducked, arms around his head, as dirt and dust billowed around him. A second later he disappeared.

"Hostiles in the weeds!" someone yelled.

The remaining security guards surrounded O'Dell and pushed him toward the road. Jacobson, eyes darting back and forth, backed away from the building. It was impossible to see anything through the dust and undergrowth.

Like a huge, black dragonfly, the helicopter thundered up the valley. As it flew toward them, a shape suddenly appeared on the roof of a distant building. Silhouetted against the light, the shape leapt off the roof and onto the rusty I-beam that stuck diagonally out of the ground. It landed on the metal and sprinted up its length. When it reached the top, it leapt from the end, arms and legs pinwheeling through the air. It was an impossible jump. The helicopter was too far away and moving much too fast, and there was no way the figure could make it. But at the last possible instant, it somehow landed inside the Black Hawk's open doorway.

For a long second nothing happened, then the Black Hawk's big, armored nose lowered. Its tail rose into the air. Instead of slowing down, it gained speed.

"Look out!" Jacobson's words were drowned by the thundering roar. "It's going down!"

He ran toward the nearest bodyguard standing in the weeds. The man's back was to the oncoming helicopter, and his wide, panicked eyes searched the tall, dry grass. The bodyguard saw Jacobson coming and snapped his weapon around. His rifle barked. The bullet cracked into Jacobson's ceramic chest plate. Jacobson staggered sideways and fell, gasping, to the ground.

The helicopter, engines roaring, dropped from the sky. Jacobson saw it coming and flattened his body against a rock. The helicopter's armored nose slammed into the ground and pitched forward with a shriek of metal as momentum fought gravity and the ground's immovable mass.

For a long, eternal second, the Black Hawk just hung there, tail in the air and nose on the ground, and then it crashed on top of him.

CHAPTER 17

Adam hobbled into the back of his shop. He should probably go to the hospital to get checked out, but he didn't have a way to get there. This Monica person had stolen his car. Without transportation, he couldn't retrieve his truck from Mesa, his Corvette from Monica, or figure out how to return the old Chevy truck to the mine, not that he could even find his way back there. He needed a new phone, but the store was at the other end of town. Running a small business without a cell phone meant lost sales, and with Monica about to call, he needed a phone sooner rather than later.

He stopped at the freight door and counted the finished bikes waiting for him to make videos. Most of his business was done online. Customers went onto the Defiance Cyclery website and customized their order. Bikers who did a lot of steep climbs needed extra low gears, and they would typically opt for a bike with an extra-large cartridge on the back and a smaller front chainring with a specialized derailleur to handle the added tension. Those who did mostly flat trails wanted a bike with a smaller cartridge set, a feature that raised their gear ratio.

Those who mostly rode cross-country would order a standard build that still gave them one extra low gear without sacrificing the high end.

As far as he knew, he was the only bike manufacturer that allowed customers to cherry-pick every part of their build. That brought him a lot of business, but it also meant sacrificing the economies of scale that the big guys enjoyed. He also didn't have a network of dealers, so he paid more for labor, materials, and shipping. In theory, assembling the bike from pieces allowed him to keep more of the profit, but in practice, he gave most of the money back to his suppliers.

He went over to the end of his small assembly line. The last step of the assembly process was taking each bike out to the practice trail he had built into the rocky hillside behind the shop. He would record a video of who the bike was for, add a quick thirty-second summary of what they had ordered and why, and then he would do a couple of climbs and drops, putting the bike through its paces. He would then splice in a canned marketing spot about how all his bikes shipped with dirty tires and end by congratulating the customer on buying the best bike on the planet. The customers loved these videos, and there were hundreds on TikTok and YouTube.

Twelve bikes waited by the backdoor for videos. With his feet in Hi-Tops, he couldn't do the videos—he'd look ridiculous to anyone in the biking community—so he would have to ask James for help.

He hobbled into his office. After running for his life from the Nightmare, it was hard to focus on anything as mundane as assembling bikes or paying bills. But that didn't mean he had time off. There was always something that needed doing. He stepped over the piles of paper, parts, and returns, and pulled out his desk chair. If he didn't pay his bills, he couldn't get more parts. If he didn't have parts, he couldn't build bikes. If he couldn't build bikes, he couldn't ship. And if he didn't ship, he couldn't get paid so he could buy more parts and pay more bills.

As he worked, his mind drifted to meeting Kate Lansing that

morning in the café. He had seen her around town and admired the way she carried herself—professional but not aloof. That morning, precision-slicing her strawberries, he had seen her in an unguarded moment, and he remembered her smile.

On impulse, he looked up the number for the Mayor's office and, before he could talk himself out of it, dialed the number.

"Mayor Lansing's office," a polite woman answered. "This is Joan. Can I help you?"

"Hi, Joan. This is Adam Barnett. I own Defiance Cyclery across the street."

"Yes, Mr. Barnett. I know who you are. My husband and I bought two of your bikes last Christmas."

"How are they working out?"

"Great. They're a lot of fun."

"That's good to hear."

"What can I help you with?"

He took a breath. "I'm calling to see if Kate Lansing is available for lunch."

He heard a rustle of paper. "The mayor generally doesn't do business meetings over her lunch hour, especially on a holiday weekend. Would you like to make an appointment for another time? She has an opening next Tuesday at three-thirty."

"Actually, I'm calling socially. I met her this morning over breakfast. My dog crashed her meeting with Johnny Kwei."

"Then your dog did her a favor."

"I got that impression. I know she's one of the judges for the Taste of Defiance today, but I had something happen last night that made me think life is short. Instead of letting the opportunity slip away, I decided to call and see if she's available for lunch."

"Oh."

Why was he rambling on? He gave a weak laugh. "This sort of feels like I'm trying to ask out a woman by talking to her mother."

The attempt at humor fell flat.

"Can you hold on a minute? I'll see if she's free." Joan clicked away.

Adam lowered his head into his hands and massaged his temples. Why was he such an idiot around women?

"Wow! Uncle Adam!"

He looked up to find Bailey grinning at him.

"You're asking out Mayor Lansing! She's really nice!"

"You know her?"

"She came to our school last week, and I got to meet her. She's so cool! You should take her over to the Pasta House! They have the best macaroni and cheese ever!"

"I don't think she'll want to order off the kid's menu, Mermaid Girl Squirrel. Besides, I just met her this morning, and I was covered in mud. The closest I'll probably get to her is when she hands me her dry cleaning bill."

He heard laughter on the other end of the phone and groaned.

"Don't tell me you heard that?" he asked into the mouthpiece.

"Is that your niece?" Kate asked.

"Yes. She helps around the shop. She says I should ask you out for macaroni and cheese."

"I remember her. After I finished my little spiel, she marched up to me and told me she was going to be the mayor someday. I think she wants my job."

"I'd take her seriously. She's already taken over here. I try to do anything, and she tells me I'm doing it wrong. In fact, she's doing it right now."

Kate laughed again. He liked the sound.

"Joan said you wanted to meet for lunch. I'm not sure today is the best day for that. I'm one of the judges for the Taste of Defiance so I already have a full plate, so to speak. We're expecting twenty-five thousand visitors this weekend, so it will be very busy. We could try something next week."

He leaned back in his chair. "I know you're busy, and I'm sorry for the short notice. It's just I had something happen to me last night that changed my perspective about putting things off. I know we just met, but I can't get your smile out of my mind."

She didn't answer for a long moment. "Well, I was going to ask for a rain check, but I must say, you have me intrigued to find out something."

"Which is?"

"Why I'm so forgettable."

CHAPTER 18

Jacobson groaned. What had happened before the Black Hawk crashed? Had one of O'Dell's men really shot him? He drew in a hesitant breath and didn't feel any pain. His ceramic plate had turned the bullet. At least he didn't have a hole in his lung.

He lifted his head. Sitting above him, the Black Hawk's armored belly lay on top of the rock. With the helicopter tilted slightly to one side, one wheel touched the ground while the other two dangled in the air. Amazingly all three of the landing wheels were still intact. The rotors still spun, flattening the weeds. Over the roar of the engine, he heard shouts and then the distinctive, flat crack of an AR-15.

He crawled out from beneath the helicopter.

"They're coming back!" someone shouted.

Above Jacobson's head, a pistol fired twice and clicked empty. A hundred feet away, an approaching wave of moving grass told him one of the killers was ready to finish them off. Jacobson brought up his rifle and fired. The M41A's jacketed rounds tore through the undergrowth. Something yowled and veered away.

"Friendly coming in!" he shouted, scrambling through the helicopter's tilted doorway. O'Dell, bleeding from a gash across his shoulder and chest, slumped on the deck. He held a pistol. Terrance stood behind him and covered the other doorway. A dead staff officer with one leg hanging from the doorway lay on the deck. He had been ripped open from his solar plexus to the top of his right leg. The smell of blood, torn intestines, and hydraulic fluid filled the morning air. The other staff officer had vanished.

"What's the status?" Jacobson shouted over the engine's roar.

"There are at least three of them," Terrance called out. "They're fast and stay out of sight in the weeds. Glad to see you didn't get crushed."

"What about the pilots?"

"I don't know."

Jacobson turned to O'Dell. "You still with us, General?"

O'Dell grimaced. "My collarbone's broken. They'd have cut my throat but I rolled onto the floor."

"Did you see them?"

"No, I was looking the other way when they attacked."

"Can you cover the door while I check the pilots?"

"My gun's empty."

Jacobson took O'Dell's pistol, ejected the clip, and loaded a fresh one.

"I'll be right back."

He hurried to the cockpit. Blood splattered the left forward window. The seatbelt's shoulder strap kept the dead pilot upright. Under his flight helmet's chin strap, his throat had been slashed. The co-pilot lay slumped up on the deck in front of his seat. His helmet had been ripped off. It usually wasn't the best idea to move a wounded man, but Jacobson leaned over the center console and hauled the co-pilot onto the seat. A bruise darkened the man's left temple.

His eyes fluttered. "What happened?"

"We're under attack," Jacobson said. "Can you get us up in the air?"

The man squinted unsteadily out the windows at the moving props.

"The sun's bright."

"You have a concussion. Can you get us airborne?"

"Yes, sir." He reached a hand toward the instrument panel. "I'll try."

Jacobson hoped the guy could figure out how to deal with the tilt. Meanwhile, Jacobson had to buy him some time.

He returned to O'Dell. The general lay propped against his seat with both legs splayed out in front of him. His ashen, bloodless face was pinched, and air wheezed in and out of his lungs.

"Hang in there, General. We're leaving."

Jacobson crouched by the helo's open door. Thick, shoulder-high weeds spun wildly under the rotors. Until the helo lifted off and they were well away, the killers could still attack. A hundred feet away, he saw something running sideways through the grass. He squeezed off three rounds, every shot late, and stopped shooting. Over and over, he had seen how they attacked from one direction to get their victims moving, then cut them off and attacked from another. He ducked across the open doorway and looked toward the tail rotor. He caught a glimpse of something coming low and fast along the fuselage. He didn't have time to do more than point his rifle in the general direction of the attack and squeeze the trigger. A shriek rang out, and the figure darted under the helicopter's tail.

"Hostile coming your way!" he called out.

Terrance fired twice.

Jacobson ejected his spent magazine, slid a replacement into the receiver, and stepped back across the open doorway. A large rock arced through the sunshine and crashed onto the Black Hawk's deck. It just missed O'Dell's legs and nearly bowled Terrance over. The FBI agent let out a shout and snapped his head around to see what had happened.

Jacobson jumped over O'Dell toward the other doorway, brought up his rifle, and fired a burst behind Terrance's right ankle. Terrance hopped out of the way and nearly fell out the door. Something screamed and whatever had been about to climb into the chopper retreated.

Jacobson looked at the pilot fumbling his helmet onto his head. This was no time for safety protocols. Jacobson stepped forward and grabbed the helmet from the man's hands.

"Get us up into the air now!" he yelled.

O'Dell fired his pistol three times. One bullet hit the metal deck and whined out the doorway. Jacobson dropped the helmet and spun around, but he was too late to stop the killer from grabbing the dead staffer by the ankle and pulling him outside.

The helicopter shuddered, lifting off at an angle. For a second Jacobson wondered if the helo was going to skew sideways, but the pilot compensated. The killers scattered, one heading toward the building and the other two taking cover further away, beneath the oblong industrial tank.

Jacobson fired, his rounds tearing holes through the metal. He grabbed the extra fragmentation grenade he had gotten from the booby-trapped network rack in Biodosius, pulled the pin, and tossed it out of the helicopter. They were about a hundred feet up and rising rapidly. The grenade fell slowly through the golden morning air, hit the ground, and bounced against the tank. Jacobson counted out the seconds and pulled back from the helo's open doorway.

The grenade exploded. Fragments peppered the Black Hawk's armored belly in sharp, metallic pings. He leaned out the door. The tank, its metal shredded, had rolled off its supports. He watched for signs of movement. Nothing. Scratch two killers.

"Where do you want me to go, sir?" the pilot called back.

"Hold for instructions at seven hundred feet," Jacobson said.

He shouldered his rifle and left the doorway to help O'Dell into one of the seats. Kneeling, he opened O'Dell's bloodstained shirt and examined the gash.

"It's not life threatening, sir," he said. "I'll stop the bleeding until we can get you to a hospital."

"I can wait," O'Dell wheezed. "I'm going to call in an Apache and additional men. Until they arrive, follow the truck's tire tracks. We need to find it before it reaches the pavement and disappears."

Jacobson stared at O'Dell's bloody face. Was a dog, even an expensive medical research dog, worth what they had gone through?

"Sir, we have a dead pilot up front, another with a probable concussion, and you've lost a lot of blood."

"We'll get medical attention after we find the truck, Major. You've got your orders."

"Yes, sir."

Jacobson told Terrance where the medical kits were located and reluctantly returned to the open door. He'd need to guide the pilot— that is, if the guy didn't pass out.

The pilot brought the Black Hawk around to fly down the valley. As they straightened, Jacobson saw two of the dead bodyguards sprawled on the ground below. He shook his head. Leaving them behind went against everything he believed in. But he didn't have a choice. If they went back for bodies, they would be attacked again. The killers had used a lethal combination of speed and stealth. The terrain gave them an advantage, and no telling how many were out here, hiding in the old mines or waiting in the weeds. The two he hoped the grenade had killed might only have been stunned.

While O'Dell issued orders on his radio, Jacobson followed the tire tracks and called out directions. As they flew, Terrance worked on O'Dell's wound. The road dropped below treeline and then wound up into the mountains until junipers and ponderosa pine replaced the desert vegetation. Earlier that morning the mountains had towered like tall, jagged teeth, but now the chopper flew among them. Jacobson kept his binoculars on the tire tracks and then leaned out, focusing on the ground. The tire tracks cut across a high, flat mesa.

"Hold here!" he yelled at the pilot.

Jacobson focused again to confirm what he had seen.

"General, there are human footprints on the road following the truck. While you have the admiral on the radio, I recommend finding out what we're up against. Our lack of information is a critical liability."

"I'll relay the message. Proceed."

"Go on," he called to the pilot.

The road reached the edge of the mesa and switched back and forth down the side of a cliff. The road was horribly exposed: narrow and steep. The tire tracks swerved as if the driver had had trouble staying on the road. Had the killer chased the driver down the switchbacks? He looked for signs of a crash, didn't see any, and breathed a sigh of relief.

At the bottom of the cliff, the tracks entered a sandy valley and traversed a string of narrow canyons, each slightly larger than the one preceding it.

Terrance, his face streaked with dirt, finished bandaging O'Dell and dropped into the seat next to Jacobson. Still holding his rifle, he wiped his face with his shirt sleeve.

"When you fired out my door, how did you know one of them was hiding outside?" he asked.

"They always feint one way and attack from another."

"When they threw the rock, I looked to see what it was. If you hadn't been there, they would have gotten inside and that would have been it."

"Did you see them?"

"No, they're too fast. Who can run like that?"

"I don't know."

As the helicopter headed west, the mountains turned to foothills, and the temperature rose. Twenty minutes later, the tracks reached the Bush Highway. The muddy tire tracks turned south toward Mesa, vanishing on the well-traveled route.

"Have we made a big loop?" O'Dell asked, his question barely audible.

"Yes, sir. We're three miles north of where Dr. Baltimore crashed into the wash."

Hoping to see the truck itself, Jacobson had the pilot continue south until they reached Arizona 202.

Jacobson rubbed his eyes, aching from the dust and bright sun. "I think this is a dead end."

"What do you recommend we do?" O'Dell asked, looking from Jacobson to Terrance.

"I have pictures of the mountain biker's tires," Terrance said. "With any luck, we'll be able to find out what kind of bike he was riding and then try and look at local sales records. We can also track down the truck."

"How will you do that?"

"We'll go through last night's security videos from the businesses along the roads. If we see a dirty truck with a bike and a large dog in it, we'll run the plates and hopefully get a name and address. The mountain biker might even have reported what happened to the police once his cell phone gets a signal."

"And if we don't get a license plate?"

Terrance shrugged. "We know what size shoe he wears and his weight. Not many people could have made that ride in the dark with the killers chasing him. I bet the mountain biking community is small enough that it won't take long to put a list together."

"That's a lot of ifs."

"I've tracked down people with less than we have now, General. All I need is time, and I'll find your mountain biker and dog."

"Unless the killers find them first," Jacobson muttered under his breath.

CHAPTER 19

Usually for a first date, Adam dressed up and tried to make a good impression, and, of course, he was grateful that Kate had squeezed him into her busy day. The Taste of Defiance was a windfall for the town's restaurants, and they would be crowded. Bailey's prompt about taking Kate Lansing out for mac and cheese gave him an idea.

Wearing the ridiculous Hi-Tops and pedaling with one foot, he rode a demo bike down to Lucky's Saloon. The saloon was in the basement of the Old Defiance Ghost Tour Company, and their Creep Tour took tourists to pubs where the spirits they encountered were rumored to not just be the kind found in a bottle.

Defiance was known for its ghosts, and he had thought it was just tourist hype until he and Cathy, on his last attempt to be romantic, had stayed overnight at the historic Gibson Hotel. They hadn't gotten much sleep. On weekends, a nearby pub had live music until two in the morning but strange and unexplained things went on in the hotel. Doors swung open at odd times, two of the pictures in their room fell off the walls, and the old building creaked with every gust of wind. Cathy had been extra clingy all night and not in a good way. By the next morning they had checked out and gone to her apartment to sleep.

Like the Gibson Hotel, Lucky's was one of the few places frequented by locals. The bar didn't look like much, but the food was good and the drinks cold. He wheeled his bike inside the saloon and leaned it against a wall so that he could keep an eye on it from his table. In a town known for its quaint, beautifully restored restaurants, Lucky's looked down on its luck. The stained oak floor was cracked, the paint shabby, and the smell of beer and burgers permeated the walls. The sign inside the door said WAIT TO BE SEATED but Adam ignored it and sat at an oak table that had been lacquered so many times it glowed. The tourists waited to be seated. The regulars seated themselves.

On a normal day, he would spend the time waiting for his food by scrolling through his emails, but since he didn't have a working phone, he bought a newspaper. Most of it was ads but there was an article on the Taste of Defiance and what restaurants would be participating. The article had a photograph of Kate Lansing. He replayed her words about "being forgettable." As far as he knew, he didn't know her. His parents might, but his phone was melted so calling them was out.

She breezed into the saloon. Along with everyone else, he found himself staring and almost forgot to stand up and pull out her chair. She sat down with a whispered thank you and smiled.

"I've never been in here before," she said. "Isn't this one of the stops on the Creep Tour?"

"It's the last one."

"Is it haunted?"

"No, but everyone thinks Stacy Heinemann, the owner, is creepy."

She laughed. He liked the sound.

Heinemann, in a dirty apron, shambled over and scowled at Adam. "It's early to eat. I don't start the grill until eleven."

"That's why I called ahead and asked if you could do me a favor and start early."

"I don't do favors. You should know that by now."

Adam smiled awkwardly. "Look, can't you see I'm trying to make an impression?"

"You're making an impression all right. The wrong kind."

Wiping a greasy hand on his apron, he slouched off.

Kate gave Adam an uncertain look. "We could go somewhere else if it's a problem."

Adam shook his head. "He's just giving me a hard time. You don't have a nut allergy, do you? The real kind, not what you'd find in here."

She smiled again. "No allergies." She put her purse on the floor. "So how are your parents doing? I've thought about calling them to say thanks for coming to my dad's funeral. It meant a lot to my mom. I asked about you, and they said you were in Malaysia trying to get parts for your bikes."

Mind turning, he frowned. It wasn't that unusual that she knew his parents. They had lived their entire lives in nearby Nostalgia Valley, and knew everyone. But where did *she* know *them* from? He went through every Lansing he could think of, trying to figure out who she was related to.

She saw his confusion. "You don't remember me, do you?"

He gave her an uncertain smile. "That's a loaded question. If I say I don't know you, then I'm a forgetful ass. If I say I do, then I'm just an ass."

"I'll give you a hint. We used to know each other in middle school. The school didn't want to have a Halloween Dance, so they called it a Harvest Dance. We went together."

That had been more than twenty years ago. He had liked a girl then, but her name had been Katlyn Kirshenbaumhein. Everyone called her Katlyn K. for obvious reasons. He had known her family since childhood. They hadn't dated for long, but he had been smitten. Her dad had been transferred out of state, and the family had moved away.

She saw the recognition on his face and laughed. "Don't look so surprised. Things change, including my last name."

"Why didn't you tell me you were back?"

"It was just one middle school dance, and it was a long time ago. Besides, I thought your parents told you."

"I was in Asia for two months. They must have forgotten. I'm sorry about your dad. I liked him a lot more than he liked me. Every time I would come over to your house, I felt guilty."

"For what?"

"Breathing."

She laughed.

"So how did you become Kate Lansing, or do I need to call my mom to get the details?"

She took a breath. "As you know, we moved to St. Louis. I eventually went to Washington University and got my law degree. I went to work for a firm in Chicago and got married. My husband was Robert Lansing. He worked for the same firm I did."

"What happened?"

"The job was demanding and the hours horrible, but we made it work, sort of. Part of it was the lifestyle. We had a lot of *nice* things. *Nice* cars, a *nice* condo on the lakefront, and *nice* vacations—when we found the time—which wasn't often. The years went by in a blur of going into work early and leaving late. I thought I was happy. But then my dad got sick. I wanted to move closer to St. Louis to spend more time with him, but Robert didn't. He'd never gotten along with my parents, especially my dad."

"I know how that felt."

"My dad liked you. Even after I was married, he kept bringing up your name. He showed me magazine articles about your bikes."

"That's surprising. I thought the only thing he liked about me was the front door hitting my backside on my way out."

She laughed. "He said you were polite, you didn't shy away from hard work, and family meant something to you. Every time you came over, he put you to work and you stuck with it. He told me he wanted to see what kind of person you were, but mostly I think he was trying to teach me a lesson. A woman must be careful. There are lots of predators out there. Even men who say all the right things vanish when times get hard. But a man who works hard for a woman, well, that's someone special."

Eyes blinking, she looked down at the table. "After my dad was diagnosed with cancer, I did a lot of commuting back and forth between Chicago and St. Louis. It wasn't fair to other people at the firm, and it affected my job performance. At that point, there were more important things than putting in hundred-hour work weeks."

"How did Robert take it?"

"We grew apart. He made partner and spent even more time at work. We barely saw each other, and when we did we fought. My priorities had changed and his hadn't. We lasted another six months before he had me served at work. He didn't even tell me it was going to happen. We got a divorce, and I left the firm. My parents and I moved back here, and then my dad died."

Her voice quivered and her dark hair dropped in front of her face. An awkward moment went by.

Trying to find a more comfortable position for his foot, Adam stretched out his leg. "You kept your married name?"

"Yes. Lansing is a lot easier to write on a political billboard than Kirshenbaumhein."

He laughed and then stopped. He met her gaze. She didn't look away. Something came alive inside him, something he hadn't felt in a long time.

"I wish you would have looked me up," he said. "I saw you around town. You reminded me of someone, but I didn't know who."

"People change a lot in twenty-five years. Besides, I thought you would figure out who I was during the election."

"I've been overseas a lot, trying to negotiate sourcing deals for parts."

Heinemann carried out their blackened chicken, clattered the plates on the table, and glowered away. Adam picked up his fork and waited for her to try the food. Her eyes widened.

"This is amazingly good! Why is it not in the Taste of Defiance contest?"

"I don't think Heinemann cares about contests. If he did, he would have to wash his apron."

"What does he marinate the chicken with?"

"I think he uses lemon juice, but he won't say."

"What's on the broccoli?"

"Almond chips, parmesan cheese, and whatever spices he puts on the chicken. You might want to write that down for your trip to the hospital later."

She snorted and took another bite.

"What happened to your foot? Every time you move, you wince like you're in pain."

"I was out riding yesterday and got struck by lightning."

She stopped chewing. "What? Really?"

"I woke up in the mud. I have a burn on my shoulder and on the bottom of my foot. It put a hole through the sole of my shoe."

"Are you all right? What did the doctor say?"

"Well, I, um, sort of haven't gone yet."

She put down her fork. "You got struck by lightning and instead of going to the hospital, you're eating lunch with me?"

"Well, don't feel special." He raised his voice toward the bar. "If I wanted to impress you, I wouldn't have brought you here!"

She barked out a laugh. "You're just as funny as I remember."

"We should eat." He held a piece of chicken on his fork. "You've got an event to go to."

"How's business?" she asked a moment later.

"Good and bad. We have a huge backlog of bike orders we're trying to get through. That's good. The bad is we're at least three months behind. Customers are canceling orders."

"Can you hire more people?"

"I'm having trouble making payroll as it is. I'm one of the little guys. They big guys have dealer networks to help them build and sell product. I only have me and three part-timers. My margins are lower, and my costs are higher, so I end up working twelve-hour days just to break even."

"What are you going to do?"

"James thinks I should license my suspension. A lot of the component manufacturers are interested. That way I get paid for every unit they ship instead of every bike I build. I could still build bikes, but that would open up new sources of income I don't have now."

"What are the negatives?"

He sighed. "I just don't know if I want to give my suspension away. I've spent most of my adult life doing this, and if I let other people have the pivot, then why would anyone want one of my bikes when they can get the same suspension from a bigger manufacturer for less money? Plus, most of the manufacturers don't want my suspension. They just don't want to compete against it. They'll give me a check for exclusive rights, and then they'll bury it so they can keep using the suspension they already own instead of paying me a couple hundred bucks for each unit shipped."

"Can you advertise?"

"That won't help. I can't build fast enough. One of the bike magazines recently ran a feature listing similar bikes, essentially pointing potential buyers to my competition."

"So, if you keep your suspension, you work like crazy and can just barely keep your head above water. If you license it, you end up in competition with yourself. Not an easy decision."

"You've stated it very succinctly."

She glanced at her watch and frowned. "I'm sorry, but I have to go."

"Can I see you again?"

She looked surprised but smiled. "I'm available tonight if you're going to the Benedict wedding. My mother wants me to take her. She doesn't do well driving after dark, and the road going into Nostalgia is terrible."

Adam groaned. He agreed with that.

"Are you going?" she asked.

"I'm supposed to."

"But you don't want to."

"No," he said. "The Benedicts are family—my niece Bailey's grandparents—and my parents want me to make nice, but the Benedicts and I don't get along."

"Please think about it. We could dance if you're up to it."

"I don't know," he said. He needed to take the old truck back to the mine and pick up his truck at the trailhead, plus he should go to the hospital. There was no way he could he get all of that done and still make it to the wedding. And if he did, what would happen with Mike Benedict, Cindy's brother? Last time they'd mixed it up, Mike had ended up in the hospital with a lacerated kidney, and Mike had pounded him so hard, Adam had wound up with a concussion. Adam wasn't afraid of Mike, but Mike outweighed him and fighting with one arm and a bad foot was not his idea of fun.

Seeing the look of disappointment on her face, he said, "I'll try. I'm not sure if I can dance but I'll try."

She got up to leave. "I'm glad to know one thing," she said.

"Which is?"

She leaned forward to whisper in his ear. "That I wasn't as forgettable as I'd thought."

And then she was gone.

CHAPTER 20

Adam rode his bike to Paul's Automotive, borrowed Paul's car hauler, and headed for Defiance's lone phone store. With any luck, he could get a replacement phone, pick up his truck in Mesa, go to the hospital in Globe on the way back, and arrive in time to put on a suit and attend the wedding. If Monica called, he might even be able to pick up his 'Vette with the car hauler and drive it to the wedding. He thought about Kate and smiled. Even though it had been twenty-five years since they'd last seen each other, it had been easy to talk to her.

Half an hour later, he had a new phone and a higher monthly bill. He drove back to his shop. From his gun safe, he removed a pistol, belt holster, and three clips of ammunition. He went to lock the safe then stopped and reached in to withdraw his old Savage double-barreled shotgun. What he really wanted was his Browning shotgun, but it was in the trunk of his car. The Savage was older than he was, but it still worked, and he kept it cleaned and oiled. It wasn't a good weapon for protection since it had only two shots, but it was very accurate for fast moving game like pheasants or quail, and that Nightmare thing moved fast.

He picked up a box of three-inch magnums, carried the two weapons downstairs, and snuck them out the back of the shop before Bailey or James saw him. They didn't know about the Nightmare, and if they saw him carrying weapons out to the car hauler, they would demand to know what was going on. He placed the shotgun on the floor behind the seat and put the pistol in the glove box.

Returning inside, he stopped in the middle of his small assembly line and made the decision he had been putting off for months. Even though he really didn't want to admit it, what he had told Kate had been true about his manufacturing. He couldn't build bikes fast enough to meet demand, and with his higher costs and lower margins, competing with the bigger guys was eating him alive. The only way he could survive was to hire more people, buy more parts and frames, and build more bikes to try and grow volume so he could get a better discount on his parts. All of that took money, time, and resources.

He went into his office and separated the contract proposals into two folders. The ones that wanted an exclusive license for the pivot he ignored. The others he signed electronically and emailed off. When he was done, he limped outside to the car hauler.

Tongue lolling from the heat, Mop followed him and, after a moment's hesitation, Adam let the dog jump up in the truck. The odds of the Nightmare somehow figuring out he had parked his truck at the Hawes trailhead were beyond astronomical, but he wanted the dog with him just in case and rolled down the windows so Mop could stick his nose out into the wind.

The roads were jammed with tourists. It wasn't easy getting through town in the big car hauler, but he finally made it and started down the mountains toward Globe. The car hauler had a reliable engine, good brakes, power steering, and everything the old Chevy didn't. He made better time than he'd expected.

He exited the highway in Mesa and took Power Road east. Almost immediately he noticed a much higher than normal police presence. Three Mesa cruisers passed him at high speed. They didn't have their flashers on, but they were going at least twice the posted speed limit. A highway patrol SUV exited the 202 Loop, cut him off at the intersection with Power Road, and accelerated, following the police cars.

He left the subdivisions behind, drove past the Tonto National Forest boundary, and headed onto the Bush Highway. Off in the distance, he saw a military helicopter fly over the Salt River.

Mop whined at the sky and backed away from the window.

"It's just a helicopter, Mop. Don't be paranoid." Boeing had an Apache plant in north Mesa. It was probably one of theirs. "Besides, I don't think you'd qualify as an enemy combatant unless they tried to take away your food."

Mop turned nervous circles on the seat.

Adam didn't know what the dog was trying to tell him, but he pulled out the pistol from the glove box and put it right next to his leg. The sun was bright and as hot as it always was in summer. He didn't expect trouble. The desert landscape was sparse. He could see anything coming from a long way off. Plus, he was in a modern vehicle. The truck wasn't a sports car, but it could easily outrun anything on foot, and there were no cliffs or hairpin turns ahead.

Emergency flashers blinked in the distance. He counted five police cruisers, an ambulance, and a tow truck. It looked like an accident of some kind. Good thing he wasn't going that far north. The traffic out to Saguaro Lake would be all backed up.

As he drove past the Hawes Trail System's gravel parking lot, he slowed and craned over, looking for his pickup. No surprise. It wasn't there. After a thief broke a window and stole his tools, he'd looked for a more secluded spot, under the shade trees near the Salt River. Nearby was a trailhead with a small connector trail that gave access to the north end of the Hawes system. If he had ridden Twisted Sister to Cat Sick, that would be where he would have left the vehicle.

He turned at a dirt pull-out and took the rutted track leading to the river. He spotted his pickup in the trees. It looked undisturbed.

He stopped behind it and felt abruptly foolish. There was no way that thing from last night could sneak up on him here. The desert trees —mesquite, acacia, and ironwood—grew fifty feet apart, and between them, in the rocky soil, grew ground-hugging plants a few inches tall: brittlebush, desert marigold, and goldenhead. Nothing the Nightmare could hide behind.

Just to be on the safe side, he belted on his pistol, put a shell in the chamber, and made sure the safety was on. He picked up his shotgun, loaded it, and put a couple of spare shells in his pocket. Mop got out and stood, sniffing the air.

"You see something, you let me know," he told the dog.

He had parked in this stand of trees dozens of times in the past without any problems, but even though he'd just seen the Maricopa County sheriff's cars whizzing past, he felt exposed and alone. The Hawes Trail System, especially the north end where the Forest Service hadn't marked the outlaw trails, was one of the best places to ride in Phoenix, and he went there a lot during the winter. His favorite trail, Cat Sick, was a nasty piece of single track that demanded blood from those who were foolhardy enough to try it. The trail had started out as a livestock trail. Fifty years of storms had washed away the dirt, leaving mostly rocks behind. Ledges, drop-off's, boulders, and cactus made the trail dangerous enough, but it had been cut into the side of a cliff, where a momentary lapse of attention could have fatal consequences.

Years ago he had come around a corner to find a bikini-clad woman sunning herself on a rock. Her appearance had been so unexpected that he'd taken his eyes off the trail and hit a ledge the wrong way. His front tire veered sideways toward the cliff. Gravity took over and he crashed into the bottom of the ravine. Standing on her rock and glaring down at him, the woman said, "That is why I will never date a mountain biker!"

It had been an eight-mile walk carrying his broken bike back to his truck. And now here he was again, hobbling back to the truck he had left parked beneath the sycamores.

A languid breeze, smelling of the Salt River, rustled the leaves. There were no bird calls, no droning insects. Even though it had rained the night before, the ground had dried. He cupped a hand against his truck's window. The interior was empty. He sighed. Nothing to worry about.

He lowered the car-hauler's ramp. The motor whined loudly in the unnatural stillness. He glanced uneasily about. Best get the truck on the hauler and book it on out of here.

He started his pickup and backed it to the end of the ramp. The sun hadn't dried the ground under his pickup, and the tires dug into the mud. When he had driven his truck all the way to the top of the ramp, he put it in park and set the emergency brake. Easing himself to the ground, he raised the ramp. Once he had it level, he chained the tow hooks to the truck bed and belted in the tires. Finished, he looked around for Mop.

"Mop! Time to go!"

No sign of the dog. Ten minutes before, the dog had been watching him back the truck up the ramp.

He whistled. A hot, listless breeze rustled the trees. The dog could be anywhere.

"Mop! I have a pretty girl to see!"

Was Mop playing hide and seek, or had something happened? A prickle of unease slid down his back. He picked up his shotgun.

One step at a time and trying not to call attention to himself, he headed for the river. The stillness was unsettling. The river attracted a lot of wildlife—quail, brown thrashers, lizards. It shouldn't be this quiet.

He heard the drone of buzzing flies. He stopped, listening, and then continued on past a big sycamore that had dropped its golden leaves. His footsteps were deafening.

Cottonwoods lined the riverbanks. At the water's edge, the willows grew thick, but at a break in the undergrowth, he saw a dead horse lying on its side. Its neck and stomach had been torn out—torn out!—and flies crawled inside its body cavity.

What had killed it? Keeping an eye on the bushes, he crouched to get a better look at the tracks crisscrossing the muddy bank. A coyote and a bobcat or mountain lion had come to the river to drink. Crows had left tracks. No human prints, though.

Mop, stiff-legged, sniffing the wind, stood in the shallows.

"There you are," he said, annoyed that he'd walked all this way for nothing. "C'mon, dog, let's go."

Mop looked at him but turned his eyes to the river.

Adam started back to the truck. Sunshine slanted down, and even though it was hot, he shivered. The highway was less than a half mile away, but with all the shrubs, he couldn't see it.

A branch snapped, the sound sharp and unexpected. Spinning toward the sound, he froze. He couldn't be sure, but he thought the sound came from a grove of green-barked palo verdes thirty yards away. He shaded his eyes. The trees had long, sharp spines, pinhead leaves, and narrow trunks, not anything a person—or thing—could hide behind.

Mop backed against his knee. "You see something?" Adam murmured.

The wind had died. Nothing moved, not even the cottonwoods' heart-shaped leaves.

If he could put the sycamore between him and whatever was out there, the dry leaves would alert him to movement. He glanced down at Mop and hoped the dog's hearing and sense of smell would give them an early warning.

Shifting his weight, he retraced his steps, replaying the events of the night before. The Nightmare hadn't employed any kind of stealth. It had attacked straight on and at full speed—like a charging bear. If it was nearby, its behavior had changed. It was staying hidden and using the undergrowth to its advantage.

"If you see anything, Mop, let me know."

Mop sniffed the still air. Adam risked a glance at the car hauler. No more than a hundred yards away, it felt much further than that. He took another step and then another, wishing he could run.

He reached the sycamore and passed a grove of mesquites with thorns the size of a T-rex's tooth. Sunshine dappled the ground, but the shadows cast by the mesquites were menacingly dark. Behind him, leaves crackled and he spun around.

Nothing there.

Backing out of the trees, he reached a clearing. The trees that shaded his truck were thirty yards away. He checked his shotgun. Three-inch magnum buckshot shells held ten .32 caliber slugs. At less than a hundred feet, that kind of firepower was a fearsome weapon. So why did he feel frightened? He had the advantage here. It was late morning, and he was better armed than most police. The undergrowth had thinned, and he could see a good distance in all directions.

He picked up his pace. He needed to go to the hospital to get his burns examined, drop off the car hauler, change clothes, and drive over to Cindy's wedding. That was a lot to get done, and he was wasting time jumping at every sound.

He reached the car hauler without further incident. Nothing hid under or behind it that he could see. He felt an abrupt surge of annoyance. He had the advantage here. Anything that came running at him, no matter how fast, wouldn't stand a chance.

"Mop, circle around the car hauler," he said. "If something's there, flush it out and I'll kill it."

Mop looked at him, hesitated, intelligent brown eyes meeting his, then walked slowly around the back of the vehicle, ears up, nose working. Adam waited, shotgun against his shoulder. Mop backed up so that Adam could keep him in sight and circled toward the front. Whoever had trained Mop had done an excellent job. The dog reached the engine, stopped, and sniffed the breeze. Adam watched him for a second then lowered the shotgun and stepped forward.

"Okay, keep watch while I climb up and check the pickup. Bark if you see anything."

Holding the shotgun in one hand, he grabbed hold of a tie-down and lifted himself onto the bed of the truck hauler. From his vantage point, he checked the trees and bushes. He couldn't see into the thicket of palo verdes, but he could see over the tops of the mesquites all the way to the river. His truck was fine. What had he thought, that the Nightmare would have opened the door and been sitting in the driver's seat taking a nap? He shook his head. Lack of sleep combined with everything else had him imagining danger when there was none. Nothing in its right mind would attack a grown man armed with a shotgun and pistol.

Jumping awkwardly down on his good foot, he opened the car hauler's passenger door. Mop hopped up on the seat. Normally Adam would have commented on the dog's muddy paws. This time he gave Mop a pass. The big diesel didn't accelerate quickly, but it had a ton of torque. In two minutes they'd be back on the main road, and whatever had made the noise would be firmly behind them. He shut Mop's door and hobbled around to the driver's side.

He started to slide behind the wheel but froze. For a second, he stared down at the muddy spot his Ford had sheltered from the sun. In the mud, he saw bare human footprints, footprints that hadn't been there ten minutes earlier.

A thought hit him, a question that made absolutely no sense but still scared him as he looked at the car hauler's door.

DEFIANCE TOWING

HONEST, RELIABLE SERVICE

REASONABLE RATES

Could the Nightmare read?

CHAPTER 21

Adam drove east past Apache Leap into the canyons leading to Globe, Arizona. Apache Leap was a sheer cliff overlooking the small mining town of Superior. Legend had it that the US Calvary had pursued a band of Apache Indians to the top of the cliff, and the Indians had jumped off the cliff rather than be captured.

When he reached Globe, he stopped at a convenience store for a gallon of water and then parked in the shade outside an urgent care that handled industrial workplace injuries. He liked Globe. The town was honeycombed with mines, interesting cast-off pieces of mining equipment littered the hills, and there were more great Mexican restaurants per capita than any town of similar size. It might not be the best place to get treated for a lightning strike, but he didn't have time to sit in a hospital emergency room for hours. He took a long drink of water, cut off the top third of the water jug, and put the improvised plastic dog bowl on the floor of the cab.

"I'll be back in a few minutes," he told Mop. "I'm going to roll down the windows, so the air can come through. Don't run off because if you get loose, someone might take you to animal control and get you snipped."

Mop yawned and stretched out on the seat. Adam hobbled inside and filled out insurance forms. In the examining room, he took off his shirt, changed into the hospital gown, and took off his Hi-Tops. Immobilizing his foot had been a good idea. It didn't hurt nearly as much as it had that morning.

The doctor came in, gave Adam a quick nod, and then thumbed through the nurse's notes. Just to be sure she hadn't left something out, Adam gave the doctor an abbreviated version of the events from the previous evening. It was almost embarrassing talking about this over and over. He was tired of hearing himself explain something even he didn't understand.

The doctor examined his shoulder and foot. When he was finished, his face turned grave.

"You're very lucky, Mr. Barnett. Another couple of inches to the right, and I doubt you would have survived. The burn on your shoulder went into your tissue but should be fine given time. It has already scabbed over. The wound in your foot, however, is infected and needs stitches to close correctly. There's inflammation around the wound which is normal for where you were and how long it took to get medical attention. But all of that is minor compared to the possible brain trauma you've experienced."

"Brain trauma?"

"Getting struck by lightning is not generally associated with memory loss unless you had a seizure. You don't have any signs of exterior trauma on your skull, so I don't think it hit your head, but you still could have hurt yourself when the lightning knocked you off your bike."

"Did it?" Adam asked.

"I presume so," the doctor said. "Were you wearing a helmet?"

"I always wear a helmet."

"Even with a helmet, falling can be very traumatic to the brain. There might be underlying neurological problems that need to be addressed. Have you had blurred vision or slurred speech?"

"No."

"Have you been dizzy? Any signs of vertigo?"

"No."

What about headaches? Does the light hurt your eyes?"

"No. But I feel all achy—like I'm coming down with something."

"That's probably from the injection you got in your arm."

"Injection?"

"In your right arm. On the bicep." The doctor pointed to the swollen spot that Adam had noticed earlier. "You have a low-grade fever. The area around the needle mark is swollen. Does it hurt?"

"Yes."

"You might have had an allergic reaction to the shot. If the reaction caused a seizure, that could also explain your memory loss. Do you know what you were injected with?"

"No. I can't remember anything from Thursday evening until I woke up in the mud early Saturday morning. I spoke with my family, and they said I went to bed Thursday night, woke up early Friday morning before dawn, and drove down to Phoenix to go biking. There's no urgent cares open that early unless I went to a hospital, but why would I have done that? In the summer, I always start riding before the sun comes up. Riding in the middle of the day is a bad idea."

"Which just confirms that you need to go to a neurological unit immediately and get examined by a specialist. I don't think you should be driving. You could have another seizure and cause an accident."

"My dog's outside. I can't leave him in my truck. The heat will kill him. Besides, I haven't had a problem since the lightning."

"That you know of."

"Are you sure it's not a scorpion sting or a wasp?"

"I'm sure." The doctor made a couple of notations on his clipboard.

"Let's get your foot taken care of. I'll write you a scrip for the infection and give you a referral to a neurological trauma unit in Scottsdale. You need to see a specialist immediately, especially if you start having headaches or light sensitivity. Soft tissue brain injuries are not something to ignore."

Adam scowled at the industrial tile. Everything he learned only led to more questions. How had he ended up thirty miles northeast of where he'd left his truck? When, where, and what had he been injected with?

The doctor numbed Adam's foot and stitched it up. When he was finished, he applied a bead of Neosporin, taped on gauze pads, and fitted Adam with a small boot. Carrying his Hi-Top, Adam hobbled outside into the heat. Mop saw him coming and stood up, wagging his tail.

"I guess nobody came by and offered you a free neutering session," Adam said.

He put his prescription and referral on the dash, and then sat on the running board and changed back into the Hi-Top. No way could he drive the hauler with a boot. With his good arm, he pulled himself up into the truck. He started the big diesel, rolled up the windows, and cranked the A/C. After he changed into his wedding clothes, he'd put out a bowl of food for Mop and hope he'd be okay without his usual walk.

Adam's cell phone rang.

"Adam?" Monica asked. "I left your car at the Licano's Mexican restaurant in Show Low. Do you know where that is?"

"Yes, I've eaten there."

"The keys are behind the left driver's side tire and the check's on the front seat."

"You don't need to pay me."

"I disagree. We can talk about that later but for right now, you need to be careful. You have a nice family. Your involvement with the animal could get you killed."

"You keep saying that Monica, but you haven't told me why." He grinned at Mop. "Except for him being a bit more flea-bitten and mangy than normal, the *animal* as you call him looks like any other stray digging in garbage cans to me."

Mop yawned.

"I don't have the time to discuss it now and certainly not on the phone," Monica said.

"Maybe you'll want to talk about the Nightmare then."

"Nightmare?"

"I saw something last night in the desert. It was big and dark and fast and followed me out of the mountains."

"What are you talking about?"

Adam gave her a generalized version of the previous night's events.

"I found its footprints this morning when I picked up my truck in Mesa. If you count this morning, it came after me three times. The first two were up in the mountains, and I couldn't do anything about it, but now I'm armed and a bit angry, to be honest. I hope it's not important to your medical research or whatever the hell you do, because if it comes after me again, I will kill it. Do you want to talk now?"

He heard a sharp, strangled inhalation. The connection dropped. Okay, so change of plan. Drop the truck at the shop. Drive up to Show Low and get the 'Vette, unload, take the hauler back to Paul's, feed Mop, skip a shower but get dressed, and blast out of there. All this was going to make him a lot later than he'd planned. He would be late for the wedding, Cindy would be pissed, but if he was lucky Kate would save him a dance.

CHAPTER 22

The Hill, as the locals called the stretch of state highway between Nostalgia Valley and Golden Gate Pass, dropped from the summit like a roller coaster and switched back and forth across the mountain so many times the road looked like a Christmas ribbon pulled across a scissor blade. Summer or winter, the hill overheated cars going up and burned out their brakes coming down. Those who drove it regularly swore the trick to reaching the bottom was to use both lanes through the curves, stay off the brakes, and cultivate a bi-directional line of communication with God. Adam had learned how to pray at an early age, but it wasn't until one winter night in his grandfather's broken-down truck, Goliath, that he learned to really mean it. There was something about the smell of brake fluid accompanied by the wail of tortured rubber that cleared the divine channels.

Standing by the Nostalgia overlook's guardrail, Adam followed the road to the bottom of the cliff where the Benedict wedding reception was in full swing. Cindy and her gal pals must have decorated Nostalgia Park's gazebo with Japanese lanterns. In the dusk the lanterns blinked like fireflies. He was late and hoped Cindy wouldn't be upset, and even more than that, he hoped Mike, her brother, had gotten bored or drunk and gone home.

Returning to his Corvette, he cinched his seat belt tight across his lap and rumbled past the yellow caution sign: STEEP HILL. No kidding, he thought. The road snaked back and forth down the cliff, and his stomach plunged with it. He squealed through the curves in second gear, the 'Vette's chrome pipes sputtering.

"Come on, old girl," he muttered under his breath. "Stay together."

The last time he and his best friend, Jeff Benedict, had gone down the Hill had been the night Goliath lost its brakes. It had been late December and the snow had been piled up on both sides of the road, so the road looked more like a bobsled run than a highway. Hoping God had hold of their souls, they made it around the first curve. Then Goliath had hit the snowbank on Adam's side with a crunch that loosened every tooth in his head. It did a couple of three-sixties before coming to a stop in the middle of the road. They'd both just sat there, too scared to breathe. Jeff argued that they couldn't very well leave the truck in the road—someone else might hit it—and they couldn't very well walk down. It was miles. Like typical teenagers thinking they were invincible, they'd kept going. By the time they'd reached the bottom, Jeff was dead, and Adam would have given anything just to have parked the truck's nose in the snowbank at the top.

But now, it was August, and the road wasn't icy. Adam reached the bottom without incident and drove to the town park. Nostalgia was a small farming community with one gas station, three feed stores, a strip mall with a sheriff's office at one end, two churches, and more horses than residents—a fact the population was quite proud of. To keep the 'Vette's new paint from getting dinged, he pulled into the gravel parking lot and stopped well away from the other vehicles. Removing the medical boot from his foot, he slipped on dress shoes and limped toward the lanterns.

Cindy, his brother's ex, waltzed with her new husband in the park's gazebo. Adam watched them from the shadows, wondering if he should just turn around and go home. But then Mike Benedict, in his hornback boots, strode crookedly across the grass. He was as tall as Adam but at least thirty pounds heavier and strong from a lifetime of physical labor. He welded pipe for Continental Gas, and the skin on his hands was split and cracked. He had lost the ligaments in his knees playing defensive tackle and walked bowlegged, his feet at right angles, like a chicken.

His brown eyes swam with the alcohol he'd already consumed. "I hoped you'd show up."

One by one, those who were close enough to overhear looked their way, but then Adam's mother, Rita Barnett, rushed over and grabbed his elbow.

"Adam! Where have you been? You missed the wedding!"

She pinned a corsage to his lapel and pulled him toward the gazebo, telling him about the ceremony and saying didn't Cindy look great? Anger moved in the depths of Mike's eyes, but Adam ignored it.

Relatives and friends said hello. His father, Thomas Barnett, gave him a quick greeting and then hurried away to carry food. Small town weddings were small town affairs where everyone helped. Cindy gave him a stiff smile, which meant she hadn't opened her Walmart gift cards yet. He grinned and winked. She glanced suspiciously at the gift table. Her parents pretended Adam wasn't there, but he didn't care. He nodded anyway and left them to eat their sour grapes.

He found himself alone at the buffet table nibbling on a celery stick.

"You made it."

He turned.

Kate Lansing smiled at him.

"I'm sorry for being late," he said. "I went down to the clinic in

Globe to get looked at. They wanted to send me to Scottsdale to this neurological unit for head injuries."

"For what? I didn't know you hit your head."

"I didn't, or at least I don't think so. The doc said I might have had a seizure after the lightning strike, and that's why my memory's like Swiss cheese."

"You didn't say anything about memory problems at lunch."

He gave her an uncertain look. "Lunch? We had lunch?"

She smacked his arm. "This isn't something to joke around about, Adam! You shouldn't even be here!"

"I told them I would get checked out tomorrow and that I had a date tonight with a beautiful woman." Her silky blue dress held his eye. "You look great by the way."

She exhaled and tried to look annoyed. "Thanks. You look handsome yourself. You're an idiot but a good-looking one."

She had pinned up her hair with a comb, and a sapphire sat in the hollow of her throat. But it was her eyes that caught him. If eyes were the wells of the soul, hers were a mile deep.

The band started playing the Cowboy Junkies' version of Elvis Presley's "Blue Moon."

"Would you like to dance?" he asked.

"Sure," she said.

He walked her to the gazebo and held out his arms. Her breasts were a polite distance from his chest. Adam noticed Bailey grinning at him from the grass outside the gazebo. She held up both hands vertically and then brought them together in a not-so-subtle hint. He mouthed at her to stop.

Adam pulled Kate closer, and she came willingly.

Rising on tiptoe like a ballerina, she allowed the full weight of her arm to fall on his shoulder. He winced.

"Did I hurt you?" Kate asked.

"Not much. No pain, no gain."

Kate laughed. He put his nose in her strawberry-scented hair. Her cheek rested against his neck.

"I have some news," he said. "Part of the reason why I was late. After talking to you this morning, I decided to license my bike suspension."

"That's huge! I hope you didn't do it because of anything I said."

"No, I should have done it a year ago."

"Are you okay with the decision? You don't seem that excited."

"It hasn't sunk in yet. It almost feels like I sold off a child. Wait a minute, do I have a kid? I can't remember."

She smacked his arm. "That is so not funny. What are you going to do with the money? Hire more people and build more bikes? I was serious this morning about the town trying to diversify away from tourism."

"Once I get the revenue from the licensing, I'll start expanding," he said, "but for the moment I'm going to compete with myself."

"Are you going to stay in your current location?"

"If I do, I want to renovate the building. We've wanted to buy it for years but James's divorce and me trying to keep my business afloat took all of my ready cash."

"It used to be such a beautiful hotel until they turned it into the boarding house. Is it really haunted like everyone says?"

"I think the ghosts moved out after the town fire seventy years ago."

"What are you going to do with all those rooms? What does it have, two dozen bedrooms?"

He shrugged. "I don't know for sure yet. I don't think anyone's ever successfully made it all the way to the last bedroom. It's not easy renovating something that has a skeleton in every closet, you know."

She laughed, eyes dancing. Then her face turned serious. "Can you tell me something, Adam? I've been thinking about what you told me on the phone this morning about how short life is. Most people don't get a second chance, and *this* is your second chance at cheating death. Have you thought about what you're going to do?"

His eyes lifted to the stretch of asphalt zigzagging down the mountain.

"I try not to think. It's easier than forgetting."

She put a cool hand on his cheek. "What happened with Jeff Benedict was an accident."

He made a face and suddenly didn't feel like dancing.

"It was the second worst mistake of my life."

She gave him a sharp look. "Let it go and move on."

He brushed his fingers along the side of her neck, then moved his lips close to hers.

"I am," he whispered and kissed her.

Knuckles struck his jaw. He heard Kate's cry. The room spun and he fell sideways. A hornback boot-heel scraped against the floor, and the boot's sharp toe drove into his backside. Panting, Mike stepped back and massaged his knee.

"Stop it, Mike," Kate snapped.

But Mike ignored her. His muddy eyes boiled.

Adam reached for the gazebo's railing and pulled himself up. In the dim lighting, faces spun and settled into place. The toe had landed on his wallet, and the blow to his jaw had made him bite his tongue.

More startled than hurt, he croaked. "That one was free, chicken. Next one will cost you."

Mike launched himself forward, but James caught him from behind and slammed him face down on the floor with a crash that shook the lanterns.

"This is the end of it, you hear me, Mike?" James said conversationally. "You have a problem with Adam, that's fine. But tonight's not the night for it. Your sister just got married. Your niece is watching. Don't do this."

Adam stumbled down the steps. Eyes furious, Cindy, in her white satin dress, stood trembling. Adam tasted blood but waited until he reached the trees before he spit it out. His father stopped beside him.

"You all right?"

Adam nodded. "Just give me a minute."

Tom exhaled. "You boys need to forget about what happened before one of you kills the other. Don't be starting anything else tonight, please. Bailey has made the Benedicts kin. Get over it."

Adam peered through the trees at the beautifully decorated gazebo. Mike stood alone at the railing staring their way. The malevolent smile on his face was easy to see.

"I wasn't doing anything."

"Neither of you ever needs a reason."

Kate hurried over, handed him a tissue, and slipped a hand under his elbow.

"Thanks," he said, wiping blood from his teeth.

"You're the mayor," Tom said, looking from Kate to Adam. "Call animal control and put him on a leash."

Thanks a lot, Dad, Adam thought.

"He's not in the doghouse as far as I'm concerned," Kate said. "He didn't come looking for trouble."

Watching his father head back to gazebo, Adam smiled wryly. Finally, they were alone. "The last twenty-four hours have been something. I should probably go before Mike dusts himself off and comes back for more. Would you like to have dinner with me sometime? I can't promise anything but hopefully nobody will pick a fight."

"I will if you'll let me take you to the hospital tomorrow. My dad kept telling my mom there was nothing wrong with him for months until she finally convinced him to go to the doctor. By then it was too late."

"Don't you have mayoral stuff to do?"

"This is more important. I'll hand it off to someone else and we'll go."

"That would be great. Thank you for the dance. It was wonderful seeing you. We can talk tomorrow on the drive to Scottsdale."

Limping away through the wet grass, he glanced back, waved, and stepped into the parking lot. The 'Vette started easily. Backing out, he headed for the Hill. He shouldn't have come to the reception, but remembering her smile, he was glad he had.

His head began to pound. The pain came next. He took his time up through the switchbacks, pulled into the overlook, and parked. He took off his jacket and tossed it on the passenger seat. Far below, Mike's jacked GMC pickup was following him up the mountain. He watched it and tried not to think about the snowy night from long ago and how it felt to know he was going to die. He hoped Mike had sobered up enough to listen. His dad was right. This had to stop.

Mike pulled into the overlook and parked behind the 'Vette, pinning the car against the railing. Sliding awkwardly out of the cab on his bad knees, he cranked some old Van Halen tunes on the truck's stereo. He had a swollen eye and a dirty scrape on one cheek, but his grin was eager.

"Until you stopped, I thought you were going to be smart and keep going," he announced conversationally as he pulled a dented aluminum bat from behind the seat. "I should have known you wouldn't disappoint."

Adam felt tired, bone tired. "I'm not here to fight but I do think we should talk."

Mike gripped the bat so hard the tendons on his hand corded under the skin. "Are you finally going to admit you killed him?"

"It was an accident, and it happened a long time ago. We need to move on."

"So, you want me to pat you on the head and tell you it wasn't your fault?" He laughed bitterly. "That's the problem with your family. Nothing is ever anyone's fault. Your grandfather was the same way until he did the world a favor and buried his ass in the lake."

Anger roared. Adam leapt forward. Mike swung the bat. It whistled past Adam's right elbow and smashed the 'Vette's taillight. Adam hit him as fast as he could, the wounds in his shoulder and foot forgotten. He aimed for Mike's face and drew blood and, after that, didn't care where his fists landed. Like lava finally reaching the moment of eruption, his anger spilled out in a moment a sudden, unreasoning fury.

Mike fell into the open door of his truck and then lunged forward. He threw his weight against Adam and drove him backward. Adam tried to break away, but Mike, in close, had the advantage. Adam planted his feet in the gravel, slowly stopped Mike's momentum, and finally pushed him off. Eyes widening, Mike backed toward the truck.

Adam cracked his knuckles and grinned. "You know what, forget about moving on. This is a whole lot more fun."

He kicked Mike as hard as he could on the inside of his right knee and heard the sharp crack of tearing tendons. Mike collapsed into the gravel. Adam grabbed Mike by the collar of his tux and dragged him toward the drop-off. Wheezing, Mike clutched the overlook's railing.

"While you were driving up here," Adam said, "I tried to remember the exact spot where the truck flipped and Jeff died but I couldn't. At first, I felt bad about it, but then I figured it wasn't *how* he died that mattered, but that he was my best friend, maybe even closer than my own brother. So you have two choices. You can stop this now, or we can both find out if chickens can fly."

Mike bellowed, tore himself loose, and lurched for his truck. He fell inside the GMC's open door and used the steering wheel to drag himself onto the seat. "Come on, Dude," Adam shouted. "Just give it a rest."

Mike slammed the door and the big V8 roared to life. Mike flung an arm across the seat and threw the truck in reverse. The tailgate crashed into the embankment. Revving the engine, he popped the clutch. With all eight cylinders pumping and the tires smoking, the truck leapt across the road like a funny car spitting fire at the Bonneville Speedway.

The headlights caught Adam and he froze. Mike had the truck's three hundred and forty horses wound all the way up, and it sounded like a hundred tons of Union Pacific coming his way. The headlights filled his field of vision. He told his feet to move, but all he could see were the lights and Mike crowing behind the windshield like the mad engineer of a runaway train.

Adam would never know if Mike swerved on purpose or if he just lost control. Later, he would remember the wind as the grille swept past his face and the truck's tail-lights soared into the summer sky. Not until two in the morning would he learn that the truck, with Van Halen screaming at full volume, had landed on the other side of the second switchback, nine hundred feet below.

CHAPTER 23

Standing in the living room and thinking of all she needed to get done today, Victoria looked at the basket of laundry, the dishes on the kitchen counter, and the pile of weapons and dirty clothes she'd dropped by the front door. That wasn't smart, but she'd been exhausted. Today, she'd carry her equipment down to the panic room and see if she could come up with a plan to either find Dark or figure out how his voice had gotten inside her head.

In the kitchen she poured water in her coffee maker. The problem with hearing Dark's voice was that she never felt safe. There was no escaping him. Valium helped blunt the sharp edges enough to survive, but what she needed was peace. Deep, restful sleep was beneficial in so many ways, according to Dr. Young, her psychiatrist. People who didn't sleep had problems achieving psychological and emotional equilibrium. They tended to be angry and depressed and had a higher predisposition toward violence. Victoria was not about to let Dark turn her into another victim. If he figured out who she was and came looking, she would put a bullet in his head and take a well-earned nap.

After folding the laundry, she picked up her weapons, dirty clothing, and the shopping bag of money. It took three trips to carry every-thing downstairs.

The panic room, on the back side of the house, wasn't really a room. Rather, it was a small cave in the canyon wall. Access to the cave was through a false panel in the wainscot. She unlatched the panel, ducked down, and lifted her gear into the cinderblock passage. Then she crawled on her hands and knees, pushing and pulling her duffel bag and guns until they fell out onto the stone floor. The cave had once been part of a volcanic lava tube. The lava had retreated, leaving the cave behind. It was narrow, with just enough room for two storage racks and a workbench, but even her father had been able to stand without hitting his head.

She put the weapons and clothing on the workbench. She wouldn't use the guns until she could remove the barrels and firing pins. For a second, she debated about keeping the money, but winter was coming and she needed propane and diesel to survive. She counted out enough to pay her bills. With the money in her pocket, she squirmed back through the passage and pushed the access panel into place. At least now she knew she wasn't crazy. Dark was a real person, not just a voice in her head. The only question was how to find him.

Upstairs making breakfast, she felt the silence press in on her. Normally she liked the isolation. During nice weather, she took her coffee outside where she could listen to the creek and the singing birds. But after yesterday, she needed something other than her thoughts to keep her company. Her boyfriend Doug had talked about getting together for the holiday weekend. She should call and finalize their plans.

Agent Doug Monroe, was the best thing that had happened to her since moving to Arizona. But like everything else in her life, their rela-tionship had started badly. He had been assigned to investigate her bombing and had come to interview her after she was allowed visitors.

There had been a mix-up about her identity, and he thought she had been blown up as part of a drug war between rival gangs. Once he realized she was the daughter of a local rancher, a respected former Marine who had been executed by the narcos, his investigation changed to finding those responsible.

Doug had kept in touch. After she'd been moved from the critical care unit at Biodosius to Mayo Clinic's burn unit, he started dropping by the hospital to keep her company. It was lonely with just the TV and nurses. He was pleasant and had a good sense of humor, and she found herself looking forward to his visits. When she had finally been released, he had driven her home. That's when she had known he was a person she could really care for. He had seen her at her worst, yet he had stuck around. Not many men would have done that. Being with him made her feel normal. After a good night's sleep wrapped in his arms, maybe she could figure out what to do about Dark.

She cleaned up breakfast and went over to her kitchen desk to retrieve her phone. Moving aside piles of bills, she knocked over a framed photo of her college roommate, Monica Belles. The two of them grinned as if they hadn't had a care in the world. Life had been a lark at college. Victoria had had a ton of girlfriends and a cute boyfriend who was always up for something fun. They went out on weekend road trips and stopped often to have sex in the back seat of his car. They had been passionate, dysfunctional, volatile, and infatuated—all the helpless, hapless hallmarks of young love. Her emotions had been so close to the surface, so ready to tumble out for good and ill, and it had been easy to let him inside her defenses. The closest thing she had to walls then had been a welcome mat.

She propped up the photograph. *That* Victoria didn't exist anymore. Tears welled in her eyes. She had lived and loved with a raw, uncaring ferocity. She could have accomplished anything, but it had all fallen apart in the reality of burying her father and trying to stay alive. At the time, and even now, she had never really stopped to think about who she had been before and how that girl had vanished. Spilt milk, she thought, dumping out her purse.

The phone and tiny battery that powered it had sunk to the bottom of her purse, beneath the post office box receipts, gas station tickets, and Kleenex. She thumbed off the back of phone, returned the battery to its slot—at least, for once, her phone was fully charged—and noticed that she had eight new voicemails.

The first message came from Monica. Her friend's voice was frantic, rambling. She needed help. She didn't say why. Just call as soon as she got the message. The next seven messages were the same. Monica needed help. Call as soon as she could.

What to do? They had been friends for years. They talked all the time. Calling her friend on a holiday weekend wouldn't arouse suspicion. It would be more suspicious if she didn't call.

Monica's phone rang five times and went to voicemail. Victoria left a message telling Monica that she was sorry to have missed her calls but with the storm the night before, the reception hadn't been good. Now the phone was showing three bars, so please call her back.

She started to set the phone down but jumped when it abruptly rang.

"Monica?" she answered. "Are you okay? What's going on?"

"Uh, sorry, this is Doug," he said. "Did you want me to be Monica?"

"Oh."

"Well, don't sound so happy to hear from me."

She heard the smile in his voice and groaned. "Sorry, my friend Monica left me messages on my phone." She tried to think of something mundane. "Car problems."

Doug didn't immediately respond, and when he did his voice changed. "I have some bad news. I can't go out tonight. I have to work. I'm sorry."

Victoria shifted mental gears. "Oh? What's going on? We've been planning tonight for weeks. I was going to get dressed up."

"I know, I know. I had lots of plans for tonight, too. You have no idea."

She stopped at the disappointment in his voice. What was he talking about? What plans? She tried to keep her emotions in check. She wasn't going to be a neurotic, needy girlfriend. If he really knew how close she had been to clocking out on Valium, he wouldn't just run in the opposite direction, he would strap himself to a rocket.

"I don't care about going out," she said. "Well, I do, but I understand about you having to work. Can I bring you something at your office so you're not eating out of the candy machine?"

The words hung in the silence before he sighed. "We never get a break, do we?"

He was right, but she wasn't ready to admit it. Better to go with the flow.

"Are you going to be in your office today?" she asked.

"No. I have to go to the Navajo County Sheriff's Office."

"Okay. How about Labor Day? I'll make some of my famous garlic chicken, plus cornbread, salad, and apple pie. We can eat in your truck and pretend we're in a fancy restaurant. Oh, waiter, there's a fly in my soup. I demand to talk to the manager!"

He barked out a laugh.

"I'm always amazed at how sunny you are," he said. "After everything that's happened, what with your folks and getting blown up. If it was me, I'd be in the nuthouse."

She almost choked but didn't.

"I'm still looking for Blackjack Joe, by the way," he added. "I'll find him, and he won't be killing anyone else after I do."

She gripped the telephone. Blackjack Joe wasn't going to be bothering anyone ever again. He and his crew of narco killers were pushing up wildflowers from a hole on the Black Knob. That debt had been repaid with interest.

"Thank you."

He didn't respond, and the silence stretched, which was unusual for them. Talking had never been a problem.

"Um, is there anything else you want to talk about?" she finally asked.

He sighed again and swallowed. "Yes. I wasn't going to say anything until later but with having to go into work and it never seeming to be the right time, well, I know I'm sounding like a food, but I just want to say that I, well, I..." he took a ragged breath.

"You're sounding like a food?"

"What did I say?"

"You said you were sounding like a food."

He groaned. "See what I mean? Now I'm sounding like a food and that doesn't make any sense at all."

Victoria smiled. "Are you wanting to be just a food or a food group? If it was me, I think I would want to be a food pyramid."

He laughed again. "Oh, man."

"What are you trying to say?"

He took another gulp of air. "I just wanted to, uh, well, I guess, I was going to tell you tonight but since we're not going out, well, I guess I should just, well, jeez, I really am a food..."

"Yes?"

He dragged air into his lungs. "I love you."

His unexpected words hit her so hard that she suddenly couldn't speak, couldn't even breathe. All the horrible emptiness gnawing at the tattered remnants of her cloudy soul abruptly vanished. Bright, warm rays of sunshine struck her. He loved her! The man was in love with crazy, senseless her!

"Hello? Are you there?"

"Yes. I...I..., I love you too, Food."

And then they were both laughing hysterically like they had never heard anything as funny. She had never been so happy.

"I was going to tell you tonight," he finally managed. "I really was. I had it all planned so I wouldn't sound like a…food. I wanted it to be special. I'm sorry."

She didn't care. She wanted to float across the room singing. He loved her. She wasn't alone in the world! Someone cared!

"But," he sighed and continued, "there've been two homicides and a kidnapping of a woman and her kids. Her husband's missing, and she thinks he's dead. That's why I have to cancel. But I'll call you tomorrow after I know my schedule. It's a long drive from your place to my office, but I'll take you up on your offer, that is, if you really don't mind. Seeing you here would be better than not seeing you at all. What a heck of a way to spend Labor Day though."

Her insides plummeted. His office was all the way down in Phoenix but if he was assigned to investigate her killings, he'd be up here all the time. Her hand shook.

"Hello?"

"I'm here," she said. Doug had been put in charge of finding her! He was smart, careful, methodical, and most of all, he didn't give up. He was a bulldog. Years could go by without anything new, and he would still be looking for her.

"Don't be upset," he said quickly. "I know we've been planning on tonight for a long time. I don't want to work."

"I'm not upset," she finally squeaked. She held the phone so tightly it hurt her hand. "Seeing you tomorrow will be great, and since it's a federal holiday, maybe the traffic won't be as bad." How could she sound so calm?

"You're amazing. You really are. I should have told you how I felt months ago."

They were almost done talking. Just hang on for a minute more and then she could fall apart.

"Well, don't make that mistake again, sir, or I'll have to arrest you."

Where had that come from? She inwardly groaned.

He laughed. "I won't. I promise."

She sagged against her desk. She had made it. All she had to do was hang up.

"Okay, the sooner you go to work, the faster you'll get done. I have some, er, food to prepare. Call me later if you can."

"You're never going to let me live that down, are you?"

"We have a wonderful memory. Neither of us will ever forget it."

"I love you. I always feel so great after I talk to you."

She wished she could say the same. "I love you, too." It came out as a whisper.

He hung up. She dropped her phone on the desk and covered her eyes. God, oh god, she thought. How did this happen? Between now and tomorrow, she had to come up with an excuse for why she couldn't make it. And then another excuse after that.

The one absolute rule she had was to never do anything that would give Agent Doug Monroe a reason to come after her. Killing the narcos didn't count. They were trespassing on her land and transporting illegal drugs, and they were armed to the teeth. When the FBI went after them, they went prepared for war. And it was war. Anyone who thought differently just didn't understand the situation of how dangerous drug trafficking had become since the US had closed the borders with Mexico. No jury would ever convict her of killing Black-jack Joe and his men, especially with them killing her father and her nearly dying in the explosion. The soulless bastards got exactly what they deserved.

But the men she had killed just this morning were a different matter. They hadn't been on her land. She had gone after them. Yes, she hadn't known what she was getting into and technically she had been acting in self-defense after they had tried to kill her, but she had still ended their lives. It didn't matter that she had saved Jan Thompson and her daughters. She had still taken the law into her own hands.

She pounded a fist against the cabin wall. Would things ever go her way? Every time she took a step forward, she didn't just take a step back, she took a leap. It wasn't fair to have gone through so much with nothing but more bad luck coming.

The house alarm suddenly wailed. She jumped in surprise and looked out the window. At the far end of the canyon, metal flashed in the sun and she heard the distant, unmistakable sound of a laboring automobile engine. She gaped at the approaching vehicle, disarmed the alarm, scooped up her .308 and binoculars, and bolted out the door. Outside of Doug and a couple of her remaining friends, nobody knew about the canyon. A visitor couldn't be good.

She hurried up the rock steps she had built into the side of the canyon wall and reached a vantage point at the top of the ridge. After crawling into her makeshift bunker, she focused her binoculars through the narrow gun slot.

A beige Mercedes sedan labored down the canyon. Her first thought was that the driver had somehow gotten lost. Mercedes sedans were expensive and low to the ground, and the road was terrible. But maybe it was some kind of moronic narco plot.

She brought up the .308 and aimed at the windshield. If the driver was a narco, it would be the last mistake the idiot ever made. She put the site on the driver's head, blinked, and then snatched up the binoculars. A minute later Monica Belles pulled up in front of the cabin. Dripping oil from a torn oil pan, the Mercedes wheezed to a stop.

Victoria hurried down to greet her guest and, holding her rifle, stepped from the trees. "You didn't do your car any favors by driving it out here."

"It was new, too!" Monica, laughing, opened the door, stepped out, and made a pistol with her hand, firing at Victoria. "Long time, no see, girlfriend, although, I must say, the hospitality leaves a lot to be desired." She covered her eyes and looked up at the sky. "Any drones in the vicinity?"

"Not today. Why? Did you rob a bank?"

"In a manner of speaking," Monica said.

"In that case, I just happen to have some camouflage netting." Victoria pointed. "Move your car under that big juniper. The car should be okay for now, but I'll come out later and cover it."

CHAPTER 24

Back at his parents' ranch, Adam collapsed into his childhood bed. Instead of falling asleep, he tossed and turned. The more he tried to understand what had led up to Mike's death, the more keyed up and jittery he became. Then he heard the bellowing of their prize Black Angus bull, Satan. The bellows, like the deep, multinote horn of a distant railroad, echoed off Nostalgia's south ridge—loud enough to wake the dead. The fence must be down. Better go fix it before the bull woke the whole valley.

He found jeans and work boots in the closet. Grabbing a pistol from the gun safe in the den and his father's keys from a hook in the kitchen, he went out to the barn and loaded a roll of barbed wire. He drove his dad's pickup down to the lake. In the light of his headlights, he saw Satan, their big Angus bull, pacing back and forth behind a break in the barbed wire.

Repairing the barbed wire normally would have taken less than an hour, but the lake held the mangled remains of Goliath, his grandfather's truck, the truck he and Jeff had tried to drive down the snowy grade—a teenage escapade that had cost Jeff his life and now taken the life of his brother. Gosh, how could he have let this happen? He should have stopped Mike, put him in a hammerlock and sat on him until he sobered up. He had wanted to talk to him, needed to talk to him, because Mike was the one person who really understood, gut level, that the pain of Jeff's death never went away. And now, he had Mike to thank for his life. If Mike hadn't swerved at the last moment, Adam would have been tossed like a rag doll over the cliff.

Adam picked up a rock and skipped it across the water, and then a second rock. The three-ton pickup lay just beyond the lake's shallows. If he angled the rock, it could hit the target with one skip. He watched a rock sink and clank against the rusted metal. Three lives cut short. All because of a stupid truck.

Dawn turned to daylight, and he still hadn't accomplished what he'd come here for. Better get to it. Winching a strand of wire tight against the fencepost, he held it in place with one hand and twisted a metal clip around the wire and the post with the other. He gave the metal clip another twist, hammered in the fence staple, then slipped the hammer into a belt loop next to his pistol. If one of Mike's hotheaded cousins took a shot at him, the pistol wouldn't help. If only Mop were here.

He was about to cut off the extra wire when Satan, his black nose snorting, wheeled his twelve hundred pounds of muscle into the wind and stomped stiff-legged through the grass. Families of Canadian geese whistled plaintively and fled the marshy hillocks at the lake's edge for the deep water in the middle, the adults in front and the goslings frantically following. The goslings were too young to fly, but their wings had developed enough so that their feet barely touched the ground as they ran. It took no more than a second or two to reach the sheltering water, but it was an eternity too late for four of the slowest. A brown blur rocketed out of the salt grass. The first gosling tumbled end-over-end and landed in a heap of feathers. Three more followed in rapid succession until the coyote reached the water and skidded to a stop.

But Mike hadn't stopped. And why not? Was Adam such a bad person that even his death couldn't steady the scales of justice? Was it his destiny to live on and on, dragging this anvil of remorse?

———

Last night after the accident, Adam had driven straight to the Gila County Sheriff's substation in Nostalgia, an office at one end of a strip mall. After listening to Adam's explanation, the sheriff, a fiftyish man with a Colonel Sanders goatee, held up a hand for Adam to stop. "Just where did this happen?"

"The overlook at the top of the grade." When the truck catapulted into space, the moon had been a sliver in the sky. "I looked over, but I couldn't see where it landed."

"Let's have a description of the vehicle."

Adam described the brown GMC pickup. "Mike's parents and sister, Cindy, they have to be told."

"Why didn't you call from the grade?"

"No cell phone service. I came straight here in case there was any chance he'd survived."

"Can you give me the name one more time?"

"Mike Benedict." Because he wanted to be truthful, he added, "His sister Cindy's my brother's ex-wife, and I would have called her except I wasn't sure how she'd take it."

Actually, he was sure.

"Were there any witnesses?"

"No. It was dark. No one was on the road."

"I don't mean that. I mean earlier when the, uh, altercation began."

Who had been in the gazebo? Not many. "Talk to my brother, James," Adam said, wanting to keep Kate out of it. "He can tell you what happened."

"All right," the Sheriff said, writing down phone numbers. "I'll send a deputy to find the truck. When he checks back in, I'll route him over to the Benedicts'. Please follow me."

Lumpy as an Idaho potato, the sheriff had a heavy-footed walk that reminded Adam of police in courtroom dramas. Out to get their man. Through the half-open door of the interview room, Mike listened to the sheriff tell a dispatcher to get on the radio to their deputy and then call the main office in Globe.

A few minutes later, the sheriff returned with a breathalyzer. Adam blew into it.

The sheriff looked at the readout and frowned. "You passed."

"I wasn't at the reception long enough to get a drink." All he'd wanted was to hold Kate in his arms. "I came, got knocked off my feet, and left. When I got to the pullout, I had to stop because my head was throbbing so bad I wasn't sure I should be driving."

"Is that so," the sheriff said, looking over the tops of his glasses. He put his notebook on the table and pulled out a chair.

"I hate to trouble you, by any chance do you have something to drink?" Adam asked. "Water? Diet Coke?" He didn't want to bother the man, but the long day, the fever, the fact that he'd had some sort of adrenaline rush and now it was going away, made him extremely thirsty.

"Really?" the sheriff said.

"Yes, really," Adam said. "I was struck by lightning two nights ago, and I don't feel all that great." He held out a hand. It was shaking.

The sheriff put his two big mitts on the back of his chair. "How in blazes did you get struck by lightning?"

Adam told him, unbuttoned his shoulder, and showed him the burn. "I can show you my foot if you like." He began to untie his dress shoe.

The sheriff shook his head. "Either you're the dangdest liar I ever heard, or you're telling the truth. I'll see what we got." He returned with Styrofoam cups reeking of stale coffee. Not wanting to seem ungrateful, Adam took a sip.

The sheriff blew on his own coffee but left it untouched. "Now, let's go over your *story* again."

Story? Adam thought. It wasn't a story. But, apparently, the sheriff thought it was.

Why had Mike hit Adam at the wedding? Adam explained about Jeff. Why had Adam stopped at the overlook? The headache and, Adam added, "When I saw him coming up the grade, I hoped we could talk."

"Talk," the sheriff said flatly.

"Yes, talk," Adam said. "But he was blind drunk."

"And why did he decide to run over you with his truck?"

"It was an impulse, not a decision," Adam said, "but if you want to know what drove him to it, it was because I insulted him." He repeated the thing he'd said to Mike about chickens flying. "I didn't go up there with the idea of us two having a fight. What I wanted," Adam said, "was for him to calm down so we could get this settled, once and for all. I didn't want my niece to get caught up in this mess."

The Sheriff asked the questions again. No, Mike's animosity had nothing to do with Cindy. No, James hadn't abused his ex-wife. Neglected her, maybe. This all had to do with Jeff—and with a dare between their grandfathers—but he though better of mentioning the second part. It would sound too much like the Hatfields and McCoys.

The sheriff clicked his pen. "Two people went off the grade, your so-called best friend and now his brother."

"He was blind drunk," Adam repeated. "Do a blood test."

"Don't worry. We will."

An hour became two and then three. The substation didn't have holding cells. The sheriff came and went, going out to talk to the deputy over the radio. The deputy found the truck, and the paramedics recovered the body. They were transporting Mike to Globe. Finally, the deputy was on his way over to the Benedicts'. He was going to have to wake them up. "Can't imagine how they're going to take it," the sheriff said in passing. "Two sons, and for what?"

"I know," Adam said. "For what?"

The acidic coffee had burned a hole in his stomach. Finally, the sheriff let him go.

———

Adam cut off the excess wire, rolled up the remainder on the spool, and started toward the well to wash his hands. Mop ran up to him. Adam turned and saw Kate walking through the fields. She had parked down the road.

He knelt and buried his face in the dog's fur. "Hey, buddy." Tears filled his eyes, and his shoulders shook. The dog pulled away and lapped his face. "Okay, okay," he said, wiping off the drool with a bandanna. Things had been bad between him and the Benedicts for years, but he hadn't wanted Mike dead.

Kate stopped in front of him. She wore gray slacks, a blue floral scarf, and dress flats that sank into the spongy ground.

Embarrassed at his show of emotion, Adam straightened up and gave Mop's head a casual scratch. "Did the pretty girl snap her fingers, and you jumped into her car?"

"What are you doing down here?" She said. "You should be in bed."

"I couldn't sleep."

She frowned. "I can understand that. But it doesn't explain why you're working. You should be in the hospital."

"You heard what happened?"

"James called me."

"How'd you know where to find me?"

"Your dad said most likely you'd be down at the lake."

"I kinda hoped he'd still be asleep."

"You know parents. They lay awake until you get home."

"It was two-thirty by the time the sheriff let me go."

"At least he didn't lock you up."

Adam laughed. "Yeah. Small blessings."

If they were going to have a conversation, he needed to wash the dog smell off. He loosened the well's plug bolt from the pipe housing with a wrench. The bolt popped free, and a clear stream of water gushed around his shoes. He washed his hands and face and then replaced the bolt and tightened it down.

"I dug this well when I was sixteen, two years after you moved away," he said, wiping his wet hands on his jeans. "I had just gotten my license, and I drove down to Globe, rented a drill pump, and purchased two hundred feet of pipe. That was a long time ago."

"I bet you wish things would have turned out differently with Jeff," she said.

"A lot of it I would sooner just forget."

Mop walked over to the fence and sniffed at the cattle browsing the salt grass. Satan dug one big hoof into the dirt and tossed his horns. Mop backed away.

"How are you feeling?" she asked.

"I couldn't sleep. It's hard to believe Mike and Jeff both died on the Hill."

"What happened with Jeff was an accident."

"What about last night? If I'd have kept going or left the moment I saw him coming up the hill, Mike would still be alive."

"What Mike did was his choice, not yours."

"That's not what most people will say. It'll be all over social media. In Defiance, I'm a little bit shielded, but my parents are from here. People will take sides."

He flung another rock into the lake. It struck the water and sank. A complete miss. A sudden wind sprang up, moving the trees back and forth. They creaked and groaned, playing another refrain in time's symphony.

"What I don't understand is how your relationship with the Benedicts got so toxic," Kate said.

Adam sighed. "It started as a dare twenty years ago."

"A dare?"

"My grandfather drowned on New Year's Eve driving his truck across the lake."

"Why was he doing that? This isn't Minnesota."

"My grandfather and Wendell Benedict, Jeff's grandfather, had a drunken five-dollar bet."

"Five bucks is nothing."

"Tell me about it," Adam said. "Anyway, it was cold that winter. The lake looked solid. Kids had been out ice skating. For some reason, Grandpa thought he could make it if he went fast enough. But the ice broke, Grandpa sank, and by the time anybody got close enough to help, he was gone. My grandmother wanted to leave the truck at the bottom of the lake, but Jeff and I winched it out that spring. We flushed the engine and got it running again, but what we didn't know was that Jeff's seatbelt housing had rusted out. Come winter, we took it down the Hill. It spun out once, but we survived. When the truck flipped at the bottom of the hill, that misjudgment killed my best friend."

"All of this happened because your grandfather made a stupid bet with Jeff's grandfather?"

"When you put it that way it really does sound crazy."

She threw up her arms. "Adam, you've spent the last fifteen years fighting over an accident! An accident that was the result of another accident that you didn't have anything to do with! We've both lost friends and family we care about. Leave the past in the past and move forward. You've almost been killed twice in the same day, but you're still alive. You've been given a gift! Most people don't get a second chance, and you've been given two." Her fingers dug into his arm. "Do you know what I would do for another opportunity to see my father again? You have a wonderful family, friends, a great dog you found running around in the mountains, a prosperous business, and maybe love if you're willing to risk it. Life isn't about what's behind you. It's about what you have in front of you if you look!"

He dropped his gaze from the lightning in her eyes and thought about the squawking geese. One second they were snapping down insects. The next they were warming a coyote's belly. Fate had a way of turning a card that was as sudden as it was lethal.

"I tried to tell Mike that last night," he said. "I think it only made him angrier. When your life is defined by a catastrophic event, it's hard to move on. I hate to say it, but I think Mike was even more damaged by Jeff's death than I was."

She sighed and exhaled the anger. "I know how it is. After my divorce, it took years before I felt like myself again."

He picked up the heavy spool of barbed wire, lugged it to his father's pickup, and dropped it onto the bed with a crash that made the springs jump.

"You must be feeling better," Kate said.

He shrugged, gathering up his tools. "Not really, but it feels good to see you. Let me drive you to your car. That way you won't have to walk back through the mud. Mop, your paws are all dirty. You ride in back."

Mop jumped up into the truck bed. Adam opened the truck's passenger door, dusted off Kate's seat, and helped her inside. The old truck smelled of hay, but she didn't seem to mind.

"Can you tell me something?" she asked as he drove. "I've thought about what you said last night, that continuing down the Hill was the second worst mistake of your life. What was the first? Was it going down the Hill, or was it blaming yourself?"

CHAPTER 25

In any accident involving a head injury, whether a stroke or a highway collision, the speed of the response saves lives. The Scottsdale Neurological Institute was one of eight hospitals in Arizona to earn a level-one trauma designation by the American College of Surgeons. It was in Phoenix's north-central corridor in one of the large, stucco-and-steel medical plazas that lined the freeway.

The Institute's staff whisked Adam into one of the trauma rooms where he was weighed, measured, and asked for samples of his bodily fluids. After getting a low score for rotational and angular acceleration trauma, he was sent to get a head MRI and a CT Scan.

Two hours later, his neurologist, Dr. Paquin, a tall man who'd spent a lifetime ducking under doorways, came into Adam's room and nodded at Kate who'd seated herself by the window. The doctor had thinning brown hair and wore a lab coat and wire-rimmed glasses.

He grabbed a stool and wheeled it over to the examining table. "I have good and bad news," he said.

Adam swallowed. "Okay."

"The good news, Mr. Barnett, is we have no idea why your

memory has been affected by the lightning. At first, I thought you had damage to your right frontal lobe, a portion of the brain that helps control nonverbal abilities, including memory. But the scans are all negative. There are no signs of blunt trauma from hitting your head, and, except for your elevated temperature, your vital signs are normal. You don't have any indicators of a concussion or swelling of the brain."

"But I do have a brain, right?" He glanced sideways at Kate. "Because someone in this room keeps claiming I don't."

Kate groaned.

"What's the bad news?" he asked.

"You might have trauma that didn't show up on the scans. Seventy percent of all head injuries remain undiagnosed. You've been riding a mountain bike in extreme situations for most of your adult life. How many times have you had a concussion?"

"Just once in July after I got in a, uh, dispute at a family reunion. I had a headache for a couple of days."

"That's an indicator of trauma. I looked you up on the internet, Mr. Barnett. YouTube has hundreds of videos of you doing things you shouldn't on a bike. Frankly, I'm surprised you haven't been here before."

Kate's mouth dropped open. The stricken look on her face made Adam lower his gaze.

Paquin tapped the chart with a pen. "There's one more thing that concerns me. Your white blood cell count is much higher than normal. Have you been diagnosed with cancer or lymphoma or a blood infection?"

"No."

"Any dizziness or lightheadedness or vision change?"

"No."

"Any numbness or weakness in your extremities?"

"My foot hurts but not as bad as it did yesterday. I carried a roll of barbed wire this morning to fix a fence for my dad. It didn't feel heavier than usual."

Paquin stopped tapping his pen. "You carried a roll of barbed wire? How heavy was it?"

"I dunno. Maybe a hundred pounds."

"You shouldn't even be able to walk. Your record shows you have third degree burns on your foot. Most people in your condition would be in the hospital."

"I don't have time to lie in bed."

Paquin pinched the bridge of his nose.

"It's good to see that I'm not the only one who gets frustrated," Kate said.

"Can you walk for me?" Paquin asked.

Adam, clutching his hospital gown so that Kate wouldn't see anything she didn't want to, got out of bed and limped back and forth.

"What is your pain level on a scale from one to five with five being unbearable?" Paquin asked.

"Maybe a two depending on what I'm doing. It was worse yesterday."

"What kind of painkillers are you taking?"

"The doctor in Globe gave me a couple of prescriptions but I haven't had time to fill them."

Paquin put his chart on a bedside table. "Lie down and let me look at your foot."

Adam settled back against the pillow.

Paquin lifted Adam's foot, unwound the tape, and examined the wound. "Are you sure you aren't feeling any numbness?"

"My foot's not numb."

"This happened yesterday morning?"

"I believe so. I don't know exactly when because the lightning melted my phone. I woke up with electricity running up and down my arms."

"I'm going to touch the bottom of your foot with varying degrees of pressure with my pen." The doctor flipped the pen upside down. "Tell me when you feel it."

Adam felt the clicker probe the ball of his foot. Then the doctor moved to the heel, and finally, to the area where the doctor had removed the gauze.

At each touch of the pen, Adam said, yes.

Frowning, Paquin sat back. "I'll be honest with you, Mr. Barnett. Either you are the most remarkable healer I have ever heard of, or your memory problems are much more serious than you know. Wounds heal in stages. The larger and deeper the wound, like what you have, the longer it takes to heal. When you get injured, the wound bleeds until the blood clots. The clots eventually dry and form a scab that protects the underlying tissue. White blood cells fight infection and repair the wound. For a wound this size, even one that has been stitched up, recovery would generally take a few weeks, depending on how bad the tissue was burned. How was the pain when I touched your injury?"

"Maybe a one or two," Adam said. "About the same as my heel."

"That's what I thought," the doctor said. "Judging from the inflammation around the wound site, I would estimate you got hit at least two weeks ago."

"That's not possible."

Paquin shrugged. "I had a patient Friday who was in a motorcycle accident, and he had a burn on his arm from landing on the bike's exhaust pipe. His wound was much smaller than yours and not as deep, and there were no signs of healing at all."

"You're saying I got hit by lightning weeks ago? I've been working every day for the past month building bikes. I would have known if I'd gotten hit by lightning."

"Your ability to remember dates and times and events may be

affected by your concussion in July or by other problems the tests haven't identified."

Adam shook his head. "My brother said I left the house to go riding Friday morning. He didn't say anything about me getting hit by lightning before then."

"If that's the case, Mr. Barnett, you heal faster than anyone I've ever heard of. Scar tissue has begun to form. You don't need the stitches any longer."

Adam felt his mouth fall open. "That can't be right. I just got them yesterday!" Adam was afraid the guy was going to remove them. And, what if this doctor was just some quack?

"Don't worry. We'll leave them be. They'll dissolve on their own. Let's just protect the wound site until you're fully healed." Dr. Paquin covered the wound with a fresh gauze pad and wrapped tape around Adam's foot.

"Gosh, thank you so much." Kate took out a tissue and dabbed the corners of her eyes. "I was extremely worried that he was seriously injured."

The doctor looked at her and then back at Adam. He returned the pen to his lab coat, placed Adam's file by his feet, and scooted the stool back toward the curtain. "Let me bottom-line this for you, Mr. Barnett," Paquin said. "Serious questions remain about your memory. You also need to see a blood specialist immediately. Thrombocytosis is a rare disease where your bone marrow produces excess platelets. You might have that or something more serious."

"Like what?" Kate said.

The doctor did not look at her. He dropped his chin, crossed his legs, and folded his arms. "Like leukemia."

Adam heard Kate whisper "leukemia."

"That's ridiculous," Adam said. "I just had a physical a month ago! There wasn't a problem with my platelets then!"

"They're elevated now. That's why you have a temperature."

"What about the shot in my arm? The doctor yesterday thought I had a fever from a flu shot or something."

"Without knowing what you were injected with, it would be impossible to guess. See a blood specialist and forward me the results. There might be a link to your memory loss."

Adam's jaw clenched. He'd wasted a day of his life. "Can I go home?"

"Yes, but I want to see you next week to run more tests. If you experience more memory loss or headaches or blurry vision, call me immediately, and I'll get you hospitalized."

"So you're saying there's no way of knowing what happened to me on Friday? My memory loss could be from the lightning causing a seizure or from falling off my bike or from when I had a concussion. There's no way of knowing for sure."

Paquin sighed and shifted on his stool.

"Given time, there's always the chance your memory might come back. Most of the time, it doesn't. After traumatic events, most people experience some kind of memory loss. That's how the brain protects itself from severe psychological harm.

"I had a patient who was involved in a car accident on a Monday morning while driving to work. He fell asleep and went off the road and hit a tree. His head hit the car's A-pillar, and that fractured his skull. He woke up in the hospital on Tuesday and had no idea where he was. The last he could remember was working in his yard on Saturday.

"Not knowing what happened drove him crazy. He went to doctors, psychiatrists, therapists, and even hypnotists. It bothered him so much that he lost his job and his marriage. By the time he saw me, he was considering suicide. I know it sounds crazy, but he just couldn't get past losing three days.

"I went through his chart and explained how the brain protects itself. I could tell that he had heard it before so I finally leveled with him. Did he really want to know what had happened? Did he really want to feel his skull fracture as it hit the A-pillar?"

Paquin stopped. Mouth open, Kate stared at him. Paquin picked up Adam's chart and stood.

"The answer is no. He did not want to know. The same thing applies here. I don't know why you lost your memory. It could be from the concussion you suffered in July. It could be from an allergic reaction to whatever you were injected with. It could be from falling off the bike.

"Most likely you suffered a seizure when the lightning struck you. Your white blood cell count is worrisome. We'll run tests and try our best to find out what is going on. But don't let this define your life. You have family, a beautiful woman who obviously cares for you, and a prosperous business. From what I read online, people rave about your bikes. That's more important than anything that happened. We'll do the best we can, but you certainly don't want to experience it again."

Adam sighed. "Thank you, doctor."

"Any time." Paquin nodded and left.

"I'll wait outside," Kate said.

Mind churning, Adam took off the hospital gown. Had the past couple of days been a figment of his lightning-blasted imagination? A dream? A dirt devil stirred up by the gusting wind? The Nightmare could have been anything. But what about Mop? The dog had obviously known something was after them when he dragged Adam down the mountain. And what about the footprints by the river?

CHAPTER 26

onica wore wrinkled sweatpants that were too long for her, a baggy sweatshirt that didn't match, and men's high-top basketball sneakers. Mascara ran down her cheeks, and her hair looked as if she had been driving with her head out the window.

"You have no idea how glad I am to see you." Smiling, she went around to the trunk, opened it, and took out a large red-and-white cooler covered in medical biohazard stickers. "I've been trying to get hold of you all morning! Someone wants me dead."

Welcome to the club, Victoria thought.

They left the Mercedes parked under the tree and went inside. Victoria listened in growing amazement to Monica's story about getting kidnapped, thrown off a bridge, and James Barnett saving her life. Monica's voice quivered as she spoke, and she kept glancing out the windows as if she wanted Victoria to lower the blinds.

"Wow, Monica, you really go to extremes to meet a guy," Victoria said. "Did you at least get James's phone number?"

Monica laughed. "Yeah, I sort of accidentally stole his phone, along with his brother's Corvette."

"What?"

"It's a long story." Monica put the cooler on the counter and unlocked it. Inside, packed in dry ice, was a two-foot-long metal cylinder. Monica put it in Victoria's freezer.

Victoria nodded at the cylinder. "Is that why they tried to kill you?"

Monica bent down, fiddling with the temperature control. "Possibly. I'm not sure."

"Make yourself at home," Victoria said.

"That's what I intend to do." Monica, grimly serious, lowered the blinds in the living room. "In case anyone's out there with binoculars, I don't want them seeing me move around. Mind if I take a shower and borrow some clothes?"

"Help yourself." This was like being back in graduate school, raiding each other's closets for the right outfit. Except, they weren't going out on dates, were they?

Monica went into the bedroom and shut the door. Outside, Victoria covered the Mercedes with camouflage netting and climbed the rock steps to her lookout. She swept the treetops with the binoculars. Dark clouds billowed up from the Gulf of Mexico, the way they always did during monsoon season, but for the moment she did not see any vehicles, airplanes, or drones.

She returned to the cabin, thawed two chicken breasts in the microwave, and put them in a baking pan. She took out a jar of peeled garlic cloves and arranged them around the chicken. Monica, emerging from the bedroom, wore a pair of Victoria's jeans, a cotton blouse, and cotton socks. Hugging a manila folder to her chest, she sat at the kitchen table.

"I'm not sure how to tell you this so I'm just going to say it." Monica's voice caught, and she swallowed. "I have the genetic marker for Huntington's disease."

Victoria frowned. "What's that?"

"It's a fatal genetic disorder of the brain where the brain cells slowly start to die." Monica sat, put the folder on the table, and weighted it down with her hands. "There is no cure. It killed my grandmother and would have killed my mother if she'd lived long enough. Until the last twenty years or so, there was no way of knowing who'd get it. I guess you could say the women of my family live just long enough to have kids and pass on the marker. And then they die."

"That's terrible! I had no idea." Victoria wiped her hands on a kitchen towel and came around to give Monica a hug. What a day. Dark had gotten into her head, and she had killed his men. Doug was investigating her for their murders. But none of that was as bad as Monica having an incurable disease. "Is there a treatment?" she asked as they broke apart.

"No. None." Leaving the folder on the table, Monica moved to a stool at the counter and reached for a box of Kleenex. She wiped away her tears. "Do you remember my Master's thesis, that thing on genetic memory?"

"I proofread it, but I can't say as I 'remember' it."

"Well, do your remember Riya Kumar, that doctor we met at the job fair in the union?"

"Can't say as I do." Graduate school was ancient history. She barely remembered the details of her own Master's in European history. Besides her thesis committee, her dad had been the only one who'd read it.

"It turns out Riya Kumar knew my advisor, and when I finished my PhD, she approached me about a job with her boss, Dr. Bill McDermott. He's sort of a Renaissance man. He's a classically trained pianist and performed at Lincoln Center, and he has a PhD in Biomedical Science from Cal Berkeley. He almost single-handedly invented the field of Cortical Neuronal Clustering. He's published over two hundred highly cited research papers, including three in *Nature*."

"Good for him." Victoria took flour and a box of cornmeal from the pantry. Trying to remember a recipe while listening to whatever Monica was going on about was straining her brain. Was it one cup cornbread and one cup flour, or twice as much cornbread as flour?

"So, I bet you want to know what Cortical Neuronal Clustering is," Monica said, leaning on the counter and smiling brightly.

Victoria felt like banging her head on the wall. This was so not a conversation she felt like having today—or maybe any day. If she just said, uh huh, maybe she could make it go away.

"All right. Go on," she said.

"Cortical Neuronal Clustering is a technique for increasing the cognitive plasticity of the cortical module in the cerebral cortex."

Tuning out, Victoria put the chicken in the oven. Then she measured the dry ingredients and took out eggs, oil, and buttermilk. Whipping them with a spoon, she felt crushed by the cascade of unfamiliar words. But this was her fault. She should have been more direct. "Listen, Monica, I have no idea what you're telling me, and I just don't have the bandwidth to deal with it. I wish you'd shut up and let me get lunch on the table."

Monica shook a chastising finger. "No, no, no. You have to understand. This affects not just me. It affects you. Cortical modules are neuronal cells in the brain that make different patterns in the cerebral cortex. They allow us to learn and solve problems. No two people have the same connections. That's why one person can learn and understand something quickly while it takes another much longer. McDermott figured out how to cluster neuronal stem cells in the cerebral cortex."

Victoria, wanting nothing more than to escape this unwelcome demand on her overburdened psyche, took a square Teflon pan from the drawer beneath the oven.

"So, someone would be smarter because of their cuticles?" She poured the cornbread mix into the pan, scraped the sides of the bowl, and licked the spoon. "I'm sorry to say, my fingernails are not feeling very smart right now."

Monica sighed, shaking her head. "Don't joke about this. Just try to understand the main concept. It's good to have lots of neuronal cells. A person with lots of them—or a dog—can connect more cortical modules."

"That must be why you scored a lot better on the GRE than I did. You had more cortical connections."

"Cortical modules. The modules connect. I don't think I have any more connections than you do. You're a lot smarter than you let on. Anyway, what I'm about to tell you is completely *off the record*." Monica put a finger to her lips.

Victoria looked across the counter. Monica beamed with her desire to spill the beans.

"Do you hear yourself?" Behind Monica, the darkened living room suggested that spilling the beans was not such a great idea, Victoria thought. "Anyhow, what *record?* Men tried to kill you, and you're worried about blowing your security clearance?"

"I guess that's right but I just wanted to give you the full background on the research, even though it is against protocol."

"Good grief, Monica. Get to the punchline. Also, we need to have lunch and put our heads together about how to keep you safe."

Victoria came out from behind the counter, slid between the table and countertop stools, and opened the sliding glass door to the patio. Beyond was the deck and the picnic table where she ordinarily ate lunch. At midday, even the birds were quiet, and the quiet made it easy to accomplish the mindless tasks that went along with running the ranch—writing out checks for septic tank clean-out, refilling the propane tank, or deworming cattle. The thoughts that disturbed her sleep never bothered her during the day.

Monica spun around, her eyes never leaving Victoria's face. "Okay,

okay. Here's why this is important. After I graduated, Dr. McDermott, who's also an admiral..."

"Hang on a sec," Victoria said. "Who's also an admiral?"

"Not in the Navy," Monica said. "An admiral in the Public Health Service."

Victoria frowned. "I've never heard of this."

"You've heard of the Surgeon *General*, right?" Monica said.

"Yeah, sure."

"Well, same military structure applies. Originally, Congress created a department that would take care of sick and disabled seamen. During World War II, Congress expanded its authority to include research, and that was when the National Institutes of Health were set up. So that explains why Dr. McDermott is both a research hotshot and an admiral."

"That's wild," Victoria said.

"I haven't gotten to the wild part yet," Monica said. "Are you listening?"

Victoria rolled her eyes. "If I must." She returned to the kitchen. Let's see what else? Maybe salad. The took down a bowl.

"So back to McDermott," Monica said. "He told me he had a research project that dovetailed with my thesis work. That was attractive for a number of reasons. I wanted to stay in Arizona. Proximity to you. But it also gave me a chance to do something about my family history. Cortical Neuronal Clustering allows me to directly manipulate the cognitive plasticity of the cortical module in the cerebral cortex."

"You're going to use that to keep from coming down with Huntington's?"

"Hopefully. Huntington's is embedded in the DNA of the brain cells. Once the genes switch on, the disease starts. I've been working to find a way to keep them from switching on."

"Super. I wish you the best. But that doesn't explain why someone would throw you off a bridge."

Monica drummed her fingers on the counter. "Let me finish, or I'll never get to the part you need to know."

"Okay," Victoria said, "but make it snappy. Lunch is almost ready."

"I will." Monica checked her watch. "Where was I? Okay, our research projects. So the deal is, we were always trying to get more money. The Defense Department has deep pockets. Admiral McDermott approached the military. They were trying to find a faster way to train service animals—bomb-sniffing dogs, drug-sniffing dogs, and whatnot—so I used my research and modified their dog embryos. One of the dogs I developed, his name is Coloso. It's short for Miracoloso. In Italian, it means miraculous. His great-grandfather was a state champion black retriever. He's an amazing dog."

Victoria, oiling the salad bowl, turned around. "You genetically engineered a dog?"

"Yes, and the last time I saw him, he was in a bike shop in Defiance."

"How did he get there?"

"James's brother was out riding his bike in the desert. Coloso must have escaped the lab."

"Okay, so that's really amazing. But it still doesn't explain why you were nearly killed. Did the dog get tired of being man's best friend and decide to take over the world?"

Monica didn't laugh. She reached around and picked up the manila folder.

"Admiral McDermott wanted to take the next step. He wanted me to research human embryos. Officially, I was supposed to find the genes responsible for Huntington's and cancer and other terminal diseases. Unofficially, he wanted to see if they could be edited out. At first, I was ecstatic. It was work I wanted to do, what I needed to do. If I could eliminate diseases at the embryonic level, it would save millions of lives. But there were ethical questions that needed to be addressed. If humanity could modify human embryos to get rid of breast cancer or heart disease or diabetes, what else could we do? Just because we can genetically engineer a dog doesn't mean we should do the same thing for humans. I suggested he put together a board of medical ethics."

Victoria put the cornbread in the oven and straightened up. She was listening intently now.

Monica's mouth flattened into a hard line. "I was ostracized. Admiral McDermott removed me from projects. I stopped getting invited to meetings. Before long he didn't want me to do anything. He just asked me *how* to do it. I would finish something and send it off, and he would give me more bits and pieces to work on."

"Did you tell him you wouldn't do anything unethical?"

"No, I went along with it. If I hadn't, I would have lost my funding. I wasn't making the progress I wanted on curing Huntington's, and there's a clock ticking in my head, literally." She propped her forearms on the counter and spun the folder in a clockwise direction. "I still had some of my other projects. The general in charge of the service dogs wouldn't let McDermott remove me from that research, but I needed measurable progress, something the government would fund so that I could find a cure." She dropped her gaze. "So, without permission, I started human trials."

Victoria froze. "You experimented on people?"

"Yes."

"Oh my god, Monica. The very thing you didn't want McDermott to do."

"Sort of." Monica sniffed and smiled. "The chicken smells good. Hand me the silverware, and I'll set the table."

Victoria opened the silverware drawer and handed across the knives and forks.

Monica moved from the counter to the table. She smoothed the placemats and laid out knives and forks. Then she turned and stood with hands on hips. "There's only so far I could go with the funding I had, and with my disease I had to continue while I still could. I was out of options. Huntington's strikes when you reach middle age. I'm in my mid-thirties. Most people don't make it out of their forties, and those who do, don't live past their fifties. I don't know how long I'll have. I won't pass on this death sentence to my kids."

"Kids? You want a family?" Victoria reared back. "With who?"

"No one. I used someone else's eggs. I have nineteen frozen embryos."

Victoria felt her mouth fall open. Her head was about to explode. She came over to the table and slid out a chair. "You have nineteen frozen embryos, and you didn't tell me?"

Monica took the folder from the counter and sat. "I didn't just cross ethical lines with this. If anyone finds out, I'd never be able to work in a biomedical lab again." She gave a little laugh. "Unless it's maybe in North Korea."

"But people get pregnant all the time using egg and sperm donors. What's the big deal?"

Monica hugged the folder to her chest. "Before I let you read this, promise me you won't get mad."

"Why would I get mad?"

"Just promise."

"But why would I get mad?"

"Will you just shut up and say you won't get mad?"

"Well, I don't know. I'm sort of getting mad about being told not to get mad."

"This isn't the time to joke around, Victoria! This is important."

"Okay, okay, I promise. Lay it on me."

Monica handed over the folder. Victoria opened it and paged through the reports. Most of the medical data she didn't understand, but then she turned a page and stopped. The folder in her hands began to shake.

"Don't get mad," Monica said. "You promised you weren't going to get mad."

Victoria stared at the picture. The man was young, probably in his early twenties, and handsome. He had fair hair, a light complexion, an easy smile, and gobs of freckles.

"He looks like me," she said.

"Yes."

"He's…he's nice looking."

"I told the broker I wanted someone who looked like they would be married to my pretty sister. This is who we found."

"You said I was your sister."

"You are my sister. I love you."

"But this guy looks like a clone of me. I don't understand why that was important."

"It's important because if my kid ever goes looking for a sperm-donor father, they won't suspect I used someone else's egg. If I use your egg and his sperm, the kid's going to be fair-haired and have freckles. That'll clear up any identity issues the kid might be having. I'm not talking about when the kid's young, but when the kid's a teenager and starts asking questions."

Victoria collapsed into a chair. What a day! "You want to have my child." It was a statement, not a question. "But why?"

"Who else would I use? I wanted someone with a good heart and soul. Someone who's smart and strong with a good sense of humor and who couldn't be beaten down no matter what. Very few people could have survived what you've been through."

"How did you get my eggs?"

"After your father was killed, you gave me medical power of attorney. Just in case. Remember?"

"Not really, but if you say so."

"Fortunately, I kept a copy. It was around the time you renewed your driver's license and signed up to be an organ donor. Anyhow, you listed me as next of kin."

"That sounds right," Victoria said. "With my mother and father gone, who else was there?"

"No one," Monica said. "So, I said I'd do it. You were very specific about the things you didn't want. No feeding tubes. No long-term intubation. When the paramedics brought you to the hospital in Flagstaff, you had burns over forty percent of your body, plus damage to almost every organ, including your brain. The doctors put you in an induced coma. If you died, the hospital was going to take you off the ventilator and harvest your organs. I drove up there and arranged for a medevac. It brought you to Biodosius. I'd seen the doctors there do some miraculous things."

"I don't remember any of it."

"Of course not. You were totally out of it, and no one thought you would live, so I...I harvested your eggs. You wanted to donate your organs, and eggs are a body part. I had thought about asking you before to let me use your eggs to have a child, but I never got the chance, and that wasn't something specifically mentioned on the power of attorney. Why would it be?"

Victoria tried to think. This was happening way too fast to comprehend. Even though she felt like screaming, she kept her voice level.

"Didn't your boss object?"

"McDermott, you mean? He wasn't in a position to object. When you were brought in, he was on medical leave."

"If he'd been there, do you think he would have stopped you?"

"Certainly, he would have. What I did would have gotten me fired."

"You said you crossed a line."

Monica took a shuddering breath. "I took the next step. Everything I did for the dogs I did to the genomes of your embryos."

"What?" She couldn't believe what she was hearing. "You experimented on my eggs?"

"I had the best of intentions. I started out doing minor things like removing bad recessive genes. Color blindness, near sightedness, that sort of thing. You have a near-fatal allergy to cinnamon. Your throat will lock up if you inhale it. You have asthmatic genes. I removed them."

Victoria had one big thing on her mind. Getting Dark's voice out of her head. That meant finding him and saving every ounce of energy for the hunt. And now this! Coming at her out of left field. How could Monica think this *wouldn't* make her angry. "I don't believe any of this!"

Monica's eyes flashed. "I did what I thought was best."

"What you thought best!"

"Yes, what I thought best! Your mother had a history of depression. You have it. Do you want to pass it on to your kids, so they'll commit suicide, too?"

Anger didn't just flash through Victoria, it roared.

"Stop right now, Monica! I won't let you talk to me like that in my own home!"

Monica crossed her arms across her chest. She started to cry. "I'm sorry. I would never knowingly hurt you. You know that."

"You have some nerve? What were you thinking? You had no right!"

"I know, but I didn't want to pass on Huntington's to my kids. And then you *did* die. No heartbeat. No pulse. As in D-E-A-D." She spelled it out. "If you want to judge me like everyone else then fine! But I stopped the curse. All of my kids and grandkids and great-grandkids from this point forward will never have to die from their brains falling apart." Her voice quivered, and a tear rolled down her cheek. "I will be the last with the disease."

Victoria stared at her friend and finally pushed herself out of her chair, walked around the table, and put her arms around Monica's shoulders. Monica stood and turned around, allowing herself to be enfolded in Victoria's arms. Victoria finally broke it off and went to the sink. She took a salad kit from the crisper and shook the package into the wooden bowl. When she was done, she leaned on the counter and stared out the kitchen window at the creek.

"I'm not mad," she finally said. "I'm just…surprised. Besides, you'll make a wonderful mother, and, honestly, I don't think I'm in any shape to do it myself." Not with Doug out of picture. Not with her scarred torso. The skin grafts on her stomach would burst if she got pregnant, and in a weird way, it was kind of nice to know a part of her would live on.

Monica covered her mouth. "Thank you so much."

"Not a big deal. I have one question though. Why would someone want to kill you for editing genomes?"

Monica blew her nose. With a tissue clenched in her fist, she stood and paced back and forth in the living room. "I made a mistake. I presented my research to Admiral McDermott after he returned from medical leave. I told him what I'd done and what I had accomplished. I should have kept it secret, but I needed the money. The government was tired of hearing about what was possible. They wanted research they could use."

"How long ago was that?"

"Three years."

"They've been using your research for three years? Doing what?"

"I don't know specifics. Like I said before, I was marginalized. They needed me, but they didn't like me. McDermott hid what I had done. If word had gotten out that I'd edited my own embryos, the scandal would have rocked medical science. There are laws in the US prohibiting that kind of work. But for me, the money kept coming. I was given pieces of projects, and I did them. Over time I heard rumors of projects at other sites. Things no one wanted to talk about. And then the accidents started happening."

"Accidents?"

Eyes haunted, Monica stared glumly into space.

"I was collaborating with a site in Atlanta and my colleagues disappeared. I had meetings scheduled with them, and suddenly they were canceled. I was told later the teams had been reassigned, but I never heard from them again. Phone calls and emails weren't answered. They just went poof."

"Were they doing something similar to what you were doing?"

"No. Officially, they were doing work on the adrenal gland. On the surface, the goal was to prevent heart attacks. Unofficially, they were working with the same military teams as McDermott. My involvement was limited to giving them information on genetic markers, so they would know how to screen test subjects."

"Test subjects—as in *human* test subjects?"

"Yes."

"Okay, all of that is disturbing, but it doesn't explain why someone would try to kill you."

Monica took an unsteady breath. "Yesterday afternoon, something happened at my job. I was in my office when my friend Will rushed in, telling me we had to go. He used to work for me before McDermott reassigned him. We carpool together. I tried to ask him what happened, but all he would say was we had to get out. I grabbed my laptop but I didn't leave. I had given up everything for my research— my career, my ethics, my self-respect, but I wouldn't give up my embryos."

Her voice cracked. She started to shake.

"We ran down the stairs to the labs. There were…bodies. Blood on the walls. People screaming. We didn't have a way inside the cryogenics lab, but we saw a dead medical tech who'd worked in that lab. Will used her badge to get us inside and locked the door. I logged into the system using the tech's badge and pulled out all my research—the dogs, my embryos, everything McDermott had taken from me. I put it all into a medical transport container."

"The one you put in my freezer?"

"Yes. We were just about to leave when something smashed into the lab's door. I don't know what it was, but the door sounded like it was going to explode. Will and I just froze. We had no idea what was going on.

"We waited ten minutes. Nothing else happened, and we eventually opened the door and looked outside. The power was off. It was pitch black. We couldn't see a thing. I have a flashlight app on my phone, and I started to turn it on, but Will didn't want to risk being seen. We heard screams.

"Will put the badge back on the dead technician, and we felt our way out. You have no idea how it feels to grope your way through the dark, tripping over dead bodies and stepping in blood and not knowing where you are or if you're going to be attacked and killed.

"We saw a light, headed toward an emergency exit, and jumped in my car. I tried to get Will to tell me what had happened and who had killed everyone, but he refused to say anything. Like I said, I had been cut off from any actual development work. I couldn't even get into the labs without an escort.

"We picked up his family and headed up here. I figured we could stay with you until we came up with a plan. No one at work knows who you are or that you exist. You were a dead woman, a project number. That's it."

"That's when you got kidnapped?"

"Yes. We needed gas and stopped to get something to eat. We didn't have any cash, and Will used his credit card. They must have been watching his account because some men jumped us outside a restaurant after we finished eating. They shot Will and grabbed his family and me. You know the rest."

"Were they military?"

"I don't know. It happened so fast I couldn't really react. They put a hood over my head and handcuffed me. I couldn't see anything, and they talked about football. They acted like I wasn't even there. I don't know who's doing this or why."

Victoria thought through everything she had been told and decided it was time to come clean. Secrets wouldn't help them. Not if they were going to survive.

"Well, about that," she finally said. "I think I know who tried to kill you."

Monica lifted her head in astonishment. "You do?"

Victoria nodded. "I call him Dark."

CHAPTER 27

Back at Williams Air Force Base, General O'Dell had gotten patched up and sent the pilot to get treated for a concussion. The platoon had returned to the old mine and found nothing, not even the body of the soldier who'd been dragged out of the helicopter. After a shower and a night's sleep, Jacobson felt rested, but also with that feeling of unreality he always had when he returned to combat. Here we go again. O'Dell had ordered a helicopter to ferry them back to Biodosius, and now the pilot was circling and looking for a place to put down.

On Saturday morning when they'd flown out to investigate Dr. Baltimore's crash site, the parking lot at Biodosius had held two dozen parked cars. But by Sunday afternoon, the parking lot was jammed with media vans, reporters, and family members demanding information about their loved ones. Police had erected barricades, and the National Guard, with their armbands and whistles, herded people to the command tent on the front lawn. Jacobson didn't envy the press liaison officer who would have to fabricate a cover story.

Lieutenant Day, in wraparound sunglasses, waved the Black Hawk down near the west entrance. Her security team, dressed in riot gear, had lined up to keep the photographers and reporters at bay.

Jacobson and O'Dell jumped out onto the hot asphalt. The rotors swirled the heat into a tornado-like blast furnace. Once they were out from under the rotors, the engines revved up, and the helo swooped over their heads.

Jacobson tried to guess what Day was thinking, but dark glasses covered half her face, and he couldn't see her eyes.

"Did you get the orders granting Major Jacobson access to Lab 6?" General O'Dell asked her as they walked toward the entrance.

"Yes, sir. Admiral McDermott sent over instructions an hour ago. He would like to discuss your progress at finding the dog while Jacobson is talking to Dr. Kumar in the lab. He's in the front conference room."

O'Dell nodded. "Okay, fine."

Day led the way to the building. The broken doors had been repaired, and when she put her security card against the pad, the doors buzzed open. Inside, the two dead security guards had been removed. Jacobson was tempted to switch on his night-vision goggles, but left them off. Given a minute, his eyes would adjust.

His phone buzzed. He checked the number and put up a hand. "Hang on," he told the Lieutenant. "I need to take this call."

He walked back toward the soldiers, and they eyed him as he cupped a hand over his mouth. No point in letting someone lipread his half of the conversation.

"I have some news," Agent Terrance said. "Yesterday, a mountain biker was reported missing in the Tonto National Forest just north of Mesa. We've located his vehicle. The police found it in Defiance, Arizona. Have you heard of it?"

"No."

"It's a tourist town up in the mountains. Small place with lots of antique shops, haunted ghost tours, and places to eat. They have the

Taste of Defiance going on this weekend. My wife and I went up there for our last wedding anniversary. I'm still paying off the tab." He laughed.

"Why would the killers go there?"

"I don't know, but a local garage owner was attacked. Same way we were. Someone named Paul Moody. He does towing and automobile repair. He's in critical condition, and a medevac helicopter took him to Phoenix. I've already notified Admiral McDermott. He's going to assemble a team."

"Is there someone in Defiance who could do that bike ride?"

"There's a bike shop in Defiance called Defiance Cyclery. They manufacture high-end mountain bikes. Adam Barnett owns the shop. There are hundreds of videos of him on the internet doing insane things with a bike. I called the county sheriff's. Barnett's well known in town. They said he's been seen walking with a large black dog."

"Can you call Barnett? His life is in danger. We need to get him in protective custody."

"I called his shop, but it's closed for the holiday. I'm going to reach out to different cellular companies and see if I can get his number. If he has a phone, we can track the signal. I'll pick you up once McDermott gets a team assembled."

"Thanks."

Jacobson returned his phone to his pocket and hoped they weren't too late.

Day escorted him past the entrance to Lab 3 and the Cryogenics Lab to the last door on the right, Lab 6. A guard stood outside the entrance with a slung M4 assault rifle over his shoulder. Day told him who Jacobson was. The guard checked his clipboard, nodded, and touched his card to the security pad. The light on the pad turned from red to green as the lock disengaged.

Jacobson stepped inside. Lieutenant Day followed, and the steel security door clanged shut behind them. His previous visit had been on

Saturday morning. Except for the dim light, nothing had changed. Patient cells stretched away on both sides of the long room, each cell with a thick glass observation wall. He stopped, skin prickling. There was an undercurrent of dread in the lab that bothered him, and he felt as if he were standing next to a humming electrical transformer.

The patient with the split forehead in the first cell saw him and launched himself at the glass so hard the wall shook. Jacobson snapped up his rifle. Day quickly stepped forward.

"No shooting, sir! If the glass breaks, he'll kill everyone in the building! You have no idea what even one of them can do!"

Jacobson removed his finger from the trigger.

He remembered the man's eyes, two ivory eggs. The feeling in the room, like buzzing bees crawling on his skin, grew worse.

"You feel it, don't you?" a woman asked softly.

Jacobson tore his gaze away from the patient. Dr. Riya Kumar looked the same as she had on the Black Hawk Friday night, except that she wore a white lab coat over her business suit. A lanyard containing her identification hung from her neck. She carried a clipboard and snapped the clip on a manila folder.

"What is it?" he asked. "That feeling."

"I don't know. A long buried sixth sense or survival instinct, perhaps. Everyone feels it."

Jacobson glanced again at the patient, then forced himself to turn away. It wasn't easy. His instincts said to get out of there. The glass shook with each blow.

"Thanks for seeing me, Doctor. General O'Dell asked me to speak to you about what's been going on. The killers are unlike anyone I've ever fought before. I need to know what I'm facing."

Kumar shifted in her sensible shoes. How long had she stood here, waiting for him to appear?

"Of course, Major, I'll tell you what I can," she said smoothly. "What would you like to know?"

Jacobson didn't spook easily but his instincts told him to toss out a few softballs.

"Why is it so dark in here?"

"The Simeon Process damages the eye's optic nerves, so we keep the lights off."

"The Simeon Process?"

"An informal name for the project. An early researcher coined the phrase."

"Is Simeon one of the researchers on the project?"

"No. Simeon, according to the Christian Apocryphal Gospels, was one of the saints raised into resurrection with Christ." She paused for a moment. "And, lo, the earth did quake and the rocks were rent and the graves broke open, and many bodies of the saints which slept arose and came out of the tombs after his resurrection and went into the Holy City and appeared unto many."

"What does that have to do with your research?"

"It's somewhat descriptive of what I do here. I was given a medical grant to preserve critical brain function until a terminally injured patient can receive medical care."

"You mean like someone getting shot in the head?"

"Not that extreme. Let's say that someone gets in a car accident that severs the femoral artery in their leg. The sudden loss of blood will kill them. I'm trying to develop a process to inhibit decay at the cellular level. I've done a lot of research with pentoxifylline inhibition."

"Never heard of it."

"In layman's terms, my research allows medical providers to chemically stabilize a patient until they can reach a proper care facility where the trauma can be addressed. Then they can be resuscitated."

"By terminal, are you saying they're deceased?"

"Yes. There's no pulse and no brain activity. I know it sounds odd, but with my process, they have a much higher chance of survival after dying than they would if they were kept alive. A patient with the severed artery, for example, would hemorrhage blood until they died. This allows medical personnel to address the injury before resuscitation."

"That sounds like a worthwhile project. What happened?"

"For all the successes, there's been a problem with a small percentage of the patients. The situation is quite unusual. It doesn't happen all the time." She flipped a page on the chart and scanned the information as she spoke. It was the kind of chart that doctors' offices always had on plastic folding arms outside the door of the examining room. "After resuscitation, some of my patients, regardless of genetic or mental health background, wake up exhibiting severe abnormal neurological symptoms. Most of those affected are violently psychotic. An unacceptably high percentage of those commit suicide. Some have killed their entire immediate families before taking their own lives."

"The process makes them crazy?"

"I don't like that term, but for some of them, yes."

Dumbfounded, Jacobson stared.

Kumar nodded. "I think you're seeing the problem. The Pentagon is concerned."

"Why continue?"

Sudden anger flashed across her dark face. "I'm a physician, Major. I help people. My research is not only about saving lives but improving them. For the first time in human history, we aren't dependent on evolution's swirling tide to extend life. My research will save millions of lives. The practical applications are enormous. Anyone with severe trauma can be helped."

"Have there been successes?"

"Yes."

"But the ones here," he nodded at the man with the bleeding forehead, "they're the ones that the process didn't work on?"

"I wouldn't say it like that. Without my research they would have died. We're trying to find a way to minimize their reaction to the process."

"Do you have any patients who aren't violent?"

Kumar nodded and turned to another cell. It held a petite woman. She lay on her mattress with her legs hugged tight to her chest. She wore a hospital gown and dark sunglasses. Her shaved head revealed a misshapen skull, and both hands were clamped over her ears.

"Her name is Anna. She and her children were bludgeoned to death by her alcoholic husband after he found out she was pregnant with their fifth child."

"She went through the process?"

"That's why she's alive."

"Why is she shaking like that?"

"The process affects the suprarenal glands. Elevated levels of adrenaline are pumped into the bloodstream. The chemical imbalance affects everything from the brain's reasoning centers to the immune system. It's especially evident in the dorsal posterior insula area of the brain."

"Which does what?"

"That's the area that controls our ability to think and control emotions. To feel and react correctly to external stimuli."

"Your patients don't feel pain?"

"They do but they can't process it correctly. Their sensory systems are overloaded."

"That's why they're so violent?"

"Yes."

"Can they be helped?"

"Neurologists, psychiatrists, psychologists, therapists, they've all tried. A priest even theorized that the mind and soul had somehow become disconnected, severing their humanity. Personally, I believe the problem is severe psychological trauma. Can you imagine what it's like to experience what Anna went through? Her husband clubbed her and her children to death because she was pregnant? Given similar circumstances, it could be any of us in there."

She smiled benignly, as if her patients were special toys she'd been given for Christmas. She obviously believed in her work.

"Why is the military involved in your research? Do they provide your patients?"

"Sometimes, but not always. Most candidates are organ donors. Every situation is looked at individually. For those I think I can help, I provide medical assistance. Time is always of the essence, of course. The faster they're revived the better."

"Do you allow your patients to see family members?"

"My work is highly experimental. I don't work with families. The family has already lost their loved one and begun the grief process. I won't put them through a second death if the process is not successful."

"In other words, it's easier if patients have no family."

"That's correct."

Trying to calm himself, Jacobson exhaled. "Then why try and help them? It's not like they have anyone to go back to. I mean, look at them. They can't function. What's the point?"

"They're people and I'm a doctor, that's why!" she insisted, her voice rising. "Given time and proper funding, I'll find the cure for the failed experiments, and they can live normal lives!"

"Failed experiments? Is that what you call them? Failed experiments?"

"Of course not. I misspoke. They're human beings, the same as you and me."

He stared at her and abruptly understood what was going on. Her patients had been declared dead. They had no rights. They had no one to object to what was being done to them. They were lab rats, nothing more.

He stepped forward, forcing her to move closer to the observation window. The man let out an enraged howl and smashed into the glass. Kumar squeaked, eyes wide as she felt the vibration. Jacobson watched the barrier bend and flex. The man bit wildly at the glass, smearing it with saliva.

"Just imagine if he got hold of you, Doctor. All your careful rationalizations and denials would do you no good." This close to the wall, he didn't just hear the man's guttural growls. He felt them. "Should we open the door? Should we have a consultation with your failed experiment?"

"You're insane!"

"That may be," he said, "but maybe we should ask him if the life you gave him is the life he wants." He pointed to her lanyard. "Will that open the door?"

Blood drained from Kumar's face.

"How do they communicate?" Jacobson asked.

"What?"

"How do your patients communicate? I've never seen anyone attack with such precision and speed. How do they coordinate their attacks?"

"I don't know! I only provide care. Why are you talking to me like this?"

"How many of your patients got out?"

She hugged the chart to her chest. "I'm not to blame for that! I'm helping these people!" The man slammed against the glass. "You need to leave. Your presence is making him agitated."

"The killers are not like anyone I've fought before, Doctor," Jacobson said. "They bend doors and climb walls. They're fast, strong, and inhumanly vicious. They feint and use misdirection. They attack from ambush and know exactly how to counter our responses. Can you imagine what would happen if even one of them got into a school or a church or a shopping mall?"

"That's not going to happen!"

The man clawed at the edge of the door, trying to get hold of it with his fingernails. His white eyes locked on Jacobson, and he howled, the sound ratcheting upward into a mad, eager wail.

Jacobson watched Kumar's reaction. His accusations had hit her like physical blows, and he was sorry to have been so blunt. He had interrogated hundreds of people over his career. Sometimes it was because he was just trying to make sense of a situation. Other times it was trying to find out something the other person didn't want him to know. Dr. Kumar was evasive, but she obviously believed she could help these people. He was beating a dead horse.

"What's your involvement in the research here?"

"I'm the senior scientist in charge of patient care."

"You help the patients that the process doesn't work on?"

"I have a staff that assists me. But yes, I try and help those that have a serious reaction. Contrary to what you might think, I'm not a monster."

"I don't think you're a monster, Doctor. I don't even think you're creating monsters. I think someone else has taken over your research, and now they've lost control. To deflect blame from their own actions, they've sent you to answer my questions. I should be talking to the person in charge."

She blinked. Her mouth opened and closed.

"You said these are the failed patients. What happens to the successful ones?"

"They're transferred to other facilities for conditioning."

"What does that mean?"

"You'll have to ask Admiral McDermott."

"How many of the patients were waiting for conditioning at the time of the killings?"

She dropped her clipboard and bent to pick it up.

"Eight," she whispered. "Eight of the patients were awaiting transfer. I don't know what happened. McDermott handles that end of things."

Jacobson nodded. "We have video of one of the research dogs helping Dr. Baltimore out of the building. Have you seen it?"

Kumar physically gathered herself, straightening her lab coat. "Yes, the dog is General O'Dell's service dog. He's trained to help those in need."

Jacobson chose his next words with care. "What was Dr. Baltimore working on before the accident? Was he working on the Simeon Process?"

CHAPTER 28

Leaving out the part where she had killed Couch, Flight, and the guy with the rifle in the RV, Victoria told Monica about the man's voice in her head. It wasn't that she didn't trust Monica. She just didn't want to put her friend in the position of keeping secrets. The less anyone knew about what had happened, the better.

Frowning, Monica asked, "Are you sure you heard Will's name?"

Victoria nodded. "Yes, but the voice called him Thompson, not Will. And he's not the only one. I've heard Dark order the deaths of other people. The two most recent were Andrew Snodgrass and Michelle Salo. Are the names familiar?"

"Yes. I worked with both at the Atlanta site. They were scientists. Michelle used to tell me about her daughters."

"They were the last two killed. There've been more. I didn't keep a tally. I thought I was going crazy."

"When did this start?"

"When I was in the hospital. I've been hearing Dark ever since."

"Why didn't you tell me you were hearing voices?"

"I don't hear voices. I hear Dark's voice. Dr. Young, my shrink, said my psychosis was brought on by PTSD from what happened to me and my dad. And, of course, that was plausible. I don't know what was worse, the day I burned alive or the day I found my dad. The narcos are really bad people, but what if they're not the only baddies?"

Monica dropped her gaze to her hands. "Admiral McDermott told me Michelle had been reassigned."

"No," Victoria said. "Dark ordered her thrown thrown off a cliff while hiking in Colorado."

The blood left Monica's face. "What about her family?"

"All killed. According to the internet, the authorities said it was an accident. They left the main trail on one of the mountains and fell trying to find their way back to their car. I tried to tell the county sheriff it wasn't an accident, but he ignored me. That's how it was with all the deaths. Dark was incredibly careful about making things look like accidents. One was killed in an automobile accident. Another drowned while scuba diving in Australia. One of the doctors killed his wife and child and then killed himself. They called it 'vengeful suicide'."

"I was just one of many, then." Monica sat back down at the counter.

"It looks that way." Victoria took plates from the cupboard. "Be glad they decided to throw you off a bridge. They could have put a bullet in your head. In your case, you had no local family, but your colleague, Will Thompson, was a different story. That's why they shot him and took his family. If they all disappeared, it would look like he'd taken off. The kidnappers might even have been able to blame him for what happened at Biodosius."

"Let me think," Monica said.

Victoria found sugar snap peas in the refrigerator, washed them, and added them to the salad. This was the meal she'd intended to bring to Doug, but she was glad to be making it for Monica. Finally, she was getting some answers.

She found an apple pie in the freezer. How strange to be staring at a steel thermos of her frozen embryos. Sighing, she put the pie in the oven.

"I need to understand how you hear him," Monica said. "Do you hear all his thoughts or just some of them? Is it an actual voice?"

"It's more of a feeling than actually hearing his thoughts. It's hard to describe. Most of the time I don't hear anything at all. I don't hear him eating breakfast, and I can't eavesdrop on conversations he has with other people. I think it has something to do with his emotions or when I'm asleep. I dream of him. It makes it hard to rest."

"Can you feel him right now? Can you tell what direction he is from here?"

"I'm not a map, Monica." The thought of getting in Dark's head terrified her. "I don't reach out to him. But sometimes I can feel him, sort of like a mosquito buzzing around in my head."

"Would you recognize him if you saw him?"

"I would recognize his voice. I've never seen Dark kill anyone, but I've felt him do it."

"Did he say anything about me?"

"No, not by name."

"Can he hear you?"

"I think so. I don't know how though."

"Could he be listening to us right now?" Shivering, Monica glanced outside the window. "Could he find us?"

Victoria was tempted to tell Monica about her visit to the cabin. Dark had asked Couch to look around for a woman. She didn't think he knew her name, and, even if he did, how would he locate her? The narcos had been looking for her for years. Unless Dark had some kind of psychic GPS, she doubted he would have any better luck. But she would have to be careful with her thoughts from now on.

"I don't know. Here. We'll need these." Victoria handed napkins to Monica. "Like I said, most of the time I hear him in my dreams. Hopefully, it's the same way for him. But even if he had a general idea of where to find me, how could he? I'm in the middle of nowhere."

"If he works for the government, he might be able to get past your safeguards. We'll have to be careful."

Victoria laughed. "How could I be any more careful? There aren't any street signs out here—just dirt roads that go nowhere. I don't have an address. All I have is a post office box, and that's an hour away. I use a satellite phone, and the service provider can't disclose my information without talking to the FBI. Believe me, the narcos have tried to find me, and they haven't."

She sliced up two lemons, put them in their glasses, and poured ice water.

"Why am I hearing Dark's voice, Monica? Did I get a tainted batch of neurons? Did you go to the brain store and get an 'Abby Normal' brain?"

Monica snorted at the movie reference. "I don't know. The military encrypted our data. To get more information, I would have to reach out to my colleagues."

"Those that are still alive?"

"Yeah, right. But if they are alive, they could get prosecuted for revealing government secrets. Besides, right now, I'd think we'd both better keep our heads down. If I'd known there were mental health issues, I wouldn't have used those neurons. I'm sorry. I didn't know."

"Can you fix me?"

"I don't know but I'll try. I'll try as hard as I can."

"How many other accidents have happened at other sites?"

"None that I know of for sure. Different teams, like the one in Atlanta, were simply reassigned. Nobody called the reassignments accidents. Money and people were reallocated as needed. That happens a lot in research. Whatever has funding gets worked on, and most of what we do here in Arizona is research. The actual development happens elsewhere. We have the dogs, but other than that, as far as I know, everything is mostly R and not much D."

"Why were the dogs at your building?"

"O'Dell refused to move me off the project. Since I was here, the dogs were, too."

"Where does the other development work happen?"

"Most of the neuron development happens outside the US. We have a big facility in Japan. There are dozens of other small sites. Projects are only funded for a short while and then disbanded."

"That's probably because it's much easier to hide things overseas," Victoria said. "They don't have the regulations, and there can't be that many people who know the big picture. The more people in on it, the more risk of leaks."

"You're sounding like this is all a big conspiracy."

"Actually, I'm saying the opposite. To have a conspiracy, you must have conspirators, and having lots of conspirators is a bad idea. In the military, if you don't need to know, you're not given access. This has the military's fingerprints all over it. I bet you were excluded because Admiral McDermott didn't want you to know what your research was being used for. If he kept you isolated, it limited his exposure and the exposure of those who funded him."

"I never thought about it that way."

"That's why this Admiral keeps his research overseas. He rents buildings and brings in equipment and hires local staff who have no idea who they really work for. If something happens, the lab shuts down. If someone objects or knows too much, they get in a car accident or fall off a cliff like your friend in Atlanta.

"My guess is that the work in Scottsdale would have kept going except the thing that happened at your building yesterday is something they can't bury, and now they're in damage control mode trying to figure out how to cover it up and what to do next."

"Four hundred people worked in my building. They can't cover up that many deaths."

"They can't, and they won't. The killers are to blame, remember?"

"Okay. So, what do we do now?"

"We eat lunch." Victoria handed over plates and took the pie from the oven. "It could be a while until our next meal, and we can't waste time. We need to see Adam and James Barnett about the dog. They need to know what kind of danger they're in."

"I'm not sure Adam Barnett wants to see me again," Monica said, "and, frankly, I'm embarrassed that I took his car."

Victoria smiled. "You didn't *take* his car, Monica. You *stole* it."

"You are unbelievable."

"He'll want to talk to you about what happened. I guarantee it."

Monica cut a square of cornbread, buttered it, and took a bite. "Yum." She brushed away crumbs that spilled down her shirt. "I'll give James a call. He's nice. He's got these blue eyes and a quirky smile. I think we had a connection."

"That's because he saw you undressed in the woods. Men would have a connection with a rock if it had breasts." Victoria tugged up her bra.

Monica smiled.

"When we finish, we'll drive to a payphone and call James."

"Can't we just call from here?"

"We could, but if the people trying to kill you know that the Barnetts have the dog, they might be monitoring their phones. It's better to find a different phone."

"I thought the FBI was protecting you."

"They are." Or were, she thought. No telling what Doug Monroe would do when she backed away. "Anyhow, I stay alive by minimizing risks."

After lunch, they cleaned up and went out to Victoria's Heavy Duty. The big truck didn't have a custom gun tray like Blackjack Joe's Rover, so Victoria put her weapons and equipment in the back seat. She started up the truck's diesel engine and drove up the canyon in four-wheel drive. The road was potholed and bumpy, but the truck had an upgraded suspension, and she had driven the canyon so many times she knew every rock. They reached the top of the canyon and turned west toward the Knob. Feeling a sudden urgency, Victoria increased her speed until the truck lost traction on a curve. Monica grabbed the door.

"Why are you driving so fast?"

"He's going to die."

"What?"

"He's going to die."

"Who?"

Victoria stiffened and hit the brakes. The truck skidded to a stop.

Monica clutched the door and braced a foot against the dash. "Holy moly. Too much excitement for one day."

Trying to keep her voice level, Victoria asked, "What just happened?"

Monica took her foot down and turned. "I asked you why you were driving so fast, and you said, 'He's going to die'."

"I did?"

"Yes."

"Did I say who?"

"No."

Victoria massaged her forehead, willing more information to come.

"Was it Dark?" Monica asked.

"I don't know. I never know what's going on until it's about to happen."

"Should we call the police?"

"And tell them what? That I said someone was going to die?"

"You really didn't hear a name?"

"Not this time."

"What if it was James or Adam?" Monica asked. "How far is Defiance?"

"Two hours."

"What if Dark knows you're onto him? What if, instead of warning them, we're leading them into a trap?"

Victoria looked in the rearview mirror. The road behind them was clear. "That's a chance we have to take. The main thing is to meet them somewhere isolated. I can keep a lookout while you explain about the dog."

"General O'Dell is going to move heaven and earth to get that dog back," Monica said.

CHAPTER 29

Adam drove Kate's Lexus home from the Neurological Institute and parked it in a designated space behind the shop. The Taste of Defiance Festival was in full swing, and hundreds of tourists wearing identical THE BEST FOOD YOU WILL EVER EAT OUT OF A GUTTER! T-shirts jammed the park across the street.

They got out of the car and embraced. Kate clung to him, head down so her dark hair obscured her face. "Sorry for being so upset," she whispered. "Listening to the doctor brought back a lot of memories of my dad."

"Don't apologize. If something's wrong, then at least I got an early warning. I'll get it taken care of and move on. The glass is half full as far as I'm concerned."

"You really are an optimist."

She gave him a kiss and slid into her car. Adam watched her drive off, waving until she had disappeared. Then he limped into the shop. Contrary to the brave face he had shown on the way back from Scottsdale, the trip to the neurologist had left him confused and depressed. Other than some pain in his foot and shoulder, he felt fine. His physical the month before had been clean. There'd been no sign of a blood disorder or memory loss.

Bailey had left the back door propped open and sat behind the sales counter on a stool. She had some of her old readers spread out around her on the floor and was pointing at the pages and sounding out words to the dog.

"Mop's bored so I'm teaching him a few more words," she said as Adam gave her an inquiring look. "Scooby Doo's his favorite. He wants us to get some Scooby Snacks."

"What about your own reading?" Adam asked. "Don't you have to fill out your reading log for school?"

"I already told Dad I'll do it tomorrow."

"Do it now, and you won't have to do it tomorrow."

She sighed. "I'll do it after I teach Mop to read."

James walked out of the back. "Hey, bro, how did it go at the hospital?"

"Great. My memory's missing, and they don't know why. My white blood cells are elevated, and they don't know why. I could have a blood disorder, and they don't know why. I might have had a seizure, and they don't know why. So why did I go?" He waited expectantly.

"You don't know why?" Bailey asked.

"Exactly!"

"Do you have to go back?" James asked.

"They want to send me to more specialists for more tests."

"I saw Kate crying as she dropped you off," James said. "Is she upset?"

"Going to the hospital reminded her of dealing with her dad."

"You can't blame her for that. Just the fact she was willing to go should tell you something." He exchanged a meaningful glance with Bailey.

Adam groaned. "Oh, come on, don't tell me the two of you have been talking about my love life. The last thing I need right now is mom calling me and giving me the speech." Adam changed his voice to a falsetto. "If you had a dollar to spend on a woman, you'd spend 86 cents on appearance. You need to put more money towards character and personality and intelligence and things that really matter."

"Did Grandma say that?" Bailey asked.

"Yes, she did, and no, we aren't discussing it."

"How much should you spend? Because Kate's much nicer than anyone you've ever dated," James said. "Maybe you need more than a dollar. I bet I could find an app on my phone that would help you budget."

Rolling his eyes, Adam gathered up the tattered remnants of his dignity. "I'm going to go take a shower and change out of this boot."

"How soon can we go?" Bailey asked. "I want a cinnamon-roll sundae."

Adam looked down at his foot. Even though it was hot out, his foot still felt like it wanted protection. He had some half-calf cushioned athletic socks. They'd fit in his old Adidas. "After I'm done, we can go."

———

Upstairs, standing under the water with his forehead pressed against the tile, he tried to reconstruct his movements. Like he'd told the doctor, he had gotten up before dawn on Friday morning and driven down to Mesa to ride Cat Sick. After that he couldn't remember anything until Saturday morning, when he'd found himself in the mining camp. How had he gotten there and why? The lightning had burned a hole through his shoulder and foot. An injury like that would have disabled most people, but he had somehow walked to the top of a hill to look around and then run back down ahead of the Nightmare.

Afterward, he had stolen an old pickup and driven it home, using his bad arm to steer and his hurt foot to step on the gas. Later that day, he'd driven down to Mesa in Paul's car hauler to retrieve his truck and then stopped to get his foot stitched up at the clinic. He had left the clinic, dropped the truck at home, and then driven to Show Low to pick up his Corvette. As promised, Monica had left James's phone on the seat. Then he'd driven back to Paul's place, unloaded the 'Vette, driven it home, gotten dressed for the wedding, and danced with Kate on his injured foot.

Maybe because he was exhausted and not thinking straight, he had gotten into a fight with Mike at the overlook. Mike was all muscle from his job welding pipe. With an injured shoulder, Adam shouldn't have been able to drag Mike to the railing and threaten to throw him off the cliff. None of it made sense.

He shut off the water and toweled. When his phone rang, he picked up and snapped, "I'm almost done. When I get out of the bathroom, we'll go."

"What are you doing in the bathroom?" Kate asked.

He groaned. "Sorry, I just got out of the shower. I thought you were Bailey. She keeps badgering me about going to the festival."

"That's why I'm calling. Are you hungry? I've got the Junior Dessert Contest to judge, but we could get a bite to eat afterward."

"Can James and Bailey come? I promised Bailey I would get her a cinnamon-roll ice cream sundae."

"Sure, bring them along. Ask Bailey if she'll share. My diet won't allow me to eat an entire one myself."

"We could split one."

"That would be nice. It's a date then."

She told him goodbye, and he put the phone down. He glanced at the foggy mirror and stopped. Wait, was he…smiling?

He shaved for the second time that day, took longer than necessary combing his hair, and hunted around in his closet until he found a clean polo. He put on slacks instead of his normal shorts. The Adidas didn't match the outfit but he had a new pair of Allen Edmonds Courtside Lace-ups. They were expensive shoes but tight, and their brown leather matched the pants.

"Wow!" Bailey said when he came into the living room.

Mop walked over and cautiously sniffed his legs.

"Since when did you start wearing pants?" James asked.

Adam felt his face flush. "You say that like I walk around in my underwear all the time. I have pants. This is not a big deal. I'm just going to get something to eat. That's all. Quit making it out to be more than it is because it isn't whatever you're making it out to be."

"What you're not making is any sense," James said, smiling.

Bailey snapped his picture with her phone. He scowled and pulled Mop's new collar out of his pocket. Mop backed down the hallway, forcing Adam to pursue him. Mop was a big dog and there wasn't much room on the narrow hallway, but the dog wove back and forth, trying to get away.

"He doesn't like collars," Bailey said.

"You think?"

Adam pinned Mop against the bathroom door. Mop pawed at the doorknob, the door opened, and they both spilled into the bathroom. Mop recovered faster than Adam did and escaped into the family room.

"You did that on purpose!" Adam picked himself up and checked his skinned elbow. "Either put on the collar or stay home!"

Bailey held out her hand. "You're not doing it right."

"Fine. You do it."

She held out her hand to the dog. "Mop, if you want dinner, you need to put on the collar."

Head hanging, Mop shuffled forward. Bailey put the collar around Mop's neck and attached the leash.

Bailey lifted her gaze to Adam. "See?"

"What I see is a bad precedent," Adam replied. "Before long we're going to have to ask him permission to do everything. Mop, can I go to work? Mop, can I go to the bathroom?"

Mop barked.

"He says you can," Bailey translated.

Adam ground his teeth. Bailey smirked and led the way downstairs. Adam locked the front door, and they headed across the street through the crowds. He almost turned around and took Mop back inside but Bailey saw some of her friends and waved them over. They fussed over Mop and scratched his ears. Mop wagged his tail and offered his paw.

Rows of food trucks filled the city park. Smoke from grills and pits and spits drifted up into the evening air. Visitors carried plates of food to tables that had been set up between the rows, while vendors selling hats and T-shirts hawked their wares. Adam tried not to trip over strollers. Bailey saw a boy she liked, made eye contact, and smiled.

He heard a woman's amplified voice and motioned for James and Bailey to follow him to the grandstand. Kate wore an apron over her business suit and spoke into a wireless microphone. She introduced each kid and dessert and joked about her failing diet as she sampled each entry. Once she was done, she met with the other judges and handed out ribbons. One kid bolted offstage without her ribbon, and Kate had to call her back.

After the judging ended, Adam called Kate on her phone.

"You're really good at this," he said. "If the next election were held today, you would win in a landslide. Are you hungry?"

"Starving. Eating all this sugar makes me ravenous. Where are you?"

"In the back under the big pine tree."

She looked up. He was taller than most, and their eyes met over the crowd.

"What's that grin for?" she asked.

"Get within reach and I'll show you."

She made a show of checking the number on her phone. "Who is this again?"

———

They met in front of the stage. Kate smiled at Bailey and James and ruffled Mop's ears.

"What are you in the mood for?" Adam asked.

"I want something healthy. C'mon." She took Adam's arm and led him through the crowds. People smiled as they went by and whispered once they'd passed. Adam felt odd being the subject of so much attention. They reached a food truck he hadn't noticed before. Kate ordered for them: stuffed peppers, kale salad with lime dressing, and Persian peas with dates and onions. Mop got four plain hamburgers from the truck next door.

James had staked out an empty table. Apologizing for having to dine and dash, Kate said that she still had the main awards ceremony to get through. She kissed Adam on the cheek and hurried away.

"What?" Adam demanded.

"If you smile anymore, your face is going to crack," James said.

"I smile like this all the time."

"You haven't smiled this much in your entire life."

Adam started to disagree, but his phone buzzed with a text. Bailey had taken a picture of Kate and him smiling at each other. His phone buzzed again. Another picture, another smile. It buzzed again and again. He swiped through the pictures and stopped protesting.

"I'm going to make an album," Bailey said, fingers moving on her screen. "I'll send everyone the link."

"Don't!" he said.

She stuck out her tongue.

They finished their food and wandered through the trucks and past the bounce houses and the "train ride" where wooden train cars had been hooked up to a tractor. The crowd at the grandstand was bigger than it had been at the kids' dessert contest. There were a lot of categories, and each had three winners, so it took a while to hand out the awards. Bailey took Mop with her to talk with some of her friends. James got a phone call and moved away where it was quieter.

Adam stepped under the grandstand to wait for Kate to finish. A cop saw him and moved to cut him off, but then Joan, Kate's assistant, hurried over.

"Mr. Barnett! Kate said you would probably drop by. I have your pass."

She put a VIP lanyard over his head. The cop nodded and stepped back by the stairs. The crowd erupted into cheers as another winner was announced. Adam's phone buzzed again. It was a link to Bailey's photo album. She had been busy. There were thirty-four pictures, most with him putting food in his mouth. He opened the last one and groaned.

"The two of you make a cute couple," Joan said, seeing his screen.

"Kate's cute. I'm lucky."

Joan laughed. "Kate said you're funny."

She excused herself and went to help Kate. Adam waited by himself. The grandstand had been built under the trees and blocked most of the light. Even though there were a lot of people nearby, it was quiet under the stage. He listened to Kate's voice and felt a tingle of anticipation.

A bush rustled. The hairs on the back of Adam's neck stood up. He spun to search the forest behind the park. A shape slid stealthily from one bush to another. All the fears of the Nightmare came roaring back. He stiffened, trying to see what was pursuing him. The darkness filled with sudden, blinding light. He staggered backwards and smacked his head on a stage support.

"Darn it," he snapped. He heard Bailey's laugh and dialed his phone. "Quit taking my picture, or you're grounded for the rest of your short life!"

"Been there, done that!" Bailey chirped and hung up.

The awards ended. Kate ran lightly down the steps. She saw him and stopped at the expression on his face.

"Are you all right?"

He clicked on the link on his phone and wordlessly handed it to her. Bailey had turned their photographs into a slideshow video complete with music and transitions featuring hearts, butterflies, puppies, and kittens.

"Did she just do this?" Kate asked.

"Give her a phone, and she'll take over the world."

Kate handed the phone back and searched his face. "So, um, does all this make you, ah, nervous?"

"Actually, it gives me a headache. Bailey just blinded me taking another picture, and I cracked my head on a post. I might lose my memory again." He peered at her. "Mom? Is that you? When did you get so pretty?"

Kate smacked his arm. "You're a nut."

Adam's phone buzzed with a call. It was James.

"I just got off the phone with Monica," he said. "She wants to get together and talk."

"About what?"

"She told me where Mop came from and what he is, and says it's urgent."

"Not so urgent we can't get dessert," Kate said.

CHAPTER 30

"Sorry about the delay," Agent Terrance shouted to Major Jacobson over the scream of the Black Hawk's engines. "We had to wait for a helo to become available."

"I tried calling Adam Barnett," Jacobson said, holding onto his armored seat. "The shop phone's going to voicemail. Hopefully, he's still alive."

"He is." Terrance brought out a tablet with a map of Defiance, Arizona and pointed to a red string of letters and numbers on the screen. "This is a signal tracker law enforcement uses to find cell phones. Every cell phone has a unique identifying MAC address that allows it to communicate with the cell towers."

Jacobson watched Barnett's phone move on the map. "What's at the top of Black Canyon?"

"It's a dead end. The Black Mansion's up there but that's it."

"Then that's our destination."

The helicopter raced east through the mountains. As they flew, Jacobson glanced around, surprised to see Lieutenant Day sitting stoically in her armored seat. One hand gripped her rifle, the other rested casually by her pistol. None of her team spoke. There were no smiles or laughter or any of the things that soldiers did when traveling. They stared wordlessly straight ahead, like robots. Startled, he realized that these must all be Dr. Kumar's successes.

Jacobson's cell phone rang. He removed it from his pocket.

"Major, this is Colonel Beardsley," his commanding officer said. "Can you talk?"

Jacobson sat up. Beardsley was a combat commander and rarely used his formal rank. When he did, it was usually trouble. Jacobson angled his mouth toward the open doorway so no one could read his lips.

"I'm in a helo, sir. I'm working with the FBI to track down the hostiles at Biodosius and O'Dell's missing asset."

There was a moment of silence as his words were transmitted to Virginia.

"That's what I wanted to talk with you about," Beardsley said. "I've received a disturbing call about your investigation. An Admiral McDermott phoned me and demanded to know if you made it a habit of assaulting civilians."

Jacobson didn't reply for a moment. "Excuse me, sir?"

"Admiral McDermott called and asked me if you made a habit of assaulting civilians. I told him no, and he sent me surveillance video of you pushing Dr. Kumar against a wall. The video has you threatening her and allegedly forcing her to disclose information you are not cleared to receive. The video is highly disturbing."

Jacobson tried to recall exactly what he had done to Dr. Kumar. He had stepped in front of her, but he hadn't touched her. There was no reason to use force. He'd have to check the helmet cam of his interview to make sure. With O'Dell injured from the attack in the mining camp and his staff dead, no one had asked him for his cam. He would have to make sure that no one took it from him.

"I'm assuming you had a good reason for your actions?"

"I didn't physically assault her, sir. I didn't even touch her. As far as forcing her to disclose classified information, General O'Dell gave me specific orders to find out what was going on at Biodosius and who the killers were. As part of those orders, I interviewed Dr. Kumar about her involvement in the attacks. She eventually confirmed that Admiral McDermott's patients were responsible for the deaths at Biodosius."

"Patients?"

"The killers are Admiral McDermott's patients. His research causes dangerous mental health instability."

"The video doesn't show any patients. It only shows you forcing Dr. Kumar against a wall."

"I would have to see the video to comment, sir. Admiral McDermott has teams of technicians. He could easily send you video that makes it look like I'm on vacation at Disneyland."

"You're accusing Admiral McDermott of falsifying the video?"

"No, sir. I'm just saying I would have to see the video before I can comment. You know what kind of man I am, sir, and what my word means. I did not touch her."

"Admiral McDermott is claiming otherwise."

"Sir, he is medically experimenting on American citizens with no oversight. He is directly responsible for what happened at Biodosius."

Beardsley drew in a breath. "He will adamantly disagree with your conclusion."

"Yes, sir. That's why the FBI should investigate."

"Be that as it may, I'm not sure you understand the severity of the situation. If you're found guilty of coercing a government employee to divulge classified information, you could and should go to prison."

"Dr. Kumar didn't disclose anything more than she was authorized to disclose. I didn't cross the line."

Beardsley spoke with someone in his office and then got back on the phone. His voice changed in tone as he resumed speaking.

"I'm not sure what to make of this, Major," he said. "You're one of the finest officers I have ever worked with. You've always acted with honor and professionalism. Why would McDermott try to discredit you?"

"He's afraid of what I know. He's afraid of what will happen when I tell the FBI what he's doing. He wants to silence me."

"He wants more than that, I'm afraid. He wants you brought up on charges. Even if you're right and he's wrong, no one will win. It will give the Rangers a black eye, and the people funding McDermott will keep targeting you."

So McDermott wasn't acting alone. "What do you suggest, sir?"

Beardsley didn't answer right away, and when he did, his voice sounded tired. "You've been up for promotion for years. Accept the promotion and go on paid leave pending a review. Given the proper assurances of confidentiality, I might be able to make this go away."

Jacobson sucked in a breath. "You want me to retire?"

"You might not have a choice. McDermott is adamant about having you charged. The only reason you aren't being thrown in the brig until this is straightened out is because I don't understand what happened and why. They want me to blindly act, and I won't do it. Not with someone with your service record."

"What about General O'Dell?"

"He's not answering my calls."

Dead, too? Jacobson tried to keep the anger out of his voice. He needed to review the video from his helmet cam before he could say anything definite, but he would never assault an unarmed woman half his size or force her to divulge classified information. He had pressed her to disclose the truth, but he hadn't touched her. He thought about telling Beardsley he had video proof of what was going on in the basement of Biodosius but didn't. His cell phone wasn't secure, and Day and her team were listening. McDermott could impound the web cam and then he could claim whatever he wanted.

"In exchange for my silence, they'll graciously let me keep my pension? Great. Just great. There are civilian lives at stake, sir. The killers are out in the population. Someone has got to do something, or the killing won't stop."

"That's not your job any longer. McDermott will get someone to assume your duties. Your involvement is over."

So that was it. He was done.

"How much leave do you have?" Beardsley asked.

Jacobson slumped into his seat and switched his phone to his other ear.

"I don't know, sir. I haven't kept track. I didn't have a reason to look."

"When can you return to Williams Air Force Base?"

"In a few hours. I'm headed to a small town in Arizona with the FBI and two squads of McDermott's men. If the killers are pursuing O'Dell's asset, my guess is they'll be there, too."

"Fine. Let McDermott deal with them. Once you're at Williams, take a commercial airline home. Don't wait for a military flight. There are lots of things about this that bother me. I tried to ask questions about what's going on, and I've never seen doors slam so fast."

"Yes, sir."

"We'll talk when you get here."

Beardsley hung up.

Averting his eyes from Lieutenant Day's, Jacobson slipped his phone in his pocket and settled back in his seat. There was only one thing that made sense about McDermott filing a complaint. Jacobson knew too much. He knew that servicemen and women were being experimented on and that these experiments permanently changed their nervous systems and brains. Jacobson knew enough to get McDermott and those who funded him put away for the rest of their lives. Discrediting him was only their first step. What else would they do to keep that information from getting out? And if they were coming after him, who else was in danger? Terrance, the FBI agent, and Adam

Barnett. Even if Beardsley wanted him to watch his step, he couldn't very well do that without giving Terrance and Adam fair warning. This was some kind of rogue operation, and he didn't know how far up the chain of command it went. He yawned and wiped a hand over his face, erasing whatever emotion might have leaked out.

"You, okay, sir?" Lieutenant Day asked.

"Helos make me nervous," he said. "Don't know if you noticed."

"I thought they might," she said. "But don't worry. I've got your back."

Under the circumstances, that wasn't reassuring.

CHAPTER 31

As Adam, Kate, James, Bailey, and Mop left the festival and drove up Black Canyon Road, the high canyon walls narrowed. James had suggested that Monica meet them at the deserted Black Mansion. Given that the town was overrun with tourists, James had told Adam, he figured the mansion was the only place they could have a private conversation. Adam had agreed, and was eager to find out what Monica had to say.

James, Bailey, and Mop occupied the truck's cramped back seat. Kate and Adam sat in the front. As Adam drove, he thought about Monica's brief phone explanation—that Mop was a government research animal. Of course, James didn't yet have all the details and he hadn't seen Mop's full capabilities, but he'd been relieved to know Mop wasn't vicious.

Adam didn't want the dog to go back to a lab. Mop had saved his life twice, three times if he counted getting his truck from the Salt River in the Hawes Trail System. Adam hadn't seen anything at the river, but he had felt an uneasiness that gave him an adrenaline rush. Whatever had been hiding in the trees had been baiting him. He didn't know who or what had killed the horse, but something had torn it apart.

He touched the pistol in his belt holster and pulled down the hem of his shirt. No point in making people worry. Hidden under his pickup's seat was his Browning automatic shotgun loaded with magnums. The first two times he had encountered the Nightmare, he had been unarmed and defenseless. It wasn't going to be that way again, and certainly not with Kate and Bailey present.

Kate gave him a sideways glance from the passenger seat and lowered her voice. "Bailey's attached to Mop. She's going to be crushed if you're forced to give him back."

"No one wants Mop to go back. He could charm the spots off a leopard."

"Maybe you could get another dog."

"That would be easier than trying to return all his stuff. Will Walmart accept a used pooper scooper?"

She smiled and rested a hand on his thigh.

Two miles up the canyon, he reached the ten-foot stone wall and metal gate that marked the edge of the Black estate. He turned right onto a mine access road and bumped past clumps of ponderosa, aspen, and oak. At the end of the road, he parked by the upper entrance to the Silent Black Mine with its large black-and-yellow sign warning of hazardous levels of carbon monoxide.

He helped Kate out of the truck and removed the cinnamon rolls and ice cream they'd brought from the festival. Defiance Mountain towered above them in the early evening sky. Far below, the brightly lit town spread out over the hills.

"This is an odd place to meet," Kate said, looking around. "Not many people come up here."

"Two men tried to kill Monica," James said. "She wanted to go someplace she wouldn't be kidnapped."

Adam looked up at the many mine shafts pecked in the canyon

walls, every butte and spire honeycombed with suffering and blood. Black and his army of enforcers had thrown claim-jumpers down mine shafts to their deaths, their blood streaming down onto the skeletons of those who had gone before. Luckily, the mansion didn't have that history. It should be safe.

"The unofficial entrance is just down the road," he said, taking Kate's hand.

"Glad I wore tennis shoes," she said.

"Yeah." He held up a foot. "My new shoes are already killing me, and it's not like we're going in by the front door."

"What do you mean?"

"You'll see."

He reached the perimeter of the estate. A few years back, falling boulders had smashed a hole in the estate's high wall. Turning sideways, he slipped through the gap, and, on hands and knees, crawled over the biggest boulder. He dropped down on the other side. Bailey and James followed but Kate stopped.

"I don't know about this, Adam. The last thing I need is to get arrested for trespassing. The Black Family Trust won't allow anyone inside the estate, even to take pictures."

"We're not going in the house. We're just going to talk to Monica and leave."

Kate didn't move. "I know I'm going to regret this."

She reached out a hand, and he helped her through the gap. Mop vaulted through the opening. Nose to the ground, the dog loped across the open ground and chased a squirrel up a tree.

Adam pointed out a half-hidden air shaft—a metal grate in a lawn that had turned to weeds. "That's one of the air vents for the Silent Black Mine. There's a myth that carbon monoxide sinks, but it doesn't. It mixes with air. Back in the day, they didn't have carbon monoxide detectors, so Black just dug shafts and hoped for the best. He kept losing miners and eventually gave up after the government threatened legal action."

He skirted the vent and cut through an overgrown rose garden, calling back to James, Bailey, and Kate that at one time, the estate had had one of the largest, most ornate, rose gardens in the United States.

"You could be a tour guide," Bailey said.

"It'd be perfect for the Creep Tour," Kate said.

"It is kind of creepy," James said, looking around. "The trees. The shadows. I should have brought a flashlight."

Adam regretted that he hadn't told James to bring a weapon. Of course, if he'd told his brother why, James would have wanted the entire story.

They crossed the overgrown lawn and stopped at the front of the house. Black had built it to show off his wealth, and even after a hundred years, it was still beautiful. Built of white brick with limestone quoins worked into the corners, the mansion's center section rose five stories. Two three-story wings flanked it.

"I've always wanted to come up here, but the Black family refused to let anyone visit," Kate said. "I can't believe such a horrible man could build such a beautiful place."

"Black said miners were cheaper than timber and treated his men like trash," Adam said. "Why build a safe mine when he didn't have to? Anyone who complained would disappear or have a fatal accident. The same for mine inspectors, labor organizers, and politicians he didn't like. He threw them down the mines, and they were never seen again."

The house hadn't been lived in since the seventies. Shingles had blown off the steep slate roof, and during the last commodity boom, thieves had stripped off the copper gutters. Birds nested in the eaves. Looking through the front windows, Adam saw water stains on the ceiling, but the stunning white marble floor and double curved staircase was still magnificent. Miraculously, the entry hall's huge crystal chandelier, once the grandest in all the Southwest, remained.

"As long as we're here, let's look around," James said.

"Where's Monica?" Adam said.

"Maybe around back," James said, taking Bailey's hand.

Adam turned toward the lawn, the rose garden, the trees, and the estate's high wall. Light was dropping behind the peaks, and he didn't want to be here after dark.

Around back on the stone terrace, three-story Palladian windows gave views of the mansion's stunning ballroom.

Kate rushed to a window and cupped her hands against the glass. "Oh, look! The grand ballroom! Can you imagine what this looked like when it was taken care of? Vivian Black was famous for her parties. The dances must have been amazing."

Smiling, she turned toward Adam and held out her hands. "Care to dance, sir?"

He smiled and took her hand. She spun gracefully and did a backwards dip into his arms. One of her shoes came off, and Mop trotted over to retrieve it.

"You do know that Mop likes shoes," Adam said, "the smellier the better."

She pushed him away. "Are you implying something?"

Mop put down the shoe and nudged it with his nose. Kate slipped her foot back in.

"He thinks you're Cinderella," Bailey said.

Kate smiled. "At least one dog around here knows how to score points with the ladies." She ruffled Mop's ears. "What are you doing next Saturday night? Want to go to the symphony?"

Mop barked.

"Looks like you have a date," Adam said.

Adam checked his watch and put Bailey's cinnamon rolls on an old metal patio table by the back door. He was almost finished passing out paper plates, plastic utensils, and cinnamon rolls when Mop barked, ears up, then bolted past. Adam grabbed Mop's collar with one hand and abruptly found himself skiing across the brittle grass.

Wearing jeans and a blue sleeveless top, Monica stepped out of the trees. The last time Adam had seen her, she'd been wearing his sweats and basketball shoes and looked half-drowned, but now her hair had been neatly styled. She was much prettier than he remembered.

Her face lit up in a smile.

"Coloso!" she cried, holding out her arms and sinking to one knee. "Come here, you wonderful dog! You'd better not growl at me like you did in the bike shop, or I won't let you have your ball!"

Mop's tail wagged so hard it felt like a weed whacker hitting Adam's leg. He let go of the collar, and Mop leapt and cavorted around Monica.

"Okay! Okay! I have it right here!" Monica dug into her purse and brought out a tennis ball. She threw it across the grass. Mop bolted after it, grabbed it before it had stopped rolling, and ran back. He dropped the ball in front of Monica, and she threw it again. He fetched it, but this time took it over to Bailey and dropped it.

Bailey looked as if she were about to cry. "You're her dog?" she whispered. "You belong to *her*?"

Mop whined and pawed at the ball. Bailey kicked it away. Mop gave chase, grabbed it, and brought it back. Bailey threw it into the trees. Mop sprinted after it, found the ball, and ran back, dropping it at her feet. She threw it again and finally smiled.

Monica gave James a hug then turned to Adam. "Thank you for letting me use your car. I'm sorry I took it without permission."

"That's okay." He removed her check from his pocket. "This is yours."

"Are you sure?"

"Yes."

"Want some dessert?" James asked. "We have cinnamon rolls and ice cream from the festival. We can eat while we talk."

Monica smiled, meeting James's eyes. "That would be nice."

They sat down at the table. James introduced Kate and Bailey, and Kate handed out spoons and paper bowls. The ice cream had melted, so they poured it onto the cinnamon rolls.

Mop dropped his ball under the table and turned mournful eyes on Monica until she gave him a piece of her roll.

"What are we supposed to call him?" Bailey asked. "Mop or Coloso?"

"Ask him," Monica said. "He'll tell you."

"What's your name?" Bailey asked. "Is it Coloso?"

Mop didn't respond.

"Is your name Mop?"

He barked.

"See, you both just figured out how to communicate," Monica said.

"Can you go through what you told James earlier?" Adam asked. "I would like to hear it from the beginning."

Monica talked as she ate, telling them of her work at Biodosius, the accident, her escape and flight, how she had been grabbed at the restaurant in Show Low and thrown off the bridge, and how James had saved her life.

"I can't begin to tell you how shocked I was to see Coloso, I mean Mop, in your bike shop," she said, licking her spoon. "I think we were both surprised."

"Why would the government experiment on a dog?" James asked.

"There's a huge demand for service dogs. Service dogs take years and thousands of dollars to train. Dogs as intelligent as Mop will make the process much faster and easier."

Adam had known there was something unusual about Mop but hadn't really put the clues together. "How smart is he?"

"I don't know. Nobody does. We still don't know what makes one person smarter than another, let alone what makes a smarter dog. We have some ideas but that's all. He scored much higher than a normal dog on some tests. On others, especially in the past six months or so, he's just like any other dog. We don't know why his scores dropped. It took him less than two months to do everything the military wanted for a service animal. For most dogs, it would have taken years. We got a lot of funding because of him. But to answer your question, I don't know how intelligent he is. There's no IQ test for dogs."

"I know a way of finding out," Adam said.

"How?"

He turned to Mop. "If a dog has five bones and someone takes away all five of them, what do you have?"

Bailey glared. "Don't answer him, Mop! It's a trick question. He wants you to say zero bones, but the real answer is an unhappy dog. 'Dad jokes' are bad, but 'uncle jokes' are even worse!"

"I'm just trying to see how smart he is."

"He's smart enough not to answer your questions. Aren't you, Mop?"

Mop barked.

"He's got you there," Kate observed. She stood and gathered the trash. "Not being compulsive," she said. "Just taking away the evidence we were here."

The sun had gone down behind the mountains, and there was a hush to the air. Bats flitted acrobatically through the twilight.

"How many dogs were you working with before the accident?" Kate asked.

"There were three in Scottsdale," Monica said. "There are more at other sites. But none of them are like Mop. He's a miracle."

"Can't they just breed more of him?"

"No, we modified his embryo, but we didn't permanently modify his DNA. He can't pass on his intelligence. If we breed him, we'll just get a normal dog. His puppies will be wonderful dogs but that's all they'll be."

"There's got to be a way that Mop doesn't have to go back," Kate said. "He's found a family who loves him."

"Before the accident, I was working on modifying his sperm, so his offspring will inherit his intelligence. We were just about to start another round of breeding. If the research works, we won't need him any longer. After the deaths at the lab though, I don't know if that's going to happen. I wouldn't be surprised if they shut the whole place down. After they tried to kill me, I thought maybe they were coming after anyone associated with the dog. I wanted to warn you to keep him out of site." She turned and faced Adam. "So, I have a question for you. How did you find him?"

"I didn't find him. He found me." Adam told her how Mop had licked the mud off his hands at the mining camp. Monica kept asking more questions, and Adam hesitantly described what he had heard and seen, including the Nightmare. James and Bailey stared in shock. Kate looked stricken.

"I didn't say anything about it before because I'm still not sure what I saw," he told Monica. "It was dark and rainy, and I thought I might have been imagining things. Whatever it was, it howled and kept up with the truck. I was going forty miles an hour."

"You should have told that to the neurologist!" Kate said. "He can't help you if you keep critical information from him! Hallucinations could be a symptom of something serious!"

"I wasn't hallucinating. I can prove it."

"How?"

He swiped through the pictures on his phone until he found a picture of the muddy footprints at the Salt River.

"I took this Saturday afternoon when I went to get my truck," he said, handing the phone across. "The ground had dried after the rain, but it was still muddy under my truck. While I was putting my truck on the car hauler, Mop ran off. I went looking for him and found him at the river near a dead horse. Something had gutted it. When I came back to the car hauler, those footprints were in the mud. The same footprints were at the mining camp."

"And you're sure they weren't there before you moved your truck?" James asked.

"How could there be footprints *under* my truck? The person who left them would have to be a foot tall."

"That makes complete sense," Bailey said.

Kate and James looked at each other.

Monica examined the pictures. "There are a lot of different research projects going on that I don't have access to, but I heard rumors, especially after Admiral McDermott started working with the military. I think they fund most of the projects at the lab."

"You think the military has something to do with what Adam saw?" Kate asked.

Monica shrugged. "A lot of the projects seem fairly mundane at first, but everything has a military application. The military isn't going to use their weapons' budgets on medical research unless it benefits them. I heard rumors about McDermott's other projects. There are six research labs in my building's basement. I only had access to Lab 2. Maybe one of the other labs was working on something that caused the accident."

"But that still doesn't answer why someone is running around in their bare feet," Adam said, "or how the same footprints happened to be at the mining camp *and* at the river. If we don't figure out why someone's missing their shoes, Kate's going to check me into a psychiatric hospital with instructions to medicate me heavily. Look at her. She's already got her phone out."

Kate snorted but put down her phone.

"I certainly don't have all the answers," Monica replied. "You don't remember anything from before you got struck by lightning?"

"No. I went to bed on Thursday night and woke up Saturday

morning with electricity going up and down my arms. I didn't know where I was, how I got there, or who Mop was."

"You have no idea how you found him?"

"None."

She let out a frustrated sigh.

"Why don't we ask Mop what happened?" While Bailey listened, she had been playing hide and seek with the tennis ball. She switched it quickly from hand to hand, then hid it behind her on the chair or between her legs. Mop always found it. "Even if you can't remember, I bet he can."

"How can he tell us what happened?" James asked.

"Ask him the right questions, and he'll tell you. He's much smarter than anyone realizes."

James and Adam exchanged dubious glances.

Bailey sighed and borrowed a pen from Kate. On a napkin, she wrote MOP. On another napkin, she wrote DAD. She put the napkins on the ground.

"Mop, remember how I showed you your name yesterday? Which one is it?"

Mop looked at the napkins, glanced at Monica, then backed away.

"Offer him food," Adam suggested. "He'll read the dictionary backwards for a chicken nugget."

Bailey glared at Adam then turned back to the dog.

"What's your name?" Bailey asked again.

Mop grabbed his tennis ball and dropped it in front of her. She ignored it. He barked and pawed at the ball. She didn't move. He grabbed the ball and ran around her.

"I'm not sure this is working," Monica said.

Adam watched Mop's evasive behavior and abruptly understood. At first glance, anyone would think that Mop simply wanted to play with the ball like a normal dog. But Adam had seen this behavior before when he had tried to get Mop to open the old Chevy's glovebox and look for a pair of sunglasses. Mop had opened the glovebox to show him the likely place for a map without being asked, but when Adam asked him to open the glovebox for the glasses, Mop had ignored him. There had been dozens of times since then that Mop had shown his exceptional intelligence, but each time Adam had tried to investigate further, Mop had concealed how smart he was by simply acting like, well, a dog.

It wasn't that Mop *couldn't* answer the question. He didn't *want* to answer it. Somewhere along the way, Mop had learned to hide his true capabilities. He'd spent his life in a cage, his only interaction with trainers who treated him like a lab animal. He was expendable. He must have grown tired of constantly being tested.

Ears cocked, Mop suddenly turned toward the trees. He took a step forward, listening. He whined and trembled and lowered his tail. Adam jumped to his feet. In the gathering gloom of early evening, it was difficult to see across the brittle grass and into the shadows cast by the trees.

"What's wrong, boy? Is something there?"

Mop whimpered.

Adam pulled his gun from beneath his shirt. "Is it the Nightmare?"

Mop sniffed the air. He shivered again.

Monica's phone rang. She removed it from her purse and put it to her ear. She listened, and the blood drained from her face.

"There's a military helicopter coming this way! I have to go!"

"What? Who's on the phone?" James demanded.

"My friend Victoria. She's watching from up on the mountain."

"Why?"

"There are people trying to kill me, remember? She's there as a precaution."

Mop barked and ran onto the grass.

Adam put away his pistol. "James, get Monica and Bailey out of here. Work your way back to my truck. My shotgun's under the front seat. If you can't get to the truck, take Buford's Bypass to Hidden Canyon and go to the bike shop."

"What about you and Kate?" James asked.

"They don't want us. Go!"

Mop raced across the lawn. The three people and the dog had barely disappeared when Adam heard the booming *thrum, thrum, thrum* of an approaching helicopter. A black shape, like a huge dragon-fly, roared across the mountain. It skimmed over the treetops, rotors flattening the pine needles, and thundered over their heads. Adam, heart pounding, watched it bank and circle the house. Soldiers carrying assault rifles and wearing body armor sat inside. The helicopter hovered above the lawn, then slowly sat down.

A soldier in full combat gear and another man wearing a black FBI windbreaker jumped out. Both men carried rifles. As soon as they were out from under the rotors, the helicopter's engines bellowed, and it lifted off.

The man in the FBI windbreaker stepped forward and reached out a hand. "I'm sorry to interrupt dinner, folks," he said. "I'm Special Agent Terrance. This is Major Blain Jacobson of the Army Rangers." His gaze shifted to Adam. "Are you Adam Barnett?"

Adam blinked. He had been expecting them to be after Monica or Mop. What did they want with him?

"What's this about, agent?" Kate asked quickly. "I'm Mr. Barnett's lawyer."

Terrance smiled. "I know who you are, Mayor Lansing. We're here because your lives are in danger."

So, Monica was right, Adam thought.

CHAPTER 32

Terrance removed a sheet of paper from his pocket and handed it across. It was a wanted poster for a missing dog. The dog in the picture looked like Mop.

"We're in danger because of a dog?" Kate asked. "Is the animal dangerous?"

"No, the dog is not dangerous. However, there are other concerns about the animal, and that's why we're here."

"What concerns?" Adam asked.

"Do you mind if we sit down? It'll take a few minutes to explain."

Were these guys going to call back the chopper and take him in for questioning? If they wanted to protect him, then why were they sitting here, out in the open, and not in some guarded safe house? Maybe he could take down Terrance, grab Kate's hand, and run like hell, but then what about Jacobson?

Rifle held across his chest and boots planted firmly on the paving stones, helmet low on his forehead, Jacobson stood watching the trees. He was taller than Adam, and his equipment made him look heavier. He also exuded an unsettling, lethal competency that gave Adam pause. He was not someone to mess with. It was one thing to get in a fist fight with Mike Benedict, but another altogether to court disaster by fighting a highly trained Army Ranger.

Terrance, his eyes dark and watchful, leaned his rifle against the table and sat.

Warily, Adam motioned for Kate to sit, too.

"Are y'all familiar with the events at a research lab in North Scottsdale?" Terrance asked. "It's been in the news."

"The phone at my shop's been ringing off the hook," Adam said. "Bikers are angry and want to know why the western half of the national forest has been closed."

"It's because of what happened at Biodosius, and there's been an assault in Defiance that has similar characteristics. Do you know Paul Moody?"

Adam stiffened. "Yes, he's a friend of mine. He owns a garage in town. Why?"

"Mr. Moody was attacked this afternoon. He was airlifted to Phoenix in critical condition."

"No!" Adam said.

"Why would someone attack Paul?" Kate asked.

"In the back of Mr. Moody's garage," Terrance said, turning to Adam, "we found an old Chevy truck. We believe you drove it to Defiance. We believe someone is looking for you, Mr. Barnett."

Mind turning, Adam stared at Terrance in growing dismay. He thought back to the tracks outside the car hauler at the Hawes trailhead. Had the Nightmare gotten Paul's information off the truck's door? Was that why he'd been attacked?

Adam reached for his phone. Terrance stiffened, his hand darting toward the pistol on his hip. Jacobson snapped up his rifle. Adam abruptly found both weapons pointed at his chest. That close, the dark mouth of the rifle looked as big around as the moon. He stopped and slowly held up his phone.

"I was about to call Paul's folks. Do you know what hospital he's been taken to?"

Terrance lowered his pistol. Without any change of expression, Jacobson went back to watching the trees.

"No," Terrance said. "We haven't spoken with the investigating officers. We came directly here because we didn't want the same thing to happen to you."

"Why would anyone come after Adam?" Kate asked. "He hasn't hurt anyone."

"No, but we think he helped someone."

Terrance waited.

Kate glanced again at Adam

Adam shrugged.

"Maybe it would be better if you started at the beginning," she told Terrance.

The FBI agent shifted on his seat. "Major Jacobson and I were brought in to assist the military with what happened at Biodosius Friday night. As part of that investigation, we've also been trying to locate a missing medical research animal that escaped the facility. The dog is used in cancer research and is extremely valuable. We've been looking for the dog and the killers ever since."

"You believe the missing dog has put Adam in danger?"

"Yes."

"As a matter of fact, I know you're in danger," Major Jacobson said, his eyes darting from Adam to the trees. "We all are. You, me, maybe even Agent Terrance. And not just because of what happened to Paul Moody. We need to put our heads together."

Kate examined the poster again. "Do you have a better picture? Retrievers are popular dogs. This looks a lot like my mother's dog."

"Here's a security video of the animal. Maybe it will help."

Terrance handed his phone across. Adam and Kate watched Mop help a man across a parking lot to a car. The man had blood under one armpit and clutched the ruff of fur on Mop's neck.

"The man's bleeding," Kate said. "Did the dog attack him?"

"No. The man was a scientist at Biodosius. We think he was wounded inside the facility, but he managed to escape before the facility lost power. He drove his SUV from Scottsdale to East Mesa where he crashed into a ravine by the Hawes trails. He owns a boat at Saguaro Lake. We think he was headed there when he crashed." Terrance turned his penetrating blue eyes on Adam. "Are you familiar with the area?"

"Yes. I go mountain biking there, usually during the winter when it's cold here. I was there Friday morning testing a new carbon bike frame."

"We found mountain biking tire tracks by Dr. Baltimore's wrecked SUV. A mountain biker and the dog left the accident and went up into the mountains. They were pursued by the killers. Did you see the accident while you were there?"

Adam waited for a missing memory to surface, but it didn't. He drew in a frustrated breath. His hands trembled. "Maybe I've repressed it, but no, nothing comes to me. I have a big time gap in my memory."

"Adam was struck by lightning Saturday morning up in the mountains," Kate explained before Terrance could ask. "The lightning hit him in the shoulder and exited out of his foot. He went to an urgent care facility and was given a referral to see a neurologist that specializes in head injuries. We drove down to Scottsdale this morning. The neurologist thinks he had a seizure that affected his memory."

She opened her purse and removed Adam's patient information and handed it across. "You can contact the hospital. They want Adam back for more tests. They said he was lucky to have survived."

Terrance looked from Kate to Adam, eyes bright with suspicion. He lowered his head to examine the papers, flipped pages, and finally looked up. "Can I see your shoulder?"

Adam unbuttoned his shirt and carefully pulled it aside so that Terrance could see the bandage. He lifted his foot. "Did you want me to take off my shoe?"

"No, that won't be necessary. We can follow up later." He sighed and rubbed a hand over his face. He looked tired. "You don't remember what happened before the lightning strike?"

Adam quietly relayed how he had woken up in the mud with Mop licking his face. He reached the part about the Nightmare, and Terrance, eyes unblinking, leaned forward in his chair. Jacobson turned to listen, mouth flattening in a hard line. Adam finished by explaining how the Nightmare had been waiting for him when he'd gone back on Saturday afternoon to pick up his truck. He turned his phone and showed Terrance the muddy footprints by the car hauler's door.

"I have no idea who left those tracks," he said. "I know it sounds insane, but it really happened."

Terrance picked up Adam's phone and showed the tracks to Jacobson. Jacobson gave the forest a worried glance, and Adam suddenly understood what was going on.

"You've seen it, haven't you? That's why you're both so jumpy. The Nightmare's out there and you know it!" He barked out a laugh. "Sorry. It's just a relief to know I'm not nuts. Can you tell me what happened? Maybe it will help me remember. Please. I need to know."

Slowly, reluctantly, Terrance explained how they had gone to the wreck of Dr. Baltimore's SUV and how they had followed the bike's tire tracks, the dog, and the killers up to the mining camp.

"They were waiting for us," Terrance said bluntly. "They killed six men. We barely escaped with our lives. We followed your truck down to the Bush Highway, and we've been trying to find you and the dog ever since."

"How many of these killers escaped the hospital?" Kate asked.

"At least five. Possibly eight," Jacobson said.

Anger crossed Kate's face. "Why was I not told? The Taste of Defiance is going on! Hundreds of people are downtown right now! If there's a problem, I need to know!"

"We don't know if they're here or not," Terrance said. "All we know is that Paul Moody was attacked, and an old Chevy that we think you were driving was found at Mr. Moody's garage. We don't know why or even if the same individuals are involved."

Kate's voice took on a hard edge. "So, again, Agent, why exactly are you here? The US government does not send heavily armed soldiers out in attack helicopters unless there's a good reason. Why are the killers in my city?"

"That's a very good question." Terrance turned to Adam. "Any ideas?"

"Do the killers want the dog?"

"I don't know. We were hoping you could tell us."

"Yes," Jacobson said. "Please tell us what you know. And I've got some intel I also need to share."

Adam rubbed his temples. "I would tell you if I could. Not knowing what happened is driving me nuts." He gave Kate a sideways glance. "Sorry, it's driving *us* crazy. I don't think an hour has gone by that Kate hasn't demanded I return to the hospital for more tests. I'm sorry Paul got attacked. If I'd known someone would follow the car hauler back to his garage, I'd have warned him."

"Why didn't you call the police after what you saw in the mountains?" Terrance asked.

"Would they have believed me? I got struck by lightning and could barely remember my name. I had no idea where I was or why I was there. I had burns on my shoulder and foot. If I'd started raving about the boogie man chasing me, the cops would have put me in a room with no windows, and I would have been eating Jell-O with a plastic spoon."

Adam's phone abruptly rang. He didn't recognize the phone number. He swiped it away. A second later it rang again.

He answered. "Hello?"

"Adam, you need to get out of there now!" a woman snapped, talking so fast she bit off each word.

"What? Why?"

"Three SUVs just stopped at the gate to the Black Estate. Twelve men wearing ski masks and armed with AR-15s just got out. They're cutting through the gate's lock. I think they're the same people that tried to kill Monica. You need to—"

The call dropped.

"Hello? Hello?"

Adam checked his phone. No signal. He relayed the conversation to Terrance. Surprise crossed the agent's face, and he stood to talk to Jacobson. A high-velocity bullet whizzed through the air. Blood spurted from Terrance's shoulder, and he collapsed.

CHAPTER 33

Adam grabbed the metal patio table, tipped it on its side, and dove behind it, dragging Kate with him. She sprawled on the ground. Jacobson caught Terrance. Another bullet hissed. Terrance gasped, clutching his leg. Adam ran out from behind the table and grabbed Terrance by his free arm. Terrance moaned, and blood from a shoulder wound dripped down his Kevlar vest. A bullet clipped the metal table and sprayed fragments across the terrace.

"Stay as low as you can!" Jacobson snapped. "The shooter's on the ground in the trees. His bullets are rising. Keep the table between us and the house."

Bending over, Adam helped Terrance hop toward the door. The FBI agent was big, easily more than two hundred pounds, and their progress felt horribly slow.

"Jacobson to Bravo Six!" Jacobson, running toward them, called into his radio. He draped Terrance's arm around his neck. "Civilian officer down! Repeat, civilian officer down! Request immediate assistance and medical evac!"

No one answered.

"Acknowledge Six?"

A bullet caught the top of the metal table and, shrieking madly, grazed Jacobson's neck. Jacobson lurched sideways, let go of Terrance, and landed on his side. Adam staggered with the additional weight.

"What is it you were going to tell us?" Adam said.

"Later!" Jacobson slapped a palm against his neck. "Keep going!"

Kate darted out from behind the table and took Jacobson's place. Adam kicked the mansion's door open and dragged Terrance across the dusty marble floor. The ballroom's tall windows gave stunning views of Defiance Peak, but, unfortunately, the shooter, especially a shooter with a scope, could see their silhouettes. Long wooden banquet tables were pushed against one wall.

Adam kicked one onto its side and lowered Terrance to the floor. His shoulder and leg bled onto the dust-covered marble.

Jacobson ran inside and crouched beside them.

"How bad are you wounded?" Adam asked.

"I've had worse." Jacobson grimaced and withdrew an adhesive bandage from a pocket on his vest. He stripped off the wrapper and slapped it over the wound. "We need to find a defensible space. Do you know the layout of the house?"

Adam pointed to a door. "We're in a wing. That hall should lead to the main part of the house. We need to find the basement stairs."

"No good," Jacobson said. "They'll trap us down there."

"The basement has multiple exits," Adam said. "The south door facing the mountain has tree cover. If we hurry, they won't see us leave. Once we're in the trees, I can get us out of here."

"How do you know this?" Kate asked.

"A bike trail goes past that side of the house."

Adam and Jacobson lifted Terrance to his feet. The agent moaned with each step, and air whistled from his lungs. The marble floor cracked and popped with their weight, and their footsteps left a trail in the dust.

"They won't have any trouble following us," Adam told Jacobson.

"No help for it. Keep going."

Kate ran ahead, opening and closing doors. She found a staircase going down.

"I'll cover," Jacobson said.

The stairs were wood, and the treads squealed under their combined weight, forcing them to go two abreast. With Terrance's arm around him, Adam gripped the railing and helped the agent hop down. The basement windows faced east, away from the setting sun, so it was much darker than it had been in the ballroom. Boxes, tools, old furniture, and piles of junk stretched into the gloom.

"We're down," Adam called up.

"On my way," Jacobson said, and when he joined them, he took half of Terrance's weight.

"Go right," Adam said, pointing through the stacked furniture. "The south exit's that way."

They had gone halfway to the far end of the basement when the floor above them creaked.

"They're above us in the ballroom," Jacobson whispered. "Can you manage without me? I want to give them a reason not to follow."

Adam nodded. Kate took Jacobson's place and put a steadying arm around Terrance's waist. Jacobson lowered his night-vision goggles and moved silently back the way they'd come.

Kate kept up a steady stream of whispered encouragement to Terrance. Trying not to trip in the dark, Adam shuffled across the basement floor. They circled around a large, ornate Victorian playhouse. At one time it had probably been outside on the lawn. The roof was shingled, and painted wood siding covered the walls. Folding chairs had been piled against it. An old-fashioned Penny-Farthing bicycle leaned against the front.

The ceiling creaked again, the sounds getting louder and more pronounced. There was more than one shooter, which meant their pursuers could spread out. Adam hoped they didn't have a schematic of the building. If they knew about the south exit, there would be no escape.

A door creaked behind them. Something metallic rolled across the floor above. A thunderous boom went off, and Adam recoiled with the force of the explosion. A hundred years of dirt and debris rained down. Terrance's working leg buckled. He twisted sideways onto Kate. She stumbled, unable to bear his weight, and he slipped out of Adam's grasp.

An automatic weapon barked, the weapon surprisingly loud. Upstairs, shouts rang out.

Adam crouched next to Terrance. "How you doing?"

Terrance didn't stir. Adam rolled him onto his back. He put two fingers to his throat and found a pulse. "He's alive but unconscious."

"What do we do now?" Kate asked. "He's too heavy to carry."

The rifle barked again.

"We can't stay here. Once they realize we're in the basement, they'll close off the exits."

Adam put Terrance's good arm over his shoulder and lifted him into a sitting position. Then he pushed his shoulder into the agent's stomach and got to one knee. Unconscious, Terrance was even heavier than he had been coming down the stairs. Grunting, Adam pushed himself upright until Terrance was draped across his shoulder in a fireman's carry.

"I can't believe you just did that," Kate said.

Pain burned through Adam's foot. He could barely stand upright with the weight. The wound must have reopened. His eyes fell on the playhouse. He shuffled back to its door. Inside, a piece of carpet had been laid down. Small toys and what looked like old teen magazines were scattered about.

Adam lowered Terrance onto the carpet. Terrance moaned but didn't regain consciousness. Adam rolled the extra carpet around him in a makeshift blanket and backed out of the playhouse, shutting the door. He looked at their footprints in the dust then grabbed a nearby canvas drop cloth from a piece of furniture. He shook the cloth, scattering the dust.

"That'll have to do," he told Kate. "Are you okay?"

She gave him a shaky smile. "You really know how to show a woman a good time. First the fight at the wedding and now this. What's going to happen if we go out on a real date?"

"We'll have to find out," he said, limping toward the south exit. His foot was bleeding. He could feel it oozing into his sock.

He unlocked the door and turned the knob until it clicked and the bolt came free. Expecting the door would stick, he pulled with all his might. The door flew open and he staggered. The old house had been blasted into the bedrock and hadn't settled an inch.

Grabbing Kate's hand, he skip-ran out into the sheltering twilight. The pines were thick and grew close to the house. He didn't see anyone.

Behind him came Jacobson, ducking and looking over his shoulder as he ran.

"At least two of them won't be chasing us," he said. "Where's Terrance?"

"Unconscious," Adam said. "We hid him in a playhouse. We'll get help and come back for him."

Jacobson didn't look happy, but nodded. "Do you know how to get off the grounds?"

"Yes, follow me."

He led them into the surrounding pines. Adam waited for someone to shout or raise the alarm, but no one did. It was easier to see in the trees than it had been in the basement, but the light was fading fast. Adam headed uphill toward the mountain and the break in the wall. Stars appeared in the sky. A bat chasing an insect flitted past. A dog howled in the distance, and a rock clattered down the mountain.

Adam let go of Kate's hand and put a finger to his lips. "Shh," he said.

"Are they coming?" she whispered.

Rifle against his shoulder, Jacobson turned to face back the way they'd come.

Adam held up a hand. "I thought I heard something."

Other than the crickets, the night remained quiet. He let out a relieved breath and turned south again, dodging through trees. A second distant howl came from high up on the mountain. It rose in pitch, becoming a crying shriek, and Adam's heart thudded uncomfortably.

"What's wrong?" Kate whispered.

"The thing that chased me out of the mountains from the mining camp. It made that same sound. We need to hurry."

He pulled Kate into an awkward run. They reached the wall and turned west. In the darkness, Defiance Peak towered like the point of a menacing, black arrow. A bullet hissed through the trees and hit the wall. Adam ducked and kept running.

"We need an exit," Jacobson said. "We can't get pinned down."

Keeping the wall to his left, Adam scrambled through the pines. The boulders that had crashed through the wall loomed in front of him. He scrambled to the top and gave Kate a hand, then waited until she and Jacobson had slid down the other side and squeezed through the gap.

"This trail will take us to my truck," Adam told Jacobson once they were on the other side.

"They'll be watching the road," Jacobson said. "They might even be trying to flank around us from below. We'll need another way off the mountain."

Adam nodded and hobbled up the road, thinking through all the hundreds of trails that snaked across the foothills. What was the best way out of the canyon? Another howl echoed on the mountain, this time much closer. The back of his neck tingled.

They reached the bike trail. Up ahead, Adam saw his truck. So James hadn't taken it after all. He hoped James, Bailey, and Mop had already started up Buford's Bypass. If they could make it over the ridge without being seen, they'd probably be safe, and the Nightmare should leave them alone. It seemed intent on tracking him.

"I have a shotgun in my truck," he whispered to Jacobson. "Should I risk it?"

Jacobson turned his night vision goggles toward the truck. "Will your dome light turn on when you open the door?"

"Probably."

"Then leave it. You'll ruin your vision, and the light will show up like a flare to anyone watching. Is there another way out of here?"

Adam pointed to a trail snaking up the western canyon wall. "That trail goes over the top of the ridge to Hidden Canyon. Once we reach Hidden Canyon, we can take it down to Defiance."

"How fast can you both run?" Jacobson asked. "The men coming after us are trained professionals, and what's making that howling noise can outrun a SUV."

"You've seen it?" Adam asked. "You know what it is?"

Jacobson took a breath, obviously struggling with what he wanted to say.

"They're failed military experiments from something informally called the Simeon Process. The scientists at Biodosius are trying to find a way of stabilizing terminally injured soldiers. The drugs they use overload the patient's nervous systems and cause problems with the adrenal glands. With all that adrenaline flooding their systems, they're strong, fast, and inhumanly vicious. I've never seen anyone kill so efficiently."

"Is that why the men at the gate are trying to kill you?"

"I believe so. I found out more about what was going on than they wanted me to know."

"Are we in danger?" Kate asked.

"Probably, if they think you know," Jacobson said. "The first bullet should have hit me instead of Terrance, but I moved at the last second. Or, who knows, they might have orders to kill all of us."

Jacobson glanced down at Adam's injured foot. "How fast can you run?"

Adam grimaced.

"Okay, then," Jacobson said. "We have two or three minutes before they get here. We might have to risk it with your truck."

Leaves crackled in the trees. A large, dark shape barreled out the darkness. Jacobson hissed out a warning and lifted his rifle.

"Hold!" Adam said. "He's friendly!"

Mop bounded up to them. He stopped and growled at Jacobson, head and tail low, muscles gathering in his shoulders. With his black fur, it was almost impossible to see anything but the dog's teeth.

"Mop, he's a friend," Adam said.

Jacobson stared at the big dog, understanding creasing his weathered face, before he finally shook his head.

Ears cocked, Mop looked up the trail toward the mountain and whined. Adam put his hand on Mop's trembling back. James and Bailey stumbled out of the darkness.

"Did you bump into Monica?" Adam asked.

"Yeah," James said. "She didn't think it was a good idea for us to go with her in case the military is after her."

"What should we do?" Adam asked Jacobson. "We can't drive out of here with the men waiting by the gate. There's no way we can outrun them through the woods. Once they see where we're going, they'll just get in front of us."

Everyone looked wordlessly at everyone else. Adam scowled. They didn't have time for indecision. They needed something unexpected.

Something to even the odds. He searched the area for ideas. There was nothing nearby but trees, rocks, rusty pieces of abandoned equipment, and the entrance to the mine. The entrance was huge, at least a hundred feet wide and almost that high. A locked sliding gate blocked a smaller side entrance.

He grabbed an old piece of rebar from the ground, went over to the hazard sign, and broke it off. He threw it into the trees and then hurried to the gate, inserted the rebar through the gate's padlock, and levered the rebar down until the lock broke. He grabbed the gate's handle and wrenched it open. The metal screeched, the sound echoing off the canyon and the distant peak.

"They had to have heard that!" Jacobson said. "Now they know exactly where we are!"

Adam nodded. "Then we'd better hurry."

CHAPTER 34

Kill Jacobson! Like a loudspeaker in her ears, Dark's voice boomed through Victoria's mind. She gasped, holding her head. Never had Dark's voice been this loud. He was nearby. She didn't know how she knew it, but she did.

Two hundred yards above the mansion, she lay hidden in the rocks. She doubted that Dark or the armed men below had seen her. Unless she betrayed her position, they had no reason to look up, but she could see the men running through the trees and the two who remained behind by the SUVs. Her pickup was parked a half mile to the east, and she had tied strips of fabric to the trees so Monica could find her way. She and Monica had only come to warn Adam Barnett about the dog, not get into a fight.

She checked her silenced phone. Monica hadn't called. No way to know whether Monica had made it back to the truck. Victoria had told her not to wait around. Well, Boy Scout's motto, she told herself. Be prepared.

She unzipped her backpack. Inside was her Kevlar vest, a black ski mask, five hundred dollars in cash from Couch's safe, a medical kit, a hundred rounds of ammunition, and a disassembled AR-15.

She slid on the vest, pulled the ski mask over her hair, and got to work assembling the AR-15. It wasn't nearly as good as her .308 for shooting from a distance, but it was a fine weapon up close, and best of all, there was no connection between it and the narcos or Monica.

She finished assembling the rifle and used her binoculars again to try to locate Monica. She saw movement and turned her gaze back to the mansion just as the FBI agent standing next to Adam staggered and fell to the ground. Victoria waited. No gunshot. The shooter had used a suppressor. Only professionals had that kind of equipment. She searched the trees. Nothing moved. She wasn't surprised. A pro would bide his time.

She swallowed, trying to quell her rising fear. She had fought the narcos for years and always tried to have the upper hand, to pick her spots, to have the advantage. But now she had no idea who the men were or what they wanted. They could be from the government or from a professional paramilitary organization. That kind of talent meant she could easily get killed: a trained sniper could put a bullet in her head from a thousand yards away.

Getting involved was beyond stupid. She should return to her truck, wait for Monica, and get as far away as possible. But even as she told herself to leave, she knew she couldn't. Dark was close. She might not get another chance to find him. For three awful years, he had invaded her mind. He had somehow known she'd been at Couch's cabin and had told Couch to go outside and look for her. Did he know she was on the mountain now?

She pushed the doubts aside. She was not a victim. The narcos knew it, and Dark, whoever he was, would soon find out.

She shrugged into her backpack and picked her way down through the trees. She reached the estate's rear wall and turned east through the undergrowth. She could have climbed the wall and cut through the grounds to the SUVs, but she didn't want to risk a dust-up with the shooters inside the wall. Dark was her target. In the past he had always been the one issuing orders. If he was nearby, he would most likely be one of the men at the gate.

She had just reached the northeastern corner of the estate and the wall that surrounded it when she heard a wailing cry. Goosebumps broke out on her skin. Was Dark using dogs to track her?

She searched for a hiding place and spotted a gap between two boulders. She squeezed into the space, angling herself sideways. Her backpack caught. She tried to move forward but couldn't. The cry sounded again, but closer. The dog was coming fast. She started to back out. The pack scraped on the rock, the sound loud in the narrow opening. If she wriggled loose, the dog might hear her. If she stayed where she was, she would be a sitting duck. Her pistol was holstered on her right hip and tight against the boulder. Her right hand held her rifle, and it was trapped as well.

She froze, turning her head to look over her shoulder. The gloom shifted. Behind her, a patch of darkness moved. Fear slithered down her back. She had a sudden, unreasoning desire to run.

Something growled, the sound low and menacing and unlike anything she had ever heard before. Not an eagle, not a catamount, not a dog. Something else. Terrified, she held her breath. Besides Dark, was there another killer on the loose?

A cricket chirped. The evening wind sighed gently through the trees. She waited, trembling, heart thudding. Another distant, crying howl cut the stillness, this one higher up on the mountain. The shadow abruptly turned and raced away.

She backed out of the boulders and sagged against the wall, her chest heaving with fear and relief. Nothing that big could move that fast. It was impossible.

Still shaking, she turned the corner and stumbled down the hill toward the mansion's gate, forcing her mind back to her main task—

finding Dark. The ground fell away in front of her, and she found herself standing on a precipice with a mere two feet between the estate's wall and a sheer drop-off. Her foot dislodged a pebble that fell silently for a few seconds until it finally clattered on the rocks below.

Keeping her backpack pressed against the wall, she edged sideways along the cliff until, fifty yards further on, the wall finally angled away. Through a gap in the trees, she saw the two SUVs, engines idling and headlights off. They were below her and by the gate. Two men stood on the road.

She slipped silently into the pines. Two minutes later the ground leveled out and the road appeared. Directly in front of her, a hundred feet away, stood the waiting men. While the men in the trees wore ski masks, neither of these men covered their faces. The man closest to the gate was tall and heavily built and stood with his hands balled up in the pockets of his jacket, face set in concentration as he listened to his radio. He wore a pistol on one hip but had no other weapon. The second man had a shoulder holster under his jacket, another pistol on his hip, and held a silenced AR-15 across his chest. Eyes scanning the road, he stood watching the canyon.

Dark could be either man or neither. She'd recognize Dark's voice, but these men were too far away to hear, and there was no way to get any closer unless she left the trees.

That left only one option.

For three long, terrifying years she had tried to stay out of Dark's thoughts. Usually, all she felt were his emotions. Sometimes she heard more, like when he'd shot Thompson or when he'd said "Kill Jacob-son"—whoever that was—but the instances when she heard his exact words were rare. She didn't like hearing him, and she certainly didn't like feeling what he was feeling: the hatred; the lust for blood.

She lifted the AR-15 and switched off the safety. She sighted on the man with the rifle, the one looking down the canyon, and took a deep breath, slowly letting it out. Deep in her mind, the place where she felt Dark's thoughts, she screamed, *Get out of my head!*

The man with the rifle just stood there watching the road. But the big man closest to the gate jumped as if he had touched a live wire.

"She's here!" He twisted around. "The bitch is here!"

Victoria fired. The second man collapsed. Dark tried to remove his pistol. Victoria shot him in the knee. He fell sideways onto his hip, trapping the pistol against the ground. He grabbed at his radio. Victoria fired again, hitting his wrist. Dark gasped and fumbled with his left hand, opening his chest pocket. She was expecting him to pull out a weapon or his phone but, instead, he withdrew a syringe. He stabbed the needle into his leg, pushed the plunger all the way down, then plucked it free and dropped it to the ground.

Rifle hard again her shoulder, she moved out of the trees onto the road.

"Too late," Dark said. His voice was the same gravely rasp she had heard on Couch's phone.

She didn't know what was in the syringe but there was no misunderstanding his expression. His face showed…triumph? Was that the word?

She checked both SUVs. An open laptop with a lighted screen sat on one of the seats. Was he reporting in to higher-ups, even while he deployed his men to kill innocent people?

"What did you just do?" she demanded. "What's in the syringe?"

He managed a smile through the pain of his wounds. "Every answer you're looking for."

"That makes no sense. How are you in my head?"

"I don't know. I only know when it started."

"What is that supposed to mean?"

"You were burned to death," he wheezed. "I was in a car accident. We were both transported to Biodosius and resuscitated. When I woke up, you were screaming in my head. I felt your burns. The pain was horrible. I had no idea what was happening. I thought it was a side effect of the augmentation process and that I had become psychotic. It happens to some of the project's patients."

"Augmentation process?"

"You've been augmented. We both have."

"I'm not a doctor. Speak English."

He shifted his wounded arm and winced. "Before you died, the people who brought you into the program augmented the neurons in your brain to stabilize the cells so they wouldn't degrade."

"That's why I can hear you?"

"Yes. We don't know what they did. That's why we've tried so hard to find you."

This was not what she wanted to hear. "Who exactly is *we*?"

"My project backers."

"The military?"

"Some, but not all."

Victoria swore. She was going to have a long discussion with Monica later.

"You need to come back to the program," he said. "The link between us is extraordinary. Imagine never having to use a phone or send emails. It will change the world."

She laughed. "There's just one problem with your new world. No one wants to hear what's in your head."

"You're not understanding the potential."

Somewhere on the estate, one of the things she had heard earlier cried out, the howl rising into a scream that made her glance nervously up the mountain. Another cry sounded, this one closer than the first. She had been standing around long enough.

Dark shifted his arm, pressing his bleeding wrist against his stomach.

"I can't help you, not until I know what was done," he said. "Who are you, and why were you brought into Biodosius?"

"Sorry," she said. "That's information you can't have."

"We can take it by force. It would be easier if you cooperated."

Victoria laughed. Dark and his backers could get in line. She lifted the rifle to kill him, but his eyes caught hers. A peculiar, oppressive pressure unlike anything she had ever experienced slid into her mind.

Tell me.

The words filled her thoughts. She flinched. The pressure grew.

Tell me.

Was he…in her head? Was such a thing even possible? She had heard his voice many times before, but this was something completely different and far more frightening.

Who are you? Why were you brought into the program?

She mentally flailed at the unfamiliar pressure and tried to stop it, but how could she? A minute ago, she hadn't even known this was possible. Hearing him was one thing but feeling him inside her was infinitely worse. She tried to aim the rifle. The weapon felt unwieldy and heavy. Her arms trembled.

Drop it.

Her hands began to shake.

"How are you doing this?" she cried out.

Drop it.

Almost as if they belonged to someone else, her hands opened. The rifle clattered to the ground.

Why were you brought into the program?

She grabbed her pistol, her reflexes awkward, as if her hands belonged to someone else. The weapon slid clumsily from her holster. With all her concentration, she tried to lift her arm and aim. Her hand jerked. It was like watching a damaged puppet in a puppet show. The pistol turned. She watched it in growing horror.

"No!"

She took hold of the pistol's barrel with her left hand and used every ounce of strength to stop her right hand from moving. But slowly, one inch at a time, the pistol rotated. He was too strong. She had no idea how or why, but he was. The pistol pointed at her temple. Her index finger trembled on the trigger. She heard someone sobbing, her own cries of anguish.

Who changed the neurons? Who brought you into the program?

"Get out of my head!"

Who brought you in! Show me!

The pressure grew. Memories moved through her thoughts, slowly at first, but gaining speed. She relived her conversation with Doug Monroe, how he felt like a food and that he loved her. She saw herself shooting Flight by the RV and freeing Jan Thompson and her two girls. Another memory, and she was speeding down the Forest Service's dirt roads in the Rover.

Show me who changed the neurons!

"No!"

The pressure, his will, pressed against her. He wanted to know how she had died so he could see who had saved her life. She shook her head, desperately trying to think of something else. He felt her fear, her growing dismay. Unbidden, the first memory, the very beginning of what had led her to Biodosius, flooded into her mind. She screamed, trying to think of anything else.

Show me!

It started with her mother. Lilly had left a note. It hadn't been long. Just a short apology before she went to sleep next to her empty bottle of Zolpidem. The intensity of the memory, of picking up the bottle and feeling her mother's dead, cold hand nearly made her faint. Dark flinched under the emotional barrage. His will wavered before it snapped back into place. She didn't blame him. No one would want to experience a parent's death.

Who put you in the program? he demanded again.

"How is this possible?" she sobbed.

His eyes bored into hers.

Who—did—it?

Each word thundered through her. He grabbed the next memory.

She saw it, moaned, and tried to push it from her mind. Anything was better than reliving that.

"No! Stop!"

Give it to me!

It was a hot, windy Tuesday afternoon. She hadn't slept, and she was exhausted. For two days she had hounded the sheriff for news, checking with neighbors, calling friends, and frantically driving every road in the area. She smelled the dust, heard the wind as it whistled across the cinders, felt the terror as she slammed her truck into a skidding stop and half fell, half lunged out into the hot sunshine. She didn't want to see what was up there, she refused to look, but she did anyway. Her father hung crucified from the cross-brace of a telephone pole. His head slumped down, chin on his chest, hair fluttering around his pain-ravaged features.

Dark flinched from her emotions. For a second, she found her mind free of his overpowering, oppressive will. Whatever he was doing in her head, it had slipped twice.

He shuddered, blinked, and found her eyes again.

Who brought you into Biodosius? Who modified the neurons?

Her finger tightened on the pistol's trigger.

Tell me!

She met his eyes, his anger hammering into her, and abruptly understood how much her life had changed. She hadn't been strong after her mother died. She had been an utter wreck. Her father's murder had destroyed her. She could barely function. But something had changed her at Biodosius. She had become the *La Puta Loca*. She didn't give up, she didn't back down, and she went after the druggies with an unrelenting vengeance that never, ever stopped.

She thought about Dark's twisted emotions, the oily, insidious way he operated. Somehow, without her knowing about it, he had invaded her mind at Biodosius. It was the only thing that made sense. Day after day, month after month, he had slid inside her like a mental penis, watching her and seeing and experiencing her most intimate thoughts.

"It was you!" she whispered. "You did this…you raped me!"

Outraged fury, the emotions he had gifted her, didn't just burst through her. They exploded like a wildfire through dry timber. She locked her eyes on his, leaning forward.

"Do you want to know how I ended up in Biodosius?" she shouted. "Do you want to know how it happened?"

She brought the memory into her mind. It was mid-afternoon. The June sun burned in the pale sky above the pines. A storm was coming. The air had a hushed, rare stillness of anticipatory waiting. She had just left the post office with her piles of bills and wondered how she was going to pay them. The narcos had killed another twelve head of cattle the night before. Her bank account was empty. Her credit cards were maxed. Winter was almost upon her, and without fuel, she would slowly starve or freeze.

She got into her truck, put on her seatbelt, and turned the key.

There was a click. A barely audible click.

The force of the explosion threw her straight up. Even with her seatbelt on, she almost hit the roof with her head. Fire shot into the cab. Her clothes caught fire. She screamed, flailing and trying to escape the inferno and feeling the fire eat her flesh. She grabbed the door handle, trying to pull it, but when she touched it, her skin melted on the metal. She threw herself against the door and, still ablaze, fell to the ground.

The panicked desperation—the misery, the agony, everything she felt as she died—tore out of her like a tornado. She spun it into his mind. He screamed, back arching. Cords stood out in his neck from the strain. His eyes abruptly turned away. His hold broke, freeing her. She jerked the pistol away from her head. It had been a mistake to talk. She should have just killed him. She wouldn't make that mistake again.

His eyes frantically sought hers. He was trying to reestablish the link. She faltered to a stop. She tried to move, to do anything, but just stood frozen. All she could do was stare.

He must have seen the expression on her face, or maybe he had read her mind. Whatever the reason, he turned his head and followed her gaze to the creature running down the hill toward them.

CHAPTER 35

The inside of the mine was completely devoid of light. Support girders, electrical cables, and railroad tracks stretched out of sight. The air smelled of dirt, rust, and mold. The mine's old-fashioned rotary power switch was mounted by the entrance. Adam turned it on. A faint blue light emanated from the ellipsoidal bulbs. As they brightened, the bulbs flickered and filaments buzzed. Another black-and-yellow hazard sign, warning of carbon monoxide danger, hung between two supports.

"You want to hide in here?" James asked, taking a step back. "Where hundreds of people have died?"

"Mine inspectors go in all the time," Adam said.

"They have respirators, and they know what they're doing," James said. "We don't."

"We don't need to go far, just far enough to hide."

A heavy, long steel bin sat against the wall. Adam used the rebar to break the padlock and lift the lid. Inside he found electrical tools, logbooks, carbide headlamps, and loose-leaf binders of handwritten notes. Dust covered everything.

A distant, screaming howl pierced the darkness behind them. Ears turning toward the sound, Mop whined.

"Whatever you're going to do, do it quick!" Jacobson snapped, watching the trees.

Adam pawed through the contents, then slammed the lid. In a dark side-tunnel, he saw a line of wall-mounted lockers. He yanked open the first locker. Hung neatly inside were four biohazard suits and accompanying respirators. He opened the other lockers. They contained more respirators and more suits. He handed out the respirators.

"I don't know about this, Adam," Kate said. "If we get lost, it could be weeks before anyone finds us. Remember the three spelunkers who disappeared in the lower tunnels? It took months to find them. The entire mountain's honeycombed with shafts."

"The men who shot Terrance are watching the road. We can't outrun them, and we have no idea who they are. Even if we get away, they'll find us and kill us later. If anyone has another idea, I'm all ears."

"What about Mop?" Bailey asked. "He can't wear a mask."

"He'll have to hide in the trees. He's much faster than they are. If they try and get him, he can just outrun them, especially in the dark."

Bailey got down on one knee and met Mop's intelligent eyes.

"Do you know what's making that howling noise?"

Mop shivered.

Bailey nodded. "Find somewhere to hide where it can't find you. We'll come back for you. Don't let anyone see you. Do you understand?"

Mop whined, shifting his weight from one big paw to another. Bailey hugged him. The big dog licked her face.

"Run as fast as you can," she told him.

He shouldered in close to her, ducked his head, and whimpered.

"I know," she whispered. "I love you, too."

She let go. Mop turned and fled into the trees. James helped Bailey with her mask. Adam pulled on a respirator and snugged the straps. Reaching up, he ripped down the biohazard sign and hid it behind the lockers. He gathered extra respirators, slammed the locker doors, and followed the rail tracks down the shaft. Abandoned equipment littered the ground. In a few places the tunnel had collapsed, making it hard to get past. The further they went, the louder the buzzing became. Some of the bulbs worked. Most did not.

Searching beams of brilliant light appeared behind them.

Adam tossed Jacobson a respirator.

"Move!" Jacobson hissed as he clipped the straps of the respirator over his helmet.

Listening to the echo of his breath in the respirator, Adam hobbled forward as fast as he could on his bleeding foot. Ten minutes later, the tunnel abruptly ended under a single light. Below them yawned a black and bottomless pit. Rusted scaffolding, girders, and a narrow maintenance walkway circled it. Steel ladders went up the walls and, he guessed, led to ventilation shafts.

Adam had heard stories his whole life about the Silent Black Mine, how it went straight down the volcano's throat for thousands of feet and how the miners had followed the rich veins of ore, but this was the first time he had seen an opening in the earth so vast and deep.

He put a foot onto the maintenance walkway and cautiously shifted his weight. One side of the walkway, the side facing the pit, had a low railing. Horizontal I-beams had been bolted to each of the pit's girders, providing lateral support. Ladders snaked up from the walkway into the darkness. To the left of him, bolted to the girders, stood an empty elevator trestle. There was no elevator, but Adam saw heavy steel cables wrapped around two large wheels.

"We need to find someplace out of sight where they can't pick us off," Jacobson said. "Make them come to us."

Trying not to think about the age of the metal, Adam stepped onto the walkway. It creaked but held. He exhaled and took a deep breath. He took another step and then a third. He held out his hand to Kate. After a moment's hesitation, she stepped onto the walkway. James, Monica, Bailey, and Jacobson followed.

Adam headed right, toward the closest ladder. He stopped under it, looking up to see where it went, but in the darkness, he saw only the next few rungs, wet and pitted with rust.

"I don't trust this ladder." He looked down the walkway. "I see another one ahead."

With the walkway vibrating under their weight, he hurried toward the next ladder. Water dripped on Adam's face. A moment later the walkway dead-ended at a roadblock of fallen beams. Adam backed away.

"This way isn't safe. Go back."

They turned around and hurried back, Jacobson in the lead. As they reached the tunnel, a bullet hissed out of the darkness. Jacobson staggered against the walkway's safety railing. He dropped his rifle, clutching at the railing with his left arm and trying to stay upright. His boot caught the rifle and sent it spinning into the abyss. Another bullet hissed out of the darkness and caught his left hand. He gasped and collapsed onto his side. Adam started to reach for the pistol hidden under his shirt but stopped. He couldn't see who'd shot Jacobson. If he held up a weapon, he'd be killed for sure.

"We're civilians!" he yelled awkwardly up the tunnel through his respirator. "There's a woman and a child here!"

A man dressed in black body armor and carrying a rifle stepped from behind a pile of toothed gears, old electrical boxes, and jackhammers. He stood swaying, chest pulling labored air into his lungs. He stumbled and put a hand against the wall. Adam tried to remember what he knew about carbon monoxide. It was a colorless, odorless gas that replaced the oxygen in red blood cells. Symptoms included headaches, weakness, vomiting, dizziness, and death.

"Where's Terrance?" the man wheezed.

"He collapsed in the basement of the mansion. We left him on the floor."

The man touched the radio on his shoulder, leaned his head sideways to speak into it and nearly fell. He took a steadying, backward step. Metal scraped. A low grunt sounded, and he abruptly disappeared.

"What the heck?" James said. "Where'd he go?"

Adam peered into the gloom. Dread paralyzed his heart. He couldn't see what was there, but he could sense the menace. He had felt it in the mining camp and when he'd picked up his truck. A shadow moved, and the Nightmare blurred toward him.

CHAPTER 36

Victoria snatched her rifle from the road and fled. It wasn't far to the pines, but each step took forever.

Help!

She staggered, regained her balance, and kept running.

Come back!

Dark fired his pistol. An eager, wailing cry howled through shadows. She felt Dark's thoughts, his growing fear.

You have no idea who I work for! They will hunt you the rest of your life! I'm the only one who can protect you! Come back! Help!

He kept shooting, pulling the trigger as fast as he could. The shots had no effect. Panic flooded his mind, making her heart race. He ran out of ammunition and screamed. Pain exploded in Victoria's head. She staggered under the mental barrage. For years, his malevolence had infected her. It felt like wasps walking across her skin, but none of it felt as bad as this. Her head about to burst, she fell against a tree. Dark let out one final, agonizing shriek of despair. Bones snapped. Limbs ripped from his sockets. His ribs broke. She collapsed, arms around her head. Just as she couldn't stand it anymore, his scream abruptly cut off. Helpless to prevent it, his death struck her in an emotional, wailing tsunami. She tasted blood. She had bit her tongue.

The link dropped. The pain vanished.

She pushed herself up, wiping tears from her eyes. She moved her arm. It was still there. Her ribs were whole. She reached out with her senses, trying to find the link, searching for Dark's presence, but found nothing. For the first time since she had woken up in the hospital, the malice, the lurking, insane byproduct of his augmentation, had disappeared.

But behind her, the creature roared, and now it came for her. Dizzy, disoriented, she lurched into a run. For years, she had fought to stay alive. Outnumbered, outgunned, she survived by using what her father had taught her, to force her adversaries into bad situations where she had the advantage. She couldn't outrun this *thing*—whatever it was. It was too fast. It had torn Dark apart. It would do the same to her. She needed a way to limit its speed, to find a place where she would have the advantage.

Rocks tripped her up. Branches whipped her face. She heard it smashing through the underbrush. Where she had dodged saplings, it barreled through. She sprinted up to the boulders. In the darkness, she didn't see the estate wall until she crashed into it.

She fled along the wall until the wind shifted, blowing up from the canyon. She had reached the cliff. Below her, far below, lay a blanket of deep and utter darkness.

Backpack against the wall, arms out and palms pressed against the stone, she scooted sideways along the ledge. With a loud crack a pine tree splintered. The creature leapt out of the trees, its dark shape smoothly jumping from one boulder to the next. In seconds, it reached the wall.

A moan escaped Victoria's lips. Quiet, she told herself. Keep moving. The ledge was less than two feet wide. In the waning light, it hadn't been any problem to sidestep along the precipice. But now? No time for caution. She ran, reaching the corner where the wall angled off to the right. Surging along the ledge, the creature let out a mewling, barbed cry of need. She looked back. In the failing light, she saw its eyes. They were white. No other color. Just white.

She spun, brought up her rifle, and fired. She heard the thud of impact, saw the shape jerk. She fired again. Trapped between the wall and the cliff, it screamed and sprang forward. She fired again. One round whined off the wall, and the next hissed away into the darkness. But her third and fourth shots struck home. The creature staggered, air hissing raggedly in its throat. The fifth jacketed round tore through its chest. It fell against the wall, took a stumbling step, and collapsed. Her rifle clicked empty. She dropped it.

Victoria backed up. An arm outstretched, the creature dragged itself along the ledge. She clawed for her pistol. It caught in her holster. She undid the holster's retention strap. Fingers reached for her. The pistol finally came free. She aimed and fired into the creature's head.

Silence fell. Gasping, covered in sweat yet chilled to the bone, Victoria stumbled backward. She fumbled for her phone. The light would destroy her night vision and signal anyone watching exactly where she was, but she had to know what she was dealing with. She aimed the screen at the shape on the ground. The sudden light was blinding in its intensity.

She stared in disbelief as the truth hit home.

CHAPTER 37

Deep in the mine, the Nightmare leapt forward, covering the distance between them in a burst of speed. It hit Adam, grabbing him by the throat and driving him backward. His feet lifted off the ground.

James shouted and ran to help. The Nightmare grabbed James and threw him to the side. Adam reached for the pistol under his shirt. The Nightmare caught his hand, twisted the weapon from his grasp, and tossed it into the abyss.

Nostrils flared in its ruined face. It sniffed, showing broken teeth, as it moved in close. Open, bleeding wounds covered its body. Its clothing had been torn away. It was big, with heavy slabs of muscle in its shoulders and legs. As it moved, its bare feet left blood on the tunnel's rocky floor. Once it had been a man. What it was now, Adam didn't know. The eyes were white and shiny, like small porcelain eggs. There was no pigment, no iris. The thing growled.

"Where is it?" The Nightmare's hand felt hard as steel.

Adam tried to pry the hand loose. He couldn't breathe.

"I don't know what you're talking about," he croaked.

"You have it." The destroyed face leaned in close. "I can smell it."

Metal scraped on the walkway. A pistol roared. The bullet caught the Nightmare in the side. It convulsed, back arching, and dropped Adam. Legs spread, both hands holding the weapon, James fired Jacobson's pistol again. The Nightmare spun. In another blur of movement, a fist struck James in the head. James's feet left the ground. He collapsed onto the walkway, unconscious. The pistol clattered across the walkway and fell into the pit.

"Dad!" Bailey screamed and ran to him.

Adam hit the Nightmare in the remains of its face. The Nightmare snapped out its right fist. The blow happened so fast Adam barely saw it coming. It struck his chest. He staggered backward against the walkway's railing. The Nightmare stepped forward, white, dead eyes locked on his.

What had the government done? What experiment had Jacobson been talking about that could tear away a person's humanity?

"Where. Is. It?" the Nightmare demanded again.

Adam felt dizzy. He couldn't breathe. The thing had crushed his chest. Fast as a coiled snake, the Nightmare hit him again. Pain exploded in his head. How could he fight a creature that could shrug off getting shot?

Kate picked up a section of galvanized pipe and swung it at the Nightmare's head. The pipe connected with a hard thud. The Nightmare snarled and twisted, its movements liquid and smooth, and grabbed her under the chin, lifting her off the ground. She started to gag, eyes widening, face turning red. The pipe clattered to the ground.

Barely able to see through the pain, Adam tried to focus. A chiming bell tolled back and forth in his skull. Kate kicked frantically, helplessly. Adam tried to move, to do something, but he couldn't breathe.

"Uncle Adam!" Bailey shrieked. "Help her!"

The tunnel spun circles. He reached for the pipe, and his fingers closed around it. Drunkenly, he got to his feet and swung. His balance was wrong, and he almost fell, but the pipe arced through the air and hit the Nightmare in the head. It dropped Kate and turned. Its white, dead gaze locked on him. It snapped its fingers at Adam's throat. Adam dropped the pipe and caught the hands before they could close. It leaned forward, bringing its superior weight to bear. It was horribly strong. Adam slid helplessly across the walkway toward the pit. He put all his strength into holding the thing back. His arms began to give way. His left foot hit one of the railing's supports, stopping him. There was no way he could withstand that terrible power.

"Run!" he gasped at Kate and Bailey. "Get help!"

The railing groaned under the stress. If it broke, there would be nothing to stop him from going over the edge. He went over every move the Nightmare had made, the way it had lashed out, the way it relied on its strength to overwhelm resistance. It had been gifted with monstrous power and knew how to use it. Skill and experience were the only way to overcome that kind of opponent. The Nightmare was bigger than he was, stronger and faster. Superior size, weight, and speed were impossible to overcome. Just ask any mouse that tried to fight a cat.

The Nightmare took another step. Adam caught the thing's weight and held it. He shifted his entire weight onto his left shoe and leaned against the railing, praying it would hold, then he snapped his right knee into the Nightmare's groin and slammed his heel down on its bare, bloody foot. Nothing happened. The Nightmare didn't even flinch. A normal man would be on his knees from that. Did it not feel pain? Was that why it could run around the desert in bare feet? James had just shot it twice, and it had shrugged off the bullets.

He let go of the Nightmare's left hand and drove his fingers into its left eye. Even if it did not feel pain, it still had to see. The Nightmare howled, the sound rising into the shriek Adam had heard on the hill above the mining camp. It shook its head, its undamaged eye locking on Adam, and threw itself forward. The movement was so fast, so insanely quick, that Adam couldn't move away from the railing. He sidestepped to his right and kicked the side of the exposed knee. The anterior cruciate ligament snapped. As its knee buckled, the Nightmare hobbled backwards on one leg. Adam pursued it. The same anger he'd felt on the overlook with Mike Benedict coursed through him in a wave of adrenaline-fueled fury.

He kept his elbows in tight against his ribs and drove his right fist into the Nightmare's throat. Air exploded from the creature's lungs. It let out a strangled croak and collapsed, clawing at its crushed windpipe. Adam picked up Kate's pipe and swung it as hard as he could, over and over, smashing it into the side of the Nightmare's head. Bone cracked. Blood sprayed across the ground. Adam kept hammering the pipe, unable to stop, until the man's skull was completely gone.

He stumbled backwards, gasping. He was covered in blood. Bits of bone and brain matter hung off him in gooey strings. Why had he kept hammering the Nightmare like that? The fight had been over. It couldn't see, couldn't stand or breathe. But he had kept hitting it. Worse, he hadn't wanted to just put it down. He had wanted to kill it, to take its life, to obliterate it from the face of the earth.

He lifted his gaze to Kate. At the sight of her, Adam's unreasoning, incomprehensible rage abruptly flared again. She backed away, pushing Bailey behind her. Seeing the fear in her eyes, her fear of him, he forced himself to take a slow, deep breath. Where had those emotions come from?

As abruptly as the rage had come, it left him. The pipe dropped from his fingers. He half fell, half collapsed to one knee, closing his eyes. Kate screamed. He heard it dimly, the sound far away, and something slammed into him. Pain exploded, searing through him in a white-hot jolt of agony. Hands grabbed him and lifted into the air.

The second Nightmare was bigger than the first. Most of its nose had been blown off, probably by a bullet. Its face had been burned so badly that it was hard to imagine it had once been human. Clothing, or the remains of it, hung off it in torn rags. It wasn't as bloody as the first, but its eyes were just as white.

It hit Adam in the stomach. He tried to breathe—to draw in air—but couldn't. His lungs refused to work. The Nightmare walked him over to the side of the tunnel and slammed him headfirst into the wall. Adam got his hands up, but the blow was too strong to stop. He tried to break away, tried to do something, anything, but all his limbs felt as if they belonged to someone else. The Nightmare lifted him off the ground, standing him up, and casually slammed him into the wall again. Pain detonated in Adam's head. The lights of the tunnel flipped sideways, and he landed on his shoulder.

Panting, blinking through blood, he reached out and felt metal. The pipe, he thought. The Nightmare saw the motion and grinned, showing burned and blackened gums. It leaned down by Adam's ear, its stinking breath washing over him.

"You can't kill me," it said. "No one can kill me again."

It picked Adam up by his belt, and with one hand, casually dragged him toward the pit. Adam dug his fingers into the dirt. No one could help him. Jacobson lay bleeding on the walkway, and James, unconscious, sprawled next to him.

"Give us what Baltimore gave you, what he promised," the Nightmare said. He opened a hand and showed Adam a small piece of white plastic. "Give us what you took, and I'll let you live. Deny me and I will kill you."

Adam peered at the plastic in the Nightmare's hand. The plastic was small, about half the size and shape of his little finger. He started to ask what it was. Then he knew. A syringe cap. It protected the needle on a syringe.

He stared, mind turning, willing his memories to emerge, but all he could recall was the thunderstorm and the blinding spike of lightning as it burned a hole in his shoulder and tore a hole in his foot.

"I can't remember," he wheezed.

The Nightmare dropped Adam to the ground. One arm snapped out, lightning quick, grabbed Bailey by the hair, and yanked her from Kate's grasp. Bailey screamed, flailing at the Nightmare's hand. Kate, hands clawing, threw herself at it. It batted her away like an annoying fly. She landed on the ground in a heap. Bailey kicked, twisting in its grasp, but the Nightmare ignored her.

"You have one choice," it growled down at Adam. "Deny me and she dies."

Adam tried to think. Dr. Baltimore must have taken a drug out of Biodosius, a drug so important the killers had slaughtered everyone at the hospital and pursued Adam through some of the deadliest terrain on earth. But he hadn't seen a syringe, much less a drug.

The first Nightmare had said he could smell *it* on Adam's skin. What was *it*? Adam remembered the bruise on his arm, how he had felt feverish Saturday morning and how the doctor at the urgent care clinic had thought he had gotten an injection of some kind. Was that why Adam's blood contained unusually high numbers of white blood cells? Had Baltimore injected the missing drug into him? That would explain a lot. A lightning strike through his shoulder and foot should have been disabling for weeks or even months. Instead, his wounds had closed by the time he'd gotten home Saturday morning, only hours after getting struck. He'd gone dancing with Kate Saturday night at the wedding. He shouldn't have been able to walk, let alone dance. Later that night, he'd fought Mike up at the overlook. Strength-wise, Mike had outmatched him in every way, and yet Adam had prevailed.

According to what Jacobson had said earlier, the drugs used by the government to stabilize terminally injured patients overloaded their nervous systems, including their adrenal glands. The body utilized adrenaline in dire, life or death situations. That's how a parent could lift a three-thousand-pound car off a trapped child or how a soldier in combat could shrug off fatal wounds and still fight. Did Baltimore's drug do the same thing? Was that how Adam had overpowered Mike Benedict on the overlook and how he had stopped the first Nightmare?

Adam tried to speak, to explain what had happened, but couldn't talk. His chest felt like there was a boulder sitting on it.

The Nightmare dragged Bailey toward the edge of the pit, lifting her over the railing. Bailey shrieked, twisting and turning, clutching at the killer's arm.

Adam heard something running down the tunnel, moving fast. He saw the darkness move, saw the muscle and determination, heard the gasping of air being pulled into powerful lungs and understood what was going to happen.

"No!"

The Nightmare opened his hand. Bailey shrieked. Slowly, inexorably, gravity took her. She started to fall.

Adam grabbed one of the walkway's supports and lunged out into the darkness as Mop hit the Nightmare with all the speed and unstoppable momentum of a freight train going downhill. The force of the impact drove the Nightmare against the railing. The steel broke.

For a terrible, awful second, time stopped. Mop turned his head, and Adam saw the love and loyalty in the dog's intelligent eyes—love for him, love for Bailey and James and Kate, and love for everyone whose life he had touched in the brief time he had been with them.

On the edge of forever, his body broken, seeing that love, Adam realized the Nightmare had been right about one thing.

He had a choice.

May the gods forgive him because he knew he would never forgive himself.

With one hand, he grabbed Bailey's wrist and let Mop fall.

CHAPTER 38

Jacobson watched both the Nightmare and the dog disappear into the pit. Blood from his wounds dripped through the catwalk's metal grate. He rolled onto his back and blinked up at the buzzing mercury vapor light above his head, his vision swimming as he regained his bearings. Stabs of pain shot through his head. He groaned and felt along the side of the helmet with his right hand and found a long horizontal crease in the ballistic Kevlar. He didn't feel any blood or excessive pain. Maybe he didn't have a head wound after all. The helmet had done what it was designed to do and deflected the bullet, but the impact of the high-velocity round had hit him like a sledgehammer.

He searched for his weapons. They were gone. He remembered his rifle falling into the pit after he got shot, but he didn't recall losing his pistol. He still had his holster, but it was empty. He snugged his respirator over his mouth. He didn't want to survive getting shot and being attacked by two Nightmares only to succumb to carbon monoxide poisoning.

"Mop!" Bailey shrieked. She scrambled to the edge of the pit, horrified tears streaming down her face. "Mop!" Head down, she shook as she cried.

Kate stumbled over to Adam and knelt beside him. James, groggy and disoriented, sat up and put his fingers to his head. A bruise darkened his jaw.

Jacobson checked his leg and tried to gauge how badly he had been wounded. His leg hurt but he could move it, so it probably was okay. The round had most likely gone through muscle without hitting bone. His hand throbbed, and he held it up to the dim light. The bullet had passed through the flesh between his thumb and first finger. Painful, but it wouldn't kill him.

He crawled to Adam. Adam rolled onto his knees, pulled his respirator away from his mouth, and vomited. Blood dripped from his forehead before he slumped back onto his side. Jacobson angled Adam's head downward so he wouldn't choke and used the fingers of his right hand to make sure Adam's tongue wasn't blocking his throat. He shook Adam's shoulder. After a moment, Adam groaned, blinking.

"You still with us?" Jacobson asked. "That was one hell of a fight."

Kate stroked Adam's arm and placed the respirator back on his face, making sure it covered his mouth. She raised her voice to make herself heard above Bailey's shrieks.

"Where does it hurt?"

"My chest," Adam croaked. "I can't breathe."

"What about your head?" Jacobson asked. "Look up. Can you see the light?"

Adam glanced up at the dim light but quickly looked away.

"Ow."

"You have a concussion. We need to get you to a hospital."

Kate's eyes filled with tears, but she stiffened her back and straightened her shoulders. Jacobson didn't know her, but he could see her resolve.

"Just hold on," she said. "We're going to get you out of here."

"Is Bailey okay?" Adam wheezed.

"Yes. You saved her life," Kate said. "You're an amazing man. I can't believe you did that."

"I couldn't save Mop."

"I know."

Adam managed a wan smile. One of his hands settled on hers. "Can we go out on that date now?"

She laughed and squeezed his hand. "As soon as you get better."

A faint smile lit his lips before he grimaced and closed his eyes.

James, wiping his mouth, stumbled over. He nodded back toward the tunnel's entrance. "Major, are more of them coming?"

"Eight killers escaped Biodosius. Two are dead. I don't know if more are here. Adam needs medical treatment. Can you find something to put him on so you can drag him out?"

James looked down at Jacobson's wounded leg. "What about you? You've been shot."

"Just help me bandage my leg and hand. I'll follow you out on my own. You won't be able to drag me and Adam. He's got a serious head injury. He needs help before the swelling cuts off blood to his brain. Every minute counts. We need to move."

Kate looked stricken.

"I know it sounds bad," Jacobson told her as gently as he could, "but we need to go before anyone else shows up. Can you help James find something to put Adam on?"

She wiped the tears from her eyes, stood, and went over to Bailey, resting her hand on the girl's shoulder and asking for her help. The two of them started searching the piles of equipment. James dragged over a piece of sheet metal. Kate and Bailey located some cable. They threaded the cable through holes in the sheet metal to form a makeshift sled. James, Kate, and Bailey rolled Adam onto it.

After they were done, Jacobson talked Kate through putting pressure-bandages on his leg and hand. She wrapped both wounds in medical tape from his first aid kit. It wasn't pretty, but it would stop most of the bleeding until he reached a hospital. As she worked, he tossed pain killers, not enough to make him stupid. After she finished, she helped him to his feet. Pain lanced through his leg. He clenched his jaw to keep from crying out and took a tentative step. His knee buckled. Kate slipped an arm around him and helped him sit.

"Can you find me a crutch?" he asked. "Something to take the weight off my leg?"

Kate and Bailey fanned out, going back toward the lockers. Jacobson waited until they were beyond earshot, leaned over Adam, and lowered his voice.

"I'm not sure how to say this so I'm just going to say it." He put his respirator next to Adam's ear and spoke as fast as he could. "The people who shot me, they're from the government. They want me dead because of what I found out about the killers. If we get out of here, they're going to ask you what happened. You can't tell them anything except this was all about the dog. The killers wanted Mop for some reason. You don't know why. Do you understand what I am saying?"

Adam blinked. His pupils were dilated.

"The killers wanted the dog," Jacobson whispered urgently, giving the tunnel a worried glance. "You were in the wrong place at the wrong time, and you almost died. Anyone asks, that's what you tell them. Understand? The killers wanted Mop."

Adam eyes fluttered and his head fell back on the sled. Jacobson silently swore, hoping he had gotten his warning through. If Adam said the wrong thing, he would be dead. Now they just had to get out of here and hope for the best.

Jacobson crawled over to the piece of pipe Adam had used to kill the first Nightmare. He used it to lever himself to his feet and hobbled down the mineshaft. The man who had shot him lay curled on his side, clutching his crushed throat.

Jacobson searched the ground until he located the dead man's pistol. Leaning on the pipe, he stooped, retrieved the weapon, and secured it in his empty holster. It wouldn't stop a Nightmare, but it was better than being unarmed.

Carrying a long length of pipe, bent at the end like shepherd's crook, Bailey hurried over. The bent end fit neatly beneath his armpit. Jacobson had her retrieve the dead man's jacket, wrap it around the end of the pipe, and then tape it in place using the last of his medical tape. Jacobson tried it, found it serviceable, and used it to hobble back to Adam. James made one last knot in the cable and spun the sled around, facing the mine's entrance. Adam groaned at the movement but didn't regain consciousness.

"Bailey, keep your uncle from falling off the metal," Jacobson told the girl, giving her an encouraging nod. "I know you're hurting right now because you lost your dog, but Adam needs you. James, you and Kate drag Adam up the railroad tracks. It'll be much easier than dragging him across the ground. When you get outside, call for help. I'll follow as quickly as I can. Once I'm out, I'll make my way down the road where the police can pick me up."

"Bailey can help you walk," James said. "She's strong for her age."

"If the men come back, she'll be a target. I'll make it out on my own. Get going before more of the killers show up. Every second counts." He turned to James. "If you come across more dead men, locate a sidearm, something small enough to hide under your clothing. The men who shot me are professionals. If you run into them, tell them you are civilians who were attacked by one of the Nightmares, and you need help. Use the pistol only as a last resort. They won't hesitate to kill you if they see you're armed."

"What do we tell them if they ask about you?"

"The truth. I was shot, and you left me behind. If I see or hear them coming, I'll take cover. Unless they have respirators, I doubt they'll be a problem. I'm more worried about the escaped killers. Go get help. We'll talk after we're out."

James grabbed the makeshift harness. He and Kate dragged Adam up the tunnel. Bailey followed, keeping an eye on Adam and nudging him if he began to roll off. The screech of metal was horribly loud, Jacobson thought, but he wanted them to make a run for it while they could.

Using the bent pipe as a crutch, Jacobson, gritting his teeth, hobbled after them, but soon found himself alone. He was trained to deal with injuries, but his wounds quickly went from a dull ache to something on fire. Blood soaked through the bandage on his leg and ran into his boot.

He came across another body. The man's neck had been snapped. His sidearm was missing. Jacobson hoped James had taken it. There were no fallen shell casings, and he wondered if the man had been affected by the carbon monoxide before the Nightmare had found him.

He kept going and found more bodies. Some lay on the ground as if they had simply fallen asleep. Others had been killed.

As he limped up the tunnel, he thought about his family and wondered if he would ever see them again. He had called his wife that morning before he had returned with Admiral McDermott's troops to Biodosius. She had been asleep, so the conversation was short. Bitterness welled up thinking about it. Before General O'Dell had gotten him involved in this mess, he had been on his way home. He should be on the lake fishing with his family instead of fighting augmented killers. Now Admiral McDermott wanted him dead for what he had uncovered. He didn't know if McDermott knew about his webcam, but odds were good he did. He needed to get out of the mine and find somewhere safe so that he could figure out his next steps. Whoever was funding McDermott would worry about the truth getting out. They would do anything to bury the news of an experiment gone wrong.

Dragging his wounded leg, Jacobson reached a fork where the main shaft split into thirds. Two shafts had signs with identifying letters and numbers. The railroad tracks continued up the main one. The second shaft didn't have tracks. A third shaft, barely large enough to stand upright in, had been blasted into the wall between the two larger ones. The two larger tunnels had lights. The third did not. It also didn't have a sign.

Air wafted gently past his left ear, and he moved his head from side to side, trying to decide which tunnel would be the shortest distance to the exit. He stopped, turned on his helmet's light, and peered up into the darkness, feeling the gentle pull of air. Was this an air shaft?

The main tunnel was where James, Adam, Kate, and Bailey had gone. It came out next to Adam's truck and the Black Estate. He didn't know anything about the second tunnel. The air shaft probably went up to the surface, but he didn't know how or if it was wide and tall enough for him in his present condition. He felt lightheaded, could only stand with the crutch, and was bleeding. He felt feverish, and his forehead was covered in sweat. He had a concussion from getting shot in the helmet and was in no shape to fight.

He switched off his light. In his condition, it was better to err on the side of caution and follow the railroad tracks up to the main entrance. It would take him toward Admiral McDermott's men, but if he saw them before they saw him, he could retreat and find some-where to hide until help arrived. The secondary tunnel was an unknown. He had no idea where it went. The same with the air shaft. Hundreds of people had gotten lost in the mine and died. He didn't want to be one of them.

He turned toward the main tunnel and was about to resume limping forward when a distant cry sounded from the second tunnel. He snapped his head around, searching the gloom. The sound came again. The Nightmare was coming fast. He needed to find somewhere to hide. The main tunnel was big, well-lit, and empty. With only a pistol, he wouldn't stand a chance if the Nightmare caught him.

Gritting his teeth and hoping the pain killer would kick in, he stumbled quickly up into the unmarked shaft. His leg felt like a knife was being plunged into it, again and again. The uneven ground and its upward slope threw him off balance. Under normal circumstances he wouldn't have had any trouble, but with only one working leg, making his way up the incline was maddeningly difficult. He climbed awkwardly, using the crutch, and heard another wailing cry, this time closer. With his working hand, he grasped at rocks on the rough-hewn walls, pulling himself forward, fear making the air hiss in and out of his respirator.

Heavy running footsteps approached. Jacobson fell against the shaft's wall, clamping his teeth over the involuntary groan in his throat. He lifted his pistol.

The footsteps stopped. Jacobson held his breath and cocked his head, listening and looking back at the junction.

A hulking shape stopped under the buzzing lights. Ragged clothing hung off the Nightmare's body in strips of ripped, bloody cloth. Blood splattered its chest, head, and shoulders. An open bullet wound gaped on the side of its face, showing bits of shattered teeth. Its eyes were white, with no irises. Its nose twitched, and it sniffed, head twisting like a bloodhound searching for an elusive scent.

Jacobson thumbed off the Glock's safety. It didn't make any noise, at least that he could hear, but the Nightmare stiffened and spun around, eyes searching the darkness. It looked up at the buzzing lights and flinched, dropping its gaze to the floor. Jacobson remembered that Dr. Kumar had ordered the lights dimmed for her patients' comfort.

The Nightmare peered at the ground. Nostrils flaring, one hand reached down. It held its finger to the light. Jacobson's heart skipped a beat. On its fingertips was his blood. Even with half of its face shot away, the Nightmare could somehow still smell.

Jacobson held his breath.

Nostrils flaring, the Nightmare turned and followed the blood down the main tunnel back toward the pit.

Jacobson returned the pistol to his holster and levered himself painfully to his feet using the side of the shaft to stand. He thought about leaving the shaft and going back to the main tunnel but discarded the idea. Help was that way if he was fast enough, but it would also mean leading the Nightmare towards Adam, James, Kate, and Bailey. He could try the other tunnel the Nightmare had emerged from, but if there was one Nightmare, there were probably more. Two were dead. That left six alive. He was better off where he was. The narrow ventilation shaft was a much more defensible position. When it returned, the Nightmare could only hit him from one direction.

But first things first. Jacobson needed total darkness, somewhere his night-vision equipment would give him an advantage. He lowered his goggles and told himself to hurry, but the uneven, sloping floor made it hard to use the crutch. Sweat stung his eyes. Air played across his face and gave him hope that soon he'd be able to remove the respirator.

The ground leveled out. Metal creaked and popped. He stopped, listening. The air changed direction, rising upwards from his feet. He leaned forward and looked down. Deep, impenetrable darkness stretched away below. He tipped his head back and saw only darkness above.

A tiny red light glowed on the wall to his right. He took a step toward it, trying to see what it was. Even with the goggles, seeing clearly was difficult. He leaned forward, squinting, and gradually made out what appeared to be a small junction box bolted to the wall. He reached toward the box. Metal popped again. He froze. Old mines had pits and shafts everywhere. Miners hadn't dug with safety in mind. They followed the ore where it led and ignored everything else. What looked like solid ground could be a quick fall to his death.

He shifted his weight, testing his footing. The creak came again. He searched the ground, trying to see past the sweat in his eyes, and made out the dim outline of a rectangular shape in the dirt. He tapped his crutch against it. It thudded hollowly. He had ventured out onto a wooden maintenance platform. He hissed out a warning to himself and willed his good leg to move backwards. Standing on anything in a hundred-year-old mine that wasn't stone, dirt, or cement was a bad idea.

He moved his crutch back a half step. The platform groaned. Metal cracked, and the platform abruptly dropped six inches. Under normal circumstances, six inches wouldn't have been an issue, but with only one working leg, he lost his balance and fell forward toward the abyss. Even as gravity took him, he threw himself backward. His crutch fell, spinning away. His hand struck something black, hard, and unyielding, and he clung to it with both hands. His other foot left the ground, and he found himself swinging out into space. Decades of dust cascaded around him, covering his helmet and face with grit. Far below, the sound muffled by a terrible distance, the metal crutch boomed as it hit bottom.

Searing pain burst through his wounded hand. The object shuddered under his weight. He swung his body around, throwing out his legs, trying to get a heel up on the wooden platform. Metal squealed, the object he clung to bending with each swing. In the falling dust, he saw only the tiny red light on the wall. Behind it, his frantic gaze caught the faint outline of a ladder leading up the vertical shaft above his head.

He angled his body toward the ladder, kicked with his good leg, missed, and swung back the other way. He tried again. His right foot touched the ladder but slipped off. He swung back across the shaft, the darkness spinning below him, and tried to catch the ladder with his boot. He missed but struck the junction box instead. A motor groaned to life above him. Slow and labored bearings started to move. He whipped his head to look upward through the swirling dust. Above his head, nearly invisible, was a huge ventilation fan. He had grabbed the bottom of the fan's housing.

Air rose slowly out of the shaft below him, languid, at first, as the fan began to pull it upward. One of the bolts holding the fan in place abruptly sheared off. The fan's housing sagged. Jacobson let out a surprised yelp. If he didn't find somewhere to put his feet, he would die.

His burning left hand refused to work. If his right hand slipped, he would fall to his death. Praying that the fan would stay where it was, he swung toward the ladder. The housing groaned. There was a pop, metal tore, and the fan motor abruptly snapped free of the housing. The motor hit his helmet and crashed down the shaft, bouncing back and forth like a bowling ball dropped down a well.

With the sudden loss of the motor's weight, the fan's housing dropped sideways, throwing him forward. He crashed against the ladder and grabbed hold of a rung. His heart thundered in his chest. With a shaking, labored breath, he found another rung with his foot. Looking up, he levered his left arm over the rung above him and let go with his good hand to reach upwards. He kept his weight off his wounded leg and lifted his right foot. The movement hurt almost more than he could bear, but he gained the next rung.

"Move!" he told himself through gritted teeth. The Nightmare had to have heard the falling motor. It would be coming, and if it found him on the ladder so close to the maintenance platform, it would kill him.

Slowly, excruciatingly, he reached up and gained another rung.

Blood trickled down his shirt sleeve. Risking a glance upwards, he saw nothing but darkness. He recalled the broken ladder on the catwalk where Adam had fought off the Nightmares and prayed this ladder was in better shape.

Hooking his left arm over each rung, he climbed and soon found an awkward, painful rhythm—hooking his left arm, pressing his chest against the ladder, grabbing the next rung with his right hand, and pulling himself up while lifting his bad leg.

Hook, pull, lift. Repeat.

He had no way to judge the passage of time, so he counted rungs. He had just reached one hundred when he heard movement below. He risked a quick look down. His heart missed a beat then hammered in his chest. Pale, all-white eyes looked up at him.

The Nightmare sniffed the air and stepped forward onto the platform. It was big, at least Jacobson's size. Wood groaned beneath its weight. It retreated, sniffing, head moving as it turned around, trying to figure out where he'd gone.

Jacobson hooked his arm more securely over the rung, forcing himself to think through the pain. The platform was flimsy. If he could lure the Nightmare toward the edge, the platform might break free. He tried to think of something that would draw the Nightmare further out toward the drop-off. He was tired, lightheaded, and every inch of him ached. Every minute he stayed where he was would only make him weaker, while the increased air flow was only helping the Nightmare purge carbon monoxide from its system. Before the loss of blood caused him to black out, he needed to find the exit. Whatever he was going to do, he needed to do now.

"Hey," he yelled down the shaft. "Looking for me?"

The Nightmare's head snapped up. It took a step forward. The platform groaned under its weight, and it retreated again.

"The trap you set at Biodosious was well done. If I hadn't gotten lucky with the chair closing the door, you would have gotten me."

The Nightmare tried to locate Jacobson's voice. The platform groaned.

Jacobson reached for the next rung. "What did Dr. Baltimore remove from Biodosius that caused you to chase Adam Barnett thirty miles up into the Tonto National Forest? Was Baltimore working on the Simeon Process? Is that why you killed everyone in the building? He had the cure, but he wouldn't give it to you. Is that what happened? Admiral McDermott wanted you to remain his lab rat?"

As the Nightmare examined the remnants of the fan housing,

Jacobson took a firm hold of the ladder with his right hand and leaned his left arm over the abyss. He shook his hand, sending blood falling down the shaft. The Nightmare's nose flared, and he audibly snorted, taking an involuntary step forward onto the platform. Wood cracked, sounding like rotten ice on a pond, but the platform didn't break.

"The ambush you set up in the mountains was well done. How many of you did I kill with the grenade?"

The Nightmare growled and took another step forward. The platform moaned, the supports creaking and popping with its weight. For a long instant, nothing happened. Time seemed to stop. The dust hung, suspended, unmoving.

Jacobson waited, praying for a collapse. He was past due for some good fortune. From the moment O'Dell diverted him to the Air Force base, everything about this operation had gone wrong. He had almost died in Biodosius, up in the mountains, and in the mine. He had gotten shot twice and nearly been crushed by a helicopter. He wasn't a believer in fate. He didn't think everything was preordained and that he had no choice in the outcome of his life. But he believed in luck, especially if he worked hard enough to put himself in a good position.

An overburdened, weakened support abruptly cracked. The platform collapsed to one side. It began to slide into the shaft. Jacobson thought the Nightmare would simply retreat to better footing, but it did something unexpected. It leapt across the shaft and grabbed hold of the fan. The Nightmare swung across the abyss toward the ladder, reaching out. The fan twisted under its weight, and, metal squealing, abruptly broke free of its mounts.

The Nightmare let out a yowl. It fell, twisting, and struck the side of the shaft. It caught frantically at the remains of the platform and started to pull itself out of the hole. The broken fan struck its shoulder. The impact wrenched the Nightmare's hands free of the platform, and the fan and the Nightmare fell screaming into the abyss.

Jacobson sagged, panting, his chin resting on a rung. He had survived. All he needed to do now was get out.

Weighted down by a bone-deep weariness, he resumed his laborious, painful climb, hooking his left arm over each rung and pulling himself up with his good hand.

Hook, pull, lift.

Post-adrenaline exhaustion flooded through him. He forced himself to keep going.

Hook, pull, lift.

One rung at a time, arms and chest burning, he climbed the ladder. Far overhead, after what felt like hours, he finally caught the faint glimpse of stars. Hope blossomed through him. He was close. Only another hundred feet or so and he would be able to take off his respirator. After being in the mine for hours, he wanted to luxuriate in the earthy scent of grass and trees.

He gained another rung. The ladder shuddered. He froze, heart thudding awake. Below, the ladder had been untouched by the elements, but close to the surface, the weather had most likely weakened the bolts that secured it to the wall. The rungs below had been smooth. But up here, they were pitted with rust.

He hooked the next rung, pulled up with his right hand, and lifted his wounded leg, trying to move gently and prevent the ladder from detaching. Another vibration thrummed through the steel, this one easily felt through his gloves. He needed to get above the loosening supports.

The ladder vibrated again, creaking. Fear cut through his exhaustion. He looked over his shoulder. Pale, white eyes shone in the darkness. The Nightmare had somehow stopped its fall and was quickly making its way upward.

"No!" Jacobson swore.

He increased his speed, climbing faster.

Hook, pull, lift.

Desperate seconds flew past. He needed more time.

Hook, pull, lift.

Heart pounding in his chest, he risked another look down. He saw the Nightmare clearly now. Unlike him, it had the use of all its limbs.

Jacobson grabbed hold of a rung with his left hand instead of hooking his elbow over it. Pain radiated up his arm. He lost his grip and then his balance and put all his weight on his left leg. Agony, unlike anything he had ever experienced, shot through his body. He screamed and somehow managed to get an elbow over the rung.

Hook, pull, lift. Move!

Even through the respirator, he could smell fresh air. Twenty feet above his head, he saw a metal grate

The vibration in the ladder was constant now. The Nightmare settled into a steady climbing rhythm. Jacobson redoubled his efforts, throwing his left arm over each rung and pulling himself up.

Hook, pull, lift.

Ten feet from the top.

Hook, pull, lift.

His helmet smashed into the grate. It was so unexpected he almost let go. He searched for a latch. The Nightmare was close enough for him to hear its eager, mewling whine.

Jacobson's eyes found a padlock. Hooking his left arm tightly over the top rung, he fumbled for his pistol. He switched off the safety, sighted on the lock, pulled in a breath, and then ducked his head to protect his face with his helmet. The weapon flashed and bucked in his hand. The gunshot was so loud in the enclosed space that he felt it as much as heard it. He lifted his gaze. The lock had been blown off.

Keeping hold of the pistol, he used his right elbow to push up the grate. It didn't move. He put his shoulders against it, pushing with his good leg. The Nightmare's rapid breathing echoed through the shaft. It was close. Rusty hinges screeched, and the grate slowly began to rise. Jacobson kept pushing. With a groaning crash, it fell back.

Jacobson twisted around and aimed the pistol down at the Nightmare. Glocks held fifteen rounds. He had shot once. That left fourteen bullets he could put in the Nightmare's head. Even an augmented killing machine couldn't survive that.

He centered the pistol's sight on the blood-splattered head. He would end this now.

The Nightmare flew up the rungs. Under the additional weight, the ladder bucked and shook. A restraining bolt, already weakened from a century of exposure to the elements, sheared off the wall. Jacobson's left elbow, slick with blood, slipped off the rung. He lost his balance and let out a surprised gasp. He dropped the pistol and grabbed hold of the ladder with his right hand. He lost his balance again, and his right foot left the rung. The pistol fell, crashing down the shaft.

For a second, he hung off the top rung by his right hand before he threw his left elbow up and over the lip of the shaft entrance. Gasping, boots scrabbling for anything to push against, he pulled himself up. The Nightmare was thirty feet below. He threw his wounded leg over the shaft's lip, made one final effort with his right arm, and slid up and out of the shaft. Grabbing the open grate with both hands, he lifted it from the ground with his remaining strength. It groaned, rusted hinges screeching. He kept lifting, ignoring the agony in his left hand. The grate reached the halfway point and started to descend. Jacobson didn't wait for it to close. He threw his body onto the grate, adding his weight. The Nightmare reached the top of the shaft and crashed into it. The metal jumped with the impact. Jacobson held on and forced it down.

The Nightmare reached up through the grate's mesh cover. Jacobson pulled his knife and stabbed its hand. The Nightmare screamed and let go. Its feet slipped off the rungs, and it slid a few rungs down the ladder before it managed to grab hold with its good hand.

Jacobson lay on the grate, gasping, nearly spent. The Nightmare was trapped for the moment, but it was too powerful, and the grate wouldn't hold it back for long. Once it got out, it would kill him. His rifle was at the bottom of the pit. His pistol had fallen down the shaft. He still had grenades, but they were too big to fit through the openings in the grate. He could set one on top of the grate and pull the pin, but it would kill him as well as the Nightmare. He searched for something, anything, to help him hold the grate in place. He saw distant lights through some trees, but they might as well be on the moon. With his wounded leg, he would never reach them, and anyway, the lights might come from the men who meant to kill him.

He met the Nightmare's pale, deadly gaze. He had a concussion, couldn't get his breath, and was shot up worse than a Texas speed limit sign. His only option was to play whack-a-mole and hope for the best. He tightened his grip on the knife.

The Nightmare surged up the ladder and struck the grate with its shoulders. The grate exploded upwards, throwing Jacobson off. The grate broke free of its hinges and sailed out into the darkness.

The Nightmare screamed in triumph and rushed up the remaining rungs. Jacobson slashed at it with the knife. He had been hoping for the Nightmare's throat but got its forehead instead. The Nightmare's head snapped backwards, and it recoiled, sliding back down the ladder. For a second Jacobson thought it would continue to fall, but it twisted like a cat and caught a rung. The steel creaked, the weakened metal popping with the stress.

Jacobson went through everything he knew about the Nightmares, trying to recall a weakness. The chemicals used in the Simeon Process caused serious complications with the adrenal gland, sending the patients into overload, giving them inhuman power and speed. It wasn't that they didn't feel pain. They didn't let it register. He remembered being in the basement of Biodosius and how the patients attacked the walls of their cells with crazed, superhuman strength, smashing their bodies against the cell doors in a vain attempt to get out. Dr. Riya Kumar tried to help them, to aid them in regaining their lost humanity, but even she knew it was hopeless. They had been created to kill, and that's what they did.

But they had to have a weakness. Even with the augmentation to their nervous systems, they were still human and with humanity's many failings.

The Nightmare gathered itself on the ladder again, glaring upwards. Muscles bunching, it bared its teeth. Jacobson knew what was coming. Combat always came down to one man against another, both wanting to survive. He had fought in a dozen countries against the best the world had to offer. Politics might take him out of a conflict, like what had happened at the end in Afghanistan, but he hadn't abandoned that fight. Minutes before boarding the last C-17 out, he had held the line against the Taliban. When fired upon, he fired back to deadly effect.

But even with his elite skills, he couldn't fight one-on-one against a Nightmare. Should he call for help? His radio was being jammed. Even if he could use it, it would simply tell Admiral McDermott's death squad where to find him. He had his grenades, but the Nightmare was too close. They would both die. Only as a last resort would he do that. He gripped his knife and waited. In seconds, it would throw itself from the air shaft.

The Nightmare had been a man once before it had been augmented. It had no family to go home to, nothing to hope for, no way of finding and regaining its severed humanity. But what about the successful ones? Were they also overloaded on adrenaline, unable to think or function? Could they have a family, a house, and find happiness, or were they also kept in dark and dim cells far from the light? He went through everything he knew, every encounter with the killers and patients as the pieces fell into place.

After gathering itself for its final triumph, the Nightmare raced up the ladder. Even with its wounded hand, it moved faster than Jacobson would have thought possible. In less than a second it was at the hatch.

large shoulders filling the entrance. Jacobson lifted his hand and found the switch on his helmet. The light lit the darkness like a solar flare. It struck the Nightmare full in its destroyed face. It shrieked. It didn't howl. It didn't wail. It shrieked. Its head snapped back. Its mouth opened in stunned, incomprehensible agony, showing broken, jagged teeth. It recoiled, its wounded arm shielding its sensitive eyes from the glare.

Jacobson stabbed the uninjured hand holding onto the ladder. The blade cut through muscles and tendons and hit bone. The Nightmare let out an agonized, despairing cry. Its feet left the rungs, and it fell backwards, twisting and screaming, flailing at the ladder as gravity took hold. Jacobson removed two grenades from his pocket, pulled the pins, and dropped them down the shaft. He covered his ears, counting out the seconds as the grenades bounced and banged down into the darkness. They exploded, shrapnel ricocheting up the shaft.

Silence fell.

He slumped against the top of the shaft, removed his respirator, and threw it into the trees. He drew in the fresh air, clutching his knife and praying that the ordeal was over. Crickets chirped. A gentle breeze moved through the trees. There was no other sound.

He turned and wearily dragged himself toward the lights. As he struggled forward, each step sent jolts of pain through his injured leg. Against all odds, he had survived the Nightmare. He just needed to get past the government's kill squad.

He followed the old mining road until it merged with a road that ran parallel to the estate's wall. In one place, boulders had crashed through, and he supposed that was how Adam had gotten in. A hundred feet further on, a large iron gate stood open. Two black SUVs were parked at a forty-five degree angle. A man he didn't know lay on the ground with a single gunshot wound to the head. Death had happened so fast he hadn't even dropped his rifle.

So worn-out he could barely move, Jacobson took his sidearm and wobbled forward. A dozen dragging steps later, he came across Admiral Bill McDermott, or what remained of him, lying on the road. Blood covered his battered face and clothing. One arm had been ripped from its socket. Broken ribs pierced his shirt. One leg lay bent at an awkward angle.

This was the man who had ordered Jacobson killed. In the beginning, McDermott had tried to help humanity, but in the end, he had only helped himself to an early death. His creations had turned on him. All he needed was an island, and he would be a modern-day Dr. Moreau.

Jacobson limped to the closest SUV. He opened the door and slid behind the wheel. He pulled his wounded leg inside and winced as it caught on the door. Two briefcases sat on the seat. The first held a radio jammer the military used to block radio signals so that they couldn't be used to detonate explosives. The second briefcase held a military-grade laptop computer. He moved it out of the way so he could sit. The screen lit up, showing a conference table with people seated around it. Some were in uniform while others were dressed in civilian clothing.

"Admiral, what's your status?" a woman at the head of the table asked, looking at him on the video call. She wore a business suit, minimal jewelry, and owl-like glasses. She peered at her camera. "We've been out of contact for almost twenty minutes. Have you eliminated the target? The committee's gone over his communications with his superiors and believe he possesses information that will compromise the project. He must be terminated and his information retrieved."

Jacobson's weary mind jolted into action. They thought he was McDermott. They must not have seen his uniform in the dark. He reached out and lowered the laptop's screen so it wouldn't show his face, but he could still see the display.

"Ma'am," he said, thinking fast, "the admiral's not here to update you. He's inside the mine confirming the target's death. There's no radio communication underground. He'll return after he's got more information. He asked my team to maintain the perimeter until he returns."

"Major Jacobson's been eliminated?"

Jacobson nodded even though the woman couldn't see him. "He was shot on the edge of the pit. The admiral's gone to confirm his status."

"We've heard screams. Horrible screams. What happened?"

"Three of the killers showed up. We've dealt with them. There were casualties in our teams. McDermott will update you when he returns."

The woman looked around at the other committee members. One of the uniformed men, a colonel judging by the insignia on his collar, leaned toward the camera on the table. He was in his sixties with graying hair and a weathered face from spending most of his career outdoors.

He scowled. "We can't see anything here, soldier. Who is this?"

Jacobson froze, his fatigued mind having a hard time keeping ahead of the conversation. If they realized who he was, they would send another team to kill him. He needed to keep reinforcements away until he could escape.

"I'm sorry, sir, but my team just notified me that multiple law enforcement vehicles are coming up the canyon toward our position. I need to direct them back to town. I'll return shortly and answer your questions. I'm closing the laptop, so the police don't see the light."

He reached out to the laptop before anyone could object and used his right finger to click off the meeting's video camera icon. He minimized the meeting but left it open. He opened McDermott's email and messaging apps and searched the subject lines until he came across the current meeting notice. He copied the names and e-mail addresses of the attendees and pasted them into a document. He then changed the computer's password. When he was finished, he powered both machines down and closed the briefcases. He put the SUV into gear and turned it toward Defiance's glittering lights.

For the first time that night, he allowed himself a smile. He had McDermott's laptop and the names of the meeting's participants. All he had to do was find the first thread to pull and unravel the entire business.

CHAPTER 39

dam woke on a gurney. Doctors shone pinprick lights in his eyes and shouted orders. He groaned and tried to sit up. His head throbbed. He vomited on himself, and the pain of throwing up hurt so much he nearly passed out. Two nurses came running. They cleaned him up, moved him onto another gurney, and quickly got him out of his clothing. He had been injured many times while mountain biking—it was an extreme sport after all—but he couldn't ever remember feeling this bad. Every body part hurt.

An orderly hurried him through x-rays and scans. Men and women in green scrubs checked Adam's cognition and neuropsychology and intracranial pressure. More lights were shone in his eyes. Each test seemed to contradict the previous one, and he was subjected to more. He had three injuries to his skull and possibly a cracked sternum. The head injury where the Nightmare had slammed his forehead against the wall was serious. He might have a brain-bleed. The doctors wanted to go in and relieve the pressure. He was prepped for an emergency decompressive craniectomy.

Lying in the emergency room, Adam remembered grabbing

Bailey's arm and pulling her to safety. He remembered her screaming and looking down the abyss. He remembered collapsing and later, being dragged out of the mine by James and Kate on a piece of scrap metal. Dead men lay on the ground. Some looked like they had fallen asleep while others had been torn apart.

Other things he knew nothing about. He didn't know how he had gotten from the mine to the hospital or even where he was. He had no idea how much time had passed. The only thing he remembered clearly was Jacobson's urgent, whispered warning. Adam needed to be careful about what he said when the authorities asked what happened. If someone was willing to kill Jacobson and Terrance, they would have no qualms about killing Adam and his family.

Footsteps approached, his privacy curtains were pulled back, and the neurologist on call stopped by his bed, an earnest young Asian doctor with an annoyingly cheerful smile.

"Good morning, Mr. Barnett. I'm Doctor Kobayashi. How are you feeling?"

"My head hurts." Adam could barely say the words.

"That's because you have a concussion and a possible cerebral edema. Do you know what that is?"

"No."

"A cerebral edema happens when bleeding or swelling in the brain causes pressure to build up inside your skull. The pressure can deprive the brain of oxygen and can be terminal if not addressed."

"Is that why I've been given so many tests?" Adam whispered.

"Yes. So far it appears you're very lucky."

"I don't feel lucky."

Kobayashi shone a light in Adam's eyes. Adam winced.

"Why does everyone keep doing that?"

"We're checking to see if your pupils are different sizes. That's a strong indicator of trauma. Do your extremities feel numb or unusually weak?"

"No."

"Have you thrown up anything since you woke up?"

"Yes."

"How is your recall of events? Do you remember what happened?"

Adam chose his words carefully.

"I was attacked by two psychos looking for a dog. I don't know why."

"Someone attacked you because of a dog?"

"Yes."

Kobayashi shook his head.

"We did an initial screen of your blood. Your white blood cells are elevated, and your blood pressure is lower than expected. Have you been diagnosed with leukemia or another blood disorder?"

"No."

Kobayashi made another note on his chart and told him he was going to order an electroencephalogram.

Adam was given the test, sent for an MRI, and then moved out of the emergency room and into intensive care. Once he was settled into his room, James, Bailey, and Kate came to see him.

"You look terrible," James said. His face was bruised from where the first Nightmare had knocked him unconscious, but he didn't seem hurt otherwise. "Of course, 'terrible' is a step up for you. Anything's better than the time you rode the saguaro."

"Adam rode a cactus?" Kate asked.

Adam hissed at James to shut up.

James ignored him. "We were biking in the McDowell Mountains. Adam lost control of his bike, crashed into a saguaro, and rode it down the side of a ravine. He had cactus spines everywhere. His butt swelled up like one of those red-assed monkeys at the zoo."

"That sounds horrible!"

"It was. Even with magnifying glasses, the ER nurses needed an hour to get all the spines out of him. One of the nurses asked me what happened. I told her I didn't know. Adam's always been the baby of the family, but I had never realized he was so small that someone would need a magnifying glass." His voice dropped. "It explains his lack of confidence around women."

Adam glared at his brother. "I nearly die, and this is the thanks I get?"

James grinned. "Just cheering you up, bro."

Adam beckoned Bailey over to squeeze her hand. "You okay, Mermaid Girl Squirrel?"

She looked down, tears in her eyes.

"I'm sorry," Adam told her. "You lost him but he saved our lives."

Bailey slumped into a chair, face in her hands as she cried. James put an arm around her.

Adam looked at Kate. "What happened?"

"Jacobson said head wounds had priority and insisted we get you out first."

"Did he get out?" Adam asked.

James and Kate looked at each other.

"We don't know," Kate said. "James and I dragged you from the mine and drove you into town. On the way we passed two SUVs and a couple of dead guys at the gate. The fire department brought Terrance out and took both of you to Banner in Mesa."

"Great! Terrance is here." Adam threw back his sheet. "Get me a wheelchair."

James shook his head. "You're staying put."

"I need to see Terrance."

"When we came in," Kate said, "we saw Terrance on a gurney. They were loading him into an ambulance. He looked totally out of it."

Uh oh, Adam thought. Adam's gut told him the ambulance had been a fake. Terrance was in grave danger.

"What about the men with guns?"

"The men in the mine? The FBI interviewed us. There wasn't much we could tell them, and they sure weren't sharing what they knew. I can't believe this happened. One minute we're eating cinnamon rolls and playing with Mop, and the next we're getting shot at. Mop must have been a valuable dog. I still don't understand it."

"I don't understand it either."

It was the first lie he had ever told her. He doubted it would be the last.

———

Two FBI agents interviewed him the next day. They were fit, had short haircuts, and wore nearly identical blue blazers that had to be hell in the Phoenix summer. He had trouble telling them apart, and, as he expected, they weren't authorized to disclose the whereabouts of Agent Terrance. But, of course, they insisted on knowing what he knew.

His story was simple—he had been attacked by two crazies looking for a dog. He didn't know why they'd come after him. He didn't even know where the dog had come from. If he would have known that any of this would have happened, he would have dropped the dog off at the humane society and let them deal with it.

The agents didn't like his responses and asked the same questions over and over in slightly different ways.

"Okay, I think I understand what you're saying," one of the clones would say, "but can you start at the beginning?"

Ten minutes became half an hour. Adam's voice went from a croak to a rasp. When they asked him to explain it again for the fifth time, he finally lost patience. Were there more killers running around out there? Were he and his family in danger? What was law enforcement doing to keep them safe?

"I'm sorry but we can't comment on an ongoing investigation," the clone on the right said.

"That's it? You can't comment?" Adam's voice cracked. "What happens if one of those psychos shows up here looking for the dog?"

The agents glanced at one other. An unspoken signal passed between them, and they stood.

"Thank you for your cooperation, Mr. Barnett." They gave him their business cards. "Please call if you remember anything else."

CHAPTER 40

Despite Dr. Kobayashi's vehement objections, Adam left the hospital the next day. Every minute he was in the hospital only heightened his growing panic. They had samples of his blood. If anyone figured out Baltimore had injected him, his life would be over. Then, he'd find himself on a gurney like Agent Terrance, knocked out and transported elsewhere.

Kate pulled her Lexus up to the entrance of the hospital, and a nurse's aide wheeled Adam to the car. Kate helped him into the passenger seat, made sure his seatbelt was secure, and got behind the steering wheel. Adam moved the seat back as far as it would go and unsuccessfully tried to find a comfortable spot where the sedan's headrest wouldn't hurt the stitches in the back of his head.

"I have to talk to Jacobson," he said.

"Call him when you're feeling better," Kate said.

"I need to do it now," he said. "Where's my phone?"

"In your gym bag," she said, glancing over. "It's in the back seat."

"Get it," he said.

"There's no place to pull over."

"Okay, but remind me to do it as soon as we get home. My head is throbbing."

It was rush hour on the expressway, and they got stuck in a river of taillights heading east toward Florence. After living for years in a small town in the mountains, Adam didn't know how the commuters endured this mess. Kate moved into the carpool lane, which helped somewhat. Daggers of late afternoon sunshine stabbed his eyes. Adam kept them closed. He folded his arms on his chest. Remember to call Jacobson, he thought. He'll know what to do. We need to come up with a plan.

"What aren't you telling me?" Kate finally asked.

Adam turned his head. "What?"

"What aren't you telling me? You're as jumpy as a stray cat at a dog show. What's going on?"

"Jacobson said there were a minimum of five Nightmares. I can't stop wondering about the rest."

"Mop is gone. They have no reason to come after us."

"What happens if the psychos don't know Mop's dead? Or what happens if it's me they want? The FBI isn't going to announce on TV what happened. Hell, we almost died in the mine! I shouldn't have brought you into this. I'm sorry."

"We're all alive because of what you and Mop did. Be happy for that."

He grimaced. "I'm not sure I even know what happiness is."

She gave him a sharp, worried look.

They left the city and reached the open desert. Saguaros and the occasional palo verde stood sentinel among the creosote bushes and spiny, red-tipped ocotillos. To the north, the dark bluffs of the Superstition Mountains loomed up in the fading light.

They reached Defiance at sundown. It was raining when Kate pulled up to the front curb. She helped Adam upstairs to his room and told him he didn't look good. He admitted it might not have been the best idea to leave the hospital and gave her a hug that might have turned into more if she hadn't pushed him gently away.

"We'll talk about that when you feel better," she said.

"I feel good enough not to talk about it now," he said.

She smiled, kissed him again, and left, teetering on her heels. The darkness made him nervous. This was too much like the mine—the dim lights, the shadows, the building's age. Was life going to calm down, or was happiness an illusion? He waited until she was gone, then picked up his phone, scrolling his contact list for Jacobson's number. What the heck? It wasn't there. Jacobson had never called him. And why would he have? They had been together, dodging bullets and trying to stay alive. But Jacobson must have Adam's number, or maybe that was Terrance. Adam swiped over to look at his recent calls. A number he didn't recognize. Then he remembered. Monica's friend had called him just before Terrance was shot. No point in bringing trouble down on her head.

He threw back the sheet and limped down the creaking stairs.

Downstairs, listening to the boom of thunder, he looked around the shop at the bike shorts and jerseys on their hangers, the helmets on pegs, and the UPS boxes of parts waiting to be taken to the workroom. So much to be done. He shuffled to the front door. Blue and white forks of lightning flashed across the sky. What was up with the dark van across the street, the one with the tinted windshield? He thought he saw shapes inside, but the rain was sheeting down, and it was hard to tell.

Well, rain or no rain, he didn't want to be a sitting duck. Going out the back door, he grabbed an umbrella, dodged raindrops, unlocked his truck, and pulled his shotgun from beneath the seat. Leaves rustled on the hill behind the shop. He spun around. An indistinct dark shadow moved across the top of the hill, but by the time he looked again, it had disappeared.

He hobbled inside, locked the back door, and set the alarm. He started to carry the shotgun upstairs but noticed his muddy hydration pack. He had dropped it on Saturday morning as he and Mop were heading to the shower. It might be a good idea to dump out the water before mildew set in. Nothing worse when you're dehydrated than a slug of mildewed water.

He rinsed out the pack's bladder in the shop's industrial sink and hung the pack upside down to dry. The bladder slid out of the pack. After it came a black case affixed with medical stickers. The case was so unexpected that for a moment Adam just stared at it. Where had that come from?

He picked up the case and set it on his workbench. Hesitantly, as if afraid it would explode, he opened it. Inside were twenty padded sleeves. Each sleeve contained a transparent plastic vial. The first two vials were empty. The remaining eighteen were full of clear liquid.

Heart pounding, he stared at the vials. The vials were what the Nightmares wanted. The one in the mine had even smelled it on him. Getting more of the elixir—craving it, needing it to maintain their superhuman strength—had to be why the Nightmares had killed everyone at Biodosius and why they had chased him up into the mountains. There was no other explanation.

The back door rattled. He snatched up the shotgun and spun around. Rain hit the windows. The old building groaned in the gusting wind. He waited, listening, then put down the shotgun, wondering if he would spend the rest of his life looking over his shoulder. It wasn't a pleasant thought.

He zipped the case shut and stuffed it back into the bottom of the pack. After a moment's thought, he put the bladder back inside the pack, filled it with fresh water, and set the pack in his locker with the rest of his biking equipment. The case couldn't stay in his shop. He would need to find somewhere to hide it, but this would work for now.

Carrying the shotgun upstairs to his room, he rested the weapon by the headboard. His twin bed was small and uncomfortable, but as he slid between the sheets it had never felt better. He turned off the lights and closed his eyes. A sudden thought struck him. Why were *two* of the case's sleeves empty?

On Friday, he had been testing his new bike on the Hawes trails, saw Dr. Baltimore crash, and rode over to give assistance. He had then somehow been injected with Baltimore's drug. He and Mop had fled more than thirty miles up into the mountains to the mining camp. That was a long way through some of the worst terrain on earth, but he was in excellent shape. His legs had been sore the next day, but that was it. But Mop had been a caged medical research animal. He shouldn't have been able to survive the heat or run for hours across the rocky terrain. It was a miracle he had made it.

Or was it?

CHAPTER 41

The next morning, Wednesday, the government released an official statement about what had happened on the Black Estate. The statement was succinct, concise, and believable. But what it didn't say was enough to attract every nutball in the country. Defiance was suddenly jammed with deep-state QAnon conspiracy theorists, UFO chasers, heavily armed rednecks, and political crazies of both stripes. It wasn't logical, Adam thought, that tourists would flock to a place where known killers were on the loose.

The official statement said that the killers were violent, mentally ill patients who had been receiving care at Biodosius. Eight of the patients had killed the hospital staff and escaped into the community. Two had died in the mine, and another had died outside the estate's walls. Five patients remained at large.

The gunmen on the Black Estate, according to the official account, had been dispatched to apprehend the fugitives. The investigation was continuing. They would update as soon as more information became available.

All wrapped up neatly with a bow. As lies went, it was plausible.

But for everything the authorities made public, it was what they left out that bothered Adam the most. There was no mention of Jacobson, none whatsoever, and no mention of Agent Terrance. They didn't talk about the project to resuscitate the terminally injured or say why the patients had become violent. They didn't mention Mop. When pressed about why dangerous patients had been at a research lab instead of at a properly equipped hospital, the officer at the briefing would only say that the remaining patients had been transferred to other facilities where they could get the care they needed. They didn't say what "care" meant. No mention was made of research continuing elsewhere.

And, most disturbing, the briefing revealed nothing about Baltimore's drug. It had saved Adam's life, but the side effects frightened him. After killing the Nightmare in the mine, Adam had been primed to attack Kate and Bailey. What would happen if he got angry at something trivial—a driver cutting him off in traffic or Bailey not putting away the milk after breakfast? The lack of emotional control terrified him.

He just wished he could forget about the entire thing—which wasn't easy after the media reported he had successfully fought off two of the "escaped psychopathic patients" in the mine.

———

"Why me?" Adam complained to James as they were helping Bailey get ready for school. "You shot the first one, and Mop saved us from the second. We'd all be dead if Mop hadn't done what he did."

It was the wrong thing to say, and Adam instantly knew it. Bailey's eyes filled with tears. She ducked her head, picked up her backpack, and left for school.

"You have to be careful around her," James said. "She doesn't eat or do her homework, and she spends hours on the phone with her friends. The only thing we can do is give her enough space to process what happened."

Adam sighed. "It's a good thing my head already aches, or this would give me a headache."

"You look better than you did last night. The swelling's gone down, and the cuts don't look as bad. The bruise on your forehead sort of makes you look like a unicorn though."

"Thanks for your support."

"Now that you're on vacation, maybe you can do something about all the paperwork on your desk."

"Great. I'll get right on it."

Downstairs, Adam limped into the office. On his desk were piles of bills, orders, and returns—and everything else that kept the shop afloat. Looking and feeling like he had been run over by a freight train didn't matter. If he didn't pay bills, he wouldn't remain in business. Sighing, he sat down and worked until lunchtime when Kate stomped into the office.

"What are you doing! You're supposed to be in bed!"

He whipped around to look at her and winced. "Ouch."

He smelled food. His stomach growled, and he grabbed for the bag in her hand. She jerked it away. He grabbed her instead and pulled her close. Her bubble of perfume enveloped them both.

"Woman bring food," he said. "Man like."

"You are obviously feeling better," she said. "But that doesn't mean you're officially off my list."

"Wow, I made your list. Score one for me."

"I'll score you all right," she muttered, but she helped him up and held his arm as they walked across the street to the park and a picnic table. The grass was trampled, but the food trucks had stayed open to serve the new crop of tourists, the circus that had developed after word got out about Biodosius. Every one of them would have been asking for an autograph if James hadn't kept Adam's picture out of the paper.

Even though he felt terrible, he was glad he could sit at the picnic table and people-watch.

Kate, of course, was the Mayor, and passersby were looking at her. Should he be worried about what some nut might do or be pleased that she looked so good in her sandals and a summer dress?

"What are you staring at?" she asked as he used a plastic knife to tear his sandwich into bite-sized pieces.

"Just admiring the view."

"You like my bruise?" She turned her head and showed him the lump on her jaw from where the Nightmare had hit her.

"It doesn't look that bad. I can barely see it."

"Joan worked on my makeup after I got into the office this morning. I had a press conference. Things have been busy."

"I heard you on the radio. You did a good job with the questions. My favorite was when someone asked you if the killers were escaped human-alien hybrids from Area 51."

She made an exasperated noise. "The more I tell people there aren't any secret bioweapon labs in the bottom of the mine, the more the idiots insist on breaking in to look for themselves. The sheriff doesn't have the resources to patrol the town and keep the crazies from crawling down the mine shafts."

"If they go into Black's mine," he said, "they won't come out."

"I'm going to ask the FBI for help."

"Will they do it?"

She took a bite of her sandwich. "I can be persuasive when I want to be. I don't want any more deaths."

Her voice changed just enough that he took a closer look at her expression. "Speaking of the FBI, two of them dropped by this morning to talk to me. They seemed particularly interested in you."

"The twins Tweedle Dee and Tweedle Dum?" he said. "I thought they questioned you at the hospital."

"They did. They wanted to know again why we were at the estate and how we ended up in the mine. They didn't seem very happy."

"I can't see why," he said sarcastically. "It's not like all of their hired killers and lab rats got killed or anything."

"They were surprised you were at home. They thought you'd still be in the hospital. I told them you had left AMA."

"AMA?"

"Against Medical Advice."

"Oh."

Her eyes narrowed. "I shouldn't have picked you up. You can barely walk, and even I can that see your pupils are different sizes."

"The doctor gave me a list of symptoms to watch out for. If things don't improve, I'll go back."

She scowled and took another bite of sandwich.

"There's one thing I don't understand. Why would these monsters follow the dog? Mop was a great dog, but he's still just a dog. Why chase him all the way into the mountains and then follow him to Defiance? It doesn't make sense."

Adam ducked his head. "I don't know."

"It's really disturbing."

With that he could agree.

CHAPTER 42

On Saturday, Adam didn't go to Mike Benedict's funeral. His parents had asked him not to—which was fine with him. He still wasn't feeling good, and rumor had it that Mike's extended family was angry about what had happened at the top of the overlook and wanted revenge—which didn't make sense. Adam hadn't killed Mike. Mike had killed himself by driving off the cliff. If his family wanted a fight, they should pick one with Mike's corpse. Knowing how ornery Mike was, even dead he would probably give them more than they could handle. That was a cheerful thought.

On Sunday, he and Kate watched a family movie on her TV. She leaned against him on the couch, and he put an arm around her.

"You're quiet," she said. "Are you okay?"

"I was just thinking about everything that happened. I was chased through the mountains by a bunch of lunatics, then struck by lightning. The next day, I went to Cindy's wedding, and Mike almost ran over me on the overlook. You and I had our first official date, and we both nearly died in the mine. Maybe we should go to Vegas and bet everything we have on black."

She laughed and twisted around to look at him. "You're an odd man, Adam Barnett. After everything that's happened, I'm just glad you still have your sense of humor."

Given the circumstances, so was he.

———

The days ran together in a blur of assembling bikes and seeing Kate. The licensing money from his suspension started coming in, and he used it to hire staff. They worked double shifts to clear the backlog, and on Halloween he opened the shop for a company pizza party. His accountant said the future looked bright.

For Thanksgiving, he and Kate had two dinners, the first with his family and the second with her mother. The two women fussed over him during the second dinner, and it felt nice to be a part of something greater than himself. Afterward, he donned an apron and started in on the dishes. Kate slipped her arms around him.

"I just spoke with my mom," she said quietly. "She says you're a wonderful man."

"Well, I guess I've fooled her," he joked before realizing she had tears in her eyes.

"Dad would have been happy. Thank you for being in my life."

Adam turned from the sink and held her as she cried. Later, as he drove her home, she asked him what he was thankful for. He turned down the radio and thought about Mop's gift.

"That's easy," he said. "I love you."

Her breath caught. She turned to search his face, glare from the streetlights crossing her face. "I was married for a long time," she finally said. "When it ended, it was like a part of me died. I'll never get those years back. It's been hard to trust again. But," she took a breath, "I love you, too."

That night, for the first time, when he took her home, she invited him to stay.

———

By Christmas Adam's wounds had fully healed, and the blowback from Mike Benedict's death had died down. Adam's parents invited Kate and her mom over for a Barnett family celebration. With James and Bailey there for the holiday, it was a noisy, chaotic, and wonderful day.

Winter grudgingly gave way to spring. One Saturday in late April, when the Gambel oaks and aspen had begun to leaf out, Adam, Kate, Bailey, and James drove up to the eastern Arizona plains. A chilly wind moaned across the cinders, tossing the limbs of the pines and whistling around a black volcanic mountain that rose into the brilliant blue sky. Here and there, tiny red-and-yellow spring flowers pushed out of the ground. It was a beautiful, raw, desolate land.

"Where are we going?" Bailey asked, looking out at the islands of pine.

"I thought it would be nice to have lunch," Adam replied.

"Out here?"

"There's a McDonalds coming up. Just the other day you said you wanted to get a Happy Meal and play in the tubes."

"The last time I played in the tubes was when I was in third grade. I'm in high school now."

"You're never too old to play in the tubes, Mermaid Girl Squirrel. Just don't get stuck like you did when you were two years old. It about killed me to crawl in there to get you out." He grinned at her in the rearview mirror.

Bailey stuck out her tongue and returned to her phone.

He steered his truck onto a dirt road and drove through a broken barbed-wire fence. The road grew steadily worse the further they traveled from the pavement. An hour later, they reached a narrow canyon. Adam put his truck in four-wheel drive. A small creek fed by melt-water rushed past the road. Sycamores lined its banks.

Kate gave him a questioning look, but he just smiled.

They reached a cabin built into the side of the canyon and parked. The cabin's pine exterior had been freshly stained and sealed against the elements. Solar panels covered the metal roof. A battered Ford F-350 and a rental SUV with Mexican plates had parked in front of the garage. Beneath an old juniper, he saw a Mercedes covered by a camouflage net.

"Who lives here?" Kate asked.

"Monica's friend Victoria. She and Monica invited us for lunch."

James stiffened. "What? When did Monica get back to the States? I thought she was down in Mexico until August."

"She was, but she came up last night. She has something to show us."

Before they could ask questions, Adam got out and went around to open Kate's door. Bailey grinned at him and waited until he opened her door, too.

"Don't get used to it," he growled as she jumped down.

Monica and Victoria emerged from the house.

"You must be Victoria." All smiles, James gave her a hug.

"The same," she said, pulling away, "but if anyone asks, make like you never met me."

Victoria wore jeans, a flannel shirt, cowboy boots, and a pistol. Monica wore a dress, a stylish leather jacket, and high-heeled boots that were out of place in the canyon. She gave James a hug, and when she went to do the same to Adam, he dangled his keys and quickly hid them behind his back.

"I'm not going to steal your truck!" Monica said.

He laughed but still put the keys in his pocket.

"You look great," James told Monica. "All tan."

Monica smiled. "Every day's a gift. I treat it as such."

"How's Mexico?"

"I love it there. There's a reef by my house. When I'm not working, I go snorkeling. I got my scuba certification. There's an island about an hour off the coast that has sea lions. The last time I was there, they were swimming through my legs. It was amazing. You should pack a swimsuit and come down. You might not want to come back."

He raised his eyebrows and smiled. "You never know."

"How's your research?" Adam asked. "You said you received a new grant from the Huntington Foundation."

"Yes. With the additional funding we've secured from the Mexican government and our private donations, we have enough money to do some testing on a possible drug. It won't stop the erosion of the nerve cells in the brain, but it might alleviate some of the symptoms."

"That's great news."

"We should catch up inside," Victoria said. "Lunch is almost ready."

Monica turned toward the garage and cupped her hands. "Time to eat! Who's ready for lunch?"

For a second nothing happened.

"Time to eat!" she yelled again. "If anyone wants food, they'd better come inside!"

The garage's side doorknob jiggled. It slowly started to turn, the motion awkward, as if a small child were struggling to reach the handle.

"That door has always stuck," Victoria said.

There was a low, frustrated moan inside the garage. The knob stopped moving, a full second went by, and then something heavy slammed into the door. It crashed open. Two dogs exploded into the sunshine. The first was big and black, with a wide skull and powerful shoulders. The second, a puppy, was fuzzy and blond, with floppy ears on a large, broad head. Like the first dog, it had long, strong legs and paws two sizes too big for its body.

Bailey let out a strangled gasp. The blood left her face. She stumbled into a run. Girl and dog crashed into each other in a pile of limbs. Mop was the first to recover and bolted around Bailey in a frenzied circle. The puppy threw himself into the mêlée.

"You're alive!" Bailey cried. The big dog licked her face, and she had to fend him off so she could get a good look.

"How is this possible?" Kate demanded. "I saw him fall into the pit, and I told the FBI I'd swear on a stack of Bibles he was dead!"

"They didn't see him fall," Adam said, "and they probably thought you were lying. They've been trying to find him for months. That's why they've been watching the shop."

"No, they're watching the shop because I asked them for protection," Kate said.

"That's what they said they were doing, but that isn't why they've stayed. They want Mop. They've never stopped looking."

She fixed him with a hard look. He spread his hands. "I'm sorry I didn't say anything. I wanted to tell you he was alive, but I couldn't risk it."

Inside, over garlicky roasted chicken, snow peas, and salad, Adam relayed what had happened. Kate had taken Adam home on Wednesday, and later that night in the rain, Adam had gone out to his truck to get his shotgun. He saw something on the hill behind his shop but went back inside.

"It was dark and windy," he said. "I didn't realize what I'd seen until I climbed into bed. I went downstairs for another look, opened the door, and there he was. He was badly hurt. His front left leg and three of his ribs were broken. I think he landed on the ore elevator. He could barely walk. Every time he moved, he whimpered.

"I didn't know what to do. The FBI had a van out front. I tried to think of someplace safe, someplace they wouldn't find him. I had Victoria's number on my phone. I used the payphone at the gas station to call her. I explained the situation. Monica and Victoria drove down before dawn and picked him up."

"I took him to a vet I use," Victoria said. "He works on livestock but he was able to patch Mop up. I told the vet Mop had been hit by a car."

"Wasn't that dangerous?" James asked. "The vet could have reported him to the authorities."

"We're almost two hundred miles from Defiance, and no one's officially looking for him. He's supposed to be dead, remember? Out here, a dog is a dog, even one as smart as he is."

"You should have told me he was alive," Bailey said, one arm possessively around Mop's neck. "I cried for weeks."

"We couldn't," Adam said. "I'm certain they went into the mine and looked for his body, but without proof of death, they had to assume he'd survived, and if he survived, he'd return to the shop. That's why they kept an eye on us. No one can ever say anything about him being alive. If the military knew he was here, they would take him away. They'd put him in a cage, and we'd never see him again."

Adam didn't talk about Dr. Baltimore's research or his suspicion that Mop had gotten injected with the second drug. Without the drug, Mop couldn't have kept up with Adam on his bike. Dogs weren't built to run through the desert in the summer sun, especially a dog that had spent his life in an air-conditioned lab. The run should have killed him. The drug also allowed Mop to handle the carbon monoxide and survive the fall onto the elevator.

After Adam finished telling them what he could, Victoria spoke about what had happened to her. She started with how she had ended up at Biodosius after Blackjack Joe had blown her up and how she started hearing Dark's voice. She told them about keeping watch on the mountain above the mansion when Monica had met with Adam, Kate, James, and Bailey, how she had felt Dark's presence.

"Wait a second." Adam frowned. "You're losing me. Dark?"

Victoria held up a hand. "Let me finish this." She described how she'd shot Dark, only enough to wound him, and how surprised she was when he gave himself an injection. "It made him invincible, and he took control of my mind until I came up with a memory that broke the connection. It was at that point a creature leapt out of the darkness and tore him limb from limb." The creature had chased her along the wall until she made a stand at the top of the cliff. "I had every advantage," she said. "The thing was trapped between the wall and the drop-off. It should have retraced its steps and tried to get to me another way, but it didn't care. It just kept coming. I emptied an entire clip into it before it died. That was bad enough, but what was really disturbing was what I found afterward." She swallowed, voice dropping. "This creature—I mean *she*—was a woman. Her entire body had been torn apart. Bullet holes everywhere."

"I call them 'Nightmares,'" Adam said.

"Aha! So Dark wasn't the only 'Nightmare' in my life!" Victoria said, smiling. "Whatever Admiral McDermott did to that poor woman, it made her crazy. Thank god he's dead."

"And who is Admiral McDermott?" Adam asked.

Victoria pointed at her chest. "The man I called Dark." She nodded toward Monica. "Actually, her boss, the head of research at Biodosius."

"Not just Biodosius," Monica said. "He had labs in lots of places, even overseas. But to answer your question, Adam, for years Victoria has been hearing this sinister voice she calls 'Dark.' She'd been trying to figure out who he was, and then, the night she took me to meet up with you, she found him out by the gate. He knew immediately who she was. For years, he'd been hearing her thoughts, too. He told Victoria he'd ended up at Biodosius because he'd been in an auto accident. Turns out they'd been there at the same time. Later that night when Victoria and I came back to the ranch, we compared notes. I knew Admiral McDermott had been on medical leave. The coincidence was just too much to ignore. I showed Victoria McDermott's picture. They were the same man."

"Turns out he's been killing off his researchers," Victoria said. "Sometimes I could even hear their names. Not always, but sometimes. They were people Monica knew."

"But why would this admiral kill his researchers?" Kate asked. "Didn't he need them for his projects?"

"The drugs used in the resuscitation process make some patients unstable and violent," Monica said. "If word leaked out about the downside of these experiments—how former soldiers and organ donors with no families were being changed into killers—the project would have been closed. McDermott covered it up instead. When anyone asked questions, he had them 'eliminated.'" She looked at James. "That's why he tossed me off the bridge. I was on his hit list, too."

"You said McDermott injected himself after you shot him," James said to Victoria. "Did he do that so he could be resuscitated again?"

"Yes. He knew I meant to kill him. I wanted him out of my head."

"But the Nightmare killed him, right?" Kate asked. "You didn't do it?"

"No, I didn't kill him. I wanted to."

"Could he still be alive?" Adam asked.

"I don't know. I can't sense him."

"He could have decided to be quiet," Adam said.

"Maybe" Victoria said, "But he isn't the only problem. There might be…others."

"What? Who?" Adam glanced at Bailey. She sat wide-eyed and still. He elbowed James to take a look at his daughter.

James leaned over and put an arm around her. "You okay, hon? Want to go outside and get some air?"

"I'm okay," she said. "I want to understand what's going on, not just for my sake, but for his." She scratched Mop's head.

Victoria pushed back from the table, stood up, and went to the kitchen. The oven door squeaked open, and she put a pie on the counter. When she sat down again, she said, "This is hard to talk about and even harder to comprehend."

"This McDermott character," Kate said, reaching for Adam's hand, "sounds like evil incarnate."

"He didn't see himself like that," Victoria said. "McDermott kept telling me how more research was needed to understand what had happened to us, how we ended up being linked. I assumed it was to try and figure out how to stop people from connecting with one another but now I don't think that's what he wanted. I don't think we were the only ones treated with the same neurons. They were injected in other patients. That's why McDermott was hell bent on knowing who brought me into the program. He wanted to make more people like us, people subject to thought control. They could already be out there."

"That's scary," Adam said.

Victoria shrugged. "I carry a gun everywhere. Mop watches over me. To be honest, he's smarter than most people."

No one said anything. Bailey gave the puppy a piece of chicken, and he gulped it down.

Monica pushed her chair back and stood up. "Let's go outside while it's still warm and eat dessert. The puppy is good about doing his business in the yard, but he's still learning."

Adam followed her to the porch. When they were outside and seated, Victoria dished up the pie. Bailey threw an old tennis ball for the puppy to fetch. It was nice to just relax and watch the little nut chase it.

"He looks sort of like Mop," James observed. "He's got a similar bone structure, the same ears, the same way of running sideways when he gets excited."

"They're not related," Monica said, scooping ice cream and pushing the tub of vanilla toward Bailey. Bailey helped herself. "The litter is a mix of the same breeds we used for Mop, but that's it. I still have embryos from Mop's parents, but I don't want to use them. If the military found a dog with the same DNA as Mop, everything would start up again."

"Is he as smart as Mop?" James asked.

"There are thousands of genes involved in intelligence, so it's hard to know for sure. It could be decades before we understand all the interactions. But yes, everything I did for Mop, I did for him."

"What's his name?" Bailey asked. "You never told me."

"He doesn't have one yet. Adam and I thought you would like to do the honors since he's going to be your dog."

Bailey's head snapped up. "What? He's my puppy? Who'll take care of Mop?"

"Mop has to stay here," Victoria said. "Nowhere else is safe."

"Can I visit?" Bailey asked.

"Sure," Victoria said. "Whenever you want."

Bailey looked from Mop to the puppy, conflicting emotions crossing her face. "But the puppy's mine? I can take him home?"

Adam glanced at James, who sighed and nodded. "If you want him. If you don't, Monica can take him back to Mexico. He's a very special dog."

The puppy returned the ball. Bailey grinned and threw it across the yard. The puppy bolted off, his oversized paws striking the cinders. He tripped over a rock and tumbled into the creek. He extracted himself, barked at the water, then picked up the ball and ran back as if he'd won the Best Dog in Show award. Just like Mop, he waited until he arrived before shaking water all over them.

"What's a good name for a dog that's really intelligent but has no brains?" Adam asked, shielding his face from the spray. "James, do you remember our old cat, D.C.? We could call the puppy D.D."

"Why would you call him that?" Bailey asked.

"D.C. stood for Damn Cat. He could be Damn Dog."

"We are not naming him Damn Dog!"

"I dunno. It would open up a lot of options. If we get tired of D.D., we could call him D.F.D."

Bailey worked it out and glared. "No! We are not calling him D.F.D."

Adam put his hand down and snapped his fingers. "Come here, D.F.D."

The puppy ran over. Adam picked him up. "See, he likes it."

Bailey snatched him away.

"Don't listen to Uncle Adam!" she told the dog, clutching him against her chest. "Uncle Adam is bad. B-A-D. You don't know your letters yet like Mop, but he'll tell you all you need to know about Uncle Adam. Won't you boy?"

Mop barked.

"Watch it, dog, or we'll have you play fetch in the mine," Adam warned. "I know exactly where to throw the ball."

An oak leaf tumbled past in the breeze. The puppy squirmed to get free. Bailey put him down, and he yapped off in pursuit, this time jumping over the rock that had tripped him the first time.

They ate their apple pie, and just for a moment, sitting in the warm sun and watching the dogs play in the yard, life was good. But later, before they left for home, Adam hiked up to the top of the ridge and stopped under a storm-scarred sycamore. A cloud sailed across the sky, obscuring the Black Knob. Blue forks of lightning danced in the cloud's dark underbelly.

He kept returning to the same questions. Why would the government create murderous sociopaths? What would the military do if they realized he had Baltimore's missing drugs? And worst of all, had that shot turned him into a Nightmare? It seemed that they craved the shots, but he did not, at least not yet. Still, he'd better hang onto them.

The day might come when he'd need to prepare himself for another fight.

Mop pushed his head under Adam's hand. The dog shivered, intelligent eyes on the empty, desolate horizon.

"I know, boy," Adam said quietly. "They're out there and they'll be coming."

ABOUT THE AUTHOR

During Michael Ewing's career as a network engineer, he has had nine jobs in five states, been outsourced, spun off, relocated, laid off, down-sized, and married twice. Characters, like the writers who create them, need a deep and tangled past. Michael doesn't write about roller-coasters—he writes about people whose lives *are* roller-coasters.

Satan's Gold, his debut novel, won the Emerging Writers Gateway award for best crime thriller. *Lightning* is his latest thriller.

Satan's Gold

The entire financial world is networked, but banks have an Achilles' heel…

An elusive ex-CIA financial analyst known only as Daemon has stolen billions from the Russian Federation, and now he's determined to plunder the richest prize of all—the US Federal Reserve. Only one man stands in his way—disgraced former FBI Agent Tyler Jackson, who is destroying all he loves in his feverish attempt to capture Daemon and prevent a worldwide economic collapse.

Jackson has been chasing Daemon for two grueling years. But can Jackson and Dixie, a female hacker wanted for unleashing a deadly computer virus, find Daemon before he makes his next big move?

If you like page-turning suspense and characters who would stop at nothing to achieve their objectives, read *Satan's Gold* today.

www.ingramcontent.com/pod-product-compliance
Lightning Source LLC
Chambersburg PA
CBHW020902060726

47591CB00004B/1043